GOBBELINO LONDON & A CONTAGION OF ZOMBIES

GOBBELINO LONDON, PI: BOOK 2

KIM M. WATT

Buy the book. Gift the book. Read the book. Borrow the book. Talk about the book. Share the book. Just don't steal the book.

Book thieves will be thrown into the Inbetween.

But still - if the cat winks, always wink back.

For further information contact www.kmwatt.com

Cover design: Monika McFarland, www.ampersandbookcovers.com

Editor: Lynda Dietz, www.easyreaderediting.com

ISBN 978-1-8380447-1-8

First Edition May 2020

10 9 8 7 6 5 4 3 2 1

To Mick,
who never asks why a cat detective,
and to the Little Furry Muse,
who proves cats have a sense of humour.
Even if it is a bit warped.

1

SCATTERED SUNSHINE & A CHANCE OF BODY PARTS

It was a spring morning of the postcard sort, all soft warm light and newly minted flowers, and we were in a cemetery. For pleasure, not work. Which probably says something about our social life.

Gentle sunshine was angling across the cemetery in those shafts of light that make everything a little magical, painting the stained grey headstones gold and turning the tatty plastic flowers nestling among them into soft-edged, pastel bouquets. Real blooms were emerging along the gravel paths, pinks and blues and reds of varying hues, and the trees were covered in a pale fuzz of new shoots. Even the slowly subsiding crypts with their leaning walls looked hopeful, the rust on the gates atmospheric rather than neglected. A car revved hard on the road outside, but it sounded distant and unimportant, less immediate than the chatter of sparrows in the trees.

I padded through the graves, smelling the deep cold musk of dead things under the fresh new grass and cool earth, the sun warm on my dark fur. Someone had left a bunch of daffodils in a cracked blue vase wedged at the base of a marker, and I stopped to investigate them, wrinkling my nose at the whiff of stale water and enjoying the fact that no one around here was likely to start throwing things at me. It was all terribly peaceful and pleasant, and I really should've been more prepared for things to go apple-shaped. Orange-shaped? Fruit-shaped, anyhow.

I caught the thunder of feet roaring across the grass behind me too late to turn and face them down. I lunged forward, heart surging into my ears, and a solid thump to my hindquarters sent me nose first into the daffodils. I gave an undignified squawk as I tripped over the vase, flowers and slimy water spilling everywhere, and something *whuff*ed just over my ears, hot breath fluttering through my fur.

I ducked behind the headstone and peered around it at my attacker, who just *whuff*ed again, and tried to follow me.

"Get away, you cornflake," I snapped, jumping to the top of the marker and perching there to glare down at a large, three-legged, and very familiar dog. Cyril. He whined and shoved his filthy wet snout at me. I bopped it, keeping my claws in. His human worked at our local greasy cafe and was generous with the bacon. One had to make allowances in these sorts of situations.

"*What?*"

He *whuff*ed again, dropping to the elbows of his front legs and nudging a stick toward me.

"Seriously? What the hell do you expect me to do with that?"

He rolled his eyes, his tail wagging so hard he was in danger of losing his balance. So unfair. I mean, dogs got the ability to eye-roll? Cats need it a lot more. You'd be amazed how often we'd like to be able to roll our eyes.

"That stick's bigger than me, mutt. What d'you expect me to do with it?"

He nudged it again, looking at me pleadingly, then got up and tried to shove his nose in my face.

"*Get out.* Old Ones take you, you slobbery garden snail. What're you *doing?*"

He jumped up and bounced in a circle, like I'd just paid him the best compliment in the world, then did the elbow thing at me again. I sighed, and looked around. There was a collection of decorative pebbles lined up around me on the top of the marker, printed with things like *Love,* and *Believe,* or painted in primary colours. I'd already knocked a few off in my scramble to safety, but there were plenty left. I tapped one experimentally. It wobbled, and I looked at Cyril.

"Ready? *Ready?* Go! Good dog!" I belted the pebble as I spoke, and it shot across the grass, spinning neatly. It didn't go far, but it was far enough to give me time to jump down and leg it in the other direction while Cyril lunged after the stone, giving little excited whines as he tried to pick it up.

I scooted down the next row of graves and jumped onto a headstone where I'd be able to see him coming. I didn't fancy any more dog drool on my neck. He wasn't far behind me, galloping across the grass at a surprising pace for an animal missing a quarter of his ambulatory equipment. He rushed up and carefully deposited the pebble on top of the marker next to me. *P.B.,* it said, in wobbly black paint on a background of red and orange stripes. I wondered if it was meant to be a sunset and who P.B. was, then looked at Cyril, who was staring at me with his tongue hanging out and his nose quivering.

"I'm not best suited to this," I told him. "You should find someone who can throw further."

He *whuff*ed, wagging his tail at me.

"Sit down," I suggested. "Stay. Roll over. Play dead."

He cocked his head to the side, his wagging easing.

"Too much, huh? Alright." I looked at the slimy rock and sighed. "So gross." I hit it, getting a bit of spin on and sending it flying across the next row of graves before it arced to the ground out of sight behind a marker. "Fetch!" But he was already off and running, ears flying goofily. I abandoned my perch and raced across the headstone-cluttered grass, heading for an intersection of the paths where I could see Callum talking to someone, his hands in the pockets of his jeans and his tatty old jacket hanging from one arm. I couldn't tell from here who his companion was, but given the sudden appearance of Cyril, it had to be Petra of the warm hands and extra bacon.

I shot up to them, my ears back and the sun running sleek fingers over my fur.

"Hey," I called as I got closer. "I'm not a dog-sitter, you know—"

Callum exploded into a coughing fit, glaring at me, and Petra looked from him to me, her forehead creased in confused lines. Humans never really hear cats, just as they never really see the more obviously magical Folk.

The bus driver can't have wings, the baker can't have horns, and cats can't say more than *meow.* These are the rules, according to humans, so that's what they experience.

But, you know. Petra wasn't most humans, not after last autumn, when she'd ended up in the middle of one of our cases. It had involved some fairly alarming issues with reality, and while she might not remember it, it did mean she might be a little more sensitive to talking cats than most people. So I just said, "Meow?"

She blinked at me, then looked at Callum and said, "Are you alright?"

"Sure," he said, giving a last, rather theatrical cough.

"You should really stop smoking," she said, and I snorted. She didn't notice, but Callum gave me another glare.

There was the now-familiar thunder of doggy feet behind me and I shot forward, scrambling up to Callum's shoulder as he yelped a complaint. Well, he should be wearing more than a T-shirt. It wasn't *that* warm.

"Drool," I hissed in his ear. "That damn dog's just a drool factory!"

He bopped my nose lightly with one finger and started to whisper something, then Petra said, "Cyril? Cyril, whatcha got, boy?" Her voice had funny, frayed edges to it, and we both looked up.

Cyril danced in an uneven circle, then dropped his prize in front of Petra and nudged it toward her, his eyes big and brown and begging for approval in that doggy way. She backed away, her hands covering her mouth. It would have seemed almost theatrical if not for the small moan creeping out of her. It was a moan that wanted to be a scream.

Cyril dropped to his elbows, hooked his nose under his trophy and flicked it in the air. Petra gave that funny little moan again, and I said, "Holy soggy Weetabix."

Cyril had fetched us an arm.

CALLUM DIDN'T EVEN SHUSH me. We just stared at the dog and his new limb as he snatched it up and shoved it at Petra. She jumped back before it could touch her and tried a breathy "Drop it!"

Cyril completely ignored that and shook his head happily, like he was a terrier with a rabbit rather than a three-legged mongrel with a slightly whiffy body part that didn't belong to him. He was gripping it somewhere around the biceps, below the point where it ended in a ragged, bloodless fringe of flesh surrounding a nub of shining white bone. A few rings and a bracelet still clung to the hand end, the pearls caked with dirt. As Cyril shook the arm, the bracelet ran back and rattled off his teeth.

"Cyril, drop it," Callum said, his voice a little more authoritative than Petra's, but no more effective. Cyril just panted at him and tossed his head a bit. Callum made a grab for the dog's collar, but Cyril shot away, prancing in a circle with the hand waving jerkily at the end of the arm.

"I might be sick," Petra said. She still had one hand over her mouth, her eyes a bit wide and stare-y above it. It was probably a good thing she couldn't remember certain portions of last year. This was pretty low key in comparison, even given the body parts.

"It's alright," Callum said, not sounding like it was very alright at all. "I mean, it's not *fresh.*"

She made a noise that suggested she was less than reassured by this fact.

"It's not that old, either," I hissed. "It's, you know. *Solid.*"

"Shut up," Callum muttered, and Petra gave him a funny look. He tried for a bright smile, which hardly seemed to suit the situation. "Don't worry. We'll sort it out."

She dropped her hands finally, took a deep breath, and turned to Cyril. "*Sit,*" she said, her voice firm. Cyril stopped his lopsided prancing and looked at her, his tail drooping. "*Sit down,*" she repeated, pointing at him with one long finger, the nail cropped short and the cuticles reddened from hot water and harsh soaps. Cyril sat, his floppy ears as pricked as they could be.

"Drop it," she said. He whined, and she put her hands on her hips, glaring at him. He dropped it. Callum hurried over and bent to pick up the limb, then hesitated. Cyril whined at him.

"Stay," Petra said to the dog, then added, "Get it away from him!"

"Um, yeah," Callum said, straightening up again. "I just . . ." he waved at the arm.

Petra gave a slightly exasperated sigh and dug in her pocket, pulling out a little bundle of white plastic bags. "*Ew,*" I muttered under my breath as Callum took them.

Although I guess they weren't used, so it was better than just grabbing a dismembered limb.

Callum wrapped a bag around his hand and picked up the arm, his cheek twitching slightly. The thing stank of mulch and chemicals and some weird perfume, and he held it away from his body as he took a step back. Cyril watched him go with mournful eyes, and I stayed on Callum's shoulder despite the stench. The ground suddenly seemed far less inviting than it had.

"How the hell did he get hold of that?" Petra asked. "He can't have dug it out of a *grave*. Out of a *coffin*." With the offending item removed, she crouched next to Cyril and rubbed his ears, giving him a treat from her pocket. I looked at Callum hopefully, but he was still staring at the arm.

"Um. No. I don't think so," Callum said, still holding the arm away from him and staring at it dubiously. "Maybe there's a grave still open or something?"

I snorted, and he shrugged his shoulder at me. "Seriously?" I whispered. "What, you think they just leave them all uncovered and fill them in every second Friday?"

Petra apparently shared my doubts, because she frowned at Callum as she found Cyril's lead and clipped it on. "That doesn't seem very likely."

"I suppose not," Callum agreed with a sigh. "I don't know, then. But we should probably put it back."

She fiddled with Cyril's leash. "Shouldn't we tell someone?"

They looked at each other, Petra with the smell of cooking oil and old coffee still baked into her skin, underlying the lonely scent of anxious nights. Callum scratched his stubble.

"We could tell someone," he agreed. "But would it really help anything?"

Petra pulled Cyril a little closer. "They should know, though. If the graves aren't filled in right or something. I mean, that shouldn't happen, right? An arm, like that?"

Callum gave a funny little one-shouldered shrug. "Stuff happens, though. And it was an accident, Cyril digging it up."

"I know." She looked at the dog, then back up at him. "Do you think he's even allowed in here?"

"I didn't see a *No Dogs* sign," Callum said, sounding a bit doubtful. I felt a bit doubtful, too. I mean, no one wants to think of dear old gran's gravestone getting wee'd on by a dog, even a three-legged one. "But it doesn't matter," he said. "We'll just put it back. We don't need to tell anyone."

Petra wiped her mouth with the back of one hand, looking around the cemetery as if expecting the boneyard police to pop out of a crypt, waving handcuffs and a writ. "Are you sure? I feel awful. But he didn't mean it. And I can't afford a fine or … or anything. What if they fine me? Or *arrest* me?"

Cyril looked up at her and whined.

"We'll just put it back," Callum said. "Really. It'll be fine."

Petra twisted the leash around her fingers as she examined Callum's face. "Alright," she said finally. "Let's see if we can find where it came from."

WE SURVEYED the rows of graves, rank upon rank of the long dead and newly deceased, lying shoulder to shoulder like soldiers waiting to rise. The hair on my tail shivered slightly.

"It can't have been that far away," Petra said. "He wasn't gone long."

"Two rows to the right," I whispered to Callum. "That's where I was. So he might have been another row over? Maybe?"

"Let's try this way," Callum said to Petra. "I think I saw him over there."

"Alright," she said. "As good a place to start as any."

Callum led the way down onto the gravel path, the arm still held well away from his body, and headed for the row I'd suggested. I glanced around to make sure we were still alone, and movement caught my eye, a flash of red trundling toward us.

"Callum," I hissed. "Near the gates. Look."

He looked around, swore, and said to Petra, "Hang on."

She turned to ask why, then nodded and pulled Cyril closer to her. He seemed pretty keen to head back to the site of the arm discovery, which was making me wonder if Callum had a point about the open graves. That seemed kind of careless, though, even for humans.

We waited, Petra and Callum pretending to look at a headstone, and the movement resolved itself into a little red car. It trundled steadily down the path toward us, Petra growing twitchier and twitchier as it got closer.

"Do you think they *saw?*" she whispered to Callum, as if the driver might hear her. "Is it a guard, d'you think?"

"I don't think there are cemetery guards," he said. "Or not during the day, anyway. I've never seen any. And I can't imagine there being cameras here. I'm sure it's just someone visiting a grave. They'll stop soon. You'll see."

But the car just crept closer and closer, until even I could see that someone had put those ridiculous plastic eyelashes on its headlights, and there was a sunflower stuck to the stubby little antenna on the roof. A shrunken woman with a halo of white hair peered over the steering wheel with great concentration, and didn't even look around as she passed us. Callum tucked the spare arm behind his back anyway, still trying not to actually touch it, although the plastic bag just wasn't that big. He made a gagging sound as his fingers slipped off it.

The car stopped a couple of rows beyond us, not too far from where I thought Cyril might have found his latest chew toy, and the woman got out. She was shorter than the car was, and almost vanished behind the headstones as she opened the boot and started pulling out a quite astonishing collection of flowers and foliage, singing rather tunelessly about not feeling like dancing. We watched her for a little while, then Petra looked up at Callum. She had Cyril pulled so tightly against her side he had one paw on her trainers. Her hand was on his back and he kept peering up at her with a furrowed brow, as if he could taste her fear.

"What do we do?" she whispered. "We can't just *wait* here. It looks really suspicious." She'd sprouted matching lines to Cyril's on her forehead, and deeper ones were surfacing around her mouth. I wondered how she'd ended up here, with the old scars of oil burns marring the warm olive skin under her eye, smelling of lingering loss and working in the rundown cafe with its greasy windows and tattered floors. Our neighbourhood wasn't somewhere you came. It was definitely somewhere you ended up.

Callum lifted a hand as if he wanted to touch her shoulder or something, then let it drop, and nodded. "We'll just go," he said.

"Go?" she asked. "But what about …" she nodded at the arm.

"We'll put it under a bush or something, and I'll come back later and sort it out."

"But what if someone finds it?"

"No one's going to be hunting through the bushes," Callum said. "We'll come back later and work out where it came from, and bury it properly. Me, I mean. I will."

"I'll come too." She didn't sound very enthusiastic.

He shook his head. "You don't have to. This is more our – *my* line of work, anyway."

"What, grave digging?" she asked, a hint of a smile starting around her lips.

"No, sneaking around in the night." He grinned at her and led the way toward the gates, detouring into the trees and patchily maintained undergrowth that lined the stone walls to stash the arm. I stayed on his shoulder and watched the old woman filling vases with flowers, doing what the living do to honour the gone. Put dead things on their graves.

We walked back to our apartment block, the cracked pavement warm beneath my paws although the air was starting to feel sticky and heavy with rain on the way. Petra and Cyril walked part of the way with us, and we stopped where their road split from ours. She looked at Callum with those tight lines still on her face.

"Are you sure this is okay?" she asked.

"You didn't do anything wrong," he said. "I'll put the arm back, and that'll be it."

She looked at him for a long moment, then touched his hand with her fingertips. "Thank you."

He looked uncomfortable, like he wanted to pull away but didn't want to be rude. "It's no problem. Really. I didn't have any plans tonight anyway."

She stared at him for a moment, then grinned and said, "Sure. Okay. I'll buy you breakfast next time you're in the cafe."

"Cool," he said, and gave her a weird wave/salute thing as she turned and walked away, Cyril hobbling next to her and occasionally looking up at her with that soppy adoring look dogs get.

"Dude," I said. "You get worse."

"Shut up," he said, shoving his hands in the pockets of his ancient jeans.

"No, seriously. You should talk to people more. Or even date one? Maybe more than one? Any variety will do."

"I'm not taking life advice from a cat."

"You should," I said, and easily dodged the gentle kick

he aimed my way. “I mean, we’re way better at it than you lot are.”

“You also think biting’s a valid form of communication.”

“It communicates what I want it to very clearly,” I pointed out, and ran ahead of him as we headed deeper into the decaying rows of old warehouses and mills that formed the broken heart of our neighbourhood.

2

MOSTLY 'ARMLESS

OUR BUILDING WASN'T ONE OF THE BETTER ONES ON THE block. Hell, there were two derelict mills just down the street that looked more structurally sound than it did. But they didn't have little bedsits (*with* en suite. I mean, we were living the high life) for rent at a price even a broke PI firm could afford. And, to be fair, it had been in better condition before the events of the autumn, when a book of power had tried to tear reality apart, with our building at the epicentre of an interdimensional storm. That takes a toll on the best of places.

We pushed our way through the main door, which had never locked. Since the whole reality storm thing, it didn't close at all. One side was higher than the other, and there were some disturbing cracks in the wall, but until it actually fell down around us we weren't going anywhere. Cheap housing-slash-office space in Leeds is not easy to come by.

Yeah, I know. Gobbelino London, but I live in Leeds. I

really wish people would stop asking me about that. Sugar in the wound and what have you. Or is it spice? Whatever, leave it alone. Some memories are best left where they are. It's not always healing to revisit the past.

We headed upstairs, taking care to jump over the gap under the bottom step. Strange winds whispered in the dark, and there was a pile of fish bones outside it. Well, they looked like fish bones from jumping distance. I wasn't going to go any closer. We ignored the gap, and so far the gap had ignored us. As I say, there were some scars.

Our little apartment door with the classy black plaque that said *G & C London, Private Investigators* was still locked, although I was pretty sure even Petra could have pushed it down with one hand. It was less the fact of it than the principle though, that thing of having a door to lock the world out. It's not something stray cats get much of, and it's not something we pine for. PI cats, on the other hand, are quite fond of having a door to protect their microwaveable bed and sardine supply.

Callum hung his coat on the back of the bathroom door and put the kettle on in the tiny cupboard that passed as a kitchenette.

"Custard?" he asked.

"Won't say no," I said, and jumped onto the desk. Callum opened the desk drawer and let out a small green snake. The snake wriggled onto the desk, hissed at me, I hissed back, and, pleasantries over, he got on with whatever snaky things he had to do. Green Snake was a left-over from the book of power thing too. I'd have preferred the underfloor heating had stayed, but snake it was. That's just how our luck tends to run.

"What do you think about the arm?" Callum asked, putting a little bowl of custard in front of me and going back to fix his tea.

"It was gross," I said, trying the custard. Callum was insisting on lactose-free versions, and I was unconvinced.

"Well, yeah. It was a dismembered arm. But did you smell anything?"

"Decaying flesh?"

"Gobs."

I licked my chops and stared at him as he sat down in the big desk chair, mug of tea in one hand. The snake wriggled off the desk and slipped onto Callum's leg, where he draped himself comfortably. "What? Was there magic involved, you mean?"

"Yeah. Or, you know, leftovers from the book thing. It seems like a bit of a coincidence, don't you think?"

Coincidence. Yeah, I don't believe in them, but … I thought about it, remembering the whiff of rot and silence and deep, still places in the boneyard. The book had been anything but still. It had been alive with power. It had been *hungry.* "I don't think so," I said. "I mean, it was just an arm. Maybe they had an oops with a grave-digging machine or something."

"You'd think they'd notice that. And it was pretty fresh – it's not like they dug into an old grave accidentally."

"*Hmm.* Grave robbers?"

"Still had jewellery on it."

"Bloody territorial moles, then. I don't know, Callum. I

couldn't smell any magic. Dead bodies are really only of interest to ghouls, and they tend to like their meat a little more well-seasoned."

"Ghouls?"

"Yeah. Ghouls." I popped my front claws out and pawed the air, baring my teeth. *"Bring out your dead!"*

"That was the Black Plague," he said.

"Ghouls loved that. Bodies were seasoned before they even hit the ground."

He wrinkled his nose and opened a packet of dodgy-looking off-brand custard creams. They hadn't even spelt the name right – the packet said *Cuttard Crems*. "Should I be worried?" he asked.

"Not unless you have the plague. Ghouls have plenty of dead to munch on. They don't usually worry about making their own."

"Usually," he said, dipping a Cuttard Crem into his tea.

"Hey, there's always a first time."

"Great," he said, and leaned back in his chair so he could put his feet on the desk. "You can keep watch for them, then."

"Sure. They don't eat cats."

"There's always a first time," he said, and picked up his book while I glared at him. The snake stared at me with eyes that matched his scales, and I tried to think about other creatures that hung around the dead. There weren't many. The living were always more interesting.

We didn't fancy being arrested for grave desecration, so we gave it until after midnight before we headed back to the cemetery, when even the champion bottle-smashers in the alley had given it a break until morning. It had started raining as the dark came in, a heavy, persistent drizzle that said it was here to stay, so we ran through it to the car, the growing puddles on the road splashing up into my face and making me snort. This is the problem with being low-slung and elegant.

Callum let me jump in the driver's side door and over to the passenger seat, then folded his long legs and already sodden jacket in and started poking and pulling things in an effort to get the car started.

"That coat's not even waterproof," I told him.

"It's more a style choice than a practical one," he said, trying the key. The car did the vehicular equivalent of sticking its tongue out at him.

"What style's that? Dead man chic?"

"Well, it's appropriate for the evening then, isn't it?" he said, and turned the key again. The car stuttered a couple of times, then caught. "There we go."

"I can't believe we still haven't got a new car."

"Well, find us some high-paying cases, then."

I sighed, and set to cleaning some of the water off my coat. High-paying cases did not seem to be in our job description. The book of power case *could* have been high paying, but we'd sort of had to destroy the thing before getting it back to its rightful owner, which had come out of our pay cheque. Then the rightful owner, the glorious and terrifying Ms Jones, had paid us a not un-generous retainer based on my passing any information I could get to her about the Watch, the cat council that keeps humans and magical Folk apart.

Unfortunately I'd had no contact with the Watch since, and people – well, clients – kept breaking things in our office, so most of our money went toward replacing chairs and stuff. And we'd ended up with a rush of Folk cases, which were all very well, but they kept paying us in waterproof goblin-hair blankets and weirdly flavoured pixie cakes, which, oddly enough, didn't pay the rent. And Callum kept accepting it, because he said who else was going to help them? I personally thought that, if that was the case, they could sort their own problems out, but that's Callum. He likes cake, even if it is hawthorn and thistle flavoured.

So old car it was. But that still didn't excuse him wearing that coat.

WE PARKED across the road from the cemetery, finding a gap in the queue of cars parked outside the terraced houses that lined the block. There were no lights on in any of them, no TV showing blue through the curtains, just the yellow of the streetlights and, down on the main road, a garage shining pale and lonely among the residential buildings. Callum switched the engine off and we sat for a little while, watching the rain on the windscreen and making sure a police car on patrol wasn't about to pop around the corner, or more body parts appear out of the bushes.

"Looks alright," I said eventually.

"Dead quiet," Callum said, and grinned at me.

I spared a moment to envy Cyril his rolling eyes and said, "Genius. Shall we go?"

"You're no fun." He opened the door and stepped out into the soggy night, pausing to grab the shovel off the back seat. We hurried across the road and into the shadow of the half-naked trees that lined the outside of the wall, hiding the dead from the living – or vice versa. I wasn't sure. My own experiences of death had been violent and thankfully short, so I wasn't sure what human afterlife looked like. As far as my own went, I was already emerging into my next life before I had time to form much of an opinion, other than the fact that dying hurt. A lot.

I crouched by the wall, then launched myself at it, skittering up the ragged stone with my claws out and my ears back. Stone was always easier than brick – more claw-holds. It didn't half hurt if you bumped your nose on a pointy bit, though. I perched on the top and peered around, the night rendered in shades of grey and violet and the rain trickling through the thin fur around my ears.

"All clear. Come on up."

"Heads." Callum chucked the shovel over the wall, then jumped to grab the smooth stone top. He muscled himself up, boots scrabbling for grip, until he could swing one leg over and pause next to me. The trees still surrounded us, even if the shelter was a bit patchier up here under their leafless branches. We scanned the long lines of markers rubbing stone shoulders with each other while the crypts hunched in silent contemplation under the cover of more leaning trees. "Looks okay," he said.

"I did say."

"So you did." He swung his other leg over and dropped to the ground, landing with a stumble and a curse.

"Alright?" I asked, sliding my forepaws down the wall then jumping after him.

"Bloody nettles," he mumbled, fishing the shovel out of a clump and scratching his hand. "*Ow.*"

"Diddums." I picked my way out of the bushes into clearer ground. "Maybe Petra can rub some lotion on for you."

He grunted as he followed me. "Where did we leave the arm?"

I stopped and stared at him. "You've forgotten?"

He covered his mouth with one hand and widened his eyes. "Oh no!"

"Don't say it," I warned him.

"We're 'armless!"

"Oh, gods," I sighed. "You cabbage. This is why you don't date, isn't it?"

He grinned, shouldering the shovel. "I also don't want to have to explain why I live with a humourless cat."

"That was not humour. That was painful."

"You have no taste." He led the way along the edge of the trees, peering into the undergrowth. "Here we go." He pulled a bin bag out of one of his over-sized coat pockets,

SHAKING it out noisily and making my ears twitch. He used the bag like a glove to pick up the arm, then turned it inside out over the limb and bundled the top closed, his nose wrinkled. *"Ew."*

I waited until he picked the shovel up again, then padded off into the graves, heading for where Cyril had been careering around earlier. "It must be somewhere around here. The bloody dog was all over the place."

"What did you do to get him digging up graves?"

"I *didn't.* I flicked a couple of stones around, then *boom,* unattached arm." I stopped by a grave and sniffed the decorative stones that had tumbled onto it. "Here. I chucked a stone from here, then ran over *here,"* I loped a couple of graves over and jumped on top of the marker. Yes, I could smell dog drool and my own faint, familiar scent. "And from here I flicked it … somewhere." I gazed over the graves.

Callum had followed me, and now he stood on his tiptoes to peer over the rows. "Well, it should be easy enough to spot."

"You'd think." We headed for the next row, but there was nothing to see except uneven lines of markers, some leaning a little forward as if ready to collapse, others leaning back as if someone was pushing them up from below, the stone dark with rain and the old flowers left on some of the graves looking brown and forlorn. We moved on, and Callum gave a little *huh.*

"That must be it."

"Looks like it," I said, and followed him as he crossed to the raw wound of earth doming out of a new grave. It was churned up and uneasy looking. The marker read, *Gladys Foster, beloved wife, sister, mother,* and said nothing about her being missing an arm.

Callum stared down at the dirt then said, "I'm not opening the coffin."

"*Ew*. No. Can't you just kind of shove it in there somewhere?"

"Well, I'll try to do a bit better than that, just in case anyone else walks their dog around here."

"I'm pretty sure that's not the done thing," I told him, jumping to the top of the gravestone to watch him. The dirt was seeping to mud in the grass, and I could feel it getting between my toes. "Why were *we* here, even?"

He shrugged. "Better than the park, isn't it?"

Well, that was fair. The park was less grass than dead earth scarred by old fires, and more cigarette butts and discarded cans than flowers. And that was before you even mentioned the duck pond full of bobbing wine bottles (but no ducks), and the fact that there were a lot of *interesting* people camping in the bushes. Some of them were human, some of them not so much, and one had grabbed my tail and tried to shove me in a pressure cooker last time we were there. It wasn't my favourite spot.

But still. A cemetery? I watched Callum as he started digging, the rain slicking his hair to his head and cheeks and running off the tip of his nose as he worked. He didn't seem inclined to discuss it further.

THE LOOSE DIRT made digging easy, and before long Callum had a trench a bit longer than the arm and almost the same depth. I say before long, but I was shivering. The rain had eased to a drizzle, but only after finding its way right through my long outer fur and the protective undercoat as well, painting cold fingers down my spine. He placed the bin bag in the trench and stared at it, then at me.

"Well?" I said. "Job's a good'un."

"Should we say something?" he asked.

"Like what?"

"A prayer, or something."

"We have no idea if she was religious. And anyway, do you know any?"

"No," he admitted, and scooped some dirt onto the shovel. "Well, sorry about all that, Gladys. Be at peace, I guess."

"Yep. Rest in pieces." I snorted, but he ignored me and kept filling in the mini grave, which was a bit off. That was at least as funny as his jokes had been.

I watched for a bit, then jumped to the ground and stretched, strolling down the row. There were some fairly fresh graves in this area, wedged in among the older ones. I guess it got crowded, and they just had to fit everyone in where they could. There were always so many dead.

I jumped to the top of a shiny marble gravestone to investigate a dripping pinwheel turning slowly under the weight of the rain, and as I leaped I felt the earth give softly under my paws. I stumbled but still made the jump, then turned to peer back down at the grave. I couldn't see anything – there must've been a pocket of loose dirt. I looked up, checking on Callum, but he was still digging. I scanned the full circuit of the cemetery again. As far as I could see we were alone.

A shiver of movement caught my eye and I looked back, whiskers twitching. A vase of flowers on the grave below me trembled, then fell over. Weird. They were definitely having some burial-related issues at the moment. I jumped off the marker, making sure I stayed well clear of the grave itself – not that I was worried about walking over someone's grave, of course, because there's nothing in them except bones, but I had no intention of falling into some coffin-filled sinkhole.

There was a whisper in the air over my head as I ambled back to Callum, and I stopped to watch a flight of bats skittering past, their movement swift and jerkily graceful, their faint squeaks making my ears flick. They were chasing tiny critters across the dim sky, and their cries of joy as they caught them were little shivers of sound running through the last traces of the rain.

Callum was patting the dirt back onto the grave carefully as I stopped next to him.

"Shouldn't there be turf on top of it?" I asked.

"I thought so too, but there doesn't seem to be any. Maybe Cyril did just dig it up."

I eyed him. "I'm pretty sure coffins are compulsory."

"You can get cardboard ones these days."

"Did you even get as far down as the coffin, cardboard or otherwise?"

He sighed. "No. But I can't work it out. If it was grave robbers, they would've taken her rings and so on. And you say it can't be ghouls. Are you sure there's nothing else?"

I sat down and scratched my shoulder with one hind

leg, the circular sucker scars from the beast of the Inbetween still itching and stinging. "Roaming packs of starving wolves. Maybe a horde of impoverished medical students. Or zombies."

He snorted. "You told me zombies don't exist."

"They don't," I said, and yawned. "The rest are possible, though."

"Sure they are." He gave Gladys' grave a last, reassuring pat, then shouldered the shovel like a rifle. "Home? I could do with a cuppa after that."

"I could do with a hairdryer," I said, and started to follow him, but I'd barely taken two steps before a flicker of movement caught my eye. I stopped mid-stride and turned toward it. Not bats, I didn't think. It had been low to the ground, deeper among the graves. Too small to be someone walking. I squinted into the rain, but it didn't come again. Had it been another cat, perhaps? That could be awkward. I mean, we weren't doing anything *wrong*, exactly. We were, in fact, righting a wrong, but if it was a Watch cat they could be … prickly. And most took a dim view of cats who talked to their humans, unless their human was a Watch-approved cat lady.

There. A flutter of movement, hard to catch in the low light. It looked like it was coming from the new grave I'd been investigating. The one with the falling flowers. "Callum," I said.

"What?" He turned back to me.

"There's something out here."

"*What?*" He dropped into a crouch, peering around anxiously. "Where?"

"Over there," I said, lowering my voice. "Down the row. About six graves along. See the big marker? There."

He swore, crouching a little lower and staring into the dark. "Night watchman?"

"I don't know," I said, thinking of the way the earth had given under my paws and the unsettling image of sinkholes. "I don't think so. Can you see?"

He shuffled back to me in his half-crouch so he could peer down our row without being silhouetted against the night. Enough light filtered in from the streets outside that he hadn't needed the torch while he was digging, but it still must've been dim to his eyes. "I think I can see something moving. It's not a person. Rats, maybe?"

I squinted. The movement was ill-defined, but it didn't have the busy industry of rats. It made me think of moles, but I hadn't seen any molehills anywhere. I kind of thought they'd be pretty unpopular in a graveyard, to be honest. Humans are kind of squeamish about such things.

The movement came again, and now I was thinking of moles it suddenly resolved itself into something that made sense, like buildings emerging from mist. Well, it made a shaky sort of suspend-your-disbelief sense, but cats aren't humans. We don't run around shouting that things can't be so when the evidence is right in front of our eyes, shaky or not. "Dude," I said. "It's a grave."

"It's a what?" Callum spoke too loudly, and when I looked at him I could see his hands were so tight on the shovel that the white of his knuckles showed even through the dirt.

"It's a gods-damned grave." Even as I spoke, the earth heaved and two arms appeared, reaching rather dramatically for the sky. A head followed them, and the hands pawed clumsily at the face as the mouth opened in a moan, then there was a pause while their owner looked around. "You know," I said, "I may have to rethink my stance on the whole zombie thing."

Callum just stared at me.

3

THE DEAD RISE. WELL, ONE DOES

CALLUM STARED FROM ME TO THE MUD-ENCRUSTED FIGURE waist-deep in its grave. It moaned again, and some cotton wool fell out of its mouth. Callum scratched a hand through his hair, then said, "That's bollocks. Zombies don't exist. You *told* me they don't exist." There was something almost put out in his tone, like I was messing with him.

"Dude, things change. And maybe it was never true anyway." There was a niggling thought at the back of my mind reminding me that sometimes there *could* be such things as zombies. I mean, we're talking legends here, but still. The walking dead are the walking dead. "There's a corpse clawing its way out of a grave over there. I'm open to the possibility that I may have been wrong."

Callum squinted down the row. The zombie didn't seem bothered by the question of its existence. It seemed to be enjoying the night air on its face and hadn't made any move to extricate itself further. "We don't know it's actually a corpse," he said.

I resisted the urge to bite him. We had an agreement about that, but sometimes I wasn't sure it was worth it. "Sure, it's just someone who's been in a really deep sleep. In a coffin. In a graveyard. Underground."

Callum shifted his grip on the shovel and said, "Maybe we should see if they need some help?"

The zombie had stopped staring around and was trying to push itself further out of the ground. I could hear it grunting with effort. "That seems like a really bad idea. Like, horror movie bad. We should just get out of here."

We looked at each other for a moment, then Callum said, "You did say they don't exist."

"Look, that's common knowledge. Common knowledge also suggests sheltering under trees in the case of a thunderstorm is a good plan."

"No," Callum said. "It really doesn't."

I growled. "Okay, well, *my point is,* common knowledge can be wrong. I bet the first human to see a sabretooth tiger pointed at it and said, hey, you can't be real, right before they got munched. It's why trolls get away with eating so many people on bridges. No one ever believes in them."

Callum straightened out of his awkward crouch. "You've heard about most things in the Folk world. I'd have thought someone would have mentioned the walking dead."

"Not if no one's survived to mention it," I pointed out, but he was already walking slowly toward the zombie. I trotted after him, and took a careful glance about before I said the next bit. "And, I mean, there are such things as necromancers. Well, there were."

Callum paused, looking down at me. "Necromancers? As in blood sacrifices and raise the dead?"

"Yeah. I never got that bit myself. I mean, couldn't they have just kept them alive in the first place?"

The zombie moaned and waved at the sky helplessly, legs still entombed in the ground. Callum rubbed his mouth with one hand and said, "You think it might be them? Necromancers?"

"I bloody hope not," I said. "They almost ended the world as we know it. They were all into enslaving humanity and wiping out Folk. But we're talking way back. Like when humans and magical Folk coexisted and you lot tended to worship anyone who promised good crops. There haven't been proper necromancers since the war of the Watch."

"Not proper ones?"

"Not ones that can raise the dead."

"How can they be necromancers at all if they can't raise the dead?"

"They wear a lot of black and wander around darkened rooms with skulls and stuff. And hang out in boneyards with black candles. That sort of thing."

He nodded. "Right. Sure." He turned back to the zombie, and I kept a good pace behind him. If he was so keen on getting bitten I wasn't going to get in his way. He came to a stop a few metres away from the churned-up grave, staring at the creature still laboriously extricating itself from the soil. It was – or had been – a woman, and she hadn't been there that long. Her flesh was still plump, if a little whiffy of raw chemicals and early rot, and her hair was partly done up in a couple of fancy clips. She was so caked in dirt it was impossible to see much of her features, but she'd managed to work herself free to her thighs.

"Um, hi?" Callum offered. "Are you okay there?"

"Dude," I said from behind him, "She's either dead, the living dead, or been buried alive. I think the answer is pretty clear in any of those cases."

He ignored me, taking another step toward the woman. "Do you need help?"

She jerked her head in his direction, as if noticing him for the first time, and whined, reaching out with both hands like a child wanting to be picked up.

"Are you stuck?" He took another step toward her.

"Callum, don't," I hissed. He ignored me.

"What happened? Did someone put you in there?" He was almost close enough for her to touch him now, and she chattered her teeth urgently. I shuffled my feet in the loose, scattered dirt, then spat and rushed forward, hooking my claws in his jeans as my tail bushed out from the smell of the thing. There was a creeping putrescence to her that I'd never smelt before, and I'd seen my share of dead things.

"Zombie, Callum. *Zombie*. You know how that works, right?"

He looked down at me. "I'm not going to touch her."

"Do you have to be so close, then?" I demanded. "If she gets loose she'll be eating your brains before you can say *Shaun the Sheep*."

"I think you mean *Shaun of the Dead*."

"Seriously? This is what's worrying you?" I gave his jeans another tug, and he finally took a step away from the woman. She gave a croaky sort of wail and wriggled her fingers at him, her legs still firmly stuck in the depths of the grave.

"What do we do about her?" he asked.

"Well, I think you're meant to go for the brains," I said, nodding at the shovel.

He scowled at me. "I'm not braining some poor woman who may or may not be a zombie."

We both looked at her. She bared her teeth, and a worm fell out of her nose. I glared up at Callum.

"Okay," he admitted. "She is quite zombie-ish. But she mightn't be dangerous. We're not exactly zombie experts."

I had always thought most horror movies just had really clueless characters, but I was starting to wonder now. "I doubt she wants to give you a hug."

"She can't seem to talk. Maybe she's just asking for help the only way she can." But he didn't move any closer to the grave, and the woman just swayed there, grunting and snapping her hands at Callum like she was pretending to be a lobster. Outside the cemetery, a car burped its way along the quiet road, and further off a siren set up an urgent wail. The bats came back, dipping and scooting through the branches of the still winter-bare trees, and I was about to suggest we just leave well enough alone when one flitted past just above my head, then banked toward the zombie.

The woman's hands shot out with the speed of a frog's tongue, clamping shut over the bat. It had time to give one terrified chirp, then she crammed it into her mouth, eyes squeezed shut in delight. The wings stuck out from between her lips at grotesque angles as she crunched happily, a little thread of blood drooling over her chin.

"Oh God," Callum said, sounding as if he was going to lose his dinner.

"Well, that doesn't seem like a good sign," I said. "*Now* can we leave her?"

"But what if she gets free?"

"Then the bats are in real trouble."

"She might want more than bats," he said, taking a step back as she stretched toward him, groaning a little louder now.

"Then brain her," I hissed.

"You brain her," he snapped back, and I narrowed my eyes at him.

"I hope that isn't a dig at my stature, or lack of thumbs. I can't help being small but perfectly formed."

"Jesus Christ, Gobs, I can't just take a shovel to her!"

"She just ate a bat!"

We both turned to look at her in the exact moment that she surged out of the earth. The batty snack had apparently been the zombie equivalent of eating her Weetabix. She planted her hands on the ground and *shoved*, pulling her knees up to her chest, her eyes still fixed on Callum and her bat-stained teeth chattering. Callum and I gave a matched set of yelps (well, his was more a scream, but I'm not one to tell tales), and we lurched away from the grave.

"Dude!" I yelled. "Brain her already!"

"Just … wait a minute," he shouted at the woman, who

was advancing in a crouch, using her hands to help her, eyes rolling and teeth bared. "You don't want to do this!"

"Seriously?" I gave him a little more space. If he was going to turn himself into a horror movie statistic I didn't want anything getting on my fur.

"Any suggestions would be very welcome," he hissed at me, not taking his eyes off the woman. She took a sudden bound forward that brought her close enough to Callum that he leaped back, slamming into a headstone and spinning off it, yelping curses and almost falling. She shot after him on all fours, her grunts building to an excited crescendo as he scrambled off, still clutching the shovel desperately.

And he might have recovered if not for that ridiculous long coat, the one I was certain he'd rescued from a bin rather than a charity shop like he said. It swirled around him as he stumbled away and he stood on the bottom of it, pitching himself face-first onto the ground.

"Oh, Old Ones take you," I mumbled, then yelled, "Hey, deadhead! Over here!"

I didn't wait for her to respond, just launched myself in pursuit as she reached for Callum, yowling like … well, like the dead were rising. She hesitated just for an instant, glancing around to see what the commotion was, and I hit her legs with all claws bared. I tore through the tissue of her tights and into the cold skin beneath, hoping you couldn't catch zombie-ism by biting *them,* and she grabbed me with that same fearsomely swift movement she had the bat.

"Hairballs," I said, as she tore me free and hoisted me aloft with a squawk of triumph. "Callum!" I stuck all four legs out as she tried to cram me in her mouth, and my claws sank into the unpleasantly squishy flesh of her cheeks. "*Callum!* A little help here!"

The sound of the shovel hitting her head was like nothing I'd ever heard before, not in this life or my three previous. It was a final *crack* and squelch that I felt shaking in the pit of my belly, and it sounded more like a rock being flung into mud than as if it should have anything to do with a living creature. Well, unliving. Undead. You know what I mean.

Her hands jerked open convulsively and I fell, flailing to get my feet under me but not having enough time. I landed hard on my side, gave a squeak, then yowled as the woman crashed down on top of me, cold and stinking and grimed with dirt and rot.

"Callum!" I wailed, trying to dig myself out as the reek of dark, festering places surrounded me and the air was forced from my chest. Every hair was trying to pouf out in panic, and for one moment all I could think of were the lost places of the Inbetween, un-empty voids between the worlds where beasts roamed and the living were nothing more than bait for vast things. Suddenly I couldn't have breathed even if there had been room for it, and my mouth filled with mud and filth.

Then the body was pulled away, and Callum stared down at me, his face pinched looking in the dim light. "Are you okay?"

"You mean other than having a twice-dead corpse on top of me? Sure, great." I scrambled clear, spitting out both dirt and memories, and we stared at the woman. Her head was a different shape to what it should've been, and

Callum looked even paler than he had when she'd eaten the bat. "You look a bit green around the gums."

He gave me a puzzled look, then said, "Gills."

"What?"

"Green around the gills."

I stared at him. "You know you don't have those, right?"

He rubbed his forehead and said, "Sure. We do have zombies, though."

"Well, one." I inspected myself. I was caked in grave muck, and possibly some zombie slime. "Told you we should've just left."

"Sure. Because that's just what Leeds needs. Zombies roaming the streets."

I considered saying something along the lines of it probably not being a big change to how things currently were, given smartphones and other mind-altering substances, then thought that might be a grand generalisation. It might be just our neighbourhood where no one would notice the difference. "Okay, so you saved the city from the zombie apocalypse," I said, and shook some soil out of my ears. "Can we go home now?"

He hesitated. "We can't just leave her here."

I looked at her. Other than the bloodless dent in the back of her head, she looked like she'd just tripped over, and might get back up again at any moment. Well, the dent and the dirt caked on her clothes and bare legs, and a couple of beetles of some sort that had just crawled out of her ear. "Really?" I said.

"Yes," he said, and bent to pull her skirt a little further down her legs.

"Hairballs," I said, and sat down to wait. Him and his *ethics.*

CALLUM WENT BACK to the woman's grave and started digging, piling the dirt as neatly as he could next to him. The drizzle had all but stopped, at least, but it still looked a bit like he was making mud castles.

"You'll have to make this one deeper," I observed. "Since it's not just an arm."

He grunted.

"It's going to take ages," I added.

"Got it, Gobs," he snapped, wiping sweat off his forehead. The troublesome jacket had been abandoned on a nearby gravestone, and I wondered if I could push it into the grave without him noticing. "Thanks for pointing all that out."

"Just, you know. If we'd left her when I said we wouldn't be in this situation."

"And we might be in the middle of an actual zombie outbreak by tomorrow morning."

"Eh. Fair point." I went back to cleaning dead-lady dirt off my coat.

"Are you keeping watch?" he demanded. "I don't fancy explaining this to some night watchman."

"Sure, sure." I glanced around, but even the bats had made themselves scarce. I didn't blame them, after what had happened to their buddy. "It's dead quiet."

Callum groaned, and went back to digging.

Well, he started it.

It did take ages. Not as long as it could have, mind, since the woman (whose name, the gravestone informed us, had been June Atkins, and she'd been seventy-three when she died. Well, the first time she died) had done a good job of loosening it all up on her way out. Callum dug down until he started encountering shattered bits of coffin, the mound of earth beside him growing steadily as he expanded the trench. Finally he stepped back with a groan, throwing the shovel down and pushing his hair out of his face with one filthy hand. The air was still heavy with damp and I couldn't even begin to get the mud out of my fur.

"Good enough?" he asked me, in that way humans have when they actually mean, *I'm not really asking.*

"Looks great," I said. "Inviting. I'm sure she'll be really comfortable in there."

He gave me a sour look, and crouched next to June. He hesitated for a moment, as if expecting her to lunge at him again, then gathered her up and carried her to the grave. He laid her down in the rough trench gently, his knees cracking as he crouched, and tidied her hair out of her face. There was some bat wing still stuck to her chin, and he plucked it off, his mouth twisting in distaste. There wasn't much he could do for the rest of her. Besides, she was about to be covered with dirt again anyway. Hopefully permanently this time.

"I suppose that's it," he said.

"Not much else we can do," I agreed.

"*We*. Huh." Callum straightened up, pressing his hands into the small of his back with a groan, then crossed to his coat and found his cigarettes. "It's times like these I wish you were human."

"I don't," I said, tucking my feet under me more comfortably. "In fact, I never do."

"Why does that not surprise me?" He lit the cigarette, drawing on it heavily, and examined his hands in the faint light that filtered through from the street. "I've got blisters. Blisters *and* nettle stings."

I opened my mouth to tell him that was the advantage of fur and paws, then movement by the wall caught my eye. "Put it out," I said.

"Hey, I've earned this—"

"No, you courgette, there's someone there." My eyes were wide, stealing every scrap of light, but all I could tell right now was that we weren't alone anymore.

Callum swore and crushed the cigarette hurriedly, smothering the telltale red eye in the damp dirt. "Is it another one? Another zombie?"

I peered into the dark. Whoever it was, they were closer now, moving slowly but purposefully with a pack slung over one shoulder. They had a torch, too, and were pausing at each row, venturing along them and playing the light over the markers. Unless there were some dramatic differences in zombie functionality, I didn't think we were dealing with the living dead. "Nope," I said, and jumped off the gravestone. "Looks human. Let's go."

"We can't just leave her," Callum whispered, waving at the grave.

"We can't *explain* her, either," I hissed back.

Callum hesitated, one hand on his head, then said something unrepeatable about cemeteries and zombies.

He snatched up the shovel and his coat and ran after me in a half-crouch as I bolted for the nearest row of crypts, which were closer than the trees. No shout went up behind us, so we might have been lucky. Maybe the intruder was still far enough away not to have seen us. It was possible, if their eyes were as bad in the night as most people's.

And, you know, if they were most people. Which seemed a little unrealistic, given the zombie and the renegade arm. Have I mentioned that I don't believe in coincidences?

4

SOMETHING'S GRAVELY WRONG

We hunkered down in the shadow of the crypt, and I backed up until I could press against Callum's leg. He was breathing hard, but I'm not sure if that was the digging or the fact that we were hiding in a cemetery from what could either be someone intent on arresting us for grave desecration, or someone heading out to see how their zombie hordes were doing. Neither seemed a great option, so I didn't protest when Callum put one long-fingered hand on my back. I figured he could use the extra support.

The thin beam of the torch danced among the graves. Whoever it was didn't seem to know where they were going, but they definitely knew what they were looking for, methodically checking each row as they advanced into the cemetery. Beyond the torch I couldn't make out much detail. Although …

"Oh," I whispered. "That doesn't seem good."

"What?" Callum whispered back.

"Hooded figure in a cemetery in the middle of the

night, dressed all in black, plus the dead climbing out of their graves? I'm not an expert, but that seems like a bit of a bad sign."

"As in a necromancer type bad sign?"

"Or some other weird human ritual. But the dead rising is a bit of a giveaway."

"You said necromancers couldn't raise the dead anymore," he hissed.

"Well, as far as I know. I mean, I'm not the bloody *Encyclopedia Cattica*." After all, who told us the necromancers were gone? The Watch. And the Watch weren't just picky about how human-Folk contact occurred. They were *secretive*. Just as individual cats have their own reasons for things, the Watch does too. Of course they do. And while the general idea may be *greater good,* we all know how that plays out. I'm not sure even cats can get that one right.

So did I trust the Watch to tell the truth about the existence (or non-existence) of sorcerers who could raise the dead? Eh.

"So never mind zombies," Callum said. "This guy could be raising an undead army?"

"Or woman. Necromancy is a pretty equal opportunity occupation."

Callum made an irritated noise at the back of his throat, then we both froze as the torch beam stopped bouncing and the black-clad figure peered around the cemetery as if they'd heard something. There was a long, terrible pause, then someone started singing *We Are the Champions* on the street beyond the trees, and the figure relaxed. They set off down the path again, and Callum took a long, slow breath.

"Do we know if they can actually raise the dead, then?"

"No idea," I said. "Proper ones aren't even meant to exist these days. They got wiped out."

We watched for a moment longer. The figure had discovered the gunky grave where we'd buried the arm and was examining it carefully. They crouched down and started muddling about with something I couldn't quite see.

"So how can that be a necromancer?" Callum asked, nodding at the figure, who had finally abandoned the arm's grave and moved on to June's. They were staring down at the freshly re-dug earth, both hands on their head.

I shrugged. "How can there be zombies?"

Before Callum could answer, the figure said, clearly enough for us to hear, "No! Oh, no! No no no!" It was a male voice, a little cracked at the edges with strain. "No!" he said again.

"Is that a necromancer incantation?" Callum asked, and I bared my teeth at him.

"Look, it's not like he's much good at it, is he? One seventy-three-year-old does not an army make. Doesn't mean he's *not* one."

"Oh my God," the figure said, and crouched down next to the grave, presumably examining the body. "Oh my *God!*"

"Shouldn't that be 'oh my Dark Lord' or something?" Callum asked.

"You do realise necromancy is *not at all* the same as Satanism?" I snapped.

"You're the expert."

The man stood up again and looked around wildly, his hood still pulled low over his face. "Hello?" he called, his voice wobbly. "Is anyone there?"

We both shut up and huddled down, hoping the maybe-necromancer didn't come looking for us. Apparently he wasn't too keen on meeting anyone either, because after a couple more half-hearted shouts he took his backpack off and pulled out a collapsible shovel, then set to at the grave.

"That's clever," I said. "You should get one of those."

"I'm not intending on needing one," Callum said. "In fact, I'm hoping my grave-digging days are behind me."

"A good PI should always be prepared."

He poked me in the side, and we fell silent, watching the shadowy figure of the maybe-necromancer frantically shovelling earth back into the grave. Every time a car passed on the road outside, or there was a clatter of bottles or the slam of a door from some late-night resident, he shot straight upright like an alarmed rabbit, peering around anxiously and brandishing the shovel like he was ready to brain someone with it.

Finally he stood back, surveying his work with a critical tilt to his head, then hurriedly collapsed the shovel, piled it back into his bag, and took off down the path at a walk so quick it may as well have been a jog.

We watched until we heard the clatter of him climbing over the gates, accompanied by an alarmed squawk and a painful-sounding thud, then gave it another couple of minutes before getting up and wandering over to the grave. We stood side by side, staring down at it. The mound of earth was raw and injured-looking, but he'd done a decent job. Callum picked up a fallen vase of flowers and set it back beneath the marker.

"Saved you some work," I observed.

"Well, we are thinking the whole thing was kind of his fault anyway, right? I mean why else would he come here in the middle of the night? And he was obviously hunting for *this* grave."

I snuffled around the place. "I just ... if he was a necromancer, if this was necromancy, the whole place should *reek* of power. There's nothing. Not a whiff."

"Maybe you just don't know what necromancy smells like."

"Fair enough, but it'd smell of *something*. Of some sort of magic." And it should have smelled a *lot*. I couldn't imagine the power it'd take to raise the dead. Even an average sorcerer, like our lovely but alarming Ms Jones, stank like a pack of toothed and furious dogs of the dark-moors-and-gates-of-hell variety. And as powerful and ancient as she was (even without her book of power), she was still no necromancer.

"So what do we do?" Callum asked.

"Absolutely nothing," I said, turning to pad toward the gate. "Nothing to do with us."

"Gobs, there was a *zombie*," he called after me.

"So? Did anyone hire us to hunt for zombies? No, they did not. This is not our business."

"Gobs!"

"Not our business." I kept walking.

This sort of thing, unknown magic seeping into the human world, was going to attract the attention of the Watch, and that was something I just did *not* need. If they were looking for a scape-cat, I was far too good a choice. And while Claudia, she of the odd-coloured eyes and excellent timing, had dragged me out of the Inbetween last autumn, she was just one Watch cat. It had been a whole pack of them that dragged me *in*to the Inbetween and ended my last life. So, no. I had no intentions of getting involved in anything that might also involve the Watch.

"Gobs," Callum called again, and I hesitated, looking back at him. His voice was strained and uneven at the edges, and he was standing on the path behind me with one hand in the pocket of his horrible coat and the other still holding the shovel.

"What?" I demanded.

He put the shovel down and fished his cigarettes out. "I ... I need to check something."

"Check *what?* And why now?"

He sighed. "A grave."

"What grave?" I turned and trotted back to him. The bats were venturing warily back into the boneyard, but they were keeping a bit higher. I didn't blame them.

He lit his cigarette before answering, the flicker of the lighter casting his face in strange angles. "The one I came to visit today."

I stared up at him, the cigarette smoke drifting in the damp air and smelling acrid and ugly above the deeper scents of wet grass and damp earth. "Better than the park, huh?"

He shrugged. "I'm not even sure where they're buried."

"Who is it?"

"Someone I used to know." He picked up the shovel again. "Will you help me find it? I just … it's recent. And, you know …" He trailed off, waving at the raw earth on June's grave.

"Sure," I said, because there was nothing else I could say. Pasts are complicated things. I didn't know much about Callum's before he'd charged in to rescue a kitten-sized me from where I'd been trapped between some prime examples of the human species and a beast that was determined to break out of the Inbetween. It hadn't seemed necessary to ask about what went before. It had been enough that he was there, even if he was so high he'd tripped over his own feet on the way in, and the kerb on the way out. The past hadn't mattered.

And he never asked me what I'd done that was so bad the Watch had felt feeding me to the beasts was a fitting punishment.

So of course I said sure.

CALLUM TURNED BACK to the graves. "The funeral was two days ago. I know it was this end of the cemetery, just not where."

"You watched," I said, following him.

"Yeah."

He didn't offer any other explanation, so I just said, "Name?"

He took a long drag on the cigarette, squinting against the smoke. "Ifan Lewis."

"Alright." I headed off over the grass, looking for fresh graves. A couple of days ago meant I'd still be able to smell the rawness of the earth, the fresh stone of the marker. It was easier than trying to read inscriptions in the low light.

We worked our way steadily through the uneven ranks of markers and spindly, still-naked trees, and I heard Callum light another cigarette as soon as he was done with the first. He kept the shovel against his shoulder, and the hair on my spine felt like it was still half-raised, even clumped with mud and damp as it was. The night – or, rather, very early morning – beyond the walls was still and near-silent, only the odd rumble of a lorry or lonely car passing to remind us that the living were still out there.

My paws were so wet that I was starting to wonder about foot-rot when I heard Callum swear from the other side of the cemetery, not far from the opposite wall. I spun toward him, half-expecting to see him fending off another unquiet corpse or hooded gravedigger, but he was just standing there in front of a marker with his cigarette hand buried in the drenched mess of his hair and the other clutching the shovel. I ran toward him, hoping he was damp enough that he wasn't about to set himself on fire.

"You found it?" I called as I got closer.

He looked up at me, his mouth twisted in an uneven line, then just nodded at the marker. I skirted it and came to a stop by his boots, staring at the grave.

The turf was torn to pieces, shattered into hills and pits, as if a small but violent earthquake had taken place. The toe of a shiny black shoe poked out near the marker.

"Oh, hairballs," I said.

Callum nodded, and leaned down to pull the shoe out. It came away easily, and he stared at it. "I don't why they put these on him," he said. "Ifan only ever wore trainers."

"Well, no wonder he left it behind," I said, and he gave me a look that suggested I was being unhelpful. "What?"

Callum didn't talk much on the way back. We left the same way we'd arrived, taking our time at the top of the wall to make sure no one was around – including his newly dead buddy – and slipping back to the car. The heater wheezed itself into life as Callum got the engine started, and I had another attempt at cleaning mud and zombie slime off my coat, but I was starting to think it was a lost cause. I worked on it all the way back to the apartment, but it didn't seem to make much difference. I felt like I might be filthy forever.

We climbed the creaking stairs with their unnerving gap and let ourselves wearily into the chilly office. Callum flicked the kettle on and peeled his jacket off, then sank into the rickety desk chair, burying his face in his hands.

"So, Ifan," I said, jumping onto the desk. The snake had been asleep in my bed on the corner, and he gave me a look that suggested he thought it was his now. I ignored him for the moment.

"Ifan," Callum agreed.

"Any necromancers in the family?"

Callum didn't answer straightaway, and when he did his voice was thoughtful. "Not exactly. Give me a moment, Gobs, okay?"

I did, but more because I didn't like that pause than because he'd asked. I watched him get up and go into the kitchenette, seeing his hand drift to the shelf where we kept the client's whisky, then move more surely to the tea bags instead. That was good. It had been a long time since he'd taken the bottle down for himself, and it didn't seem a great time to start, what with the whole undead thing and all.

He slopped water into his mug, put some biscuits in a bowl for me, then found some dry clothes in the bottom of the filing cabinet.

I waited until he sat down again before I said, "Not exactly?"

He sighed. "Magician."

"He was a magician?"

Callum nodded, and opened the packet of Cuttard Crems. "So's his dad."

I blinked. "You know magicians."

He smiled, just slightly. "I know lots of people."

"You never said."

"You never asked." He dipped the biscuit in his tea.

I crunched one of my own biscuits, thinking about it. Okay, so I'd never said, *know any magicians, then?*, but surely that was something you mentioned. I mean, magicians – *proper* magicians, not pull-a-coin-out-of-your-ear magicians, although they do that sometimes, because everyone's got to make a living – were closer to Folk than human. Not to the extent of sorcerers, who were ancient enough to have lost most of their humanity over the centuries, but still. That level of magic wasn't exactly common these days.

Then again, neither's Callum. He accepts the world of Folk without question, and while he's no magician he's got more old magic in his bones than any human I've met before, sees more and understands more. Sometimes I think there's more magic in him than he realises – or than I've realised. I'm not sure which.

"Alright, so I'm asking now. How do you know magicians?"

He sighed. "I just do. You weren't exactly my introduction to the idea that there's more to the world than humans, you know."

I sat up straighter. "How come you're so clueless about it, then?"

"Nice."

"You are."

"Just because I see it doesn't mean I understand it." He slurped tea. "Look, that bit doesn't matter. Ifan's *gone.* That woman was dead. We don't even know what happened to Gladys – whether she's running about with one arm or if she's still in the grave and the arm just kind of …" he trailed off, waving vaguely.

"Dug itself out?" I asked.

"Maybe."

I really wished that seemed as implausible now as it would have that morning. Well, yesterday morning, now. I yawned. "Dude, we can't do anything about it."

"We can find out who that guy in the cemetery was. If he's the one doing it."

"I didn't smell any magic. And he didn't exactly strike fear into my heart, like a decent sorcerer should."

"Right, so, we talk to Ifan's dad. See if he knows anything."

I snorted. "I can see that going well. 'Hey, you didn't happen to raise your son from the dead, did you?'"

"We have to start somewhere."

"*Why?*" I complained. "No one's hired us to look into it. And I almost got eaten. I'd rather avoid that in the future."

Callum rubbed his face with both hands and fished a new box of cigarettes out of the desk drawer. If we didn't get munched by the undead I was going to be showing him some NHS articles on lung cancer. "Other people could get eaten. This could spread."

"As I said, no one's paying us to be interested in this."

"Civic duty, then," Callum said, lighting the cigarette and leaning back to try and persuade the smoke to escape through the window. The chair creaked ominously.

"I'm a cat. We do not have civic duty."

He sighed, and looked at me for a long moment. There was still mud on his face, caught in his stubble and smeared on one of his eyebrows. "Ifan was a friend."

I glared at him. "Who you were so close to that you watched his funeral from … where? Behind a crypt? The top of the wall? The gates?"

He looked away. "The gatehouse. It's empty. I watched the procession go past, then left before they finished."

"Because you didn't want to be seen by any of your dear friend's family."

He jammed the cigarette in his mouth and crossed his arms over his chest. "And you don't have parts of your past you miss but had to leave behind?"

We were both silent for a while then. Under the damp must of wet clothes and muddy skin I could smell that lost part of him that was always there. Nothing filled it, but at least he'd stopped trying. You had to, eventually. Some losses just have to be borne.

But there were ways to make the bearing of them easier.

"Hairballs," I said. "You're a soppy damp carrot, but *fine*. Let's go hunt zombies. But in the morning. Now will you move that bloody snake and heat my bed? It's not a snake bed. He doesn't understand boundaries."

Callum snorted and got up. "Like you do."

"I *so* do," I said, and he scritched my head, his fingers gentle and warm between my ears. Friendship is such a strange and complicated thing, but good humans are hard to come by.

Even if they do come with zombies.

5

THERE'S A FINE LINE BETWEEN COLLECTOR AND … SOMETHING

THE NEXT MORNING WAS NO IMPROVEMENT ON THE NIGHT before. True Yorkshire spring, it was. I half-opened my eyes to drizzle on the window and Callum cursing the electric shower, which stopped working any time someone in the building flushed a loo, or washed their hands, or rinsed a glass, or, you know, *looked* at a tap. I snuggled down into the soft fabric of my bed, watching the bare branches of the tree outside scratching the low sky, and didn't move until Callum emerged from the tiny bathroom barefoot, already pulling a hoody on. His hair was wet and stuck up at strange angles.

"Breakfast?" he asked me.

"Cafe?" I suggested. I fancied some bacon.

"No. Cat biscuits."

"How dare you?" I said, but with no real heat. They weren't so bad, but it was the principle of the thing.

"I'll put some cat milk on them."

"I'd prefer custard."

"You do know that's not one of the feline food groups, right?"

"It is mine." I sat up as he snorted and wandered into the little kitchenette, putting the kettle on and shaking biscuits into a bowl. "So are we off to see dad magician?"

Callum came back and put the bowl on the desk. "I suppose so. I mean, you're right, we can't exactly accuse him of doing it, but he should be told what's happened to Ifan. Imagine if he came to visit the grave, and ..." He trailed off, his mouth twisting.

I stepped my front paws out of the bed and stretched, pushing my hindquarters up and arching my tail toward the ceiling. "You kind of sound like you *want* to accuse him of it."

Callum shrugged. "He's not a necromancer. But he's not exactly a nice person. Or a nice magician, conjuring up pretty flowers and sunny days."

Well, this sounded like fun. I set about my biscuits. I had an idea I was going to need my strength.

IT MIGHT HAVE LOOKED like drizzle from inside, but by the time we got to the car my paws were sodden and Callum's coat was dripping. Again.

"Dude, just buy a raincoat," I said as he threw it in the back seat and folded himself behind the wheel.

"I could say the same to you," he said, and I bared my teeth at him.

"*My* coat looks good even when it's damp."

"So does mine."

"You look like a flasher."

He gave me a disgusted look. "Do you even know what one of them is?"

"Hey, I'm a cat of the streets."

"Sure you are," he said, pumping the accelerator and doing weird things with knobs. I was half sure that the car only started through his sheer willpower alone. "That's why you need a heated cat bed."

"Even a stray's allowed to like the finer things in life."

He snorted, and tried the key. The car whined, coughed, and spluttered without catching. He tried a different combination of levers and knobs. "You reckon the Watch knows about all this?"

"I'm not about to ask."

He nodded at that, and the car finally burped its way into life. Humans, like most other creatures, can't shift, can't step into the endless void of the Inbetween and back out again somewhere else entirely, the way cats can. So he'd never known the empty cold of the Inbetween, but he'd glimpsed the monsters that lived there, and seen the scars they left behind. He never asked why I didn't fancy getting close to the cats that had thrown me to them.

OKAY, call it prejudice, but I pretty much expected Callum to drive us to some run-down corner of Leeds, all boarded-up windows with things moving in the darkness behind them, and corner shops with faded posters on the walls, doing a brisk trade in spells and curses out the back door. The magical equivalent of our neighbourhood, basically. Those are the sort of places Folk and those humans who drift on the edges of the Folk and human worlds tend to congregate, where it's easier to pass unnoticed.

These little pockets are everywhere, faded leftover villages and tattered streets in cities where humans never go. There aren't any signs or anything. People just … don't go there. And Folk can live pretty openly, which is nice when you spend the rest of your time overheating with your woolly legs stuffed in jeans or trying not to take root when you stop for a coffee. Not that most humans notice, but there's always a risk.

Those are the sort of places I'd go looking for a magician, but Callum drove us out toward the outskirts of the city, where terraced houses and red brick semis gave way to grey stone homes set behind high fences, the sort that have electric gates with alarms on them. The gardens looked lush and self-satisfied, even in the cold rain, and there were summerhouses and water features in at least half of them. I even saw some dubious topiary.

"Dude," I said. "Magic pays well."

"He does something in finance," Callum said, turning down a street lined with spreading trees. "Ifan's dad, that is."

"Magical finance?"

"No, I think just regular finance. Folk clients, though." He pulled over just before a pair of large metal gates and leaned his forearms on the wheel, peering up at the stone wall. A plaque said *43*, but there was nothing else to identify the house, and the wall was too high to see beyond it.

"Will he let us in?" I asked. I didn't fancy sneaking this

one. I was willing to bet there were guard dogs around the place, and there's no reasoning with them.

"Let's go and see," Callum said, and got out of the car. I followed him, my ears back against the rain, smelling wet grass and leaf mulch and a vague, unfounded superiority.

The gate had a little call button with a camera above it, and Callum rang, then waited. After a moment, there was click, then an impatient voice said, "Yes?"

"Mr Lewis," Callum said. "My name's Callum North. I was a friend of Ifan's."

I blinked. I'd never really considered the fact that Callum had adopted my name. I'd sort of forgotten that he hadn't been Callum London until he met me.

"Great," the voice beyond the gate said. "What d'you want?"

"We have some information I think you need," Callum said.

"Yeah? How much are you charging?" Lewis' accent was broad and Northern, and didn't seem to sit well with the fancy gates and flash vehicles drifting past on the road outside, their occupants peering at our tatty car suspiciously.

"Just some information in return."

There was a pause, then Lewis sighed. "Fine. Come in."

The intercom clicked off and a hum started up in the walls as the gates unlocked themselves and swung softly inward, revealing a potholed drive leading up to a broad sweep of gravel in front of the house. There was a garage off to the left with a rusting ship of a Rolls Royce sitting in front of it, the driver's side dipping wearily toward the ground at the front. There was a water feature coughing green water near the doors, and the grass on the lawn was about nose-high to me. I looked up at Callum as we headed for the house.

"Skimping on maintenance a bit here."

Callum smiled slightly. "Ifan said his dad fell out with the tiddy 'uns who looked after the water, as well as the dryads and gnomes who looked after the garden, and he never really worked out that you can hire humans to do it. He doesn't like humans."

"Magicians *are* humans."

Callum shrugged. "Lots of humans don't like humans."

Well, that was fair. We climbed three wide stone steps to the front door, the house squatting uneasily above us, its harsh lines softened by the wilting ivy that climbed the front and ventured around one of the towers. There were quite a few towers. The whole thing looked a lot like a child's sandcastle – boxy on the bottom and topped with lopsided spires.

The door opened as Callum lifted his hand to knock, revealing a short man in a lime green tracksuit. He glared at me.

"You didn't say anything about a cat."

"Yeah, I'm not delighted to be here myself," I said, glaring back.

"He's not Watch," Callum said.

Lewis sniffed. "They're all dodgy, cats."

I opened my mouth to tell him how little I appreciated that slight on my kind, and Callum nudged me with his boot. I subsided, and he said, "I want to talk to you about Ifan's grave."

"What about it?"

"Can we talk inside?"

Lewis grunted. "Sure. Why not? May as well have all his junkie mates around with their conspiracy theories, right?" He stepped back to let us in, and I wondered how dangerous it might be to bite a magician. Callum didn't reply, just walked into the vast entrance hall and stood there with his coat dripping on a zebra-skin rug. Actual zebra skin, not print.

"Gross," I announced, jumping off and onto the old, scoured wood floor. "Oh, dude. What is *wrong* with you?" Taxidermied heads lined the walls, glaring down at us with glassy, furious eyes, festooned with dust-encrusted antlers and horns and moth-eaten ears. Dead birds were pinned to the walls and hung from the two-story ceiling on wires, a painful imitation of life, and there were two human skeletons posed with cups of tea and feathered hats arranged on chairs in the corner.

Lewis looked around as if seeing it for the first time. "My family have always been collectors."

"You know there's a fine line between 'collectors' and 'mass murd—'" I was cut off by Callum nudging me again, and I narrowed my eyes at him.

"Come into the study," Lewis said. "You can tell me how sorry you are, and how you wish you could have been at the funeral, and did I know just how close you were to Ifan, and then you can ask me for money, right?"

I huffed in disgust, but didn't say anything. Neither did Callum. He just followed Lewis through a low door at the back of the hall, under the staircase that curved its way up to the first-floor landing. I followed, eyeing a side table with giraffe legs. I suppose you couldn't accuse him of being species-ist, at least. Not with the skeletons there.

The room beyond the hall was dimly lit, curtains drawn tight against the dull day and only an old-fashioned brass lamp with a green shade spilling light on the cluttered desk. Lewis waved Callum into a high-backed leather chair and lowered himself into a matching one on the opposite side of the desk. There was a fat bottle of brandy and a half-finished glass sitting in front of him, and he nodded at it. "Suppose you want some of that, too?"

"No," Callum said. I jumped to the arm of the chair and examined the room. It coursed with whispers of low-level magic, charms and spells and the sort of curses that got you a month of stubbed toes and bitten tongues and flat tyres. Old books with cracked spines lined the walls, interspersed with jars in which half-seen things moved in murky liquid. There seemed to be fewer dead things in here, but I wasn't sure the half-life in those jars was any better.

"So what do you want, then?" Lewis asked, taking a gulp of brandy.

I waited for Callum to do his patented, quiet-voiced, softly-softly approach, where the person ended up confiding in him while he nodded and made sympathetic noises, and sometimes even patted their hands.

"Ifan's grave's been dug up. Did you do it?"

Lewis snorted brandy out of his nose, and I stared at Callum. "Dude," I said, but he ignored me. He was watching Lewis.

"What … how …" Lewis slammed his glass back onto

the table and wiped his face with the sleeve of his track-suit. "What in the name of the Old Ones are you *talking* about?"

"You didn't do it?"

"That's my *son,*" Lewis hissed, leaning over the desk and jabbing one finger wildly at Callum. "My *son!*"

"Ifan told me once that those skeletons in the hall are his great-aunts. And he showed me the room with the others. The preserved heads and the sarcophagi."

Lewis fell back in his seat and grabbed the bottle, slopping brandy over the desk as he tried to fill his glass. "That's family business. He had no right to show you."

"So did you take him?" Callum asked.

"No." Lewis wrapped his hands around the glass, but didn't drink from it. He just stared at Callum with his face set in hard lines. "No," he repeated finally, his voice quieter. "We preserve the heads of our elders to preserve their knowledge. We store the bodies for those who want to rise again. We don't do anything for children who turn their backs on their birthright and destroy themselves."

I snorted. "Yeah, I've been here five minutes and even I don't think it was his birthright he was turning his back on."

"He was a waste," Lewis spat, and gulped brandy. His hand was shaking.

A muscle twitched in Callum's jaw. "Then who dug up the grave?"

"Are you sure that actually happened?" Lewis asked. "You didn't hallucinate it?"

"I saw it too," I said. "And it wasn't the only one."

The magician looked at me properly for the first time. "There were other graves?"

"At least two others," Callum said.

"Well, then, *obviously* it's not me. Why would I dig up other graves?"

"You sure?" I looked around the dark, cluttered room. "Business going alright? Grabbing your son's body didn't start you thinking about other avenues of income?"

"What, you think I'm selling body parts?"

"More involved in a little light reanimation."

"Reanimation?" Lewis looked from me to Callum. "The corpses were moving?"

"Biting, too," I said, before Callum could answer.

"Dammit," the magician said, and put his glass down. "*Dammit!*"

"What do you know about it?" Callum asked. His hands were clasped together in his lap, and his knuckles were white with pressure. I wondered if he wanted to bite Lewis as much as I did.

"Nothing." Lewis got up, rubbing his hands over his tight grey curls. "You have to go."

Callum didn't move. "What do you know?"

"Why would I tell *you?*" Lewis demanded. "Some junkie friend of my kid, just turning up talking about reanimated corpses? You probably think this is *funny*. And where were you? Where were you when he overdosed in some damn back alley somewhere?"

That muscle was jumping in Callum's jaw again. "I'm sorry I wasn't there to help. But I can help now. I can at least make sure no one's ..." He trailed off, and swallowed hard. "No one's done anything to him. So you can help or not, but you're only slowing things down by not."

Lewis glared at Callum, his hands clenched into tight fists, and I said, "We're professionals. G & C London, private investigators. Just tell us what you know, then you can go back to your taxidermy or whatever."

The magician sniffed. "Yeah, you look like professionals."

Callum got up and rested his hands on the desk, leaning forward to glare at the older man. "Fine," he said. "Why would you do more for him now than you did when he was alive?"

And he turned and walked out into the hall of dead things, his shoulders drawn high and tight and his footfalls dull on the skins covering the floors.

We were halfway to the gate before the gravel crunched behind us, and we turned to find Lewis puffing down the drive, his tracksuit glaring in the dull grey light.

"You really care about this?" he asked us.

"Do you?" Callum asked.

The magician crossed his arms and rocked back on his heels, frowning at us. "Look, I wasn't the greatest dad, I get that. But he didn't *want* help. What was I going to do, lock him up? He was a natural magician. He'd have escaped from anywhere I put him."

"Sometimes it's not about it working," Callum said. "Sometimes it's about the trying."

Lewis tried to hold Callum's gaze, then examined the

ground instead. "He got in with some weird lots over the years. Spell-casters and druids and dream-walkers and all sorts. The last thing was this group of … well, mostly they're not even magicians. Half of them I doubt have even seen a sprite, let alone cast a spell."

"And?" I said, when he seemed unsure how to continue.

He glanced at me. "They're calling themselves necromancers."

"Oh, dude," I said. "But if they're so useless—"

"I know. But Ifan was involved. And now you're saying corpses are being reanimated, including maybe him? That's quite a coincidence."

"Where do we find them?" Callum asked.

Lewis shrugged. "Ifan used to go to Headingley to meet them. I think they have some sort of meeting space there."

"Names?" I suggested. "A phone number? *Anything?*"

"We weren't exactly close," Lewis said.

"Awesome," I said. "That really narrows things down."

Callum took a card out of his pocket and handed it to the magician. "Call us if you locate them."

"Alright," Lewis said, and watched us head down the drive, avoiding the larger puddles. Eventually he called after us, so quietly I barely heard him, "Thanks."

I looked up at Callum as he hit the button to let us out the gate. "Nice guy."

"Yeah. And that was him actually being pretty civil. You know why Ifan showed me the room full of heads and bodies?"

"Why?"

"His dad used to lock him in there when he was a kid, if he forgot a spell or wouldn't turn a frog inside out."

"*Urk.*"

"Pretty much."

I was quiet as we clambered back into the car, which after a couple of days of us being damp and muddy was starting to take on a distinctly swampy smell. Callum coaxed the ancient motor into life, and we coughed and backfired our way down the road as it warmed up.

"You think he was for real?" I asked. "About the necromancers?"

"I'm not sure," Callum said. "Not much point in him pointing us at people *he* doesn't even think can do it."

"There is if he wants to distract us."

He glanced at me. "You smell anything in there?"

"Magician stuff. And a *lot* of dead things. I mean, the magic didn't smell powerful enough, but maybe he did do it. He really likes dead things. He's a, whatchamacallit, necropotato. Necrophiliac."

Callum snorted. "That has slightly different connotations to just liking dead things."

I stared at him. "Humans are so weird."

"Yeah, I know. But we gained something."

"A new fan?"

Callum fished in his pocket and waved an unfamiliar mobile at me. "A phone."

"You *stole* it?" Well, this was a new, shiny Callum. Or maybe an old one, I wasn't sure.

"It was on the desk." He put it on the passenger seat next to me. "It might be Lewis', but I don't see him holding the back on with gaffer tape."

"Oh, I like this Callum. Can we keep him?"

Callum snorted, and rolled his shoulders in the wet coat. "Don't get too excited. There might not be anything in there related to necromancers."

I wondered if it was a bad thing to hope that there was. One didn't usually hope for raisers of the dead.

6

THE SPHYNX CAT CAFE

THE MOBILE CALLUM HAD ACQUIRED REALLY WAS IN A BAD way. It looked like it had been dropped on something hard, from a good height, and the dog had given it a decent chew before it had been rescued. I mean, our phone was pretty ancient and ugly, but even it looked fresh from the shop compared to this one. But it worked, and we were currently staring at a square of dots on the screen.

"A spiral?" I suggested.

"But which way?" Callum asked. "And starting where? It locks you out after a few goes."

I sighed. "Was he a spiral sort of person? Perhaps we're overcomplicating this. Can you draw a spiral when you're high?"

Callum scowled at me. "Uncalled for."

"Well, just try something. I'm hungry, and this car stinks."

Callum tried a zig-zag pattern, then a U, then an L,

and the phone came up with a warning that he only had two attempts left. "This could take ages."

"We need a hacker. All good PIs should have a hacker."

"You watch too much TV."

"I wish," I grumbled. The only TV we got was when the decrepit laptop agreed to connect to next-door's Wi-Fi – and when they didn't notice and change the password again. Luckily they were pretty uninventive. It was always some variation on *PorkPies4Eva.*

Oh, yeah. Wi-Fi was one thing Callum *did* steal, because his theory was that there was sort of spare Wi-Fi lying around going to waste, and it didn't cost anyone else anything. Plus he'd give the round, bespectacled man in the apartment next door the odd bottle of wine on the rare occasions we were feeling flush.

I imagine the unexplained bottles of wine probably seemed pretty weird to the neighbour, but our whole neighbourhood was pretty weird. A free bottle of wine was welcome-weird, unlike the man on the third floor who, every other month, ran naked through the halls throwing frozen peas everywhere.

"Can we get lunch?" I asked, putting my paws on the window. "There's a cafe right there."

Callum looked up with a sigh as the phone screen went blank and it locked him out. "Why not."

We'd parked a couple of streets over from the straggling centre of Headingley, outside a hair salon offering cheap haircuts for students, and across the road from a series of old houses that had been chopped up into flats. Beer cans and wine bottles overflowed from the recycling bins, and someone had put a traffic cone on the roof of a porch. Students carting bags of books and cradling take-away cups of coffee washed past us, dressed head to toe in black, or flowing pastels, or the sort of pleated beige trousers that made a hairball catch at the back of my throat. We wound our way through them and slipped into the cafe, where a woman with three lip piercings looked at me and said, "Out!"

"Aw, man," I muttered.

"Takeaway?" Callum asked hopefully.

"If the cat stays outside." She wrinkled her nose. "Shouldn't you have it on a leash?"

Callum hurried me out the door before I could express my opinion on leashes or being referred to as *it*, and we stood looking at the ambling passers-by.

"Bet she's a dog person," I said.

Callum snorted, and turned down the road. "Come on. Try the next one."

The next one was so dimly lit that I doubt they even saw me, although I kept myself tucked behind Callum's legs as we went in, just in case. He ordered a coffee and a tuna sandwich while I inhaled the ghosts of old cigarettes and late nights baked into the scarred wood floors. Callum found a small table at the back of the cafe, and I jumped onto the seat against the wall, peering out at the small room. There were only a couple of other tables occupied, each by people on their own, and there was low music playing that kind of sounded like cow bells.

"Jeez," I said. "You sure you want to eat here?"

"You're the one who was starving."

"Eh. I'm rethinking that." I watched him pull the phone out of his pocket again and examine it, and as he did a pale, skeletal shape detached itself from the shelter of the curtains at a small window above us and jumped to the table. I gave a squawk of alarm, and Callum jerked away as the creature landed in front of him, pale flanks all but glowing in the low orange light of the wall lamps. A tail, thin and bald as a rat's, whipped softly behind it, and it regarded me with pale, narrowed eyes.

"What?" it said, and now I could smell it. It smelled like a cat. It moved like a cat. It also *sounded* like a cat, and a she-cat at that, but there wasn't a hair on it. Even its – her – whiskers were nothing more than nubs. And that *tail* … Ugh. Bald tails are the one thing about rats that I just can't get on with, and this one was cat sized.

"Old ones take us," I said. "What happened to you?" I wondered if you could get zombie-cats. She kind of looked like you'd imagine a zombie-cat would look.

The cat breathed out rather heavily through her nose. Her poor, naked nose, with a little line of scar tissue twisting over the very end. "*If* you are referring to my lack of hair, a) rude, and b) I am a Sphynx cat."

"Sphynx? You come from ancient Egypt? You're a mummy cat?"

The Sphynx cat tipped her head to the side slightly, and the orange light shone through the skin of her ears, highlighting the twisting blood vessels. Her tail whipped a little harder, and I tried not to look at it. "A Sphynx cat is a breed, you peanut."

I stared at her. Her skin didn't seem to fit properly, and hung in naked folds from her shoulders. "You're meant to look like that?"

She sat down, and now I didn't know where to look.

Cats aren't exactly fussed about the human concept of modesty, but there were nipples everywhere. "Dude. You come into *my* cafe and insult me?"

"Your cafe?" I asked.

"The Sphynx Cat Cafe," Callum said, tapping the drinks menu on the table. The cat stared at him. "Hi," he said.

"Hi," she said, a little cautiously. "You one of them?"

"One of who?"

She examined him, turning her back on me. At least I didn't have to look at her nipples now, but her tail was dangerously close to my nose. I shifted back in the chair a bit. "You can hear me, but you don't smell like one of them."

Callum nodded. "Pretty certain I'm not one of them, although I still don't know who you mean."

"The mothy cabbages with their ridiculous robes and rituals," she said. "My human got caught up in it for a bit, but she got over it pretty quick."

Callum and I looked at each other. "A coven?" I suggested.

"No. Those are kind of fun, at least. I was in one, a couple of lives back." She examined a paw, the knuckles huge and claws looking alarmingly long without a little fur protection.

"Is this a guessing game?" I asked. "How many goes do I get?"

She gave me a flat, sour look. "Why're you even interested?"

"We're looking for someone," Callum said. He pulled our phone out of his pocket and flicked through it, then turned the screen to the naked cat. “Have you seen him?”

I peered around so I could see it too. It was a screenshot off a website, and I put good odds on it being the obituary page. It showed a man a bit younger than Callum, with a heavy jacket buttoned up to his chin. He was laughing at something the person taking the photo had said, his eyes narrowed in delight and his skin shining dark under some winter sunlight. I looked up at Callum, but he was watching the cat. She examined the picture.

“He’s not been around for a while,” she said. “But, yeah. He used to meet that silly lot here. Some of them have a bit of magic, some don’t. He did. And he used to bring me cat treats.”

Callum nodded, and took the phone back, glancing around the cafe. The skinny, bearded man with the topknot behind the counter was staring at his phone, and neither of the customers were looking our way. “They still meet here?” he asked.

“No. When Katja – that’s my human – quit the group she kicked them out. I think Hairy there’s still in it, though.” She nodded at the man behind the counter. “He used to let them in sometimes when Katja was out, though he hasn’t for a while.”

“That’s brilliant,” Callum said. “Thanks … what’s your name?”

“Pru,” she said.

“Gobbelino London,” I said, before Callum could call me *Gobs* in front of her.

“Callum,” Callum said.

“Got any biscuits?” she asked.

"Not on me, no."

"Useless." She got up and slipped away, a wraith in the shadows.

"I second that bit about the biscuits," I said.

"You would." He waved me under the table as Hairy came over with a plate piled with a chunky sandwich, salad and crisps in one hand and some cutlery in the other.

"Tuna on granary?" he asked, as if he had so many orders on he couldn't possibly keep them straight.

"Thanks," Callum said, then added as the man put the plate down, "I was hoping you could help me out with something."

"Dude, I'm strapped," Hairy said. "Whatever you're collecting for, I can't do it."

"No, nothing like that." Callum dropped his voice a little. "I'm looking for a group that used to meet here. My friend was always talking about it."

Hairy wiped his mouth. "There's scrabble on a Monday. Knit'n'Chat on Thursdays."

"Not that sort of group. This one was … special. Exclusive."

Hairy looked at Callum carefully. "Who's your friend?"

"Ifan Lewis."

The other man frowned, glancing around uneasily. "He's … he doesn't come around anymore."

"He's not around anywhere," Callum said. "Which is why I need to talk to your group. I hear they get up to some interesting activities."

"I don't know anything about it," Hairy said, his voice rising.

"About what?" Callum asked pleasantly. "Him not being around, or the group activities?"

"You're … you need to talk to someone else," Hairy said. "I'm not even really part of the group anymore. And Ifan left like a month ago, about when Katja kicked us – them – out."

"Not really part of it? So you still go sometimes?"

"Um. Yes." He looked around. "Sort of. Not much, though. It got a bit weird."

"Weird?"

"Yeah." Hairy straightened up. "Look, Ifan was a pretty good guy. After he and Katja both quit, it stopped being so fun. It was just meant to be a bit of a joke, you know? Dress in black, do a few incantations, nothing serious."

I curled my lip back off my teeth. *Nothing serious.* This was the problem with humans. Always messing in stuff that they didn't understand, and thinking it was *nothing serious.*

"So it ended up being serious?" Callum asked. "How serious?"

Hairy shook his head. "Look, I quit before anyone *did* anything."

"What were they trying to do?"

Hairy waved vaguely. "I don't know, okay? And I don't want to know." He pulled his phone from his pocket, the tattoos on his forearms shifting in the dim light. I could see at least two that no one with any sense would want carved on their own skin. Not because they were ugly, but because they were dangerous. He thumbed the screen a few times, then turned it toward Callum. "That's the address of where they meet now. Oli runs it. Go, join up, whatever. Just leave me out of it. And don't tell them I sent you. I don't want anything to do with them."

"Alright," Callum said, punching the address into our ancient phone. "Thanks."

"Whatever," Hairy said, and I lifted my head over the edge of the table.

"Get your tattoos redone," I told him. "You're going to attract hinky-punks with that red one."

He stared at me, then looked at Callum. "You shouldn't have a cat in here. We've got a resident one, and they might fight."

"I'll keep an eye on him," Callum said.

"You can't even hear me," I said to Hairy. "Well done, you furry runner bean."

"He's noisy," Hairy said, and wandered back to the counter.

"You are," Callum agreed.

"The man's clueless."

"True." Callum scraped the tuna off half his sandwich and piled it onto his coffee saucer. "But we have an address."

"If he's even got that right."

"Shut up and eat your tuna."

I did. It wasn't bad.

THE NECROMANCER GROUP hadn't exactly gone far when the cafe kicked them out, and as the rain had stopped, leaving the day dull and bored looking, we left the car where it was and walked. We headed deeper into the ranks of converted houses and 24-hour shops and off-licences, leaving the centre behind us and finding quieter streets. The houses shrank down, and the odd B&B appeared, all wearing *Vacancy* signs. Students gave way to dog walkers and grey-haired women dragging shopping bags, and the windows sprouted boxes filled with last year's half-dead flowers and, in a few cases, some bright new spring growth.

We stopped in front of a narrow terraced house with a small paved patio area between the gate and a faded red front door. Black curtains decorated with silver stars hung at the windows, and someone had drawn teeth around the doorbell.

"Classy," I said.

"We can't talk," Callum said. "We still don't know what's living in our stairs."

"Yeah, but we didn't put it there."

He scratched his fingers through his stubble and said, "I guess we should see what they know."

"Hang about. Necromancers, Callum. You know why they're meant to be extinct? They tried to wipe out the Folk and enslave humanity. We fought a war over it, and it's what put Folk into hiding from humans, because they were too scared of us after that to do anything but hunt us. And the necromancer bloodline was meant to be destroyed after. So if they're not extinct, and they're back ... well, we probably shouldn't go charging in there shouting that we know what they are." I thought about it. "In fact, we probably shouldn't go in there at all."

Callum looked at me levelly. An elderly woman in fetching green boots went past with a pit bull, who glanced at me and huffed. I huffed back. "So what do you want to do?" Callum asked, once she was out of earshot. "Go to the Watch?"

"Gods, no."

"Then what? We just leave them here, possibly raising the dead? Raising Ifan?"

I wrinkled my nose. "You just had to know someone in the graveyard, didn't you? Couldn't just leave well enough alone."

"I'd rather I hadn't. And it's a cemetery, anyway. Graveyards are around churches."

"Oh, well. Consider me corrected."

We stared at each other for a moment longer, then I sighed. "*Fine.* But if I get eaten by a zombie I'm holding you entirely responsible."

"That seems fair," Callum said, and climbed the steps to ring the toothed doorbell.

THE BELL BUZZED RATHER UNDRAMATICALLY INSIDE, and after a moment someone yelled, "Just a sec!"

There was some hurried scuffling behind the door, and I braced myself to face down some sort of creature from the crypts, a tantrobobus or a black shuck or something even more horrifying.

Then the door opened to reveal a woman with an abundance of dyed black hair tumbling over her shoulders and spilling down the back of her long dark robe. The hood hung loose behind her, and she placed one hand on the doorframe, lifting her chin and chest as she narrowed green eyes at us. Then she slumped, and dropped her hand.

"Shoot. Sorry. I thought you were someone else. Are you here about the boiler?"

"Um, no," Callum said. "We're looking for Oli."

"That's me," she said.

"Right." Callum shot a look at me where I was snuffling along the wall, just out of sight, and I shrugged. I could smell laundry soap and carpet shampoo, and not a lot else. "I heard you run a certain, um, niche interest group?"

"Oh!" She struck her pose against the door again. "A new disciple!"

Callum scratched his head. "We just want some information, really."

"We?" she asked, and caught sight of me as I ambled back. "Oh, no. No cats. I'm allergic."

"I'm not Watch," I said. "Kind of the opposite, to be honest."

She stared at me. "Is that supposed to make me not allergic?"

"You were serious?"

"Of course. Why else wouldn't I want a cat in here?"

Callum interrupted before I could answer. "He won't come near you. Just let us into the hall so we can talk a bit more easily."

"No," Oli said, and sneezed rather pointedly. She wiped her nose. "See? I'm really very allergic."

Callum sighed. "Okay. Look, do you know Ifan Lewis?"

"Why?"

"I'm a friend of his."

She examined him, sniffling a bit and rubbing her nose again. "He stopped coming to meetings after we left the Sphynx Cat Cafe."

"We heard you got thrown out," I said.

She sniffed. "A difference in values. Katja was never truly committed. She was just a dabbler. Ifan too."

"Ifan's dead," Callum said, his voice flat.

Oli stared at him. "I'm sorry," she said. "Truly. He ended up not being the right fit for us, but he was nice. I liked him."

"So you don't know anything about his grave being dug up and zombies running about the place?" I asked, and Callum looked at the filthy welcome mat, shaking his head.

"Zombies?" she demanded, almost laughing. "Zombies don't exist."

"They did once," I said. "Or something like them. You know, when necromancers were meddling about in things." She just looked at me blankly. *"Like you,"* I said, wondering if I was going to need to draw a diagram.

"Like me?" she looked at Callum. *"Like me?"*

"Well, I guess there's no point being polite now," Callum said. "We've heard you're necromancers."

Oli straightened her sleeves. "We are," she said. "But that has *nothing* to do with zombies."

We were quiet for a moment, waiting.

She sighed. "I should give you a leaflet. We just had some made up." She rummaged on the windowsill and handed Callum a glossy black flyer printed in tight white font. "There's a website, too, if you want to learn more.

It's on the back. Necromancy isn't *raising* the dead. It's conjuring the spirits of the dead. We do it to offer solace to the living, who are the ones suffering."

"You're a medium," I said.

"In a way. I'm High Priestess Olivia." She extended a hand to Callum, who shook it. Her nails were painted black with little glittery skulls on them.

"Callum," he said.

"Pleasure. Look, you're very welcome to come back without the cat and attend a couple of sessions to try it out, before you commit to anything—"

"Commit to what?" I asked. "Blood sacrifice?"

She frowned at me. "No, investing in robes and paying a membership fee. Honestly, what sort of monsters do you think we are?"

"Necromancers," I said. She scowled at me.

"So you know nothing about Ifan's grave?" Callum asked.

"Of course not. And I'm very sorry to hear he's passed. I can try and contact him for you, if you like?"

"No," Callum said. "No, I don't think so." He took a step back. "I'm sorry to waste your time."

"Not at all. Come back if you change your mind." She gave us a little wave then stood in the door and watched us go. When I looked back from the corner she was still there, her robes blending into the shadows of the hall so that she was nothing more than a disembodied face floating in the uncertain dark.

7

FANCY MEETING YOU HERE

"Well, that was a bust," I said as Callum climbed into the car. "I guess that's all avenues exhausted, isn't it? Such a shame."

Callum gave me a sideways look. "We can go back to the cemetery tonight and see if anyone turns up. You could ask Susan if it's happening at other places."

I sighed. "We *could* do that. But do we really need to? Our so-called necromancers are really just mediums. Old Lewis is nasty and up to all sorts of filthy magic, but I don't think he's got the power for this. And *zombies don't exist*."

"I seem to remember you complaining about almost being eaten by one," he said, pulling into the road in a belch of exhaust smoke.

"*One.* One maybe-zombie. We don't know about the arm. And Lewis might have had second thoughts and dug up Ifan to put him in a jar somewhere. There's not exactly a contagion going on here. It could've just been an aberration."

"That's a pretty big aberration, and a *lot* of coincidences. And then there was our hooded cemetery visitor."

I huffed. "We could have a proper case right now. You know, one that pays actual money. But no, we're chasing around after walking corpses that we don't even know actually exist."

"Humour me," Callum said. "If Susan comes up with nothing, and there aren't any other zombies tonight, then fine. We'll go back to finding lost sprites and settling gnome grievances."

"We could find something more profitable," I said. "Like, you know, *anything*."

THINGS WERE LOOKING PRETTY sparse in the bribe department when we got home, so Callum went down to the shop and bought some pre-cooked chicken bits with fake-looking grill marks on them. They smelled faintly of disinfectant and plastic.

"That's below standard," I told him. "She won't be happy."

He gave me a sour look. "It's better than picking over the bins, isn't it?"

"You tell her that." But I took the chicken breast gingerly in my teeth, trying not to drool on it too much – hey, breakfast was a long time ago and I'd been busy – and trotted downstairs, out the front door, and around the corner. The grate near the bins was swimming with run-off and clogged with old crisp packets and a couple of over-strength beer cans (among other more unpleasant things), but there was a metal vent that let into the depths of the building on the wall nearby. I set the chicken down and waited for a moment, then decided it was too wet for hanging about. I wanted to warm up before we went traipsing around graveyards – sorry, *cemeteries* – again.

I leaned over to the vent and bawled, "Hey, Susan! *Susan!*"

A soft pink nose appeared almost immediately, whiffling at the air. "Gods, Gobbelino. Don't *shout.*"

"Sorry," I said. "Didn't realise you were right there."

She peered out, wrinkling her nose at me. "Pass it here, then."

I picked up the chicken and pushed it against the grate. There was some busy scuffling, and for a moment it looked like it wasn't going to fit, then it was dragged through, leaving a pale film of grease on the edge of the pipe. I waited.

Before long Susan reappeared, careful to keep her paws away from the chicken sludge. "How long's that one been in the fridge?"

"Look, I told him it was substandard. But the corner shops, you know ..." I shrugged at her, shuffling a little closer and trying to keep my paws out of the toxic-looking puddle. Fat globs of leftover rain slipped off the broken drains above us and splatted around me.

Susan sniffed. "It's barely safe to eat."

I flattened my ears and gave her a big-eyed look, and she sighed.

"What d'you want?"

"Information."

"Well, there's a revelation. That's what you always want. *What* information?"

"Hey, I come for chats," I protested.

"And ruin my street cred at the same time." But she wriggled her ears as she added, "Must be important for you to get your feet wet."

"Fairly. You got any contacts in the boneyards?"

"Which one?"

"All of them."

She gave me a long, evaluating look. "This sorcerer stuff?"

"Hopefully not."

"It better not be. There's still some really soft patches in reality around here from last time."

"I know," I said. "But around here's safe. Honest. I just want to know if there's been anything weird happening in the cemeteries."

"Weird? Like humans doing their chanting at the moon rubbish, you mean?"

"Eh. That, and …" I took a breath. "Reanimations."

"You what?"

"Reanimations. Premature burials, perhaps. That was popular a few hundred years back, right?"

She just stared at me as someone started screaming abuse at a street sign at the end of the alley, and the day darkened from dull morning to gloomy afternoon. "Gods, Gobbelino. What in the name of the popcorn demons of Bezmatog are you mixed up in now?"

I opened my mouth, shut it again, and shrugged. That was the hell of it. I just didn't know.

And I was also never sure if she was making these demons up or not.

I LEFT Susan with a promise that there'd be no more substandard chicken, and padded back to the apartment. Most cats don't rate rats as the truly excellent information network they are. Show them a little respect, offer the odd bribe, and you can find out pretty much anything. I mean, cats get most places, but rats get *everywhere.*

And, as it happens, I am at a slight disadvantage when it comes to getting places, because I can't shift. Shifting is how cats appear in rooms you swore you locked them out of, and turn up sleeping in beds in cat-less houses. It's how we walk your human halls of power and no one's ever sure if we're meant to be there or not, and it's what makes Schrödinger so bloody hilarious to us. Well, hilarious in the *let's-do-it-to-you-and-see-how-you-like-it* sense. Which did actually happen, but you won't find that in the history books. The Watch cover their tracks. You might notice no one's repeated that particular experiment, though.

But, anyway – shifting. I mean, you can trap a dog in a box. A cat, not so much (although a cage is different. It's to do with the structure, and we can't shift out of them, more's the pity). To shift, we simply step out of this world into the Inbetween, the space that runs between all the worlds, maybe even between all realities, and step back again wherever we fancy.

I, however, can't shift. Or I can, but the creatures that

cruise the Inbetween like otherworldly sharks have my scent. They've had it since the Watch had trapped me in there and fed me to them, and if my tail so much as slipped into the void now they'd chomp it off. Which means I have to be a little more inventive than most cats, hence my excellent working relationship with Susan. The only thing I can't get behind are those tails.

Back in our tiny apartment, the day passed slow and grey and reluctant. We had nothing to do and no money to do nothing with, so I hogged the heater and slept while Callum alternated between reading one of his trashy bargain bin books and poking the computer to see if it'd let him on the internet. Petra called and Callum told her he'd buried the arm and not to worry, although she probably shouldn't walk Cyril in the cemetery for a while. He neglected to mention that this was due to the risk of zombies rather than being worried about the three-legged dog digging up any more body parts, but she still agreed.

By the time the noises in the alleyway went from daytime drunk to after-work drunk the rain hadn't restarted. The air still felt dull and heavy, the clouds too close to the tops of the buildings, but when I jumped onto the windowsill to peer out into the dimming day I didn't land in the usual puddle that seeped through the frame. So that seemed like a good sign.

"How's it looking?" Callum asked, even though the window was right behind him and he could see perfectly well. Humans are weird like that. They always ask questions they know the answers to, or questions they don't actually want answers to.

"Great weather for zombie hunting," I said. "Or necromancer hunting."

"Great." Callum got up and stretched. "You going to check if Susan knows anything before we go?"

I pressed my nose to the glass, watching a scraggly pigeon in the tree. "She won't know anything yet. Isn't it a bit early to head to the cemetery? There'll still be people about."

He nodded. "We don't know when the dead tend to surface, though. They might be early risers."

I lifted my lip to expose one tooth. "What about dinner?"

"We'll get fish'n'chips."

Well, I couldn't argue with that. I jumped off the windowsill and followed him out the door and down the dingy stairs. The evening outside was painted in damp colours, everything rendered in muted and unfamiliar shades, and I could smell car exhaust and old oil and the dank scent of unspooling lives as the night drew down on the edges of the cracked orange streetlights and uncurtained windows.

It seemed as good a night as any to look for the dead.

Given that it was around dinnertime and the houses outside the cemetery had cars coming and going and people putting bins out or taking bins in or shouting at each other in the tiny front yards, we couldn't very well just park up and sit there. Even if a cat and a guy in a dodgy coat just hanging about the place didn't look kind of suspicious anyway, our car was too much of a wreck to pass unnoticed among the newish cars along the street. So we parked a couple of roads over and walked back, Callum with the shovel under his coat in case we needed to re-bury anyone.

As we ambled along, trying to look inconspicuous, some little girl rushed toward me shouting, "Kitty, kitty!"

I shot onto Callum's shoulder and perched there, trying not to hiss at her.

"Sorry," Callum told her. "He's a bit antisocial."

She squinted at him. "My brother's like that."

"Is he?"

"Yeah, he's got a thing from the police to say."

Callum nodded, said, "Cool," and kept walking, both of us hoping her antisocial brother wasn't home and about to take exception to his little sister talking to strangers and their cats. The little girl just stood there scratching her belly and watching us go, until someone screamed her name from the house and she turned and ran inside.

"Antisocial?" I said.

"Sounds better than *don't touch him, he'll bite you.*"

"Eh." I stayed where I was in case of further children, and also because there were a couple of dog-walkers out and I couldn't be bothered with them. I'd already had my week's worth of dog drool from Cyril. And see where *that* had got us.

The cemetery gates were still open, and there was no one around. I guess people don't get too precious about the dead these days. Callum ambled in for all the world as if he had no intention of braining anyone, and we found a quiet spot among the trees and bushes that lined the wall to keep an eye on things. We were close enough to the gates to spot anyone coming or going, and not far from a grave that looked newly dug.

The cemetery was big, rolling up a gentle slope from the gates to an area of bigger markers and more posh-looking crypts, while below the gates it stretched all the way down to meet the main road, everything a jumble of old stones and new cut through with gravel paths and punctuated with solitary trees. It was probably nicer in summer, when the trees would have all their leaves. For the moment they looked unpleasantly skeletal, the new spring shoots nothing more than nubs in the orange light seeping in from outside.

Callum pulled the trussed paper packet of fish'n'chips from one of his pockets and set it on the ground next to us. The snake was wrapped around it, chewing on one corner.

"Great," I said. "You brought the snake. Now we have to share."

"I didn't bring him," Callum said. "He just comes along sometimes. Anyway, it's you that has to share. I don't think he eats chips. And I need my strength in the event of grave digging."

I gave him a sour look, and stared at the leaning shadows of the headstones while he shared out the fish, peeling the batter off mine and the snake's. The cemetery didn't look ominous. It just looked lonely.

We crept back into the bushes when a woman in a black jacket drove slowly past in a tiny, battered Ford Ka, doing a precise circuit of the cemetery without ever getting out or shining a torch into the corners. Why would you? As we'd seen last night, it was easy enough to get in if you wanted. It was probably more to make sure they didn't lock in some old dear who'd lost track of time while chatting to her sister than any worry about intruders.

We went back to our spot on the grass once she was gone, and listened to the clang of the gates shutting and the car puttering away down the road outside. The houses began to quiet down and darken, and the traffic on the main road at the bottom of the cemetery thinned. The snake wriggled back into one of Callum's pockets, and Callum tried to read a book in the dim light, then gave it up as a bad job and stretched out on his back, staring up at the bare branches above us.

I stayed with my paws tucked under me, eyes wide in the low light, scanning the graves for movement. Someone had to keep an eye on things, and I waited patiently enough until Callum started snoring, then I got up and wandered off. Bad enough I had to listen to it at home, when I was snuggled down in my own cosy bed. If I was out here getting damp toes anyway I could find better things to do.

I was investigating one of the crypts when the clatter of the gate stopped me mid-sniff. The old stone stank faintly of ghouls, but that didn't bother me. Humans worry too much about dead things. It's the living you have to watch out for.

Especially when they're climbing into cemeteries in

the middle of the night. I scooted out of the crypt and ran across the path to where Callum was still snoring steadily. I slapped him in the face with one damp paw and hissed, "Quiet!" as he sat up with a grunt of protest.

"What?" he whispered, wiping drool off his cheek.

"Someone's here." I nodded toward the gate, and we ducked for the cover of the trees as a hooded figure hurried down the path, a bag swinging from their shoulder. "Same as last night?" I asked Callum, my voice low.

"Don't know," he said softly. "They look about the same size, and they're dressed the same, so probably."

"Unless midnight grave-digging's really popular."

He shushed me, and we watched the figure scurry among the graves while the moon fought to break out from the clouds and somewhere out in the real world a car alarm squalled into the silence.

The figure found what they were looking for somewhere in the middle of the rows and a little closer to the gates than we were. They took their bag off and dropped it on the ground. I still didn't entirely believe we had a necromancer, but my fur started to prickle anyway, anticipating murmured chants and arcane rituals, stinking candles and the whiff of blood – or worse. Maybe there'd be the scream of a sacrifice, although given he'd only been carrying a backpack it couldn't be much larger than a chicken. But, whatever other garnishes he had, there'd definitely be the greasy reek of the nastier types of magic.

After a moment there was a plasticky rustle and the sound of a packet tearing, and I wondered if you could buy your sacrifices pre-packaged these days. Then there was some loud crunching that definitely did not sound like bones or anything particularly nefarious, followed by a satisfied sigh. A bottle cracked open, and a phone started to make little beeping game sounds.

I looked at Callum. "The terror value of necromancers seems to have been slightly overstated."

He peered around his tree, then shrugged. "I guess even raisers of the dead have to eat."

"Do we just wait?" I asked. "Or do we talk to him?"

"Let's see what happens," Callum said, sitting down cross-legged. I settled next to him, pressing against his leg to steal a little warmth. Our evil sorcerer pumped their arm triumphantly and crunched another handful of crisps as the phone gave a whistle. They took another drink. Started the game again. We listened to it beep and screech as a few bats danced cautiously above the trees.

I looked up at Callum. "This is thrilling. Are those necromancer games, d'you think?"

"Just give it a bit longer," he said. "If nothing happens in …" He checked his watch. "Half an hour. If nothing happens by then, we'll go talk to them."

"Fine," I said, and set to grooming between my toes. It passed the time. Very slowly, mind, but it did.

By the time I'd finished cleaning my belly I was bored, and the chill of the night was starting to seep up from the grass into my bones. "That's got to be half an hour."

"Pretty much," Callum admitted. "Why aren't they *doing* anything?"

"Maybe they're just staking it out, like us," I said. "We

should talk to them. At least find out if they're working for Lewis, or the necromancers, or are some sort of freelance reanimators."

Callum sighed, and got up. "You're right. Let's get this done." He brushed off the back of his coat and straightened the sleeves as we started out from under the trees. The maybe-necromancer gave a whispered cheer as the phone binged excitedly. I lifted my nose, trying to catch their scent over the quiet dark mulchy smell of the dead.

And caught something else entirely. Something familiar, rich and feral and dripping with the sort of power old Lewis probably had dirty dreams about.

"Back!" I hissed. "Get back!"

Callum didn't even question it. He threw himself back into the shadows as the gate clanged open with a hard, angry sound. The hooded figure gave a squawk and flung themselves flat on the ground, the phone beeping in muffled alarm for a moment before it was turned off. The cemetery fell silent. Even the bats had gone, and no cars passed on the road outside. The world retreated and the faint breeze fell to utter stillness. There was a pause, then gravel crunched under the deliberate step of heavy soles, approaching down the path with the inexorable tread of an advancing army.

8

DEAD CROWDED AROUND HERE

We crouched in the undergrowth beneath the trees, Callum hissing as he found the nettles again, and listened to the sure, unhurried footsteps coming our way. I didn't have to see to know who it was, not with that rich, muscular scent rolling toward me, but I heard Callum's breathing hitch as he caught sight of our latest cemetery visitor.

"Ms Jones?" he whispered, his voice barely a breath. "What's she doing here?"

Ms Jones, the sorcerer whose book of power had just about torn the world apart last year. Ms Jones, who had paid us to pass her information on the Watch. Ms Jones of the changeable eyes and, currently, glossy purple Doc Martens. Ms Jones, who I still harboured suspicions could probably change me into a smoked mackerel.

She stopped in the centre of the path, her hands in the pockets of a heavy blue jacket, and pivoted slowly on her heel. I flattened myself to the ground, and Callum stopped breathing. I couldn't tell if she saw us, or maybe had heard that one tiny whisper, or, gods knew, *smelled* us. Who knew with sorcerers?

She lifted her chin just slightly, eyes narrowing as if she was cutting through the dark with some sort of magical super-vision, and I hoped Callum didn't pass out from holding his breath for so long. Then the gate clanged, whether from the last of its own momentum or something else, and she looked that way instead. Callum exhaled very softly, and the hooded figure leaped up and legged it for the opposite wall.

Ms Jones spun back just as the figure flattened themselves behind another grave.

"Hello?" she called. "Anyone there?" She sounded gentle, maybe even a bit nervous, but she had the prowling movement of a stalking cat as she started down the path in our direction again, scanning the graves. Hoody abandoned their backpack and started elbow-walking toward the cover of the nearest crypt.

"What do we do?" Callum breathed, under the sound of her footfalls.

"We can't let her see us," I hissed. "What if she's behind all this? What if *she's* raising the dead?"

"Really?"

"She's the strongest sorcerer I've come across."

We were both silent for a moment as Ms Jones continued her survey of the cemetery, then Callum said, "We've got to go, then. We can't stay here."

"She'll see us if we move."

"She'll find us if we stay."

We were both right. There was no way she'd miss us

scrambling back over the wall, but she was barely twenty metres from us now.

"Maybe she won't notice us if we're really quiet," I suggested.

"Maybe a passing comet will save us," Callum muttered, and in that moment there was the sort of ominous creak from one of the crypts that would have made my tail bush out if Ms Jones hadn't had that effect already. She turned toward it just as Hoody threw themselves away from the metal gate they'd tried to open and sprinted for the wall.

"Stop," Ms Jones said, her voice barely carrying to us, but the word echoed through the taut air of the night. Hoody stopped so sharply that they pitched face-first to the ground with a painful-sounding thud. They whimpered, and Ms Jones looked around the cemetery again.

"Ready?" Callum whispered. I didn't even bother to answer. My paws were already gathered underneath me, ready to launch an assault on the wall. I had no idea what she was planning to do to our maybe-necromancer, but I was less worried about that than the possibility of being turned into a piebald shrew if she decided we were spying on her.

Ms Jones started to turn back to the hapless figure still flopping about on the grass, unable to get up, then paused and looked directly toward our little scrap of shelter. The fur on my spine joined my tail, puffing up wildly.

"Who's been having a picnic?" she asked, her voice laced with amusement. "A midnight feast in the graveyard?"

"Cemetery," Callum muttered, and I would have bitten

him, agreement or no agreement, but Ms Jones was still staring at us.

Well, not at us. At the abandoned fish'n'chip packet bundled up on the grass, marking our position like a nice big *You Are Here* arrow.

"Hairballs," I mumbled.

"COME OUT, come out, wherever you are," Ms Jones called in a cheery, sing-song voice that made me glad I hadn't stalked anything for sport recently. Not if this was what it felt like to be the stalkee. She flexed her fingers absently. "No point hiding. I know you're there."

Callum's hand wrapped around me, and I stifled a hiss of protest. "Shh," he breathed. "I'll lift you onto the wall. Make yourself scarce, alright?"

Before I could point out that I had not agreed to being picked up, let alone to running off and leaving him to face a Doc Marten-clad sorcerer, the gates clanged again. We both froze, and Ms Jones looked around, a scowl twitching her mouth. The fat beam of a powerful torch washed across the headstones, cutting stark shadows on the ground, and the sorcerer raised her arm to protect her eyes as she was lit like an actor stepping on stage.

"Alright, then," a tired voice said. "What're you doing in here at this hour?"

Ms Jones hesitated, and for one moment I thought she might fling out some terrible curse and crush the man and his light to dust. Then she lowered her arm and smiled, clasping her hands in front of her.

"I'm *so* sorry," she said. "I thought I might have dropped my purse when I was visiting my mum earlier. And I *know* it was silly to come back at night, but, well, the gate was open, and …" her voice faltered. "Well, I can cancel my cards, but there are photos in my purse. Of my mum. I'd hate to lose them."

The torch beam dipped a little, flooding the path rather than her face. "You really shouldn't be here at night. We get some weird sorts."

"I know. And I'm really very sorry."

"Did you find your purse, at least?"

She toed the ground with one boot. "No. But … well. I'm *so* absentminded sometimes. I might have left it at work."

Torch-man heaved a rather large sigh. "I suggest you check there first next time. Come on. Out you come."

"Of course." Ms Jones took one last look around, her smile curling down at the edges, then walked to the gates. We listened to the clatter of the chain going around the frame, and the click of the padlock, and the mutter of Torch-man telling off a woman who could probably turn him inside out with a glance. Before long a car started up and drew away, and another followed it.

Then there was silence. We waited where we were for a moment longer, then Hoody scrambled to their feet and took off toward the wall. Callum launched himself in pursuit, sprinting across the graves, and I pelted after him. Hoody glanced back, apparently catching the sound of boots on grass, squawked, and ran faster.

"Stop!" Callum yelled. "We only want to talk to you!"

Hoody apparently wasn't up for conversation, and

they were too far ahead of us. I overtook Callum, paws light on the damp grass and across the broken gravel of the path, but even I wasn't going to be quick enough. Hoody threw themselves at the wall, scrabbling so clumsily that I thought we had them trapped, then gave a desperate little running-on-terror jump and clawed themselves up. I reached the wall just as they teetered at the top on their belly, then plunged head-first to the other side with a yelp of alarm.

I skittered up the wall after them, hearing Callum yelling behind me, and would've been straight over, too, but there was an enormous *arf!*, and Hoody screeched as security lights flashed on around a solemn stone building and the edges of an empty parking lot. *Arf* was joined by a cacophony of snarling and short, angry barks, and Hoody raced screaming across the tarmac below, chased by three large dogs that, temperament-wise, appeared to be as entirely unlike Cyril as it was possible to be. They were also quite unlike him in the number of legs, which didn't bode well for Hoody. I watched them go. Discretion is, after all, the better part of valour.

Callum pulled himself up until his waist was resting against the top of the wall, arms holding him up and his boots dug into the stone, and said, "No?"

"Hey, you want to have your toes chomped, go for it," I said, as Hoody swerved away from one of the dogs and headed off in a different direction, still screaming.

"They look like they're just chasing, not attacking. They're probably trained not to actually bite."

The hooded figure tripped over a kerb and went sprawling, their screams taking on a new note. The dogs snapped at them, and I could hear cloth ripping even over the snarls.

"Sure about that?" I asked, and we both watched Hoody stagger up and run for the gates of the enclosure. They made it up and over with the dogs barking in delight behind them, and sprawled on the ground in relative safety, both hands over their face.

"Well," Callum said. "Not entirely sure."

We dropped back to the ground on our side of the wall and picked our way back among the graves. Hoody had left their bag abandoned next to a shiny new marker, the turf still showing seams where it had been laid on the replaced earth. A crisp packet had spilt its contents across the grass and a bottle of diet drink was lying on its side where it had rolled against another headstone. Callum picked up the backpack and peered inside.

"Black candles?" I asked. "Stone knives? Sacrificial chicken?"

He took out a small Tupperware container and opened it, frowning at the contents.

"Sacrificial goldfish?" I suggested.

He crouched down and held the tub out to me, still frowning. I padded over and peered at two little glass bottles of liquid and a syringe, a plastic cap pulled over the needle. I looked up at him. "Drugs?"

"Of some sort," he said. "Nothing that looks familiar to me, though. Those are proper medical vials."

I sat down and scratched an ear with one back paw. "You think it was a doctor of some sort? Some magical beat-the-dead serum?"

"I have no idea what to think," he said, putting the lid

back on the tub and replacing it in the bag. He shouldered it, then picked up the rubbish and went to collect our traitorous fish'n'chip packet and the shovel.

It was late, cold, and damp. I wanted to go home, have some custard, and fall into my bed for a minimum sixteen hours. But as Callum reached for the top of the wall, a small but very discernible sound crept across the silent graves. I stopped, the fur along my spine starting to creep up.

"Callum," I said softly, and he paused, looking down at me. Neither of us moved again for a moment, and I strained for the sound. Callum opened his mouth to say something, and I heard it again. A moan, drifting on the still night air, and my tail went to full attention. I spun around, and Callum swore.

It wasn't even coming from the grave Hoody had been sitting on. In fact, I had no idea what grave the thing had emerged from, as it was just wandering down the path in a dirt-encrusted suit and socks, giving voice to a questioning groan now and then.

"Where the hell did he come from?" Callum asked. "There's no one *here.*"

"There was no one here last night, either," I said. "Or not till after the dead started wandering around, anyway."

"Ugh." Callum put the backpack down and picked up the shovel. "I *hate* this."

"Can't we leave it? I mean, the gates are locked. What's it going to do?"

"Bite the night-watchman when he comes back? Or whoever opens up tomorrow?"

"You're severely hampered by your ethics," I said, and followed him as he advanced on the zombie. It turned toward us, and put its arms out in proper zombie-approved fashion, making little clutching gestures. Callum hefted the shovel, shifting his grip on it, and he and the corpse walked toward each other like a couple of mismatched gunslingers. I hung back a little, since there didn't seem to be a lot I could do. Cats weren't well equipped for zombie fighting, judging by the night before.

Callum stopped, and the creature did too. They stared at each other, and it dropped its arms, something like a grin hoisting its lips up. It tipped its head from side to side, as if cracking its neck, then dropped into a crouch, hands brushing the ground.

"Gobs," Callum said. "Do you see this?"

I eased forward, my eyes on the thing. "What's it doing?"

"I don't—" he broke off as the creature bared its teeth and rolled its eyes. It gave voice to another moan, but it sounded less confused, more gleeful.

"I don't like this, Callum. Let's go." I started to back up, my eyes on the zombie. Callum didn't move. "Callum, come *on*."

The zombie chattered its teeth at me then looked back at Callum. It advanced a couple of paces, using its hands to help itself, moving with an uncanny, liquid grace.

"We can't just leave it," Callum said.

Thank the gods for kitty senses. Even as I started to say, *Of course we can, you soft cauliflower,* there was a whisper of movement behind me, felt more than heard. I bolted forward without bothering to look back, yowling, "*Run!* Callum, *run!*" and the night exploded with the muted clatter of skittering hands and feet.

Callum charged with me, taking one hard swing at Zombie One's head as it lunged at him. He caught it a glancing blow and the thing was thrown sideways, but was up again before Callum had taken more than a couple of paces.

We pelted across the raised backs of the graves, sprinting for the dubious refuge of the crypts, and the night filled with hisses and moans and the slide of shoeless feet on gravel behind us. Callum was running all out, hurdling flowers and dodging markers, and I slowed to his pace, stealing a look back.

Our first zombie had been joined by two buddies, all of them loping after us with that uneasy grace, jumping to the tops of headstones and teetering there before leaping away again, teeth chattering with delight and eyes wide and staring. They were keeping up with us effortlessly, not even trying. Old June must've been the early, not-quite-perfected version. These were new and improved, and as the lead one reached almost lazily for Callum I leaped at it, teeth bared. It knocked me away, both of us hissing, and I hit the edge of a grave marker hard enough to turn my hiss into a yowl. Callum slid to a stop, spinning around and brandishing the shovel.

"Keep going!" I yelled at him, ignoring the pain in my side and struggling back to my feet. The zombie was stalking toward me, mud dribbling from the corner of its mouth. At least, I hoped it was mud.

"Gobs, get here," he snapped, and I glanced at him. He'd put his back to some monolithic marker, a great carved slab of stone that the inscriptions had all but weathered off. I ducked left, then right, keeping the movements a little slow, and the zombie followed me. I feinted left one more time, then shot to the right, launching myself almost vertically up and over a headstone, feeling the wind of the thing's hand almost catching my tail before it headbutted the stone with an enraged moan.

I kept going, dodging a second walking corpse then skidding to a stop at Callum's feet as he stepped forward and swung the shovel like a cricket bat – which he was used to handling. We have that sort of clientele.

The shovel slammed into the face of a tall, thin zombie, sending it flailing backward. Its head hit a marker with an ugly, final sound, and we both said, "*Ew.*"

There was no time to savour that particular victory, though. My zombie had recovered and scampered over to us, its nose off at a funny angle from running into the headstone. The other remaining zombie moaned, and it moaned back.

"They're communicating," Callum said. "That's—"

"Really not important," I snapped, as the two undead examined us, their fingers creeping through the grass like creatures with minds of their owns. The first one, the one from the path, bared its teeth and hissed, a portly, balding man in a three-piece suit caked in dirt and muck, stinking of embalming fluid and old-school cologne and the sort of never-ending hunger that makes your heart break, because you know nothing will soothe it, not in this world or the next. If there is a next.

I've smelled that sort of hunger before, but not normally in dead things. Callum had a whiff of it on him once upon a time. It came in needles for him, but it has so many different forms. They all smell the same, though. Lost and desperate and hurting, with a gap that can never be filled.

Then the thing leaped, and I stopped feeling sorry for it, because its teeth were bared and its not-breath smelled just the way you expect a dead thing to smell. Plus it was drooling down its chin.

Callum met it with the shovel, slamming it across the creature's face, knocking it back to the ground. As he swung, the second zombie charged forward, and I threw myself to meet it, tearing my claws across its cheeks, trying to keep clear of its mouth. Callum spun toward me, jabbing the shovel hard into the thing's belly. I leaped clear again as it doubled over, and spotted Zombie One already on its feet and hunching toward us. Callum jerked the shovel back and aimed a hard blow at the back of Zombie Two's head, but the thing ducked away and he caught its neck instead, knocking it to the ground. I lunged at Zombie One's legs, trying to trip it before it could reach Callum, but it just stumbled over me and kept going. Callum turned to meet it, raising the shovel to swing, and Zombie Two grabbed him from behind, dragging him to the ground with a groan of triumph.

"*Callum!*" I yelled, tearing my way up Zombie One's back, my desperation tasting like bile at the back of my throat and the whole night standing stark and clear and empty around me. There was dead flesh under my claws and dead stars above me, and both zombies were on top of my partner, and he was yelling with fright and fury, and there was nothing I could do. Nothing at all.

Then there was a whisper at the edge of hearing, as high and taut as crystal on the verge of breaking, and a soft, harmless sort of thud, then nothing but the sound of Callum swearing.

9

WHEN A BAD DAY GETS WORSE

I STARED AT THE SPOT WHERE MY CLAWS WERE SUNK DEEP into cold flesh, my ears echoing with the silence. Well, I was looking at a point a little ahead of my claws, actually. The skin there was a bit dirty and nasty-looking, as could be expected from someone who's just crawled out of a grave, and, more importantly, there was nothing attached to it.

There *had* been something attached to it, just a moment before. There had been a head attached to it, and the head had been very intent on biting Callum's face off. Now I was staring straight past my claws at Callum, who had the shovel raised in one hand as if he'd been fending off the aforementioned head, and the elbow of the other arm was driven down into a throat that had presumably also been attached to a head not a second or two before. Callum blinked, and shifted his gaze from me to something just over my shoulder.

There was that high, sharp sound again, like a blade on glass. My fur, which I thought had reached maximum volume, tried to expand further, and I turned my head toward the noise almost against my will. It felt the same as hearing an unseen dog growl. You might not be able to do anything about it, but you wanted to know where it was.

There was a new hooded figure standing next to us, only this one wasn't munching on crisps, and it seemed to favour robes over a tracksuit. Its face was hidden in shadow and it was holding … well, a scythe, not to put too fine a point on things. Although the scythe looked to have a *very* fine point, judging by the way the light was sliding off it. My fur gave leaving my body a seriously good attempt.

"Callum," I whispered.

He swallowed. "What?"

"Do you see that?"

"Yes," he said, not taking his eyes off the figure, which prodded something with the handle of the scythe. I peered around to see what it was.

It was a head, which snapped hungrily at the wooden handle. The figure tutted, and I wondered if *this* was the necromancer, and we were about to witness some terrifying ritual, the rules of nature and the universe being turned on their heads. Again. I'd had enough of that last year.

"This is not right," the figure said, the voice distinctly feminine. "This is not right *at all*." She lifted her head to look at us, although I still couldn't see past the shadows of the hood. "What have you been doing?"

"Us?" Callum managed, his voice a little high. "We haven't done anything."

"Are you sure?" she asked. "Someone's done something. These things don't just *happen*, you know."

"We're trying to find out what happened," Callum said. "That's all."

I had the sense she was frowning at us. "And you, cat? What are you doing playing around with human bodies?"

I just stared. It was the scythe. There was only one kind that carried scythes, and I'd never come across one before. We tended to move in different worlds. You know, the living and the dead.

She tutted again, and dug through the pockets of her robe. I waited to see if she was going to produce some sort of magical restraints, or a parchment to read us our sins from, or maybe even an hourglass, but she didn't. She produced a mobile instead, and quite a nice one by the look of things. It was in a pink plastic case with cat ears. She poked the phone a few times, and I heard it ringing on the other end. The whole place was silent. Not even wind whispered around the graves. Callum's breath was harsh and ragged, and the head snapped a couple of times, but that was all.

Someone picked up on the other end of the phone.

"Emma?" the figure said. "Did I wake you? I'm so sorry. I've run into …" She trailed off, looking at us, then said, "Complications, I guess. Can you take the brownies out of the oven in ten minutes? Yes, I know I shouldn't leave them in when I go out. Yes. Yes. I'm sorry. No. Yes. Okay." She hung up and put the phone back in her pocket, then looked around the cemetery. "There's no one else here. Are you *sure* you didn't do this?"

"Very sure," Callum said. "Would you mind?" He nodded at the body.

"Oh. Of course. Off you get, kitty."

I jumped off the body, staring at her, and she lifted it away with one hand, laying it gently to one side. Callum rolled off the re-corpsed corpse of Zombie Two, coming face to face with a detached and still snapping head, and pushed himself up onto his knees.

"Thank you," he said.

"You're quite welcome," the hooded figure said, nudging Zombie Two with one bare foot that gleamed like bone in the dull light. "What happened here?"

I opened my mouth to say something, but nothing came out.

"Are you alright?" she asked me.

I blinked at her.

"Oh dear. You might have shock, you know." She examined me for a moment longer, then snapped her bony fingers. "I know! I have just the thing." She went back to her pockets, and after a moment there was the rustle of paper. She pulled out a small bag and shook it at me. "Homemade cat treats! Would you like some?"

I wondered if it was safe to take treats from the dead.

She checked another pocket. "I also have cookies, but they're probably not good for you."

"That never bothers him," Callum said, not moving from his knees. The snake was peering out of his pocket, but when he spotted the head he dived out of sight. Some help *he'd* been. Although I was still trying to decide whether he maybe had the right idea.

"Emma won't let me give our cat treats," the figure

confided. She'd leaned the scythe against her shoulder, and was looking from the cookies in one hand to the cat treats in the other. Her fingers were thin and painfully white. "Well, she's not *our* cat. She's more of an acquaintance, I suppose. We don't see her much these days. She prefers Whitby. Do *you* want a cookie?"

Callum looked at me doubtfully. I shrugged at him. "I'm not sure," he said.

"Oh! Very sensible," the figure said, and stuffed the snacks back in her pockets. "Never take sweets from strangers and all that." She knelt in front of me, her robe pooling around her like a slice of the universe, colours that were almost blues and purples but not quite swirling through it. She held out her free hand with the palm up. "Gertrude. Reaper Leeds."

Reaper. Well, this was a turn up for the radio. TV? Whatever, it was a turn up for something. And also probably what you got for hanging about boneyards looking for the dead. "Gobbelino London," I said, finally finding my voice, and nosed her palm. She smelled of cold high places and deep silence and, oddly, vanilla icing. "PI. You may have heard of us."

"Um," she said. "Well. I've never needed a PI." Her face was still mostly hidden by the hood, but I could see a small neat chin and thin pale hair, and a necklace with a silver kitten holding a ball of yarn on it. She got up, and extended her hand to Callum in the human manner. "Gertrude."

"Callum London," he said, shaking her hand and still looking a little confused.

"Would you like that cookie now?" she asked, digging

in her pocket. "Sugar's very good for shock, I've heard. And I've been trying a new recipe. Gluten free *and* vegan. It's important to offer options for everyone, don't you think?"

"Um. Yes?" Callum said. He eyed the scythe, which was sitting steadily against her shoulder while she fished the cookies out. Somehow, even though the cemetery was unlit, it still seemed to be reflecting light from somewhere.

Gertrude handed him the cookies and deposited some biscuits in front of me. "My own recipe. Do tell me what you think."

We stood there, Callum munching a cookie and me nibbling cat treats with the bodies of the zombies strewn around us, the reaper watching us with the scythe leaning against her side and her hands clasped in front of her. She looked from one to the other of us eagerly.

"Fantastic," Callum said around a mouthful.

"Excellent," I agreed.

Gertrude clapped her hands, a flat hard sound. "Wonderful! Oh, I'm so happy. I never want to test things out on customers, you see, and most of the people I meet in my night job are, well." She gestured around the cemetery. "Beyond cookies."

"Customers?" Callum asked, taking a bite of a second cookie.

"Yes! We have a lovely little place in town." She fumbled back in her robe, and produced a business card, which she handed to Callum.

"Dead Good Cafe," he read aloud. "Home-baked cakes, fresh-brewed coffee, and pets." He looked up. "Pets?"

"Ghoulets," she said. "Baby ghouls. It's amazing how many people think they're just weird dogs."

"Humans," I said, and she smiled at me.

"Indeed."

We were silent for a moment, a strange little trio in the middle of the night, then Gertrude's phone rang, a bright little tune that I half-recognised. She fished it out of her pocket. "Yes? Oh. Yes, just stick a toothpick in the centre. No, not clean, there should be some crumbs on it. Not too gooey, just a bit. I know, dear, but not *everyone* likes gooey brownies." She listened, then sighed. "Okay. Yes. Take them out. You can have the gooey middle and we'll sell the rest." She hung up, and rubbed her arm thoughtfully as she gazed around the cemetery. Her sleeve rode up and I spotted cartoon cats with mermaid tails dancing on the sleeve of what looked like pyjamas underneath. "Well," she said. "Are you feeling better?"

I made a non-committal sound, and she glanced at me, her eyes bright in the shadows.

"Yes," Callum said, like the cabbage he is.

"Then you'd best explain to me what's happening to my souls," she said, pointing at the bodies. "They've gone all squidgy."

"Squidgy?" I asked.

"Yes. They're not attached right anymore. They didn't leave when they should have, and now they've stuck to the vessel and gone all gooey, like bread dough." She sighed, a gentle, aching sound, and Callum and I exchanged glances.

"We don't know what happened," Callum said. "But we're trying to find out. A friend ..." he swallowed, then kept going. "A friend of mine may have had this happen to him, too. Have you ever come across it before?"

Gertrude shook her head firmly. "Never. It's all quite automated. Usually DHL collect the souls, but if they miss any, I reap them manually. The last week or so quite a few have gone missing, and I haven't been able to find them. I can feel they're here, but they won't come out. And I guess this is why. They're stuck."

"DHL?" Callum asked. "The couriers?"

"Yes – oh. No. Not those couriers. Departed Human Logistics. It is a bit confusing, but it was our name first."

"I see," Callum said, not sounding as if he did at all.

"And you've really never seen this before?" I asked Gertrude.

"Absolutely not. Sometimes souls can be a bit slow, if they've got unfinished business or just haven't quite accepted things yet, but I can usually sort it out with a quick chat." She frowned. "I'll have Grim Reaper North on the phone if this keeps up. What a pain. He's already a bit dubious about the cafe."

I decided I didn't want to get into too much detail regarding the internal workings of either a baby ghoul cafe or reaper politics, so before Callum could ask any of the things he was obviously dying to ask I said, "Is it magic doing this? Can you tell?"

She picked up one of the heads and examined it, and when she answered I could hear the frown in her voice. "I can't imagine any magic that could do this."

"Not even necromancers?"

The head stuck its tongue out and tried to lick her

hand, and she put it back down gently on the stump of its neck. It promptly pitched forward onto its face and started pulling itself toward Callum with its teeth. I gagged.

"Necromancers have been gone for thousands of years," Gertrude said. "Well before my time."

"What about zombies?" Callum asked. "Have you come across them before?"

She wrapped both hands around the handle of the scythe. "Zombies aren't real. I've been reaping for …" She hesitated, and I could almost see her adding things up. "Well, a good few centuries, anyway. I've never even heard of zombies except as those awful movies. All gore and screaming. Not my thing at all."

"Anything's possible," I said. "I'm sure you must know that too, if you've been around that long."

She picked up the head and set it on its stump again. "You poor thing," she said to it as it fell over once more. "Your soul's quite ruined."

"Aren't a lot of souls?" I asked.

She gave me a disapproving look. "I hope you're not talking about human notions such as damnation and so on."

"As if," I said. "I just mean everyone's a bit ruined. It's life."

"The soul never is," she said. "Not in that sense. It's like saying a pebble's ruined because it's become worn. It's still entirely beautiful, just a different shape. This is different. Something's been *done* to them."

We were silent again, considering what might have been done to the souls, and by who. Callum climbed to his feet, watching the two heads trying to drag themselves towards him.

"Thanks," he said finally. "You know, for saving us."

"Oh, no problems," Gertrude said, and dusted her hands off. "I'd best be going." She nodded at Callum, and gave me a quick scritch behind the ears. "Do try not to get eaten."

"Don't you want to find out what's doing this?" I asked her. "I mean, we *could* be dealing with zombies here."

"Or necromancers," Callum said.

"I think zombies might be better," the reaper said. "You know, if one had to choose."

"Well, help us find out which, then," I said. "Or aren't you interested?"

She frowned at me. "Of course I'm interested. Souls should *not* be treated like this. Plus, it's going to completely throw off the annual lost soul statistics. Grim Reaper North is going to be most unhappy about it." She glanced at the sky. "But I'm already late."

"So you're just going?"

"I have banana cake *and* millionaire shortbread to make," she told me. "And two other cemeteries to check for missing souls. I might be in time to save those ones if I hurry."

Callum rubbed the back of his head and looked at me. I shrugged. I didn't fancy an argument with a reaper.

She examined us, then nodded as if reaching an agreement with herself. "Look, maybe we can help each other. Come and see me tomorrow. I'll have checked the other graveyards and cemeteries by then."

"Okay," Callum said. "That sounds good."

She nodded. "Mind those heads."

I shuffled away from one that was getting a bit close to my tail. "Will do."

"Nice meeting you," Callum said.

"You too," she said, her smile flashing in the shadows of the hood. "See you tomorrow."

We watched her move fast and fluid across the grass without seeming to actually take a step, and something weird happened with the wall. It was there, then not there, then she was gone and the wall looked just as it had before.

"Dude," I said.

Callum looked from the wall to the bodies and sighed.

AND THAT WOULD HAVE BEEN plenty for the night, really. You know, almost being caught by a sorcerer, chasing a mysterious maybe-necromancer across a cemetery, discovering strange vials, being tag-teamed by zombies, *and* meeting a reaper with a fondness for baking and kitty pyjamas. It was enough. And I would have been fine with following Gertrude out, but of course Callum wouldn't hear of it while there were three bodies just lying about the place.

And, to be fair, there were still two heads trying to eat their way across the grass toward us, which I suppose might've been a bit much for someone to come across tomorrow morning while visiting Great-Aunt Fran. Plus, there was something weird going on with the bodies. Well, weird*er*. They kept twitching and making little creeping motions, as if they were trying to rejoin their heads. I didn't *think* that was possible, but then I hadn't thought any of this was possible a couple of days ago.

I found a grave for a Cheryl Jones that looked very much as if someone had exploded out of it like a particularly hungry jack-in-the-box, and as the intact zombie was the one that looked most like a Cheryl we decided to put her in there. I found the other two graves while Callum re-interred Cheryl, and wandered back to meet him by the snapping heads and their restless bodies.

"This is gross," I said, as Callum held both heads up, looking from them to the bodies and back again as he tried to decide which one looked like a match. "Just pick one. I mean, does it really matter?"

"It does to the people who buried them," Callum said.

"Well, that's us right now," I pointed out. "And, for the rest, they can just be happy Great-Uncle Mitch doesn't come knocking on the door wanting brains for supper."

Callum sighed. "I suppose," he said. "It just seems a bit off."

"It's *all* a bit off," I said. "Just get them in the ground before any more turn up."

He didn't answer, just set one of the heads down, muttered an apology, and drove his shovel into the skull. Or would have, if he hadn't closed his eyes at the last moment. The head rolled away and he almost stabbed his own foot. He glared at me, daring me to say anything, but I didn't. We looked at each other for a moment, then he took another swing at the head. This time he got it, and we both checked the bodies. One had stopped twitching.

"Well, that's something," I said. "I mean, even if they're in the wrong graves, at least they're a matched set."

He gave me a disapproving look, and I shrugged.

"Whatever. I'm going to go make sure no one else is looking like going for a midnight ramble."

"So helpful," Callum muttered, grabbing the dead body's arms and starting to drag it off toward one of the graves.

"You couldn't do it without me," I said, and wandered off.

I was nosing around a fresh grave, ready to jump back if the turf so much as trembled, when I heard a yelp, a thud, and a clang.

"Callum?" I yelled, already breaking into a run. "Callum, you alright? *Callum?*"

"Yeah," he called back after a moment. "It's nothing."

I loped down the rows and stopped next to him. He was sitting on the ground, stripped down to his T-shirt and staring at the remaining body and head with the shovel clutched in his hands. There were smears of blood on the handle from his blisters, and what looked like zombie bits on the blade.

"What happened?" I asked.

"Tripped," he said, waving at the head.

I looked from him to it. There was a clean, blood-less cleft in the skull. "Well, you told it, right?"

"Yeah." He pushed himself up, pressing one hand to his side and puffing air. "Last one."

"Good," I said, watching him. "What happened to your side?"

"Bumped it," he said, swinging the shovel in his free hand.

We looked at each other.

"You going to finish checking the graves?" he asked me.

"You going to finish burying that zombie?"

"Just having a breather."

We stared at each other a moment longer, then he sighed and let his hand drop away. His T-shirt was torn, dark stains blooming over the old material.

"Oh, Old Ones with hairballs and hangovers," I said, as he lifted the shirt to expose a ring of teeth marks, red and raw against the pale skin of his torso. "Three-day-old soggy Weetabix. Demons in tutus. *Hairballs.*"

"Yep," he said. "Pretty much."

"Are you changing already?" I asked. "Are you hungry? Do I look tasty?"

He scowled at me and dropped the shirt back into place, wandering over to where his jacket was slung over a headstone to dig out his cigarettes. "No, Gobs. Jesus. We don't even know if that's how it spreads. *If* it spreads."

"They're *zombies*. We know how that works."

"We don't know if they're that sort of zombie."

I stared at him, then said, "It's affecting your brain already, isn't it? You should go to hospital."

"You don't like hospitals."

"Well, true." I knew the sort of things that hung around hospitals. I'd stayed awake the whole time watching the damn things when Callum was kept in overnight after that goblin punched him in the head. I didn't fancy repeating the experience. "We need someone to suck the poison out, then."

"What? No!"

"It's what you do with snake bites." I nodded at Green Snake, who'd just poked his head out of the coat pocket. "Isn't it?"

Green Snake flicked his tongue unhelpfully and vanished again.

"No one's sucking anything," Callum said, and picked up the shovel, the cigarette wedged in the corner of his mouth. "Let's just get finished. I'll put some hydrogen peroxide on it when we get home."

"Right," I said. "I'm sure that'll do it. Well-known anti-zombie properties, peroxide."

Callum ignored me and kept filling the grave in, cigarette smoke drifting around his face in the still air of the cemetery, and I dug my claws into the grass and listened to the bats squeaking on the far reaches of hearing, the night suddenly dark and heavy and full of fright.

10

OH, NO. NOT SCIENCE

I WASN'T SURE HOW LONG SOMEONE HAD BEEN KNOCKING by the time I realised what it was, because I was putting all my mostly asleep willpower into ignoring it. I redoubled the effort as I heard Callum stumble over and drag the door open.

"Yeah?" he managed, sounding like he'd been out in the desert for a month, running on cigarettes and caffeine.

"Morning," a woman's voice said, in rather brighter tones. "Breakfast?"

I opened one eye as the scent of bacon drifted across the room. Petra stood in the doorway with her work clothes on under her jacket, clutching a paper bag with some pretty enticing grease stains on it, as well as a big thermos mug that gave off a whiff of coffee. Callum made some not-very-articulate sound and waved her in. His T-shirt was on back to front, and his hair was partly in his eyes, the rest tangled around a persistent twig. I yawned.

"You alright?" Petra asked as she came in and

deposited the bag on the desk at the opposite end to my bed. "Rough night?"

Callum bundled the duvet back onto his armchair-bed and headed into the kitchenette. "Late one. Tea?"

"No." She waved the mug at him. "I didn't get you one. Sorry. I've never seen you drink coffee, so …"

"I don't," he agreed, and stared down at his shirt as if trying to figure out what was wrong with it. His jeans were on the right way around, at least, but they were about as filthy as you'd expect after a night of zombie fighting and grave digging. He also hadn't made any move to bite her, which I figured was a good sign.

"I just wanted to say thanks, really," Petra said. "For the arm, I mean. I thought you'd come by the cafe, otherwise I'd have popped in sooner."

I weighed up staying in bed and trying to sleep a bit more, or investigating the bag. The bag looked good, but it felt like we'd barely got home. Twelve hours sleep is a bare minimum for any decent PI work, and I was certain I'd barely had a fraction of that.

"S'okay," Callum said, dropping the box of teabags in the sink. "No problem. Really."

"Even so." She unpacked the bag, releasing a waft of gloriously meaty air. "I don't know what I'd have done."

"You'd have been fine." Callum managed to pour the kettle without burning himself, although he did slop water all over the tiny worktop.

Petra watched him for a moment, an amused little quirk to her mouth, but it faded as she said, "Was there anything else … weird?"

Callum glanced at me, and I blinked.

He cleared his throat and said, "No. It was fine."

"Really?" She took a sip of coffee, and took her phone out of her coat pocket. "I'm on a couple of local Facebook groups. You know, buy and sell, that sort of thing."

"Okay." Callum splashed milk in his tea and made it back to the desk, where he removed the snake and his cigarettes from the drawer. I'd been too tired to deal with Green Snake trying to crawl into my bed last night, and had got a little snappy. Callum had put him in the drawer for everyone's safety.

Petra stared at the snake. "Does he bite?"

"Not usually." Callum forced the sash window up a bit, wedged it with a book, and lit a cigarette, inhaling like it was the only thing keeping him alive.

"Great. Anyway." Petra took another sip of coffee, and kept her eyes on Green Snake as she said, "People were talking about disturbances in the cemetery. Last night *and* the night before."

I opened both eyes and sat up, stretching the stiffness out of my spine. My ribs ached from being thrown against the headstone.

"*Our* cemetery?" Callum asked, stopping with one hand reaching out for his tea.

She smiled. "That's a weird way to put it. But, yeah. At our cemetery."

"That's, um, odd," Callum said.

Petra nodded. "And this morning someone posted this video of … well, I don't know. I'll show you." She flicked through her phone, and I ambled over, rubbing my face on her hands until she petted me, so that I could keep an eye on the screen. Callum leaned over the desk, his forearms heavy on the scarred top, and she hit play.

At first there was nothing but the dark shapes of trees stretching above the cemetery wall and the streetlights sliding off parked cars, and a voice said, "They came out just there … seriously, what're they *on?*" The camera shuffled side to side, catching the edges of an upstairs window, then stopped as an indistinct shape moved across the street. The camera stilled, and the voice said, *"There!"*

I tensed, waiting to see Callum caught on camera, clambering over the wall with his face lit by the yellow light. Or Hooded Figure running down the road, or even Gertrude sliding effortlessly through the stone. One of those. It *had* to be one of those.

The shape emerged into the light, and the hair on my tail lifted softly. The figure moved bent over, using its hands to help propel it along, legs half-bent and back curved. It was too far off and the light too bad to get much detail, and when it paused again and its pale face swung toward the window, the person videoing jerked back with a curse. By the time they had it focused on the creature again, it was loping down the road, headed away from the lights and deeper into the houses.

I looked up at Callum, seeing tight lines around his mouth. He had one hand cupped over his side, and I could smell the rough tang of hydrogen peroxide. He'd been in the shower for about an hour in the small hours before dawn, and I think he'd basically bathed in the stuff.

"Weird, right?" Petra said.

"Weird," Callum agreed. "Probably just a prank, though."

"I suppose," Petra said, but her fingers tapped lightly on the phone as she looked at him. "And you didn't see anything?"

Callum shook his head as he retrieved his cigarette from the windowsill.

Petra looked at me, her eyes dark and thoughtful, then got up. "I've got to get back to work," she said. "Be careful, alright?"

We watched her go, and Callum exhaled softly as the door shut in her wake. "This is not good," he said.

"I think we already knew that."

"But one got out, Gobs. That means there's more than just the ones we've seen. That's *really* not good."

"It could have been Ifan."

Callum shook his head. "Not unless they did him up in clown make-up."

I tipped my head to the side. "Good point. So if we count Ifan, we've got at least two zombies out there."

"If they're zombies."

"What d'you prefer, the living dead?"

He rubbed his face with his hands. "God. I thought maybe we got them all last night. I mean, no one *did* anything. We were there all night."

"We don't know how they're doing it. No one did anything in the cemetery, sure. But they must be zombifying them before they go in the ground, or at a distance or something."

He groaned. "So what've we got? Lewis tried to reanimate Ifan, and it kind of spread? Or the necromancers did it?"

I sat back and scratched at one of the scars on my chest. "We're talking seriously strong magic," I said. "I really don't think Lewis could've done it. And High Priestess what's-her-face may be able to hear cats, but she smelt more of mung beans than blood magic." I paused, then added, "There was only one person there last night who *might* be able to raise the dead. *Might.* And I'm still not saying she did."

Callum stubbed his cigarette out and picked up his tea. "So, shall I call the scary sorcerer who once threatened to throw you into another dimension and ask her if she's starting the zombie apocalypse, or do you want to do it?"

"I'd rather keep my fur on the outside," I said. "We should tackle everyone else first. And maybe she *is* behind it, but maybe she was actually investigating. Gertrude's had missing souls for a few nights, and not just there. So maybe this is more widespread than we realise. Maybe other people know about it."

"Oh," Callum said. "Well, that makes me feel much better. You know, that there could be whole packs of the undead out there."

"All running around biting people," I said, and he wrinkled his nose. "How's it feel?"

"A bit sore."

"Any cravings for lightly sautéed cerebellum?"

"Not so far."

"Well, that's something. It's evidently not instant, then."

"We don't even know if it spreads like that."

"We don't know that it doesn't, either." I yawned. "Susan might have found something out about the other boneyards by now. Can we eat first, though? I'm starving."

"I think you've got worms," Callum said, opening the paper bag and pulling out a sandwich and a foil packet that oozed the scent of bacon and sausages.

I sniffed. "Well, you've got sticks in your hair." I ignored him tugging at the offending twig and scratched the foil pack till it tore. If we were going to be hunting zombies, I'd need my strength.

WHILE I GNAWED my way through two rashers of bacon and one large sausage, Callum emptied the cemetery backpack out onto the table. There was nothing in the main compartment but the Tupperware with its vials and syringe, and the pockets yielded nothing more interesting than an empty packet of Haribo and a few coins. He took a large bite of his bacon butty and stared at the vials again.

"Are you analysing them by thought alone?" I asked, licking my chops.

He snorted. "I can't work out why anyone would be carting some weird drug around a cemetery."

"Maybe he was a dealer," I said. "Maybe he had nothing to do with the zombies."

"Says the cat who doesn't believe in coincidences."

I sighed, and abandoned my last piece of bacon. I'd need it to bribe Susan with later, anyway. I snuffled around the plastic tub and cautiously whiffled across the vials themselves, then sneezed and sat back on my haunches.

"And?" Callum said.

I sneezed again. "And nothing. All I can smell is disinfectant and rubber gloves."

"And the bag?"

I checked it. "The same. It's pretty new. Books, a bit. Maybe an egg sandwich. Dead things. But that could be from last night."

Callum sighed. "Well, unless we stick someone with a needle, I guess we won't know what's in here. We'll have to go back tonight, see if they turn up again."

"Oh, good," I said. "That sounds fun."

"And in the meantime, let's talk to Susan, then go and have another word with the necromancers. Properly eliminate them as suspects before we worry about Ms Jones."

"Really? What about naps? I barely slept last night!"

"Neither did I."

"In human terms, four hours is a short night's sleep. In cat terms, it's not even a snooze. I need my sleep!"

"Sleep in the car," Callum said, adding a piece of bacon he'd saved from his sandwich to my foil packet and wrapping it up.

"Hey, you kept some? I could have eaten all mine, then."

"The chicken was substandard, remember? We need to look after our informants." He grabbed his coat from the back of the bathroom door and shrugged it on. "Come on."

I sighed and got up. "I don't feel on top zombie-fighting form."

"You ate too much bacon."

I tried to protest, and burped instead. It was possible.

THE SUN WAS OUT, albeit in a slightly begrudging manner. I led the way around the side of the building, and Callum unwrapped the packet of bacon, setting it next to the grate then retreating a couple of paces. We waited, Callum crouching on the pavement next to me with his forearms resting on his knees and his hands hanging loose between them, a cigarette dangling unlit in one. The sun hadn't made its way down among the buildings yet, and it was damp and a little chilly.

It wasn't long before Susan pushed her nose out of the grate to examine us, her little pink paws gripping the rusting iron firmly while she checked for scents. Then she slipped out through the skinny gap and investigated the bacon, her soft fur bright and glossy.

"That's more like it," she said.

"We aim to please," I said.

"Then can we have some fruit next time?" She pushed the bacon toward the grate. "We'll all get scurvy at this rate."

"Cats don't need fruit," I said.

"Your human probably does," she said, and I shrugged. It was true, our diet had kind of gone downhill since our across-the-hall neighbour, Mrs Smith, left on a trip to

Tibet to find herself or whatever. I wasn't sure how you lost yourself in the first place, but that's humans for you.

"I'm healthy," Callum protested. Susan stared at the cigarette in his hand pointedly, and he flushed. "Fairly, anyway."

Susan groomed her whiskers and said, "Well, I asked around. All as quiet as you'd expect in most places. Ghouls, of course, and the usual imprechauns after any valuables that get dug up, but that's normal."

"Imprechauns?" Callum asked.

"Leprechaun-imp combo," I said. "They've turned into quite a distinct kind. Small, blue, and seriously into anything shiny. They run most of the pawn shops in town."

"Huh." He scratched his stubble. "Most places?"

"Most places," Susan agreed. "Morningside had a lot of freaked out crypt rats."

"Crypt rats—" I started, and Callum interrupted me.

"Rats that live in crypts. Kind of got that one."

"*No,*" I said. "It's a sub-kind of faery that—"

"They're rats that live in crypts," Susan said. "You're thinking of bonetown rats, Gobbelino. And they're more a clique than a sub-kind."

"I thought bonetown rats were a band," Callum said.

Susan looked at her paws, whiskers twitching. "Yes, because that's exactly what we went looking for. Do you want to know what's got them freaked out or not?"

"Yes," I said. "Sorry."

"It seems you were right about the reanimations. A couple of nights ago, two corpses just dug their way out of their graves and wandered off. The first one got hold of two rats before they knew what was going on."

"Oh, no," Callum said.

"These are not the sort of threats rats are used to," Susan said. "We don't appreciate it. We have enough trouble with living humans. So I hope you're going to sort this out."

"We are," I said, with more conviction than I felt. I still had no idea how to deal with a potential zombie outbreak, but I didn't fancy sharing that information with Susan.

"Apparently no stink of magic," Susan said. "But I don't know how that would work."

"Science," Callum said thoughtfully. He'd brought the backpack with him, and was fiddling with the straps.

We both stared at him for a moment, then Susan sniffed. "Rice cakes," she said, and slipped back into the grate, leaving us to wonder if that was an insult or a request. Insult, I thought. But it wasn't always easy to tell with Susan.

"Science?" I said, arching my whiskers at Callum.

"No one's smelling any magic," he said. "We found what look like medical vials at the cemetery. What if this is a human problem, not a magic one?"

"Then that's just frigging fantastic," I said. "I think I'd prefer a necromancer to some rogue scientist. At least we know what rules apply to magic."

"Do we?"

"Well, we've got an idea, anyway." I stood and stretched. "Let's go and see what our necromancers say."

I DID my best to sleep all the way to Headingley, but given the rattles and belches of the old Rover, it wasn't easy. Oh, and the fact that my partner might turn into a zombie at any moment, and we had no idea either how to stop it or even where the zombies had come from in the first place. That did make a restful nap a bit tricky to settle into.

Plus I was still worried about the Watch. Even if Callum was right, and it was a human problem, it was too close to magic to rest easy with the Watch. After all, their main goal in life was purportedly to keep humans ignorant of the unseen world swirling through the borders of their own, and once humans accepted the existence of the walking dead, all bets were off.

And even without my history with the Watch, they get pretty strict about keeping things separate. They wouldn't hesitate to deal to both of us with, as the humans put it, severe prognosis. Prudence? Whatever. I'd be back in the Inbetween and on the monster munch menu, and Callum ... well, who knew. I wondered if I should try and get ahead of them, contact Claudia myself and get her help to deal with this. But I still didn't entirely trust her, and I had no way of getting hold of her, either.

If I'd been able to shift I could have stepped into the Inbetween and found the faint dusty traces of her scent where she'd left it behind her, following her trail as it unravelled like a deep indigo thread in the darkness. I probably couldn't have gone straight to her, as all cats cover their tracks, but I'd have been close.

As it was, I'd have to amble up to a Watch house in person and take my chances that they heard me out before they chucked me back to the beasts. Which didn't sound like an amazing idea. And maybe Callum was wrong about the science thing, anyway. Maybe it *was* necromancers, and we could find a cure and sort the whole thing out before the Watch even heard about it.

I was starting to worry about how often I seemed to be hoping for necromancers.

CALLUM PULLED up a few houses down from the necromancer's house, and I sat up, yawning. "What now?"

"Now you stay here," he said.

"I what?"

"She won't let me in with you there."

"I don't believe for a moment she's allergic."

"That's irrelevant," he said. "The only way I'm getting in is without you."

"Pig snot," I said. "I'll climb in a window."

"Just wait here. You said you wanted a sleep, anyway."

"What if she decides to use you as a sacrifice? What then?"

Callum rubbed the back of his head. "I'll take my chances. I think I'm less likely to get sacrificed without you being rude to people."

"Who's going to get me custard if you get sacrificed?"

He snorted. "It's so good to know you care, Gobs. Stay here." He swung his lanky form out of the car, moving a little more stiffly than usual. "I'll leave the window open."

"I'm not a *dog*," I spat, and he waved his fingers at me then headed down the pavement to the house. I put my paws on the dashboard to watch him ring the bell, and a moment later someone in black robes answered. I couldn't see their face from here, but their head was shaved, so unless Oli had had a haircut since yesterday, there was a new necromancer on the block.

I jumped out the window and padded to the end of the row of terraced houses, slipping down a footpath that ran between the red brick walls of the necromancer's row and the next one along.

Well, I wasn't going to stay in car, was I?

The brick walls of the houses gave way to high wooden fences, the old wood full of claw holds. I scuttled up the one at the end of the necromancer's row and paused at the top, checking the yard beyond for dogs. There was nothing but a child's playhouse and a half-hearted veggie patch, so I jumped to the grass and ran across it, scaling the next wall and repeating my surveillance. This yard had the rusting corpse of a washing machine and two tricycles slowly disintegrating on moss-covered concrete. I kept going.

Two yards. Three. The fourth had a yappy little dog with a pink bow stuck between its ears, and I spat at it then circled the yard on top of the fence, throwing my most inventive insults at the creature and wondering if Callum had been sacrificed yet, or if they were just going for brainwashing.

Then I was peering into the fifth yard, and the stink of magic rose out of the ground like a heat mirage on tarmac. I wobbled on top of the fence, breathing the reek of blood and wax and the sort of power that sets your skin crawling, not wanting to touch my paws to the over-lush grass below. Wildflowers grew up through it, but they were strange and twisted things. Anything would be, in that.

A door slammed somewhere in the depths of the house, and I took a deep breath of nearly clean air. Whatever was in there, Callum couldn't handle it alone. I threw myself off the fence and bolted across the yard, my eyes on the upstairs window that was open just enough to admit someone small, sleek, and determined.

11

ATTACK OF THE ZOMBIE CHICKENS

THERE WAS A SMALL OVERHANG AT THE BACK DOOR, protecting it from the rain, and I jumped to it from the downstairs windowsill, the glass blocked off with more black curtains. The tiles on the overhang were a bit mossy, but with the dry morning it was easy enough to keep my footing. I settled myself on the edge, ears back as I squinted at the upstairs window. Painted wood sills. It'd be slippery, but the brick beneath the window had good grip, so as long as I kept momentum I'd be fine. Plus, it was only the first floor. I could land a fall from that with a drunk pigeon on my shoulder.

I bunched my legs under me and launched myself at the window, tasting that moment of pure pleasure as I became airborne, the movement effortless and made of absolute grace. Then my paws hit the edge of the sill and a hideous pale face popped up between me and the black curtain. I squawked, kicking wildly with my back legs, suddenly very much wanting to test my theory that I could land back in the garden quite happily, but I'd judged the jump too well.

My momentum carried me straight through the gap under the window, my claws offering nowhere near enough resistance going forward. I belly-flopped onto the sill, still trying not to shoot straight into the room beyond, but it was too late. I careered into the monster beyond.

We landed in a tangle of limbs and claws and curtains, and someone bit me very firmly on the ear. I yowled, kicking out with my back legs, my claws scoring soft flesh, then a voice I'd heard before hissed, "Stop it, you pretzel!"

I stopped kicking. "Pru?"

"Yes. Gods." She wriggled in the grip of the curtain. "Help. My claws are stuck."

"Um." I tried to pull myself away from her, and panicked for a moment when I couldn't get my front paw free. "*Ow!*"

"Shut up!" We thrashed around for a moment longer, both of us panting, then she rolled away from the curtain and sat up on the carpeted floor beyond. "Come on, hurry."

"I'm trying," I hissed, and tugged hard at the curtain. My paw gave a flash of pain, then I was free. "What're you *doing* here? I thought you were a … well, never mind."

She gave me an insulted look, even though I hadn't actually said what I'd thought. "I'm looking for Katja."

"Katja? Your human?"

"Yes. She started acting really weird yesterday, and

today she went out and hasn't come back. I think they've *done* something to her."

"Like what?"

"Dude, I don't know." She glared at me, her tail thrashing. "Whatever it is you think they're doing to your human, probably. Anyway, what's with the wild entrance? There aren't any shift-blocking charms here, you know."

"Just didn't fancy shifting into a necromancer's house," I said, examining the room. It didn't look like the lair of a sorcerer with violent tendencies. There were pony posters on the wall and a purple desk with a small pink chair pushed up against one wall. "You find anything?"

"Not up here. Not sure about downstairs – too many people."

"Okay." I headed for the door.

"Where're you going?" she asked, trotting after me.

"I think my human's down there. My partner, I mean."

"He's not joining up, is he?"

"No. But I don't think he realises what he's getting into. Have you smelled that backyard?"

Her whiskers twitched. "Wait till you get a whiff of downstairs. Someone around here has real power. Or did. It seems pretty old."

We took the stairs shoulder to shoulder, our paws silent on the old carpet. Magic rose and drifted around us, lazy scents that were baked into the walls and floors. Paintings above us shifted just on the edge of vision, and I wondered how I hadn't been able to smell it yesterday. Someone was good at shielding themselves.

The hall stretched before us, one door lying dark and open to the left and back of the house, another closed closer to the front door. To our right, a door hung open and warm yellow light spilled out across the deep red of the hall runner.

I crept toward the open door, belly slung low to the ground, my ears twitching as a deep voice said, "Terribly sad, of course."

Callum's voice was quieter as he said, "I was wondering if anyone else had gone missing recently?"

"I hope you're not *suggesting—*" a woman's voice started, and the deep-voiced man spoke over her.

"Of course not. We're spirit communicators, not murderers or kidnappers."

"And you don't think anyone might have targeted you?" Callum asked. "Thought you were dangerous, perhaps?"

"Well," the woman said. "Now you mention it, we *did* have a couple of threatening phone calls just yesterday."

"Really?" Callum asked. "What did they say?"

I had settled myself to listen in the shadows of the door, my ears pricking, and I'd almost forgotten Pru. Until there was the sudden, too-loud pad of sprinting paws on the hall floor, and she skidded to a stop next to me, the runner bunching under her feet.

"The kitchen!" she yelped, loud enough that all conversation ceased beyond the door. "The *kitchen!*"

"*Shh!*" I hissed, but it was already too late. Heavy footfalls rang on the wood floors, and light washed over me as the door was jerked wide. An enormous man with a bald head glared down at me.

"Cats?" he demanded. "You brought *cats?*"

"Not intentionally, and not plural," Callum said,

crossing the floor on softer feet to look down at me, rubbing his side as he came. Tall as he was, the bald man was even bigger, and at least twice as broad. "Gobs. Really?"

"This place *reeks,*" I said. "As in blood magic, not like drains or anything."

"And the kitchen!" Pru insisted. "The *kitchen!*"

"Oh, gods, it's Pru," High Priestess Oli said, appearing behind the two men. Then she sneezed, and looked at me accusingly. Okay, so maybe she was allergic.

"Yeah, it's me," Pru snarled. "Where's Katja? What did you do to her? Was it like *them?*" She jerked her head toward the kitchen.

"Like who them?" I asked. "What them?"

"You need to leave," Big Man said to Callum, leaning toward him like he was about to use his chest to pin him against the wall.

"What's in the kitchen, Pru?" Callum asked.

"Look," she said. "I let them out."

"You *what?*" Big Man yelped, forgetting about Callum. "Oh, you ugly mutt!"

"Hey!" Pru and I said together.

"Oh, no," Oli said. "Oh, it took *ages* to get them back in the coop last time!"

"Coop?" I asked, and Callum stepped past me, finding the hall lights and flicking them on. I took one look behind me, in the direction of the kitchen, and shot to his shoulder, my tail bushing out wildly. "What in the name of all that crawls are *those?*"

Big Man scratched his head. "Chickens?"

"Headless ones," Callum said, and we watched the five

chickens sprinting back and forth across the kitchen floor, moulting as they went, slamming into cabinets and rebounding, then heading off again in whatever new direction they found themselves in. They were astonishingly fast, but removing the heads hadn't done much for them. One was stuck in a corner and just kept bouncing from one wall to another. The others were doing better, and, as we watched, one finally found the door and raced toward us, feathers raining to the floor as its wings waved wildly, trying to keep itself upright.

Pru shot straight for Callum's other shoulder, and he sighed slightly but didn't protest. Big Man made a grab for the chicken, but it just rebounded off his hands and went ricocheting into the nearest wall then took off again, legs pedalling like an Olympic cyclist.

"Zombie chickens," I said. "Sure you don't have anything to say to us?"

"Not zombie," Oli corrected me. "Just reanimated. The brain's trickier. We were just trying to keep the bodies going after death to start with."

"To start with?" Callum asked, finally looking away from the chickens. Three of them had made it into the hall now, and were tearing back and forth, bouncing off the walls and each other, while Big Man made clumsy grabs for them.

"Well, yes. So many people mourn their pets, you see, and we've never been able to contact non-human souls. So we thought that if we could just reanimate them, it'd really help. I mean, people are already cloning pets, and this would be much cheaper." She tipped her head. "Cheap*er*. Still profitable, though."

Pru and I gave voice to matching hisses from Callum's shoulder, and he winced. "Can you not do that so close to my ears, please? And less claws would be nice."

"Where's my human?" Pru demanded. "Where *is* she?"

"How would we know?" Oli asked, as Big Man finally grabbed a chicken with a whoop. It promptly kicked his wrists so hard that he swore and let go, and the creature raced off into the nearest wall. "We haven't seen her since we left the cafe."

"Were kicked out," Pru said.

"You're *reanimating* things," Callum said.

"Well, only chickens so far. And a few cockroaches. But we were never sure if we actually reanimated them or if they never died in the first place."

I gagged. "That is disgusting."

She looked at the chickens. "I admit it's not very pleasant right now, but we're still ironing out the details. Once we can work out how to do the brains, it'll be perfect. No one ever need lose a pet again!"

"No, because they can just have zombies," Callum said, and pinched the bridge of his nose. "So you know nothing about any human zombies?"

Big Man looked around at that, and burst out laughing. "You've been watching too many horror films," he said. "Zombies don't exist. And trust me, reanimating headless chickens is hard enough. A whole human would be impossible."

"And you haven't seen Ifan," Callum said. "Or Katja."

"Look, Ifan was a nice lad," Big Man said, giving up on the chickens. "Lot of magic in him, too. But he had issues we couldn't help with. I don't think anyone could, really.

We weren't exactly surprised when he left. Whatever he was looking for, we weren't it."

"And I think Katja really only joined because she'd just bought the cafe and we'd been meeting there for years," Oli added. "I wasn't surprised when she quit."

"But she's *gone,*" Pru said. "Where's she gone?"

"I'm sure she'll be back," Oli said. "She's probably wondering where you are. You're not allowed out, are you?"

"I go where I want," Pru muttered, pointedly not looking at me as I peered around Callum's neck.

Callum looked from Big Man to Oli, and sighed, then jumped as a chicken ran into his legs. It bounced off, hit another zombie chicken, and came back at him again. He made an *urk* sound and backed up to the front door. "No one else in your group could have been messing around with the idea of human zombies?"

Big Man chuckled. "Not a chance. We use them to make up the numbers we need. Other than Ifan, they're about as magic as a plum pudding."

"Great." Callum nudged the chickens away from him with one boot. "You have to stop this, you know."

"We're not doing anything wrong. We're not *hurting* them," Oli said, crossing her arms.

"They're *dead chickens,*" I yelled. "They're not supposed to be running around!"

"Ow," Callum said, rubbing his ear. "He is right, though."

"And what're you going to do about it?" Big Man asked, looming toward us. "You think you can stop us?"

"RSPCA," Pru suggested. "Or the Watch."

"They're *dead* chickens," Oli said. "it's hardly cruelty."

"Tell that to the RSPCA," I said. "And the Watch? No chance."

"Who?" Big Man demanded, and Pru and I exchanged glances.

Callum let out his breath in a low whistle. "Well, one won't believe they're dead and will do you for cruelty, the other *will* believe they're dead and will do you for bringing magic into the human world by getting people into this little group of yours."

"Personally, I'd go with the RSPCA," I said. "More likely to come out with all limbs attached."

"Get rid of these," Callum said. "And don't make any more. This is not okay. Not even slightly."

Big Man did the loom again. "You're not going to report us to *anyone*."

Callum looked up at him calmly enough, but I could feel his pulse pounding in his neck. "Not if you stop it right now. Otherwise I most certainly am."

Big Man grabbed the front of Callum's hoody. "Let's rethink that," he hissed.

I took off from Callum's shoulder as I felt him move beneath me, glimpsing Pru hitting the floor at the same time. There was a commotion of limbs and fists going on, and somehow Callum was out from under it and slamming Big Man face-first into the front door.

"No!" Oli shouted and started forward, and I jumped straight at her face. She shrieked and fended me off, staggering away and tripping over one of the chickens. She lurched toward the wall, put one hand out to save herself, missed, and plunged into the living room.

I chased her, hissing, *"I will shed on you!"*

She screamed and covered her face, but that might have been the three headless chickens that were running up her legs, moving purposefully but in weird silence, necks jerking awkwardly.

I turned back into the hall in time to see Big Man throw Callum away from the door. Callum stumbled, caught his hip against a black sideboard, and dropped into a crouch as Big Man rushed him, roaring. Callum twisted aside with a grimace, somehow finding room to sidestep the larger man, who tripped over a braced Pru and crashed to the ground with a thud that shook the walls. Callum bolted for the door, grabbed the handle and threw it open just as Oli ran past me.

"Heads!" I bellowed, and Callum flattened himself to the wall. She should have at least bumped into him as she rushed past, but he just watched her go past with a slightly quizzical look on his face. She plunged through the door with a scream, which was matched by the scream of the man standing outside in a red polo shirt with a box in his hands. They crashed to the ground together, and two chickens ran past into the road, where they vanished under a passing bus and didn't re-emerge. Well, not in the same shape, anyway.

Pru joined Callum and I at the door, and we stared at Oli as she disentangled herself from the postman.

"Dreadfully sorry," she was saying, trying to dust him off. "I thought you were my husband."

"Okay," he said.

"It's a game we play. Ambush."

"Okay," he said again, and handed her a crushed box

that was starting to grow a wet patch on one corner. "This was fine when I got here."

"Sure," she said, nodding eagerly. "Of course it was."

He walked back to his bike, glancing at us doubtfully, and pushed it away, limping slightly.

Oli narrowed her eyes at us, and Big Man grabbed Callum's shoulders, jerking him back into the hall. "You're not going anywhere," he hissed. I crouched to launch myself at his ridiculous face, and the final three chickens shot past us and down the stairs to the road.

"Stop them!" Oli shrieked, shifting the box to her hip and waving her free arm wildly at the birds. "Don't let them escape!"

Big Man let go of Callum and rushed after the chickens, and just as the dead birds reached Oli the box exploded in a roar of pastel blue powder and pink glitter.

I dodged behind Callum's legs, bouncing into Pru as she did the same, and we both stared from relative safety as the powder slowly settled. It drifted across the steps and crept onto the paving stones, coating the two black-robed necromancers in a luminous slick. The chickens wobbled, then collapsed halfway to the gate, looking like threadbare feather dusters, and the glitter danced softly up to the walls of the house. It flowed and twisted, like a half-legible signature or a replicating virus, and I pulled my tail closer as a small drift approached the door.

"Let's go," I said, and added, "Don't touch that," as Callum extended a curious finger to the blue stain creeping up the steps.

"I'm not magic," he said. "It can't hurt me."

"*Whatever,*" Pru said. "Move it, skinny. And give me a

lift. I don't know what it might do to cats, and I'm not going to be a shiftless wonder like cat burglar here."

"I *can* shift," I insisted, scrambling up to Callum's right shoulder as he picked Pru up and deposited her on the other side. I could smell sweat and weariness on him, and a deeper whiff of something unpleasant, milk on the turn or a bad orange at the bottom of the bag.

"Don't touch it," he said. "Really?"

"Really," I said, and nodded at the twin twisters of powder lifting off the two stunned necromancers, the pink and blue deepening to bruised purple as they twined together in the sky, forming a miniature storm cloud. "I think this is where old Lewis gets his magic from. He steals it."

"Eh," Callum said, jumping over the steps and onto the stained pavement. "I'm not feeling too heartbroken."

"Me either," I said, looking behind us as he shoved his hands in his pockets and ambled toward the car.

"Is that them done?" Pru asked. "Someone's taken their magic?"

"I don't know," I said. Oli was helping Big Man up and hurrying him into the house. She shot a furious look after us, and I could feel the heat of it. The purple of stolen power had been thickest over her, and I wondered if she was the one who had been doing the cloaking. Or maybe not. Maybe there was someone else, hidden in the attic or off about their business, someone who leeched that terrible power into the very earth around them. The pale blue stain was hesitating at the threshold of the house, the glitter already fading. It couldn't get in. "Maybe not entirely," I said. "But the chickens are done, anyway."

"Gross," Pru said.

"Entirely," Callum agreed, reaching through the window to open the car door. "Gobs, anyone could've stolen this when you left."

Pru snorted. "Unlikely."

"D'you want a lift or not?" I asked her.

"Eh, I might just shift," she said, jumping to the pavement. "Look, if they didn't do anything to Katja, what's happened to her?"

"What's wrong with her, exactly?" Callum asked, and Pru wrinkled her nose.

"She smells wrong. She went to town yesterday afternoon to get some meat for me and some stuff for the cafe, and when she came back she said someone *bit* her."

"Bit her?" we echoed, and she arched her whiskers at us.

"Yes. Their teeth, her skin, you get the picture?"

"You said *someone,* right, not *something,*" Callum said, pulling his coat around him despite the sun.

"Yeah. I mean, I'd have asked more, but she can't hear me. She's very human." There was a softness in Pru's voice, and I shifted uneasily.

"And she's gone," I said.

"She went out this morning and never came back."

I looked at Callum. He wiped his mouth, nodded, and said, "Okay. Go and see if she's back. If not, come with us. This might be connected, even if it's not to do with the necromancers."

"Yeah, what about them?" she asked. "Should we report them to the Watch?"

"Probably," I said. "I'm not exactly on first name basis with them, though."

She gave me an evaluating look. "Not on first name basis, and can't shift. What'd you *do?*"

"It was totally a set-up."

She shook her head. "Look, there's a Watch house I know. I'll tell them about the necromancers. I won't mention you," she added, as I opened my mouth. "Then I'll see if Katja's home. If she's not, I'll come find you."

"Good plan," Callum said.

"Good as any," I agreed.

Pru nodded slightly, then was gone, the world opening and closing around her as if she'd never been, only the whisper of air filling the empty space to mark her passing. Her momentum would carry her across the unfathomable void of the Inbetween, the space that runs between and behind the worlds, as vast as loss and as directionless as sorrow. And before the beasts – the leviathans in the far reaches of the abyss, the flashing toothed hungers in the shallows – could so much as realise she was there, she'd step out again, at the Watch house or somewhere similar, and go about her business.

Old ones take me, I missed shifting. It made life so bloody *easy*. Well, it had. No use moping over lost lives, though.

I looked at Callum. "What now?"

"Cemetery," he said.

"Oh, joy," I said, and jumped across to the passenger seat. "Can't we go somewhere more fun?"

"There's zombies," he said. "What could be more fun?"

12

SHAKING DOWN THE MORTICIAN

"It's *daytime*," I complained as we pulled up outside the cemetery. It was a lot easier to find parking during the day, with the kerbs outside the houses empty of cars.

"I'd noticed," Callum said.

"Why're we here now?"

"I want to check something. And you never know. Maybe we'll catch someone doing some raising of the dead while we're here."

"Of course. It's notoriously a broad daylight activity," I said, then added, "We're not going to stay here all day, are we?"

"Not sure. But it's sunny, at least," Callum said.

"Eh." I jumped out the driver's side door after him. "I prefer sun through a window, to be honest."

Sunny was pushing things, anyway. The sun was about, but high cloud turned it a little weak and murky, and there was a chilly breeze working fretfully around the trees, shaking their branches and making them whine.

We'd swung by Lewis' grand old wreck of a house on

the way here, but he hadn't even let us in the gate. He'd just shouted over the intercom that how he got his magic was no one's business but his own, and if any filthy necromancers had so much as touched his son's corpse he'd know, and he was going to peel them like a banana. I said he meant an apple, as people skins weren't as loosely attached as banana skins, and he should know that given his creepy hobby, and Callum said no, we both meant grape, and Lewis had let loose with some swearwords even I hadn't heard before, then hung up. No amount of ringing on the intercom got him back.

So that was kind of a bust.

"You think that necromancer lot really are sticking to chickens?" I asked Callum as we ambled through the cemetery gates. There was a small bent man in a brown jacket reading a book aloud next to a weathered headstone and a groundskeeper tidying up Cheryl's grave, but otherwise the place was empty.

"I don't know," Callum said. "Both Ifan and Katja going missing seems suspicious, but they seemed pretty sure it was impossible."

"There was a lot of power in that place," I said. "It felt kind of old, though. Like it was more part of the house than of anyone in it."

"More power than Ms Jones?" Callum asked, stopping next to the grave of Lillian and her missing arm. He typed something into the old phone, frowning.

"Maybe? It's hard to tell when it's stagnant like that." I thought about it. "I wonder if Ms Jones can fix zombie bites?"

He shot me a glance. "We're still thinking she might be behind it, though."

"Yeah, but maybe she'd take pity on you. You could look a bit bedraggled and pathetic. More so than usual, I mean."

Callum grunted. "She's more likely to brain me as a precaution, either way." He led the way to June's grave and fiddled with the phone some more.

"What're you doing?" I asked. "And what about lunch?"

He glanced at me. "I'm serious about the worms thing."

"I'm very serious about the lunch thing. Cats need to eat regularly, you know. We get grumpy otherwise."

"Oh, is *that* the problem?"

I lifted my lip to expose one tooth. "What're you doing, anyway?"

"Hang on. Ifan ... Lewis ..." He had to mash the phone particularly hard to get the S to work, then muddled around for a moment longer while I sat down and scratched the sucker scars on my shoulder. They'd healed well, but jeez. Some days.

"There," Callum said, sounding pleased with himself, and crouched down, turning the screen toward me.

I squinted at it. "*Williams & Son Funeral Directors. Non-denominational ceremonies, cremations, and embalming.* Gah. Why can't you just leave your dead as they are, like normal creatures?"

Callum shrugged. "I like the idea of a Viking burial, myself."

"Noted. Why are we interested in Williams and his offspring?"

"Because they buried Lily, June, *and* Ifan."

I stared at him. "What's the betting they buried our buddies from last night, too?"

"Checking now," Callum said. He wandered off in that loose, slouchy stride of his, then stopped abruptly, looking down at a different grave. "Wasn't this the one Hoody was sitting on last night?"

We both stared at it. The neat seams of the turf were gone. The *turf* was gone, churned into the erupted soil.

"Oh," I said. "That seems bad."

"Definitely not good." Callum stared for a moment longer, then typed the name into his phone while I sniffed around curiously. It smelled the same as the others. No scent of magic, no lingering whiff of power. Just a few soggy crisps and a faint hint of panic.

"Gobs," Callum said, and there was an edge of excitement in his voice. "It is. It's the same place."

"Well then," I said. "I'd call that a pattern, with or without the others. Let's go and ask them if they've been having some mishaps with the embalming fluid."

WE HAD a small moment of alarm when the old car, apparently feeling it was being overworked, refused to start, but Callum eventually coaxed it into life and we puttered our way to Williams & Son, possible originators of the zombie apocalypse.

It was about fifteen minutes' drive from the cemetery, nestled in among a collection of new buildings mostly given over to small business offices and 24-hour gyms, bisected by carefully landscaped green areas and tightly trimmed trees. The mortuary sign was discreet, pale grey writing on a glossy black background, and we parked up in the corner furthest from the front doors. The rest of the parking area was empty, and there was a fountain by the doors with three sparrows washing themselves in it. My ears twitched toward them as we got out of the car and I dropped my belly low to the ground, tail flicking.

"Hey," Callum said, and I looked up at him, whiskers trembling. "Inappropriate."

I straightened up with an effort. "Really? It *is* a place of the dead."

"Yeah. Of the dead, not of the bloodbath on the front step."

"Whatever." I kept my gaze away from the sparrows as we skirted the building, following the drive around the back to where two hearses were parked, noses pointed out at us. There were double doors behind them, and another single side door off to the right. Callum ambled up to it and knocked. There was silence for a moment, and I spied a camera nestled above the door, black eye staring at us.

He knocked again, and this time steps rang hollow on concrete inside, a lock clicked over, and a man stared out at us. He looked a bit younger than Callum, probably in his twenties, with messy dark hair and a white coat pulled over a slightly fussy jumper.

"Yes?"

"Hi," Callum said, smiling in an *I'm-totally-harmless* way. "I'm looking for the person in charge of preparing bodies? Specifically Ifan Lewis and June Atkins?"

"Why?" the man asked.

"I'm an assistant groundskeeper," Callum said, which I thought was a pretty good explanation for the state of his jeans. And, well, the rest of him, to be honest. "We've noticed a few anomalies."

"We follow very strict protocols," the man said, drawing back, and even hidden behind the door I caught a whiff of fear from him. "There can't be anything *wrong.*"

"I didn't say wrong," Callum said. "Why would there be something wrong?"

I started to ease around the door, hoping to do a little solo investigation, but ducked back again as heavier footfalls rang on the concrete floor inside.

"Jan?" the newcomer said. "What's going on?"

"Nothing, Dad," Jan said. "Just, um, someone from Harrow Hill."

"The cemetery?" his father asked, coming to the door to examine Callum. He had the same slim build as his son, but was a little heavier, the line of his shoulders softer. He wore a suit instead of the white coat. "Is something the matter?"

"I've got it," Jan said. "I'll deal with it. You head home and have lunch with Mum."

Lunch. My stomach complained at me, and I shuffled my feet. I was sure low blood sugar was bad for PIs.

"Are you sure?" Williams Senior looked at Callum's long threadbare jacket with its stained hems, a frown twisting his mouth. "What's this all about?"

"We share similar research interests," Callum said with a smile.

"Research?" Williams asked, looking puzzled, and Jan

tugged at the neck of his jumper like it was a size too small

"Dad, I've got this," Jan said. "Really. You always tell me I need to be more proactive. Well, I am."

"How?" his father asked.

"Well, um, it's … it's …"

"It's about advancements in embalming techniques," Callum said. "More eco-friendly options for the discerning client."

"Oh," the older man said. "I see." He examined Callum again, and I kept to one side of the door. He didn't seem like the sort of person who'd be too keen on a cat in the workplace. "Yes. That does sound interesting. Well, don't get behind, Jan. We've got Mrs Appleton being picked up at three."

"She's ready," Jan said, still pulling at his jumper. "And I'm about to start on Mr Borski."

"Alright. Well, make sure you get some lunch." Williams retreated into the building, not without a couple of backward glances at Callum, who smiled encouragingly and tried to look like an environmentally aware gravedigger.

Jan waited until an internal door clicked shut, then said, "What's this about?"

"I told you," Callum said. "We've had some anomalies with a few of your corpses."

Jan glanced nervously behind him, and I took the chance to slip inside. The room beyond was cavernous, the roof high and strung with yellow lights. Glossy coffins were stacked neatly in racks to one side of the room, some with *Sold* stickers on them. The other side had various trolleys and contraptions parked up and ready to use, as well as a few gravestones wrapped in protective sheeting.

"I really don't know what you're talking about, but fine. Come into the preparation room."

He led us across the warehouse-like space as Callum's phone started to whistle. Callum glanced at the display and thumbed it off, and we followed Jan through another door into a smaller room. The walls were painted stark white, tiled below and above the stainless cabinets that ran along two walls. The floors were tiled too, and the overhead lights were painfully bright. I padded in behind Callum and jumped onto one of the worktops that capped the cabinets. It was stacked with packets of latex gloves and boxes of cotton wool, and tubs labelled *foundation* and *filler*. The opposite wall was glossy metal and lined with rows of oblong doors. Some of them had neatly printed labels on them, and the hum of refrigeration came from behind them. There was a coffin on a rolling table in front of the doors, a pink-cheeked woman lying in it with her eyes closed and her hands folded on her chest. The smell of halted rot washed across the room in waves.

Callum stayed well back from the coffin. "You haven't done anything to her, have you?"

"No! I mean, I prepared her, but what else would I do?" Jan pulled a pen from his coat pocket, fiddling with it, then spotted me. "Hey! Where'd the cat come from? It can't be in here!"

"Not an it," I snapped, and Jan's mouth dropped open.

"You," he started, then shook his head. "Is this some

kind of joke? Have you got a speaker in that thing's collar?"

"*Definitely* not a thing," I said.

"Shut up, Gobs," Callum said, then said to Jan, "You have no idea why there might be a problem at the cemetery?"

"No," he said, looking at his pen. "We're very careful here."

"Any chance you were *in* the Harrow Hill cemetery last night?"

"No," he said again, his voice a little high, and glanced at me. "That cat really shouldn't be in here. It's unhygienic."

"Dude, I'm *way* more hygienic than you are," I said, nodding at a plate smeared with crumbs and tomato ketchup that was sitting on the counter, a half-full mug next to it. "Plus, everyone's dead. I don't see the issue."

"Please stop doing that," Jan said to Callum. "It's weird."

"*You're* weird," I muttered, and Callum shushed me.

"The graves have been disturbed," he said, watching the mortician carefully.

Jan rubbed his mouth. "That's terrible. I've said for ages that security should be better."

"We found a backpack," Callum said. "It had some vials in it. And a syringe."

"Really? Well, I imagine it'd be quite an attractive place for drug users. Quiet, you know." Jan shoved his pen back in his pocket. "Terrible that they'd desecrate the graves, though. The dead should rest in peace." He lifted his chin as he said it, like he was giving an interview and wanted the camera to get his good side.

"Yeah, they *should*," I said. "Except when someone's zombifying them."

Jan twitched, glancing at me. "How are you *doing* that?"

I huffed and jumped to the floor, scouting the edges of the room for scents. Everywhere was bleach and disinfectant and the gut-heavy chemical stench of embalming fluid. Here and there – at the drain in the middle of the floor and around the edges of the refrigerated doors – I could smell the mellower trail of natural rot, but it was almost banished entirely. This wasn't a place of death. It was the denial of it.

"Look," Callum said, "I know this sounds weird. But we're not accusing you of anything. We just want to know if the bodies were linked in any way, or if something was done differently to them. Maybe a new chemical, a new technique – anything."

"We?" Jan asked. "You and your animal?"

"Oh boy," Callum said.

"*His animal?*" I demanded, glaring at the mortician as I abandoned my investigating and prowled toward him. "Ex*cuse* me?"

"Stop that," Jan said, stepping back and flapping his hands at me. "Get away!"

I bared my teeth. "You better be allergic, talking like that."

"No, cats just freak me out," he said, then shook his head. "And now I'm *talking* to one."

"You spend all day with dead people and *I* freak you out?" I demanded.

Jan turned back to Callum, who was leaning against the door with his hands in the pockets of his coat. "Look, I don't know how you're doing this talking cat thing, and I don't care. We're a very professional outfit here, and I don't appreciate these sorts of pranks and accusations. You need to leave, and if you bother me again I'll call the police."

"That'd be interesting," Callum said, not moving. "I wonder if they'd find some vials that match the ones in here?" He took the little tub from his pocket and shook it gently.

"You should get some help," Jan said, his voice tight. "Professional help." He looked around, and spotted me nosing across his desk. There was nothing on it but a monitor and a packet of Hobnobs. "Hey! Get off!"

Callum raised his eyebrows at me, and I shrugged. I'd circuited the whole office, but even the laptop bag on the floor by the desk chair just smelled sterile and impersonal. Every sliver of personality and life was drowning under the stink of chemicals, and I didn't even bother trying to steal a biscuit. They'd taste as dead as the rest of the place smelled.

"Alright," Callum said, and took a card from his pocket. He handed it to Jan, who just stared at it as if Callum had handed him a small oblong frog. "Call if you change your mind about nothing being out of the ordinary. We can help."

Jan swallowed, a little click sounding in his throat, then said, "You and the cat?" He was trying to sound mocking, but it just came out confused.

"Yeah. Me and the cat." Callum tipped his head and

opened the door, and I jumped off the desk, running past him into the empty room beyond.

JAN HAD OPENED the front door of the mortuary and was peering out at us when we got back into the car. Callum raised a hand to him, but he didn't wave back, just watched as we puttered out onto the quiet roads of the industrial estate in a blue-grey cloud of exhaust fumes.

"Well?" Callum asked.

"I couldn't smell anything," I said. "I *still* can't smell anything. I may never smell anything ever again. It's just all chemicals and grossness."

"So no magic?"

"I seriously don't know. There could've been a genie in the Hobnob packet and I wouldn't have known unless it popped out to say hi."

Callum sighed, and his phone vibrated in his pocket. He didn't take it out.

"Aren't you going to see who it is?" I asked. "It could be an actual, real, paying client. Even a non-Folk one. A cheating spouse, if we're lucky."

"It's not," he said.

"Well, I know our odds have been poor lately, but there's always the off-chance our luck might change."

He pulled the phone out of his pocket and put it on the seat in front of me without looking at it. I blinked at the display. Six missed calls, all from the same contact.

"Ms Jones?" I said, my stomach twisting. Although I

still hadn't had lunch, so that could've had something to do with it.

"Maybe she's just checking in to see if you've got any info on the Watch for her," Callum said.

"It's possible, right? I mean, she didn't *see* us last night."

"The first missed call was this morning," Callum said. "Before we were even up."

I stared at the phone. "So what do we do?"

"Nothing. Go stake out the cemetery again. See if Jan shows up, or Ms Jones, or anyone else."

"And we just ignore her calls?"

"For now." He glanced at me. "I don't know what else we can do, Gobs. She was *there*. Maybe she did know it was us. And if the mortician didn't do it, and the necromancers didn't, and Ifan's dad didn't ..."

"But why call us? Surely she'd just show up and turn us into earwigs or something."

"We haven't been home all day," Callum said. "Maybe she *has* turned up."

I thought of the last time a displeased Ms Jones had turned up in our office, and hoped my bed had survived this encounter. Although, with any luck, she might've scared the snake away. There had to be an upside, right?

"Even if it is her, we can't tackle her," I said. "There is no way that ends well."

"I know," Callum said. "We need some help."

"The Watch? I mean, for a start, they'll *definitely* want to brain you. But I'm not sure even they'll be too keen on tackling a sorcerer."

"Well, that's reassuring to know," Callum said. "But I

wasn't thinking of them." He fished around in his pocket again, then popped a card in front of me.

I looked at it. "I know our cards are classy, dude, but I fail to see the significance."

"Oh. No, not that one." He fumbled in his pockets again, then put another card in front of me.

"Dead Good Cafe? Gertrude?"

"She said she'd help. She was upset about the souls."

I considered it. Ancient, powerful sorcerer against … well, a reaper. There wasn't much describing them. They just *were*. "You know, you've had worse ideas," I said.

"Thanks."

"Plus, she might have more biscuits."

He gave me an amused look, and as we rattled on down the crowded roads I took a deep, slow breath. The chemicals of the mortuary were receding, and I could smell exhaust fumes and the damp of the old seats, and Callum's own deep scents, familiar and comforting and not quite as they should be.

"Jan didn't make you fancy a nibble?" I asked him. "You know, a bit of fresh meat for lunch?"

He made a face. "No. And you're making it sound really weird, Gobs."

"It *is* weird." I settled into the seat and listened to the rattle of something loose in the door, and Callum scritched my head as the world flowed past, human and beautiful and oblivious.

13

TO MARKET, TO MARKET, TO CATCH THE UNDEAD

WE LEFT THE CAR A FEW STREETS FROM OUR APARTMENT, AS parking in Leeds for an afternoon cost about as much as our food budget for the entire month. But we didn't get too near the creaking building itself. The idea of walking into the apartment to find Ms Jones standing amid the devastation of all we owned was too much to consider on an empty stomach. Besides, it wasn't far to walk into the city centre, where the Dead Good Cafe was.

Not that it was a pleasant walk. The route was through part of the city that hadn't had its turn at regeneration yet, and it was the sort of blasted landscape you slipped across fast, with your ears back and your whiskers twitching. Human progress had trapped the earth beneath sheets of broken asphalt, and the weeds that pushed their way through the cracks had a twisted, poisoned look. It wasn't the sort of land that was going to recover in any of my lifetimes.

I suppose you could argue humans hadn't known any better in the past, and were trying harder now, but if they'd actually looked up at some point in their sprint into industrialisation, they might have noticed. You know, what with the deadly fogs in the cities and drowned fish in the canals and half of them dying from inhaling their own factory filth. But no one ever accused humans of having a lot of perspective.

Callum ambled through it all with his head down and his hands in his coat pockets, doing that unnoticeable thing that meant we probably wouldn't be mugged before we got to busier streets. Probably. Nothing's guaranteed, and humans don't have a monopoly on muggings. Not that it'd net them much, though, which was a deterrent in itself.

"D'you think this is the best approach?" I asked him.

He glanced at me, then rummaged for his cigarettes. "What? Gertrude?"

"Yeah. I mean, some backup sounds great," I said, skirting an abandoned fridge with its door hanging open on one hinge. "But maybe our main goal should be discovering if we need to amputate your ribcage or something."

Callum half-smiled, cupping his hands around the cigarette to light it. The sun ran through his hair and picked out threads of copper among the brown. "Remember we talked about that civic duty thing?"

"Remember I told you it doesn't apply to cats?"

"Yeah. Mind the glass," he added, crunching onto a spray of multi-coloured shards where someone had apparently been smashing bottles against a stone wall for the pointless joy of it. I picked my way across the street, trying not to step on any splinters, but the shattered glass was everywhere, and I stepped on one that stuck between my toes.

"Ow," I complained, stopping to examine it.

Callum looked at me and said, "Lift?"

"If you want me walking at the end of this."

He ambled back, picking me up in one hand without answering.

"Thanks."

"Sure," he said, and set me down when the pavement was clear again. "Look, you may not feel we have any civic duty, but this could affect *everyone*. We still don't know how many are out there. We don't know if the bite's infectious. Or … or treatable. The best way to find all of that out is to figure out where it started."

"Eh," I said. "I think you should have threatened to embalm Mr Mortician, and see how that went."

"We'll try that tonight if he shows up and Ms Jones doesn't."

"And if she does show up?"

"I don't know," he said. "If Gertrude'll help us, maybe we can confront her. If Gertrude won't, then I don't know."

"We leave it," I said. "We *have* to. We can't go against her. She's too strong."

"Mmm," he said, and stubbed his cigarette out on the nearest wall. He looked at the ground, littered with ground-in gum and crushed cans and plastic wrappers, then tucked the butt back into the packet.

We walked on in silence for a while, and as the half-abandoned industrialised area began to fade at the edges, filling with tatty buildings of the sort that housed cold, lonely apartments upstairs and grimy stores beneath, I said, "You still haven't said how you knew a magician. Well enough to go to his house for tea or whatever."

Callum gave a one-shouldered shrug. "We didn't go there for tea," he said, and left it at that.

The past is the past. As long as it stays there.

THE CITY GREW up around us, sprouting vaping stores and barber shops with kids hanging around outside them puffing on those weird electronic pipes everyone's into. Broken walls and graffiti gave way to red brick and self-conscious murals, and shops selling phonecards and off-brand booze gave way to record stores and coffee shops.

We skirted the centre proper, with its glass cliff of a shopping centre and humans with clipboards asking everyone to sign up and save the world while the city's lost slept a few paces away, curled up next to overflowing bins and presided over by the window displays of clothes no one could really afford, but bought anyway. Everything stank of perfume rolling out of shop doors and leaking car exhausts and corn in filthy water at the street stalls and fear and hunger and hope and sorrow, and feet thundered on the pavement all around us, drowning thought with momentum.

Cities never bothered me, but the sheer volume of people always seemed to make Callum uneasy. He dropped his head even further between his shoulders and watched his feet as the crowds around us swelled, shrinking in on himself while I trotted along next to him, trying not to be stepped on by any of the masses charging along with their eyes on their smartphones.

A pair of broken trainers attached to stained army trousers stopped in front of me, and I looked up at a huge man with an exceptionally luxuriant black beard.

"Happy travels," he said, touching a hand to his forehead

"May your beard be glossy and toes stay warm," I replied, and he gave me a broad, slightly crooked smile. He wasn't Folk. Folk know Folk. They have strange edges, as if they're more clearly part of the world than non-Folk. But he saw me and heard me, and he had the whiff of cold nights and lost days to him. Those on the edge of things always see more clearly than those in the centre.

"Tip for you, little cat," he said. "Don't go down the market."

Callum had stopped, and we both looked at the big man with his pack tucked protectively close to him. A sleeping bag leaking a wisp of stuffing poked out of the top. "Why not?" he asked.

"Bad, bad stuff happening down there, man," the bearded man said. "Like, worse than police. Worse than drunk kids. It's *bad*."

"Bad how?" Callum asked, and I scrambled up to his shoulder so no one stepped on my tail.

The man scratched his beard, examining us carefully. He seemed to make a decision, and lowered his voice slightly, despite the fact that no one was paying any attention to us. "It's … I don't know. It's weird, man. There's a closed stall down there where we sleep sometimes. Me and some others. It's safe. No one usually bothers us." He looked around, and lowered his voice. "Frankie went out last night to use the toilet, and when she came back she was *scared.* Someone was chasing her. Only it wasn't *someone*. Not really." His smile had gone.

"What was it?" Callum asked, his voice dropping as well. The crowd flowed around us, hurrying to or from or away or whatever, and we were locked together in the invisibility of animals and the lost.

The man shook his head. "I don't know." He held up a hand wrapped in a bloodied cloth. "I trapped it, but the rest of us barely got out."

"Oh," I said. "Oh, *hairballs.*" Then I tried out a couple of the choicer human swearwords I'd picked up along the way.

"Agreed," Callum said, then added to the big man, "Will you show us?"

He studied Callum, his eyes sharp and glittering in the uncertain sunlight. "Can you kill it?"

"Yes," I said, before Callum could answer. "He's killed one before."

"If it's the same thing," Callum said.

"Really?" I asked. "You think there are two varieties of bite-y monsters out there?"

"Well, I've got one on my shoulder," Callum said, and I bared my teeth.

The big man snorted, and held his bandaged hand out. "Theodore Large. Usually known as Big Ted."

"Gobbelino," Callum said, pointing at me as he shook hands. "And Callum."

"Alright, then, Callum and Gobbelino," Big Ted said. "I'll show you where our monster is."

Big Ted led the way through one of the low, unassuming arches that open into Kirkgate Market, emerging into a confusion of plants spilling from overcrowded stalls, orchids and lilies and ferns and ... stuff. I'm not a botanist. The market swept away from us, curving downhill, the arched ceiling criss-crossed with metal frames that held up a glass roof. Sunlight washed in on the florists and food stalls and places selling phone cases and spices and clothes on rickety racks and reclaimed furniture on the tacky side of cool. A wooden mezzanine floor circled the walls, pocked with offices, and the whole place smelled of cooking and incense and far-off places and magic.

I spotted a faery trying on a long black coat with roses embroidered on the back while a human woman exclaimed over how lovely it looked. Outside a stall packed with plastic bins of spices, a human man with crinkled skin bought big bags of cardamom pods and cinnamon sticks from a tusked gnome, while a parrot watched over the transaction with a clinical eye. In a greasy-windowed cafe, a dryad and a faun were giggling together behind the counter while a small group of young humans ate cake and drank tea, oblivious to the faun's hooves and the dryad's seamed, softly wooden skin. It was a mishmash in here, Folk and human all muddled up in a pleasant confusion.

There are places like this everywhere. I mean, sure, a lot of Folk like to stick to their pocket places, and the Watch tend to frown on too much mixing, but they can't stop it where it's unnoticed. So Folk are everywhere.

They're outnumbered by humans something ridiculous because there are just *so many* humans, but there are plenty of Folk around still – and that's not even counting cats and the other creatures that straddle both worlds.

And some places always attract *more* Folk, and if you want magic, you go to the market. Not the once-a-week ones, although they'll always have a few, but the ones that have been there since the beginning, when the city walls grew up around them. That's where you find Folk, amid the mess of gloriously weird and beautiful things. That's where you find magic.

We drew to the side of the main thoroughfare, under the metal dragons fixed at regular intervals below the mezzanine overhang. Cheap DIY tapestry patterns and luminously coloured feather boas dangled around us, and the stall they belonged to was crowded with an eclectic mix of human tat and jars behind the counter that practically dripped with magic. Big Ted was rubbing his bandaged hand.

"That okay?" I asked him.

"It's sore," he said. "I hope it's not going to get infected. Human mouths are really dirty, though."

"You said it was a monster," Callum said.

"It was both."

"Are you hungry?" I asked.

Big Ted frowned at me. "I had a sandwich earlier."

"So, you're not craving something a little different? Lambs fry, maybe? Liver? Hearts?"

The big man looked puzzled, and Callum poked me. "Shut up, Gobs."

"Look, we don't know how this works. I'm just asking the important questions."

"Even for a cat, you're a bit weird," Big Ted said, and headed deeper into the marketplace, towering head and shoulders above the shoppers. I hoped he wasn't about to turn into a zombie. The small ones had been hard enough to deal with.

WE WOUND our way through the narrow bottleneck at the top of the market where the open roof gave way to a low ceiling, and headed down the barely perceptible slope through a thicket of tiny shops, hairdressers and jewellers and clothes stores and greengrocers. Stalls lined the walls as well as forming free-standing clusters wound about with pathways and alleys, and humans and Folk scurried from one to the other with laden shopping bags and take-away cups clasped in their hands.

Big Ted veered left, skirting the wall and heading for an area of boarded up stalls, all wound about with yellow caution tape and warnings to wear hard hats and boots if entering. There was an expanse of bare concrete floor between the last of the central, occupied stalls and the wall, as if no one wanted to get too close to it, and the lighting was dimmer here than elsewhere. There were no doors to the outside world, and the overhead lights were almost as patchy as in our apartment block. The work site was silent despite the signs, no shouting or whining of tools or even the flat glare of work lights beyond the boards. Shoppers skirted the area, sticking to the populated stalls, and everything felt cold and dull and forgotten.

"Here we are." Big Ted stopped where the caution tape ran out. "It's that one." Most of the stalls against the wall were still boarded up with sheets of plywood, but a few had white-painted shutters pulled down over their fronts, and he was pointing at the one closest to the construction site. I stared at the door and shivered, wondering if something had *happened* here. It had the feel of it, one of those places carrying echoes of old, unpleasant things, reverberating loud enough for even humans to catch their whisper and want to stay clear.

Callum took a step forward, then stopped. "Do you think it's still in here?"

Big Ted nodded. "I put the padlock back on. It's not locked, but you can't roll the shutter up without taking it out from this side."

I'd jumped to the floor once the crowds thinned, and now I snuffled along the edge of the door. There were so many market scents, so much food and so many people, plus the distinctive (and not unpleasant) reek of everyday magic and Folk, and all I could really smell was more of the same. Maybe a richer vein of human scents, warm bodies and cold nights and some mildly illicit substances, but not much else.

"I can't tell," I said.

"Some help you are," Callum said. He took a breath, then stepped up to the shutter and put a hand against it, listening.

"Dude, if I can't hear anything, there's no way you're going to," I said.

He shrugged, then slipped the padlock out of the lock. It clattered, metal against metal, and no one moved for a moment. I strained my ears, but I still couldn't hear anything, and eventually Callum rolled the door up far enough that we could both peer in.

The funky smell of old blankets and humans in close quarters rolled out, and I wrinkled my nose at a whiff of stale curry and greasy chip trays. There was no light inside, and the patchy illumination sneaking in around us didn't reach far. Everything was rendered in shades of grey and near-black, and even with my low-light super-sight there wasn't an awful lot to see. A pile of books against one wall, almost as battered as Callum's collection. Some bottles of water that looked like they'd been refilled a lot of times. A couple of torn travel posters on the wall, stained where they'd been recovered from bins. Some candles stuck to a crate, wax forming stalactites down the sides, and a collection of rumpled blankets and sleeping bags that could have hidden half a dozen people, or no one at all.

"Hello?" Callum called. "Anyone in here?"

No one answered, and we exchanged an uneasy glance.

"It must be in here," Big Ted said, making us both jump. He'd crept up and squatted down next to us, looking like a pro wrestler about to tackle an opponent.

"Anything yet?" Callum asked me.

I breathed in the cold stale air, trying to sort one scent from another. "It's such a jumble," I said. "There's too much going on."

"Remind me again why I have a feline partner rather than a canine one?"

"Well, I don't dig up zombie arms, do I?"

"Eh." Callum rolled the shutter up a little further and ducked beneath it, waving to Big Ted to stay where he was. I slipped after Callum before he eased the door back down again, and we both stood there staring around in the dark. I couldn't hear anything but our own slightly uneven breathing and the market noises filtering to us from about a million miles away. Callum fished in his jacket and a moment later there was the click of his lighter. Light flared into the breathless space, and I narrowed my eyes against it. "Hello?" Callum said again.

The blankets swelled motionless at the back of the stall, and he took a step to the side, the lighter out in front of him like a weapon. "I'll light one of those cand— *Jesus frigging Christ!*" He dropped the lighter and the shadows jumped up again.

"*Old Ones take you!*" I yelped, shooting backward until my tail fetched up against the shutter. Every scrap of my fur felt like it was trying to go in a different direction, and my ears were so far back I thought I'd strained a muscle. "*What in the realms is that?*"

"Gobs! Can you see? I dropped the lighter!"

"I can tell you dropped the lighter, you tomato! *Get it!*"

"I can't *see* it!"

"Should I come in?" Big Ted shouted, not sounding too keen. "What's going on?"

"It's okay!" Callum yelled. "Stay there!"

My eyes had readjusted already, and I stared around wildly, my heart too loud in my chest, trying to understand what I'd seen. Something was moving among the blankets now, thrashing like some trapped beast, but that wasn't what had my fur so pouffed up it was almost physically painful.

No, that was due to the arm flopping about not far from Callum's feet, as well as a foot, a few internal organs, some hair, and half a hand, all jumbled up into some monstrous new organism, wriggling about the place as if trying to figure out how they all fitted together. I wrinkled my nose against a new stench.

"Man, you do *not* want to see this."

"Is anything going to bite me?" Callum asked.

I took a couple of shaky steps forward, sinking low to the ground. My shoulders were shaking. "I can't see any teeth." The foot was still in a knock-off Adidas sneaker, and the toes were wriggling through a hole in the cloth uppers. The hand was opening and closing hopefully, but didn't seem to be about to launch an attack on anything.

"Where's the lighter?" Callum crouched down, patting the ground in front of him tentatively.

"Dude, don't—"

Callum *urk*-ed as his fingers sank into something that might have been a spleen. Or a kidney. I never thought I'd have to tell the difference. He straightened up hurriedly, wiping his hands on his jeans. "I don't need it."

"You definitely don't want it," I agreed, creeping forward another few paces. "This is so gross." I was by his feet now, staring at the disassembled human in front of us. It was both more awful and more *abstract* than the zombies from the cemetery. It was hard to believe that any of this had once been a person, worried about where the next meal was coming from and how to pass unnoticed in the world and if it'd rain tomorrow. And believing that, if nothing else, at least they had a safe place to sleep. My whiskers twitched.

There was still a lot of thrashing going on in the tangle of bedding on the floor, and I supposed there had to be at least three other limbs in there somewhere. My nose was full of the claggy scent of blood and old fear, and I skirted the carnage carefully, trying to ignore the quivering organs. "Callum, take a step to the left, then— No, my left," I added, as something squidged under his boot and he gagged.

"Jesus, Gobs." He recovered, went the other way, and bumped into the wall. "Ow."

"Two steps forward." He edged forward, using the wall as guidance. "Okay, candles are just in front of you. There's some matches in the middle." There was a pause as he fumbled on the crate. The blankets were still thrashing, and I started to hear a sound that made my already raised fur tremble. Light flared. Callum touched the match to the two candles that still had enough wick left to light, then straightened up, shaking the match out.

"Okay, better— *Gobs, move!*"

I launched myself off the floor as the blankets exploded upward, and the half-heard noise became a moan that reverberated in my bones.

14

A SMALL PROBLEM WITH BODY PARTS

THE WIND OF SNATCHING HANDS PASSED BEHIND ME AS I crashed into the wall, ricocheted off, touched down among the bloodstained bedding just long enough to launch myself forward again, and hit the rough floor already running. I almost went nose first into the shutter, and recovered just in time to spin myself around, put my tail against it, and yowl, "Callum! We got a live one!"

"Kind of guessed that!" he yelled back, snatching the crate up and using it like a lion-tamer's chair to fend off the very much intact zombie that was trying to extricate itself from the blankets. It had them so firmly tangled around its legs that it was mostly towing itself after Callum with its arms. The candles had tumbled off the crate and winked out on the floor, which was better than a fire but not great for Callum and his human vision.

"What's going on?" Big Ted yelled from outside.

"Shut up!" I shouted back. "Callum, from the left!" I winced as he turned in the wrong direction. "*My* left!"

He spun back just in time to crack the crate across the zombie's arms as it reached for him. "Jesus, Gobs—"

"Your right! Again! Quick!"

He lashed out with the crate, and this time caught the zombie's head, sending it sprawling.

"It's down! Run! *Run!*"

"Guys?" Big Ted called. "Should I come in?"

Callum staggered toward me, still clutching the crate, and stepped in some unidentified body part. His foot shot out from under him and he yelped, landing hard on his bum with his good leg half-folded underneath him.

"*Swing!*" I bellowed, and he swung the crate wildly. It slammed into the zombie's belly as it finally hauled itself clear of the bedding and pounced, moan-roaring all the way. Callum grunted with the impact, dropping to his back and shoving hard against the zombie's weight, using its own momentum to carry it over him. It tumbled across the stall with an indignant moan, fetching up against the shutters and setting them shaking violently. Callum scrambled to his feet, waving the crate threateningly.

"Where is it?"

"*Guys?*" Big Ted asked, sounding slightly panicked.

"*Wait,*" I snarled. "Callum, ahead and left!"

"My left or yours?"

"Yours! No, mine!"

"Goddammit—" Callum ducked, raising the crate to catch the zombie in the belly again and pivoting neatly on his heels as he pushed the creature away, sending it plunging back into the bedding, where it moaned and thrashed and sent loose body parts scattering across the stall floor as it tried to right itself.

"Nice!" I called. "Now *move!* Big Ted, open up! *Now!*"

Callum bolted the few strides across the stall as Big Ted ripped the shutters up. Callum landed on his knees so hard I hissed in sympathy, then threw himself to his belly and rolled out into the market. I shot through the gap as the zombie moaned and scampered toward us, body parts still spilling from the blankets.

Big Ted slammed the shutter back down just before zombie crashed into it, the impact so hard that the metal bowed outward, and all three of us yelped. The creature moaned urgently and started to scrabble at the door, the sound of its nails on the painted metal making my whiskers twitch. Callum grabbed the padlock and shoved it through the latch, clicking it closed firmly, then rocked back on his heels and took a deep, shaky breath.

"Dude," I said.

"Yeah," he agreed, and we watched the zombie poking raw, bloodless fingers between the door and the concrete, still moaning. There seemed to be a pleading note to it now.

"Aw. Poor thing," Big Ted said, and I blinked at him, then looked back at Callum.

"You bitten?"

"More than before, you mean?"

I shrugged, and he stood up, inspecting the bloody marks on his jeans where he'd wiped his hands. "That's just so unpleasant."

The zombie shook the shutter and whimpered.

"So what do we do with it now?" I asked.

"I lost my lighter," Callum said, staring glumly at his cigarettes.

"Could've been worse," I pointed out, and he shrugged, putting the packet back in his pocket.

"Smoking's bad for you anyway," Big Ted said, adjusting the bloodied bandage on his hand.

"So are zombies," Callum said, turning around to face the market. He froze.

I looked up at him, then followed his gaze to two young women in hijabs standing between us and the nearest stall, which had its locked back to us. The women were clutching phones and each other's arms, but they looked less frightened than intrigued.

"What's that?" one of them asked.

"Um. What?" Callum asked, trying on his dimples. They tended to be pretty effective, although I had a feeling these two might be a bit young to be quite so easily charmed. When it came to women, the dimples seemed to work best on those of a certain age. Men were less predictable.

The woman took a step forward, pointing with her phone hand, her nail long and carefully polished. "*That.* The … thing."

"Hand," her friend supplied. "Well, most of one, anyway."

We all stared at the offending (and mildly twitching) digits while the zombie took its moaning up a pitch, and went back to the throwing-itself-at-the-shutter technique.

"Also that," the first woman said, and gave Callum a suspicious look which said the dimples hadn't worked. "Is there someone in there?"

"Not exactly," Callum said, at the same time as Big Ted said, "Yes."

They exchanged glances while the zombie crashed into the shutter and moaned unhappily. The women looked at each other, and for a moment no one spoke. I glanced around, wondering how bad things looked.

Pretty bad. As well as the hand, a couple of loosely connected toes, a gnawed bone (possibly a femur, but again, I'd never thought I'd have to identify one), and a patch of featureless skin had followed us out into the marketplace. There was also …

"Callum," I hissed, and he shot me a warning glance. I pointed my nose toward the corner of the shutter, which was being partially held up by a head, the face turned away from us and the hair matted with blood and muck. Callum followed my gaze and winced. He turned back to the women.

"It's all fake," he said. "I mean, obviously. It wouldn't be real, right?"

"Are you an actor?" the first woman asked.

"He doesn't look like an actor," the second one said, regarding Callum critically. "Although the big one might be."

Big Ted swept a bow. "I've dabbled," he said.

"It's for Halloween," Callum said.

The women stared at him, and I looked at my feet.

"It's March," the second woman said. Her hijab was pale blue, and it matched her nails rather nicely.

"It's, yes," Callum said. "Yes, it is, I mean. But, you know. Everything starts earlier every year." He gave a shrug, just some worker who can't control his boss' demands.

The women looked at each other again. Then the first woman grinned. "It's one of those events isn't it? Are you rehearsing?"

"Yes?" Callum offered, as the zombie pawed at the shutter. It was concentrating on the closest point to where we were standing, and hadn't investigated further yet. I hoped it didn't get bored and wander off to find the head-induced gap before the women left.

"Oh, *wow*," the woman said, turning to her friend. The light caught the small red stone in her nose piercing. "Hessa, this is the coolest! You remember, they did that zombie one last year? It was like a live action thing, and you had to run around Leeds surviving zombies. My cousin did it."

"Umair?" she asked. "That sounds like him."

"No, Jana."

"Really? She's into that zombie stuff?" Hessa shrugged. "I prefer that murder weekend we did. That was fun. *And* required actual thought, not just running around screaming."

"You would," her friend said affectionately, and linked an arm through hers. They turned away and we watched them wander off, Big Ted looking confused and Callum scratching his hand through his stubble. At the last moment the woman with the red piercing turned back and said, "Can I get a photo?"

"No! Um, no. I mean …" Callum shot a desperate look at me.

"Confidentiality," Big Ted said. "Very important with these events."

"Yes! No." Callum nodded eagerly. "What he said. Confidentiality, yes. You know, wouldn't want anyone finding out about the setup."

"Oh," the woman said. "Okay. Cool." She gave Callum a little finger-wave, and the women vanished among the stalls, heads almost touching as they whispered to each other.

Big Ted looked at Callum but didn't say anything.

"Dude," I said. "Practise the talking, okay?"

"Why, when you do so much of it?" Callum asked. He'd gone a bit pink.

WITH OUR LITTLE corner of the market empty again, we stared at the head holding up the corner of the shutter.

"Do we just kick it back in, or pull it out?" I asked.

"What do we do with it if we pull it out?" Callum asked.

"Maybe we can take it to someone," Big Ted said. "Someone must know how to fix this."

Callum and I looked at each other. "That's not a bad idea," I said.

"But who?" Callum asked, and neither Big Ted nor I answered. Behind the shutter, the zombie moaned and scratched at the floor. Callum pressed his hand against his side, and I thought I could see a darker patch on the faded cloth of his T-shirt when he released it.

"Is it bad?" I asked him.

He shrugged. "It hurts a bit."

Big Ted looked at Callum. "You're bitten too?"

"Yep."

"Have you tried peroxide?" the big man asked. "Peroxide fixes everything."

I stared at the ceiling. "Sure it does. Look, we need to get moving." *Before either of you start getting snacky,* I thought, but didn't add. "Let's take the head with us. Just in case."

"You want to carry a severed head around *just in case?*" Callum asked.

"We don't know. Gertrude might have figured something out. Ms Jones might turn out to be on our side. The stuff in those vials might end up being an antidote. It gives us something to test on."

"I hate it when you have good ideas," Callum said.

"You might have an antidote?" Big Ted asked.

"No idea," I said. "But it's worth a shot. Better than peroxide, anyway."

"Nothing's better than peroxide," Big Ted said, and went to his backpack. He found a bottle of the stuff in a pocket and offered it to Callum. "Want some?"

"Sure." Callum took the bottle and pulled his coat out of the way, peeling his T-shirt up to examine the gauze taped over the bite.

"Gods," I said. "Have you two got shares in the company or something?"

ONCE THE PEROXIDING had been done (and Big Ted had given Callum a lighter, with a further warning that smoking was bad for his health), Callum put all the twitching scraps of person in the crate he'd brought out of the stall with him, his face wreathed in smoke from a cigarette. I was pretty sure smoking was illegal in the marketplace. Then again, zombies probably would be too, if anyone knew about them. That done, Big Ted banged on the shutter next to the lock and insulted the zombie's ancestry to keep it occupied while Callum crept to the other end to grab the head.

The zombie realised what was happening at the last moment and raced to reclaim the head, seizing it by the hair just as Callum tried to jerk it away. There was a brief, heated struggle, then the zombie's grip slipped, and Callum stumbled back with a yelp. The head snapped eagerly at him, and he chucked it away before he could fall over and land on it, so adding to his infectious bite collection. I jumped clear as it rolled toward me, wrinkling my nose at the scent of rot and emptiness, while at the other end of the stall the zombie gave a despairing sound of loss. Its arms were still stuck out under the shutter, and it waved them like a very hopeful and rather unpleasant sea anemone.

Big Ted picked up the head and placed it carefully in the crate, and Callum started kicking the zombie's hands back under the shutter. The hands grabbed hopefully at the air, trying to catch hold of him, oblivious to the impact of his boots.

"What're you *playing* at?" I demanded.

"Trying to stop it climbing out," Callum said. "What does it look like?"

"It's only trying to get out because it can see you!" I regarded the heavy metal shutter. "Well, smell you. Or hear you. Whatever. Just move away!"

"If it gets out, I'm throwing you at it," he warned me, retreating a few steps.

"Shh," I said, and we watched the arms. The hands opened and closed, and the zombie moaned questioningly a couple of times, then fell silent. It patted the ground in a questioning semi-circle, picking up scraps of rubbish and discarding them. I tapped the shutter over by the lock. "Here, *zombie-zombie-zombie*."

The hands jerked, and the creature moaned. I called it again, scratching my claws over the metal of the shutter, and the arms slid back inside like a hermit crab retreating into its shell. There was an almost-silent pause, far too short, where I barely heard its feet on the floor, then it moaned next to my ear and sent my half-settled fur shooting back to action stations. It pawed at the door. I pawed back. It pawed and moaned.

"Oh, very clever," Callum said.

"You know I'm the brains of the outfit," I said, sitting up straight and wrapping my tail around my toes. The zombie gave a questioning little moan next to me.

"I know you like to think that," Callum agreed, and took his coat off to cover the box of body parts.

"What now?" Big Ted asked.

"Now we see if someone can fix this," he said, and wandered over to the construction wall. He pried one of the *Danger Do Not Enter* signs off and propped it up next to the padlock, then picked the crate up under one skinny arm and looked at Big Ted. "Can you keep an eye on things here? Make sure it doesn't get out?"

"Of course," Big Ted said.

"We'll be back as soon as we can," Callum said, and headed for the market entrance.

I took a final look at the shutter then followed him, the zombie still whiffling softly to itself. "Sorry," I said to it, but it didn't reply. Or not in any way I understood.

OUTSIDE, we stood blinking in the afternoon light, buses and cars thundering past and belching exhaust at us, shoppers charging in all directions, intent on spending money and acquiring things as a matter of urgency. Callum kept the crate safely wrapped in his jacket, holding it at his side with one arm as he squinted against the smoke from a new cigarette. I wondered if he thought he could smoke out the zombie-ism or something.

People gave us a wide berth, and I didn't blame them. Even for the unperceptive, Callum looked rough enough to notice. He had blood smeared on his cheek and hands, and there was some stuff stuck in his hair that I was pretty sure used to belong to someone else. Together with the large tear in his T-shirt and the new rips in the knees of his jeans, he looked like he'd just stepped out of a bear-wrestling contest. Well, a mild one. Maybe goat-wrestling or something. Less claws, but plenty of being knocked down.

I clambered up to his shoulder, as it was easier to talk

and it wasn't like it was going to make him look any more suspicious. "You think Big Ted's okay in there?"

"It shouldn't get out," Callum said.

"What if there are more? I mean, we know some are loose. We don't know where they went."

"I know." He puffed smoke, shifting the crate so he could hold it a little more securely. I coughed pointedly, but he ignored me. "We'll just have to be as quick as we can."

He turned away from the market, and we made our way down the grey pavements with their posters pasted to grimy walls, trains rattling on the raised rails above us and pigeons strutting in the gutters. The busier roads gave onto awkward streets that used to be almost as rough as our neighbourhood, and still kind of remembered it. The memory was soaked into the red brick walls and stained tarmac, persisting despite the stark modern sculptures in newly formed courtyards and the triple glazing pressed into reformed window frames. There were a couple of fancy restaurants, the kind even a cat couldn't sneak into, as well as a pub that still stank of ancient pints and daytime drinking, clinging on grimly amid the microbreweries and boutique coffee roasters. The canal ran through it all, slow and green and muscular, filled with squabbling ducks and the shadows of lost crimes.

We cut past a few cafes with signs outside advertising vegan and gluten-free cakes and coconut milk turmeric lattes and some sort of new superfood that I couldn't pronounce. I did try a few times, until Callum told me to stop spitting on his neck. We also walked past a cat cafe with a burly tabby and a large ginger tom who looked like he'd just walked straight in off the street scrapping in the window while a little girl bawled and a panicked-looking young woman tried to get a pillow between them. Behind the humans, I could see three other cats flopped to their sides, wheezing with cat-laughter, and a tangle of kittens gulping cream off someone's scone.

"You lot are so weird," I observed, and Callum nodded.

"I know. Here we are."

On the corner of a side road on the next block was a mint-green door with a neat *Open* sign pinned to it, and a hanging sign above it which said *Dead Good Cafe* in pretty, curling text. There was a set of little wooden chairs and tables to either side of the door, all adorned with inviting-looking cushions and plants in pots. Under the *Open* sign, a smaller one read, *Please remember to close the door! We are a pet cafe, and we don't want anyone to escape! Thank you!* There was a smiley face underneath it, and a brass bell above the door that would tinkle when we opened it.

"I'm having second thoughts," I said.

"Because reaper?"

"Because ghoulets. Full-grown ghouls like their meat dead and well-seasoned. I'm not sure baby ones are so picky."

"Well, stay there. They're not going to climb me to eat you."

"What if they eat you first?"

"I feel that might be bad for business," he said, and opened the door.

15

GETTING OUR HEAD AROUND THINGS

THE DOOR WAS PLATED WITH STAINLESS STEEL SHEETING ON the inside, and it opened into a dimly lit interior, the walls painted in deep greys and the sofas and chairs done out in dark blues and purples. Sheer indigo curtains shot through with glittering threads hung at the windows, keeping the natural light down, and there were lights on the walls imitating gas lamps. Overhead, bare yellow bulbs on black metal chandeliers added to the gentle glow, washing off skull vases holding little bunches of wildflowers, mugs featuring cats in bows, doilies acting as place mats, and a surprising array of cushions printed with the sort of cutesy kittens that suggest the designer had never actually met a cat. Low, cheerful music played, and about half the tables were occupied. There was a distinct prevalence of dark clothing and big boots and silver jewellery going on.

It should have felt oppressive, even intimidating, but with candles flickering in jars on tables and the scent of coffee and cake wafting everywhere it was like stepping into the warmth of your favourite aunt's living room on a dark night – familiar and welcoming and just a little on the weird side of quirky.

"Hello," someone called, and as my eyes adjusted I saw a woman in a bright sundress and an apron (again printed with kittens – Gertrude was obviously a terrible influence) coming out from behind the counter. "Take a seat anywhere. First time here?"

"Um, yes," Callum said. "But—"

"Any open wounds? I know it's an odd question, but it's an issue of infection, you see."

"Um—"

"Any open wounds and we'll have to ask you to come back next time. For your safety and the safety of the animals."

"Well—"

"Otherwise, all we ask is that you don't disturb the animals, or pick them up. They'll come to you if they fancy a snuggle. Management bear no responsibility for any bites, scratches, or other injuries sustained through interaction with the animals. But that's unlikely," she added brightly. "And please don't feed them anything other than the food we provide. Or touch their bellies, even if they look like they want you to. And you don't have any meat of any sort on you, do you?"

"Okay," Callum started again, and I spied a couple of shattered bones sitting under one of the chairs. They looked like they belonged to something large. A sheep, at least.

"Also, if they start growling, please step outside until we can sort the situation out. Rescues, you know. One has to be understanding." She smiled at us in a way that said very firmly that we *would* be understanding, or we would be taking our coffee elsewhere.

There was deliberate, pale movement under a table, and a ghoulet pushed his way out, eyeing us up with flat white eyes. Soft fur covered its body, like the sort of fluff you get on newborn mice, the skin showing through underneath. It snuffled toward us with its flat nose raised, a thread of drool descending from one fang.

I pressed a little closer into Callum's neck and whispered, "The body parts, Callum. I think the body parts may be a problem." Which, you know, they generally are, but it seemed a little more urgent right now.

"Ah," Callum said, clutching the crate a little tighter. The ghoulet advanced until it ran into Callum's boot, then pawed his leg. He retreated a couple of steps, and it followed. More were emerging from under the tables, their eyes wide and their noses quivering.

"Oh, no," the woman said, her voice sharpening as she spotted me. "Oh, you *haven't* brought another animal in here! They're very territorial—"

"Lady," I hissed, as the ghoulet pawed Callum's leg again, with more claws this time, "these are *baby ghouls,* not *animals,* and I personally would rather not be referred to as an animal myself."

"Oh," she said, and sighed. "It's you, isn't it? From the cemetery? Gertrude said you might be coming by. She's in the kitchen, through that door and second on the left. Get a move on, would you, before you get them all wound up?"

We were already in the centre of a ring of baby ghouls,

their eyes fixed on the crate, all flabby pale skin and staring eyes and an unnecessary amount of teeth and claws and drool. A chorus of low growling started up, and the woman rubbed her face with one hand.

"Oh, honestly," she said. "Can't we have one day without someone bringing a sausage roll in or something?"

"I'm not a *sausage roll,*" I said.

She scowled at me. "You don't need to be. You realise you're snack-sized to them?"

"It had crossed my mind."

"So get moving before I have to close the whole bloody place to calm them down!"

"Callum, I think she's got a point," I said, as one of the ghoulets tried to bite his boot.

"No. Really?" he said, and I clung on a little more tightly as he picked his way carefully through the drooling monstrosities and hurried across the room. I didn't relax until he'd closed the door behind us, and I could hear fretful growling on the other side of the metal plating.

And even then, *relax* was a relative term. We were still carrying a boxful of undead body parts, on the way to see a reaper.

THE HALLWAY we found ourselves in was more brightly lit and warmly coloured than the darkly cosy cafe, and offered us a door marked *Toilets* to the right and two marked *Private* to the left. Callum pushed open the second one, opening it onto a kitchen that was all gleaming stainless worktops and slick spotless floors. It wasn't as brightly lit as might have been expected, but it was more than enough to see the reaper, with another kitty apron on over her robes and her sleeves rolled up to her elbows. She was decorating a cake at the island in the middle of the room, swirling pale icing into thick, appetising whorls with a palette knife.

"Ems," she said, without looking up. "Do you think I should make some sugar flowers, or just pop a bit of fresh lavender on it? I know the lavender isn't really edible, but we could just have it on the display rather than serving it."

"Personally, I'd go with custard," I said. "Or squirty cream. Everything's better with squirty cream."

Gertrude looked up. "Ah," she said. "There you are." She examined us, then went back to the cake. "You look like you've had a rough morning."

"You could say that," I said.

She stepped back to scrutinise the cake. "Have you found out anything about my souls? I've already had Secretary Reaper on the phone. DHL are getting most concerned."

"We're working on it," Callum said. "We sort of ran into a complication."

"Two," I said, and he glared at me. "What? Two's the minimum, really."

Gertrude frowned. It was a little alarming, in the harsh light of the kitchen with her hood pushed back. I could see her skull through her thin hair and taut skin. "What sort of complications?"

Callum pulled the coat off the crate and set it on the island. "This, for a start."

The head snapped a few times, some stray skin poking out of its mouth, and rolled its eyes at us. Gertrude pinched the bridge of her nose, the palette knife dropping icing on the spotless worktop. "I'm quite sure this isn't covered by my food hygiene certificate," she said. "And what exactly do you expect me to do with these?"

We stared at the crate, watching the hand trying to climb the sides.

"I don't know," Callum admitted. "But we didn't really know what to do with them."

"I'm pretty sure we couldn't just pop them in the bin," I said. "I don't even know which bin they'd go in. Garden waste, maybe?"

The reaper sighed, and pulled a big catering bucket with a lid from one of the open shelves under the island. "I imagine that if we kill the head, these will die too."

"It does seem to work that way," I agreed.

"So I assume you have a reason for not killing the head yet?" She started transferring the zombie scraps into the bucket.

"We're hoping someone can use it to work out how to fix this," Callum said.

Gertrude tugged on the fingers. They'd wound themselves into the sides of the crate and didn't want to let go. "Do you have any idea what's causing it yet?"

"Not exactly," I said. "Did you find anything at the other cemeteries?"

The reaper sighed and popped the head into the tub, then sealed the top and carried the whole thing to the big stainless doors of the walk-in fridge. She found a space for it at the bottom, moving some smaller tubs of yogurt and sour cream away to make room. Then she straightened up and looked at us. "Nothing but more missing souls. Not even the bodies, although there were some empty graves."

"Oh, cool," I said. "That's just fantastic." I looked at Callum, who was inspecting his coat. It had some new and rather unpleasant stains on it, and the snake was hanging out of one pocket looking queasy. "Dude, throw it out," I said to him.

"Do I ever say that about your coat?"

"No, because my coat is glorious. And also attached."

"Your coat is patchy and may have fleas."

I jumped from his shoulder to the worktop and drew myself up into my full indignant height. *"I do not have fleas."*

"Off," Gertrude said. "Just because I've had a head on my worktop doesn't mean I want a cat on it, too. It's unhygienic."

"Why does everyone keep thinking I'm unhygienic?" I complained, jumping to the floor. "It's species-ism, that is."

"I'm not species-ist," Gertrude said. "I like cats. Well, I thought I did."

Callum had been about to lean on the wall, but he thought better of it and just shoved his hands in the pockets of his jeans. "So, you don't know how we might be able to stop this?"

Gertrude was washing her hands, the scent of disinfectant and herby oils drifting across the kitchen to mix with the warm smells of cake and lavender. She turned to look at us before she answered, drying her hands on a towel. "To do that, we need to know how it started," she said. "If we can't find that out, all we can do is put them down."

Callum started to say something, then stopped and just looked at the polished surface of the worktop, his hand pressed to his side.

"We've got some leads," I said. "But time's getting a little tight, you know?"

Gertrude stepped back from the island, examined the cake, and swirled the palette knife over it a couple of times, getting the icing just so. "Because there are more every night?"

"Yeah," I said. "And because someone got himself bitten, and we don't know how long before he starts fancying a snack of deep-fried frontal lobe."

Callum sighed as Gertrude looked at him. "You were bitten?"

"Yeah. One of the heads last night."

"That was rather careless," she said.

"I know. But that's why we kept this head. If someone can think of a cure, maybe we can test it on that."

Gertrude scraped the last of the icing out of the bowl and smeared it on the sides of the cake carefully. "I'm just going to go with the lavender flowers," she announced.

"Sounds like a good choice," Callum said, and I jumped to the top of the bin so I could at least see a bit better. Gertrude glanced at me, but didn't say anything. She reached behind the drawn curtains, squinting at the light that sneaked in, and lifted a potted lavender plant onto the worktop, snipping a few flowers off before putting it back.

I looked from Callum to Gertrude, but no one said anything. The reaper arranged the lavender carefully on top of the cake. "How does it look?" she asked.

"Lovely," Callum said. "Really pretty."

"Good. Wait here." And she left, carrying the cake.

I looked at Callum again, arching my whiskers, and he shrugged. It wasn't like we had any better options right now.

GERTRUDE CAME BACK in before I'd got bored enough to start walking on the worktops, although it was near thing. It would have been nearer if Callum hadn't threatened to leave me downstairs with the ghoulets if I did it. I didn't think he was serious, but I wasn't certain. And I didn't fancy taking my chances with mini ghouls.

Emma followed the reaper in, and they both examined us as if we'd tracked mud across the spotless floors of the kitchen.

"Gertrude said you've been bitten," Emma said to Callum.

"Um. Yes," he said, not quite looking at her.

"Well, show me. I bet you're being just like a man, aren't you, and pretending it's all fine?"

"It is fine," he protested. "I've been putting peroxide on it." He thought about it. "Anyway, I *am* a man."

"I'm not sure you should be boasting about that around here," I said, and Gertrude snorted as she carried the bowl to the sink and came back to wipe some practically invisible crumbs off the worktop.

"*I'm* not sure peroxide is the recommended treatment for zombie bites," Emma said. "Show me."

"Told you," I said, as Callum peeled his shirt up with a sigh.

Emma picked the tape off and pulled the gauze away carefully, exposing pale puckered skin. The teeth marks still looked raw and bloody, and around it the flesh had a damp, unhealthy look. Redness spread across his torso like a stain creeping across carpet.

"It's infected," she announced.

"That's why I'm putting peroxide on it."

She straightened up and glared at him. "Do you really think that's going to work?"

He shrugged a little awkwardly. "We don't actually know if the bite's infectious."

"Something's infectious." She poked the reddened skin around the wound, and he flinched, sucking air in. "See?"

"Well, you stuck your finger in it!" he snapped, pulling his shirt down. "Anyway, what do you suggest? Go to A&E and ask them what antibiotics are best suited for zombies?"

"That may not have the desired result." She looked at Gertrude, who was leaning against the sink with her arms crossed. "Do you know?"

Gertrude shook her head. "This has never been a problem before. Not in my time, anyway." She examined Callum. "I can ask Secretary Reaper tonight, but I rather think we might want to try and move more quickly than that."

"Ooh." Emma clapped her hands lightly. "Do we have clues? What've we got?"

"Necromancers," I said. "But they say the most they've managed to reanimate are headless chickens and some cockroaches."

"Gross," Emma said.

"So gross," I agreed. "Then we've got a magician, with a dead and presumably zombified son, who likes taxidermy and keeping heads in jars. He *might* have dug his son up, but we can't figure out why he'd do the rest."

"Then there's Ms Jones," Callum said.

"Ms Jones?" Gertrude asked.

"Sorcerer with a thing for skinny jeans and Doc Martens," I said. "She was at the cemetery last night too. Honestly, she's the only one I think might be powerful enough to do it. I mean, *maybe* the necromancers could, but only their house really smelled of magic. They didn't so much."

"There was no taint on the corpses," Gertrude said.

"Yeah, I didn't smell anything, either," I said. "It's like it wasn't magic at all."

"They all came from one mortuary," Callum said. "But we went there. Gobs couldn't smell anything, and the mortician was …"

"A potato," I said, while Callum looked for a decent descriptor.

Emma tapped her fingers on the worktop. "If someone's going to raise the dead, they're going to want to be there to see if it worked, right?"

"You'd think so," Callum agreed.

"So your sorcerer was there. Anyone else?"

"Just someone in a hoody," I said. "We never got close

enough to see who it was, or even if it was the same person."

"But they dropped some stuff," Callum said. "Vials and a syringe." He dug into his pockets and pulled out the little tub he'd taken from the backpack, opening it to show Gertrude and Emma. "It may not even be connected."

Emma picked up the syringe, examined it, then went into the fridge and pulled out a tub. She set it on the island and pulled the lid off to reveal a few whole trout.

"What're you doing, dear?" Gertrude asked. "That's for the fish special."

"I only need one." Emma took the cap off the needle, slipped it through the rubber seal on the vial, and partly filled the syringe. I jumped to Callum's shoulder to watch her jab it into one of the trout and depress the plunger, then step back.

We all stared at the fish. It just lay there, eyes glassy and body slack, and my stomach rumbled.

"Well," Emma said. "Maybe it doesn't work on fish. Or maybe it's nothing to do with it."

"I can't use that now," Gertrude said. "I'm going to have to throw it out."

Callum sighed. "Well, we're still no further on, anyway." He looked at me. "Maybe we need to do the rounds again. See if we can shake anything else loose."

We were quiet for a while. Emma had rescued the bowl from the sink and was licking the palette knife. Now she put the knife down and said, "Look, human perspective and all—"

"I'm human," Callum muttered, but with even less conviction than he'd said he was a man earlier.

"And also serious zombie fan—"

"She makes me watch *all* the zombie movies," Gertrude said, looking pained. "Even that one with the lawnmower."

"Oh, I know that one," I said. "Wasn't it meant to be ironic or something, though?"

"It was disgusting," Callum said, and Gertrude nodded vigorously.

"Anyone else like to interrupt?" Emma demanded, glaring at us all. "No? Good. Look, this is obviously a bit of an unknown for everyone. And if there's any chance they're infectious, we need to act quickly. Which means we need all the information we can get." She pointed at me. "Gertrude says the Watch deal with stuff like this. Ask the Watch."

"I can't," I said. "They have some issues with me. And they'll probably blame me for it."

"For zombies?"

"They'd blame me if you lot started a nuclear war."

Emma frowned. "Well, they'll certainly blame you if there's a zombie apocalypse and you kind of failed to mention walking corpses to them."

I growled at the back of my throat, and Callum said, "She does have a point."

I opened my mouth to ask whose side he was on, and there was a fleshy thump from the island. We looked at the tub of dead fish. They just lay there, looking fishy.

"Look," I started, and stopped again. The top fish *moved*. It hitched itself up and flopped down again, giving another thump. Then it opened and shut its mouth a few times, eyes swivelling in its sockets.

"Holy cow," Emma said. "It worked."

"Hoody's the one, then," Callum said, watching the fish wriggle a little more enthusiastically, the tub juddering on the stainless surface. "But who *is* it?"

"It's the mortician," I said. "It has to be. No magic. Just vials of chemicals."

"Science," Callum said, a little smugly.

"The upside is that, if he made it, he should be able to figure out an antidote," Emma said.

Gertrude leaned over the tub and poked the fish, which tried to bite her. "Then I think we should take him the head. I'd rather not have it in my fridge. All I need is Environmental Health making a surprise inspection."

"Alright," Callum said, and opened the fridge to take out the bucket. "Can I borrow this?"

Gertrude wrinkled her nose. "Well, I don't want it *back*."

"Right. Of course." He set it on the floor at his feet and looked at me. "Let's do this, then."

"I'll drive you," Gertrude said.

"Really?" I asked.

"Of course. You're doing quite enough damage on your own, what with getting bitten and so on. Just give me a moment to get ready." She hurried out of the kitchen, pulling her apron off as she went, and after a final peek at the fish Emma followed her, leaving us alone in the kitchen. Something was scratching at the inside of the bucket with a slow sort of desperation, and the trout was chewing on one of its tub-mates.

Callum looked at me. "Do you think I should call Ms Jones back?"

I shrugged. "Maybe. But what was she doing in the cemetery, really? And how did some wilted lettuce of a mortician figure out how to raise the dead? That bit all seems a bit weird."

He rubbed the back of his head. "It does. But we're going to need some help. We don't know how many more zombies are out there."

"We've got a reaper. That seems like a good start."

He snorted, and bundled his coat up, snake and all, as Gertrude pushed the door open. She had pulled the sleeves of her robe down, and was wearing an enormous, floppy-brimmed straw hat with a wide pink ribbon, her bony hands encased in pink gloves embroidered with white flowers. She picked up her scythe from where it was leaning by the fridge, next to the mop and broom.

"Ready?" she asked.

"For what?" I said. "A reaper garden party?"

"You can walk," she said, and took a set of car keys from a hook on the wall. "Callum, come on."

16

BEHOLD, THE CREATOR OF ZOMBIES

I HAVE DIED THREE TIMES. NONE OF THEM HAVE BEEN gentle, surrounded-by-loved-ones deaths. Last time, my flesh was flayed from my soul by the creatures of the Inbetween.

And I was fairly certain that death four was going to be the most terrifying of them all, and, rather than being zombie-induced, was going to result from a fiery inferno of a car crash, courtesy of a reaper who learnt to drive when the fastest things on the roads were steam-powered unicycles. Or something. My grip of human vehicular history is a little wonky.

Gertrude had one of those white trade half-size vans, with a cab in the front and the back all sealed off for carrying cakes to events, or ghoulets back from graveyards. Which seemed less hygienic than a cat sat on your worktop, if we're going to choose hairs.

It also meant I couldn't escape into the back seat, so I just sat bolt upright in Callum's lap, watching wide-eyed as Gertrude changed lanes with careless confidence, slipping into gaps in queueing traffic that I swear the aforementioned unicycle shouldn't have been able to fit through. She sailed through red lights, took one-way streets the wrong way, and overtook turning buses. Buses turning *toward* us, I mean. And I'm pretty sure I heard Callum whimper when she turned right onto a roundabout instead of left. Which was actually not so bad, as she then changed her mind and went straight over the island in the centre, bumping through the flowerbeds with the van's suspension protesting wildly.

We rejoined the traffic without even a touch of the brakes and plunged down a side street at about twenty miles over the speed limit.

"Um, Gertrude?" Callum said. He was holding onto the door handle with one hand and the dashboard with the other, and his feet were jammed onto an invisible brake. "I'd rather not get stopped by the police while carrying a severed head in a tub."

Callum had a patchy history with the police. It wasn't as bad as my history with the Watch, but it was the sort of history which meant I did most of the breaking and entering, and also had annoying knock-on effects when it came to things like putting up with ancient phones rather than acquiring new ones. Even if I would have been the one doing the acquiring.

She gave him a puzzled look as she swerved around a rubbish collection truck and narrowly missed hitting a Range Rover. "Why would they stop us?"

Callum shrieked, "*Look out!*" and Gertrude spun us onto the wrong side of the road to get around a horde of cyclists, then pulled back onto our own side with what felt like two wheels in the air. She looked back at him.

"I've never had so much as a parking ticket. Why would they stop me?"

Callum appeared to have lost the power of speech, and I decided I preferred the reaper with her eyes on the road. Neither of us spoke.

SOMEHOW WE MADE it to the mortuary as visitors rather than customers. Gertrude pulled across the road and into the drive a breath in front of a lorry, and I swear I heard the whisper of metal on metal as we flew past the nose of the truck, over the speed bumps and around the drive to the back of the building. She braked for the first time in the whole trip, slamming us to a halt just before we hit the rolling doors. I was flung off Callum's lap into the footwell, and he yelped as I gouged his legs on the way past.

Both of us sat there shaking quietly, and Gertrude turned the engine off.

"Here we are," she said, peering through the windscreen at the sign. "Traffic was a bit awful, wasn't it?"

"Traffic," I said. "Sure."

She frowned at me. "Well, come on. No time to waste."

Callum managed to unpeel his hand and open the door, and almost fell out onto the drive. We wobbled up to the building, Callum carrying the bucket and Gertrude following with her head down, keeping her face sheltered from the pale spring sun.

It took Callum two goes before he managed to actually ring the bell, and he clawed his cigarettes out while we waited for someone to answer. He managed to get one lit, the flame of the lighter wavering around wildly, and was dragging on it desperately when the door opened and Williams Senior frowned at us.

"This is a no-smoking property," he said.

"Sorry," Callum mumbled, and ground the cigarette out, tucking the butt back into a pocket. "Is Jan here?"

"He's busy."

"This won't take long."

Williams looked past Callum at Gertrude, who raised a glove-clad hand rather elegantly. Her face was lost in the shadows of her hood and hat, and the robe hid her bare feet, the not-quite-black fabric absorbing the sun.

"Are you with him?" he asked (I was hiding behind the door again. Humans and their *hygiene*).

"I'm an interested party," the reaper said. Williams stared at her for a little longer, and she added in a rather reproving tone, "I have a sun allergy. It's most uncomfortable, even when covered up."

"Oh," Williams said, then, "*Oh!* Yes, sorry. My apologies. Do come in."

"Thank you," Gertrude said, and breezed past both men. I saw Williams stare at her feet, but he didn't say anything. He just led the way to Jan's office, knocked once, and pushed the door open for us. Then he left before Gertrude could be reproving at him again.

Jan stared at us. "What're you doing here? I told you, I'll call the police if you keep this up. I mean it!"

"Look at that," I said. "Our mad mortician's going to call the police."

"*What* did you call me?" he snapped, and waved what looked like a putty knife at me before recovering himself and waving it at Callum instead. "*Stop doing the cat thing!*"

"Oh, believe me, I wish I could," Callum said. "But you really just have to put up with it." He set the bucket of body parts on an empty rolling table and said, "These are yours, I believe."

"What is it?" he asked.

"Your Christmas present," I said, jumping to one of the counters.

"It's March."

"No baby goats," I said, and everyone looked at me. I shrugged.

"Kidding," Callum said finally. "No *kidding.*"

"Baby goats are kids."

Gertrude shook her head almost sorrowfully, which seemed a bit harsh. Jan poked the bucket. "You're harassing me," he said.

"You're *making zombies,*" Callum said. "Just admit it and we can figure out how to stop it. That's all we're here for."

"What are you, twelve? Zombies don't exist."

Gertrude sighed and took her hat off, setting it on the counter next to me. "Are we sure about this? He does seem a bit … potato-ish."

"Who are you?" Jan demanded. "Why are you people *here?*"

"*Zombies,*" I said. "You made *zombies,* you soggy onion."

"Stop *doing* that!" he yelled.

"Dude, if you don't get your act together I'll bite something sensitive," I snapped.

"I do need to know what happened to my souls," Gertrude said, folding her arms. "Is this definitely the man from the cemetery?"

"He certainly yelps the same," I said, and Jan huffed like we were the ones being ridiculous.

"*What* cemetery?" he demanded. "Why would I be in a *cemetery?*"

We all stared at him.

He folded his arms over his chest. "I just prepare the bodies. I don't *bury* them."

"Open the tub," I snarled at him. "Open the tub and tell me you know nothing about zombies."

"Excellent point," Gertrude said. "And show me your shoes."

"My *shoes?*"

"I want to see if they're got graveyard dirt on them. I'll know."

"Look, I've had enough of this—"

"I've had enough of the undead," I snapped.

"And I've had enough of squidgy souls," the reaper added.

Callum rubbed his forehead. "Gobs, shut up. Gertrude—"

"*Me* shut up?" I demanded. "He's—"

"He's doing this in *my* cemetery," Gertrude said. "All of Leeds is my cemetery. I hope you're not going to suggest *I* don't talk to this man."

"All of Leeds is your cemetery?" I said. "Creepy."

Callum took a deep breath, one hand drifting to his

side in a gesture that was already too familiar. "Jan, just open the tub."

"Look—"

"Open the damn tub!" Callum bellowed, and Jan gave a little yelp and grabbed the bucket, ripping the lid off. The fingers promptly scrambled over the lip, making a desperate grab for his sleeve. He shrieked and dropped the lot, scattering twitching zombie bits all over the white tile floor. The head rolled toward me, snapping eagerly, and I jumped back with a hiss. Callum grabbed it by the hair and swung it back into the bucket.

Gertrude stooped to pick up two dancing toes and handed them to Callum, who gave an *urk* of disgust and dropped them in with the head. "Now," she said. "Are you going to talk sensibly?"

"That's a trick," Jan said. "They're clockwork or something."

I looked at Callum. "*Now* can I bite him?"

"I'm starting to see the sense in it," he said, and Jan backed up until he bumped into another of the rolling tables, this one with a sheet-draped shape on it.

"You have to leave," he said again, and behind him the shape sat up with a groan.

"Oh, *bollocks,*" Callum said, and grabbed Jan by the front of his jumper, hauling him away just as the sheet slid down, revealing a young man with rough stitching holding his bare torso together. The corpse looked around and moaned questioningly, and Jan gave another shriek.

"Get it!" he squawked. "Get it, *get it!*"

"Oh, now you know what it is," I said, as the corpse swung its legs off the table and stood up.

"Jan?" someone called from outside, and the door started to swing open. "Is everything—" They were cut off as Callum shoved the door closed again. "Hey!"

"Tell him it's fine," Callum said, his voice low.

Jan nodded, swallowing hard. "It's all good, Dad," he called. "Nothing to worry about."

"Why won't you let me in? I heard a shout." There was a rattle as Williams Senior tried the door again. "Jan, open this!"

Gertrude stepped forward to meet the corpse as it took its first couple of shaky steps, the scythe appearing in her hands as if it had always been there.

"No," I hissed. "Don't kill it. Re-kill it. Whatever. We might need it."

She looked at me, then just used the blunt outer edge of the scythe to force the creature against the wall and hold it there. It waved at her vaguely.

"Dad, it's all good, really," Jan called.

"Then *let me in.*"

Gertrude picked up the sheet, flung it over the corpse, and stood in front of it, still holding the thing pinned there with her scythe behind her back. She nodded at Callum, and he stepped away from the door, offering Williams a broad smile as I dived behind a bin.

"Sorry. Locked it by accident, I think."

Williams gave him a suspicious look, then stared at Jan, who looked like he was on the verge of throwing up. "What's going on here?"

"Nothing," Jan squeaked, in about the most suspicious way imaginable.

The zombie groaned, and Williams stared at Gertrude. She patted her belly. "Sorry. I don't think my lunch agreed with me."

No one moved for a moment, and a bell rang in the room outside, a buzzing, impatient thing. Williams looked over his shoulder, then back at his son. "Tell me the truth, Jan. Is this one of your LARP-y things?"

"Um," he said, and the bell went again, ringing for longer this time. "You better get that."

Williams tutted, and glared at us all. "You should be ashamed of yourselves," he said. "Here of all places you should have respect for the dead."

The bell went again, and didn't stop this time. The dead might be patient, but not customers.

"For God's sake," Williams muttered, and jogged out. Callum closed the door after him, and Gertrude turned to check on the zombie. It was eating the sheet, stuffing it into its mouth hopefully.

"You poor thing," she said.

GERTRUDE LIFTED the zombie back onto the table and held it there while Callum tied it down with some cable ties Jan produced from the desk drawer. The mortician seemed a bit dazed.

"I didn't think it was really working," he said, once the creature was secure.

"It depends how you define *working,*" I said. "You

know, if the zombie apocalypse was your intention, then yeah. Job well done."

"It's not an *apocalypse.*"

"Yet," I said.

"This is a scientific endeavour," he insisted. "One must make sacrifices for science."

"These are souls," Gertrude said. "You're trapping them and making them go all squidgy."

"Squidgy?" he asked.

"That seems to be a reaper technical term," I said, and Callum nudged me with his boot. "What?"

"It's the biting I'm worried about," Callum said. "Is it infectious?"

"Of course not," Jan said. "They're not *zombies.*"

"Just the walking dead, then?" I asked.

"It's nothing more than an unfortunate side effect of treatment. Trial and error is the natural way of science, after all."

"The zombie apocalypse seems like a pretty big error," I said. "And what sort of name's Jan, anyway?"

He gave me an irritated look. "It's Janson. My mum was really into Swedes."

"Like, in soup?" I asked, and Callum nudged me again.

"No, as in the *country,*" Jan snapped.

"Oh," I said. "So, are you a doctor? Or professor? You know, you kind of need the title to really get the whole mad scientist thing going."

"*No,*" he said. "That's really very offensive."

"Oh, good. So no medical training, then?"

"I'm a mortician! There's training! And I've been studying neurochemistry myself for years!"

"Gobs, shut up," Callum said, then added to Jan, "You're sure it's not infectious?"

Jan put his hands on his hips and let out an aggrieved sigh. "How can it be? It's not a virus. It's a formula that's injected straight into the brain."

Callum let out a long, slow breath, and wiped his mouth. "Well. That's good to know."

Gertrude tapped the bucket of body parts. "But you do know *how* to reverse it, don't you? You didn't just bring all these bodies back to life with no way to stop it?"

"Um," Jan said. "Well. I mean, I wasn't even sure it'd work …"

"You don't know," I said. "You cabbage. You made them, and you don't know how to stop it."

"Well," he said, tugging at the front of his coat. "Well, I didn't think I'd need to …"

"You sodden lump of half-eaten—" I was cut off by a voice from the door.

"There's a way to stop it," the new voice said, and my stomach twisted with the familiarity of it as we turned to the door. I hadn't even heard it open. Over the sharp harsh stench of bleach and antiseptic and other things I couldn't name, her scent rolled to me, muted at the edges but still rich and raw with power. I stepped behind Gertrude, and Ms Jones looked at Callum. "Have you lost your phone?"

"Um. No," he admitted.

She leaned against the doorway and folded her arms. Today's Docs were an old, faded red, scuffed at the toes, and her hair tumbled dark and heavy over her shoulders. "No?"

"Um."

Ms Jones' gaze drifted to Gertrude. "Reaper Leeds. May your scythe be sharp and your souls be sweet."

"Ms Jones, I presume."

The sorcerer raised her eyebrows. "You were expecting me?"

"I heard you might be involved." Gertrude's voice was level, the scythe leaning innocently against her shoulder, and I scooted toward Callum. The smell of old power rolling against eternal spaces was making my fur prickle, and I didn't fancy being caught in the middle of it all.

"Involved," Ms Jones said.

"My souls are going squidgy," Gertrude said. "It's not acceptable."

"Ah. I see." The sorcerer looked at me as I scrambled to Callum's shoulder. "So that's why you didn't answer my calls."

"You *were* at the cemetery," Callum said.

"And, seriously. How did peanut here figure out how to raise the dead?" I added.

Ms Jones looked at us for a long, still, moment, then smiled. It tilted the corners of her eyes, and showed teeth that were just a tiny bit crooked. "I'd also like to know that," she said. "I had hoped you two would help me find out. You *are* still on retainer, you know."

"Sorry," Callum said. "It's just …" he trailed off uncertainly.

"It's just that we thought you might have told him how to do it, and then figured we were onto you, and so were going to turn us into woodlice," I filled in. Well, she was already unhappy with us. What was a bit more?

"Well, that's a little insulting, assuming I was involved with that sort of magic. But I see the concern," she added, in a way that made me think we weren't entirely safe from the woodlice issue. She nodded at Jan. "So you're the one, then. I hadn't thought you'd be human. I was searching everywhere for … something else."

"Who're you?" he asked. "You shouldn't be back here. My dad—"

"Is having a little nap. He's quite alright," she added, as Jan clutched his hands to his chest. "I had hoped to talk to you privately, but I can see that isn't happening."

"How did you find him?" Gertrude asked. She still didn't look entirely convinced by the sorcerer.

"They all came from the same funeral home," she said. "I'd have found him quicker if I'd realised he was human."

Jan made a funny little squeaking noise.

"That's how we found him, too," I said. "And it's definitely him. He doesn't know how he did it, though. Or how to stop it."

"I do know how I did it," Jan said, apparently talking to the floor.

"But *you* know how to stop them," Gertrude said to the sorcerer. "Can the souls be saved?"

"That isn't my area," Ms Jones said. "But as long as the brain's killed, the body follows. How many are out there?" she added to Jan.

"Ah. Well. I …"

"You don't know that either?" Callum asked.

"Dude," I said, and Jan shot me a panicked look.

"Well, I know how many I administered the formula to. I just … well, some of them I thought it didn't work on, but now I think maybe it did, and some of them reanimate immediately, and some take ages, so …"

"How many?" Gertrude demanded. "How many souls have you ruined, you horrible little man?"

Jan looked from her to the scythe and said, "Maybe twenty?"

Callum sighed. "Great. We dealt with four. So there's sixteen more out there somewhere."

"Maybe," Jan said. "Maybe not so many as that. I don't think the early ones worked."

"Wonderful," Ms Jones said. "Do I have to issue any dire warnings about how there won't be any more?"

Jan looked from her to Gertrude. They both looked like they wouldn't mind following up on dire warnings, so he nodded firmly. "No. Got it."

"I should hope so," Ms Jones said, looking at the zombie on the table. It had almost finished eating the sheet. "How *did* you manage this?"

"Research," Jan said, drawing himself up. "I've always been interested in the brain."

"I do believe such research is usually carried out in laboratories," Gertrude said.

Jan sniffed. "Those places never think big enough."

"I told you. Mad scientist alert," I said. "Or mad mortician, I suppose."

Jan glared at me. "That's really *very* offensive."

I shrugged. "I'm pretty offended that a dead person tried to eat me."

Callum picked up the bucket of body parts. "I guess we don't need to worry about antidotes, then," he said, and pulled the head out. "We just need to round them all up before too many people find out about it."

Jan made a strange, strangled noise.

"What?" Callum asked.

Jan pointed at the head, his hand not entirely steady. "Who's that?" he asked.

We stared at the head. My stomach was suddenly tight and hot, like I'd eaten too quickly despite the fact breakfast was so long ago I couldn't even remember what I had.

"You don't recognise them?" Callum asked.

"No." Jan's voice was uneven, but sure. "It's not one of the originals."

"Oh, good," I said, as Callum rubbed his mouth with one hand. "Look at that. It *is* infectious. You utter rotten potato."

Ms Jones shook her head. "Humans," she said. "*Men.*"

Gertrude made a small noise of agreement, and the head snapped hopefully at thin air.

17

CALLUM'S GETTING HUNGRY

MS JONES TOOK THE HEAD OUT OF CALLUM'S HAND AND dropped it in the sink, then pointed at Jan. "I want to see the formula."

"But it's *impossible,*" he said. "It *can't* be infectious!"

"Dude, you *just said* you don't recognise the head," I snapped at him. Callum was silent, hugging his arms tightly about himself. "Get over yourself! It mutated, or you were wrong, or *whatever,* but this is a new zombie. It's spreading somehow."

"That's not good," Jan said.

"No baby goats," I snapped, and the mortician looked puzzled, which suggested all the chemicals were tainting his short-term memory. "*No kidding*. This is how the zombie apocalypse starts, you know."

"Oh, come on—"

"You need to make an antidote," I said. "Gods know how many of the living dead are actually running about nibbling people, and my human's already been bitten. *I want an antidote.* I mean, what if he goes full zombie and bites *me?*"

"Jeez, Gobs, I thought you really cared there for a minute," Callum said. His face was a little pale and sweaty looking.

"You should know better," Ms Jones said, poking the head with a pen. "Where's that formula, mortician?"

"On my computer. Look, I can't make an antidote for what is, essentially, a stimulant."

"So make a de-stimulant," I said.

"You mean a relaxant?" he asked, and I bared my teeth at him.

"*Honestly,*" Gertrude said. "Stop being so difficult. You've made an absolute pig's ear of this, and we need to get it sorted out."

Ms Jones straightened up. "I'm rapidly losing patience," she said. "I want that formula. Then you are going to help me make an antidote."

Jan lifted his chin. "Oh, are you a scientist now?"

"Aw, man," I said, and even Gertrude put a little more distance between the mortician and her. "*You're* not even a scientist. And she can turn you into a pumpkin at three paces."

Ms Jones nodded, and gave that crooked-toothed smile again. "Maybe a butternut squash. Depends how I feel."

Jan fiddled with the front of his coat. "I still maintain this just isn't possible. And the whole trying to eat things is just a side effect of—"

Callum moved so fast I pitched straight off his shoulder to the floor. He grabbed the front of Jan's jumper and hoisted him onto his tiptoes. "I don't *care* what you think is possible," he hissed. "I've been bitten. And I'm *hungry*. So *make the damn antidote.*"

Jan gave a horrified squeak, and Callum shoved him away. The mortician crashed into the restrained zombie and pushed himself off with a little wail, tripping over his own feet and stumbling to the floor. For a moment there was silence, then Ms Jones said, "Get that formula on the screen, mortician. Callum, come with me."

She marched out, and Callum scratched his chin. "Is she going to brain me?" he asked no one in particular.

Gertrude sighed. "Come along. I'll make sure she doesn't." She followed Ms Jones.

Callum and I looked at each other. "I don't know," I said. "But not listening seems a good way to get brained."

"I suppose." He ran his hands back though his hair, and we followed the reaper and the sorcerer out into the empty room beyond.

Ms Jones had stopped in the middle of the big room, next to a dark, glossy coffin set on a trolley. Shiny cream fabric lined the inside, and Williams Senior was lying in it with his legs slung over the sides and his eyes closed. One of his shiny shoes was on the floor, and his black sock had a small white ghost embroidered on the toes.

"I thought you didn't kill him," I said, as Callum stopped behind me.

"Gods. What've I done to deserve all this slander?"

Jones asked, and prodded Williams in the side. He snorted, and started snoring. "Of course I didn't kill him."

Callum and I looked at each other. Okay, maybe she hadn't *done* anything, exactly. Well, other than destroy our office. It was her book of power that had done the real damage last year. But still, that reek of old power was enough to make me nervous. She beckoned to Callum.

"Show me."

He gave me another uneasy glance, then stepped forward, pulling his coat back and moving the torn T-shirt out of the way. She pulled the gauze off in one quick movement that made him suck his breath in, exposing skin that had gone a bit pale and gunky looking, as if he'd been in the bath half the day. Each tooth mark was a bloodless purple crater, as dead-looking as our latest zombie. The bite looked raw and unhealed and the red rash of infection was gone, but I liked this even less.

"That seems worse," Gertrude observed.

Ms Jones wrinkled her nose. "It doesn't look too good."

"I'd prefer you didn't brain him," I said, and she gave me a quick, unreadable glance.

"Thanks," Callum said to me, then added to Ms Jones, "Can you do anything about it?"

"Maybe." She laid a hand on Callum's belly, to the side of the wound. Her eyes seemed to have paled, reflecting the pallor of his skin, and I shivered as I smelled the ozone-tang of old power. Callum flinched and put one hand out to steady himself on the coffin, his face tightening. Fluid bubbled to the surface of the bite mark, clear and gloopy, forming beads and spheres that trembled where they sat. Ms Jones closed her eyes, lines digging their way into her brow, and I could see warmer skin tones creeping across Callum's belly, emerging from under her fingers.

There was a long, taut pause, then she gave a little gasp and dropped her hand. Callum staggered, grabbing Williams' leg to steady himself. The mortician grunted but didn't wake up.

"Did it work?" I asked.

Jones shook her head. "No. The infection's too well set in. Maybe, if you'd called me back this morning, I might've been able to do something." She arched her eyebrows at both of us, and Callum pulled his shirt back down.

"I'll put some more peroxide on, then," he said.

"Good luck with that," Ms Jones said. "I'm going to see if I can scare an antidote out of the mortician."

"What do we do?" I asked.

"Find the rest of them," the sorcerer replied.

"We should go back to the market," Callum said. "There might be more there, and we can check on Big Ted."

"Why would there be more?" Gertrude asked.

He hesitated, and when he answered it was like a reason that wasn't a reason. "We don't know how many other people that zombie might have bitten."

"It bit that one a lot," she observed. "Considering it's mostly just a head."

"I just ..." he shook his head, and pulled his cigarettes out of his pocket. "I just feel we need to go back there."

"Feel how?" I asked, and he shook his head again, scowling this time.

"I just do, okay? Intuition or whatever." He looked at Williams, then found his lighter.

"Your zombie-sense kicking in?" I asked.

"Hilarious, G." He cupped his hands to light the cigarette, and I looked up at Ms Jones. She shrugged.

"Good a place to start as any," she said. "And you might want to find Claudia."

"The Watch? I thought you didn't trust them."

"I don't. I'm not even sure I trust her. But I think we might need all the help we can get." And she turned and marched back into the preparation room, leaving us in the echoing room with the sleeping mortician.

I looked at Callum. "I promise that if you do turn into a zombie, I'll make sure someone brains you as painlessly as possible."

He examined the end of his cigarette and said, "Thanks, Gobs. I appreciate it."

"I thought you would," I said, and followed Gertrude as she led the way to the car, shaking her head as she went.

THE DRIVE back to the cafe was no less terrifying than the drive out had been, and I was trying out the theory that keeping my eyes closed was less frightening than seeing what was happening when Callum yelped, "Bus! *Bus!*"

I opened my eyes in time to see the bus pass *through* the side of the car, and yowled like a dog had my tail as a large man in black leather whipped past me. I'd have buried my nose in his gut if I hadn't flung myself sideways and landed in Gertrude's lap. It was distinctly uncomfortable, but still better than sitting with Callum, who was gripping the dashboard with both hands, his eyes wide. An old lady with lime-green hair came through the windscreen, merged with him, and passed on into the back of the van, followed by a teenager clutching a pack of Maltesers. Then the bus was gone, and the road was clear in front of us. Well, free of buses, anyway. Gertrude was merrily dodging cars as she used the wrong side of the road.

"What the *hell?*" Callum managed.

Gertrude glanced at him, then down at me. I was fairly sure I was doing a good impression of one of those puffer fish. "Oh, sorry. The van inhabits my reality when I'm driving, not yours."

"What?" I asked, which was about as coherent as I could get.

"Well. I'm not technically alive, which means I don't technically exist in this reality. So when I touch things, they have to merge with my reality, which isn't technically the same."

"Technically," Callum said.

"Exactly!" she smiled at him, and drove neatly through a bus shelter. "People sometimes glimpse the van, but it's not technically occupying the same space as them."

"This is making me technically motion-sick," I said.

"Well, get off my robes, then," she said.

I did, and went back to keeping my eyes closed until I

felt the van finally come to a halt. The engine switched off, and there was shaky silence.

"Well," Gertrude said. "Are you hungry? By my understanding, it's well past human lunch-eating time."

"Starving," I said.

"I think I am," Callum said. "But we need to go back to the market." He was rubbing his thumb into his opposite hand, a restless, insistent movement.

Gertrude opened her door. "Come and have some lunch, then we'll go."

"Good idea," I said, and jumped out as Callum opened the door. He followed me, took his cigarettes out, frowned at them, and put them back.

"You alright?" I asked him.

"Sure. Just, you know." He shrugged, and his hand strayed to his side.

I heard a *psst* from the alley, and peered around. For a moment I couldn't see anything, then the *psst* came again, and I spotted a pale face staring down at me from on top of a big commercial recycling bin. The face jerked its head. *Come here.*

I thought of biscuits, and jerked my own head. *No, you come here.*

The face narrowed its eyes, glanced at Gertrude, and shook its head. I sighed. So close to biscuits, yet so far.

"Catch you in a bit."

"Where're you going?" Callum asked.

"To see a cat about a zombie. Find me some tuna or something?"

"Sure," Callum said, and as I trotted toward the bin I glanced back at him. He was rubbing his forehead with one hand, and when he followed Gertrude there was something slow and painfully hesitant about his step.

I turned away, my heart hurting.

I SCRAMBLED up to the top of the bin and sat down next to Pru.

"Is that a *reaper?*" she asked.

"One who makes excellent biscuits," I said.

"Huh." She thought about it. "That's why I couldn't find you, then. I've been looking for you since lunchtime, but the trail just stopped here. You must've been in some reaper shadow or something."

"Sorry," I said. "What's up? More human problems?"

She wrinkled her nose. "Human problems and Watch problems."

"Oh, dude," I said. "You didn't mention me, did you? Guilty by association and all that."

"Not a dude. And no, I didn't. I told them about the necromancers, and they were all, *hmm,* interesting, thanks for telling us, etc etc. But then I got home and my human was there, but she was still being weird." She hesitated, her naked nose wrinkled.

"Weird how?" I asked, when it seemed she wasn't going to continue.

She looked at me, her pupils scratches in the green of her eyes. "This is going to sound really gross."

"We just watched headless chickens running about the place yesterday. Try me."

"She didn't really *do* anything at first. She just wasn't

herself, you know? Next thing I know, I walk into the kitchen and she's eating the chicken necks she bought me. Raw."

"Chicken necks? Gross," I said, before I clicked with the rest of what she'd told me. "Wait, *she* was eating them?"

"Yes, you cabbage. Do you listen at all?"

"Sorry. Just … chicken necks. Ew. So what then?"

"Tell me about it. And she didn't even leave me any. Anyway, I'd seen on the news about the cemetery … what'd they call them? Desertions? Debutantes? De … Whatever, there was that, and talking to you, and the maulings—"

"Maulings?" I asked.

"Yes, maulings. It's been all over the news. People getting set on and savaged. They're calling it wild animals, but after Katja getting bitten and tucking into the chicken necks I just … well, it all adds up, doesn't it?"

"It does," I said. "Do you remember how many maulings?"

"No, I was more worried about making sure Katja didn't go full zombie. So I thought, well, I'll go back to the Watch. I mean, no offence, but you two …"

"Oh, thanks."

She shrugged. "Well, you better know what you're doing, because the Watch say it's a human problem. Nothing to do with them. Their advice is, and I quote, '*don't get eaten*'."

I stared at her, my stomach churning so badly I thought I might throw up a hairball, although that seemed a bit off when in the company of someone who'd never had to deal with them. There was a sour taste at the back of my throat, all burned things and old memories, and I spat at a pigeon that was posturing at us.

"'Don't get eaten'? That's it?"

"That's it. And oh, too bad about the human, but they're sure there'll be some others left."

I opened my mouth, shut it, then finally managed, "Old Ones take them. Old Ones take them and suck their rotting bones."

"Yep," Pru said.

I wondered if it was possible to hate the Watch any more than I already did. Trapping me in the Inbetween to die, stripping me of the ability to shift, and *still* holding me accountable for acts undertaken three lives ago was bad enough, but now they were basically taking a look at the potential end of humanity, giving a collective *eh,* and going back to grooming their tails. They suck worse than goblin poetry, and that stuff makes your ears bleed. Literally. And I'm using that word in its correct sense here.

I looked at Pru. Just because she was angry at the Watch didn't mean she'd help us. Cats don't tend to have a *with you or against you* mentality. We're more *with you if it's interesting and/or until something better comes along.*

"You know this is spreading," I said. "More humans are going to turn if we don't stop it."

She shrugged. "All I know is what I was told: this is human business. The Watch will not get involved. And, you know. Preventing the extinction of humanity has never exactly been a guiding principle for them. Fewer humans'll just make the job of keeping the Folk secret a hell of a lot easier."

She wasn't wrong, but it didn't do anything to ease the furious tightness in my limbs. "Look, I get that's the official line – well, I don't get it, actually, because if the zombies do take over, not only will they try to eat us, we won't have anyone to open our custard. But, you know. No one ever accused the Watch of trying to make anyone's life easy."

She wrinkled her nose. "Do you know, there are cats that go their entire lives without having a packet of custard opened for them?"

"Well, that sucks. They should try it some time."

She tipped her head, and I couldn't tell if she was amused or not. The skin of her face was furrowed with wrinkles and bumps that could have meant anything, and the hairless knobbles of her knuckles exposed her claws in a way that was both threatening and unthinking. I hesitated, not wanting to get into a fight with a cat whose allegiances were unknown. Not that I was angling for a fight, but Callum had pointed out more than once that I had a tendency to talk my way into them.

Then she said, "I'm partial to vanilla yogurt, myself."

"Yogurt?"

"Yes. The probiotics are very good for you."

"Okay," I said. "Okay, so, who's going to get vanilla yogurt for you if the humans are all busy running about biting each other's brains out?"

"I imagine the Watch feel that either enough humans will survive, or that we will have to cope without yogurt. Or custard."

"And you're okay with that?" I couldn't get my head around it. Cities emptied, becoming echoing, treacherous shells peopled by the dead. Bodies torn apart in the streets, filling the air with the stench of decay and loss. Fires roaring unchecked through villages and towns, tearing the heart out of everything. Packs of dogs roaming the alleys, bringing down the weak and the hurt. The world given over to old, savage laws.

I mean, maybe I should have been more comfortable with those laws, given that I am, at heart, a wild animal (as are all cats), but I didn't fancy it.

"No yogurt," I said. "No custard. No heating. No fluffy blankets. No safe, sunny windowsills on a cold winter's day. No hot water bottles. No roast chicken. No shrimp. Ugh, no *shrimp.* No—"

"Yeah, I get it," she said. "I never said I agreed with them." She sighed. "I don't want my human turning into a zombie. She's just bought these new cushions that feel like fluffy marshmallow clouds."

I sat down and scratched my chin with one back paw, my heart suddenly easier in my chest, although my words felt stuck somehow. Finally I said, "Where'd you say your human got bitten?"

Pru's wrinkly forehead wrinkled even more. "The hand? Why's it matter?"

"No, where as in, at a cemetery?"

"Oh. No, in town. The market. She tells me everything." Pru straightened up, a purr in her voice. "She'd just bought me some liver when this other woman ran up, bit her hand, and took off with the meat."

"The market." Funny how much kept coming back to the market. It wasn't as if it was close to any of the cemeteries. But then, certain places have a pull. And there had been a butcher's row seeping blood and flesh into the ground there for centuries. It was as old as the city itself, if not older. That had to set up quite the stink, if one had the nose for it.

I looked up at the sky visible between the buildings. It was a deep warm blue, and I could smell tarmac heating in the afternoon sun. A train chattered somewhere out of sight, slowing as it came into the station, and the scents of muddled lives and jumbled needs and the raw, rich urgency that underlie any city drifted around us like musk.

I looked back at Pru and said, "You want to help?"

She looked at me with those pale eyes. "As much as I want to bite the Watch on their collective tails."

"It might get into that guilty-by-association territory."

She considered it, the nubs of her whiskers twitching and that unsettling tail curling around her toes like it had a life of its own. I know humans have this thing about being *so ugly it's cute*, but I'm unconvinced. I mean, I have a *great* coat, other than the sucker-mark scars and the smaller, nastier ones from a crappy human's cigarette. I didn't fancy not having it. Still, it's all just window dressing, right?

"Vanilla yogurt's *really* good," she said finally. "And Friday's fish night. I'm not happy about missing fish night. It's not right."

"That would suck," I said.

"Yes. We had Scottish salmon last week. Wild, obviously."

"Obviously," I said, trying not sound sarcastic.

"So?" she asked.

"Find a cat called Claudia. Calico, one blue eye, one green one. If she'll help, bring her to the market."

"Alright," Pru said, and got up. She stretched, muscles and tendons moving against the skin, and I looked away. It made me feel weirdly voyeuristic. "I'll catch you soon, but just so you know – I'm totally blaming you if the Watch get their tails in a twist."

"That's fair," I said. "They'll blame me anyway."

"Yeah, you have that look." And then she was gone, setting the pigeon cooing in alarm. I wondered if it was fair, getting her involved like that, but it wasn't like we had much choice. As Ms Jones said, we needed all the help we could get now.

I jumped to the ground and headed back to the cafe, wondering if Callum had found me any tuna.

18

WHEN YOU'RE HUNGRY, YOU'RE HUNGRY

No one answered my scratches at the door, so I had to climb to the kitchen window, fending off the pigeon who had apparently decided my toes might be edible. After some dedicated scratching on the glass Gertrude finally heard me and let me in, and I shoved my nose straight into the bowl of water she offered me, even though it was on the floor. I wouldn't normally let my standards slip that far, but it seemed a bit risky to argue the point with a reaper who was particular about her worktops.

However, now it seemed she'd lost my human.

"Gone? What d'you mean, he's *gone?*" I demanded, water dripping from my whiskers.

"He said he was going to the loo," Gertrude said. "What did you expect me to do, chain him to the fridge?"

"He's been *bitten,*" I said. "Who knows what he's up to!"

"Do you think he might be looking for brains?" Emma asked. She was leaning by the door, eating a very gooey piece of brownie. It looked more like dough than cake.

"No I don't think he's looking for brains," I yowled at her, then took a shaky breath and sat down, thinking of Pru and her chicken necks.

Gertrude clicked her tongue. "There's no need to shout."

"He's upset," Emma said, and crouched down next to me, licking the last of the brownie off her fingers. "I'm sorry, Gobbelino. That was a bit unthinking."

I looked up at her, wobbly with hunger and fright. "I need to find him. Right now. I just … anything could happen."

"Of course." Emma looked at me for a moment, then said, "Can I scritch your ears? Would that help?"

"You *can,*" I said. "It won't help, though."

She rubbed the top of my head, smelling of chocolate and coffee and some warm, unknown scent. I closed my eyes slightly, my heart still running too fast and a little tremor making its way down one leg. "G," Emma said, and I looked up at her before realising she was speaking to the reaper, "I think we have some tuna in the cupboard. Will you give some to Gobbelino while I shut up the cafe?"

"Why are we shutting, dear?" Gertrude asked. "It's only two o'clock."

"I think we have more important things to take care of," Emma said, still working her fingers gently into the short fur on top of my head. I rewarded her with a small purr, my heart slowly retreating from my ears back down into my chest.

"It's not good for business to just close up willy-nilly," Gertrude said.

"I hardly think one early close in three years is willy-nilly, love," Emma said, and got up. "I'm going to go and sort it out now."

I watched her go, my legs still shaking a little, and when Gertrude put a bowl of tuna in front of me I said, "Sorry about the shouting."

She sniffed. "I suppose if anything will make you shout, it's zombies. That Jan made me feel a bit shouty myself."

"Let's just hope they're getting somewhere with the antidote," I said. *And preferably before Callum bites anyone.*

IT WAS ONLY a few streets to the market, and in the normal order of things it would've been quicker to walk than drive, but that was without Gertrude's technically-not-in-this-reality driving. We shot the wrong way down a cobbled street (Emma closing her eyes when a Vespa with a delivery box on the back tore through the middle of the van, me burping tuna at the driver), rocketed around a corner and through some bollards onto a courtyard area between two bars, then pelted across a pedestrian bridge, the van barely skinny enough to keep both wheels between the rails. Gertrude was humming *Pour Some Sugar On Me*, and Emma was mostly looking at her hands.

"At least we live above the cafe now," she told me. "We used to commute."

"That seems needlessly stressful," I said, perched on the bench seat between the woman and the reaper with my claws firmly embedded in the fabric. Gertrude hauled the wheel over and we thundered up another cobbled street, through more bollards, and out into the streets of Leeds. Well, through the centre of an Uber, and *then* onto the streets.

"You're both very rude," Gertrude said, adjusting her sleeves with one hand. "I'm a very safe driver. Even when I was alive I was."

"What did you drive back then?" I asked.

"Oh, horses sometimes," she said, waving vaguely. "Although mostly goats. We had a lot of goats."

I looked at Emma, and she shrugged.

We pulled onto the pavement at the bottom end of the market, where the outside stalls formed rows across the paved square, and Gertrude drove straight into the middle of them, parking next to a stall selling T-shirts emblazoned with old band names and passive-aggressive slogans. We sat there for a moment as she shut the engine off, the shouting of the veggie seller filtering in through the windows.

"*Strawberries!*" he bellowed, as if personally offended by them. "*Lovely English strawberries! Two pound a punnet! Two punnets three pounds! Get your strawberries! Berries-berries-berries!*"

"That's a good price," Emma said. "We should get some on the way back. Victoria sponge always sells well, especially this time of year."

"I could make jam," Gertrude said. "I've got some spare jars."

"Lovely," Emma agreed.

"Excuse me?" I said, looking up at both of them. "Zombies? Callum?"

"The world can't stop just because of zombies,"

Gertrude said, opening her door. "Particularly not when it comes to cake."

I swallowed a huff and followed her out as she pulled her hood forward against the sun.

"Where's your hat?" Emma asked, climbing out the other side of the car. "You know you burn!"

"I'll be inside in a moment," Gertrude pointed out.

Emma frowned at her. "You never know. We could end up outside again."

"I'll be fine," Gertrude said, and took her scythe from behind the seats, tucking it into her robes somehow. "Let's go."

Finally! I wanted to shriek at both of them, but I didn't. For all that I wished I could bite their heels to get them moving, there was something reassuring about being accompanied by a reaper wielding a scythe that could cut through reality itself.

I led the way through the arched doors and into the market proper, weaving my way around hurrying feet and catching the scents of old meat and fresh fish and plasticky wrappings and hair dye and hopes and hungers of all shapes and sizes.

"Do you know where you're going?" Gertrude asked me.

"I have a hunch," I said. No one paid us any attention. There are weirder things in most markets than a reaper and a talking cat.

A scent swelled around us as we walked, eclipsing all others. It was old and strong and not exactly unpleasant, if you're okay with where the meat on your plate comes from. I could hear new shouting now, this one a mechanical drone.

"Pork-chops-ten-pounds-pork-sausages-three-pounds-pork-ribs-pork-shoulder-pork—"

"They like their pork, don't they?" Emma said.

We emerged from the crowded side alley into a wider thoroughfare, each side lined with brightly lit refrigerated stalls. The glass display cabinets were stacked with rippling trays of mince and round rows of sausages, heaped with bone and meat and gristle and blood, all neatly garnished with bunches of parsley and spiked with labels on plastic cards. Cleavers rose and fell, and customers pointed, and butchers in immaculate aprons shouted prices, and in the centre of it all stood Callum, gnawing on a very large and very bloody bone.

"Ew," Emma said.

"Hairballs," I agreed.

I WOULD HAVE THOUGHT a tall skinny guy in a long coat gnawing on a large raw bone would have at least attracted a few interested looks, but … you know. Cities. A young woman stacking the round discs of burger patties in a display case kept looking at him, but more with a *could I get away with filming him and putting it on YouTube* fascination than *oh God he's eating a raw bone* horror. Some little kid was pointing at him and saying *he* wanted a bone, and a rather toothy Folk with yellow predator's eyes was drooling slightly as he watched. I wasn't sure if it was envy over the bone or if he just thought Callum looked tasty.

I scooted up to Callum and put my front paws on his leg. *"Hey!"*

He looked around with the distracted air of a someone surfacing from deep and serious work, then spotted me. "Oh, hey, Gobs."

"What're you *doing?*" I hissed at him. He wasn't exactly centre of attention, but still – weird builds. Between a bone-munching human, a reaper, and me, someone might actually start noticing things, and no one wanted that.

"I was hungry," he said, waving the bone vaguely.

"For *flesh?*"

He looked at the bone in a puzzled sort of way, as if he couldn't really see the problem, then looked up and saw Gertrude. "Hey," he said, and hid the bone behind his back. "Sorry. I just didn't fancy a hummus wrap."

"I could have made a panini," she said.

"I'm not sure roasted veggies would have done it," Emma said.

Callum wiped his mouth, discovering some scraps of meat still on his chin. "Um, yeah. I just needed something … else."

I supposed we should just be happy he wasn't sitting on the floor with a tray of lamb's brains. Or, you know, helping himself. "So, did it scratch the itch?" I asked him. "Are you feeling better?"

He brought the bone out of hiding and turned it over a few times, looking for leftovers. "Sort of? I'm still hungry, though."

“Do you want another bone?” Emma asked, and I glared at her. “What? It seems better to keep him well fed.”

“I rather think Emma has a point,” Gertrude said, and headed to the nearest meat counter, leaning over the display case. She inspected the contents then turned back to us. Callum was gnawing on the bone, trying to get to the marrow, and Emma was keeping a safe distance between them. “Any preference?” the reaper called. “Pork, lamb?”

Callum waved the bone at her. “The lamb was nice. Maybe I’ll try pork, though.”

Gertrude nodded, and plucked a customer ticket from the dispenser.

I looked up at Callum and said, “I don’t suppose you’ve noticed anything else while you’ve been here, have you?”

Callum licked his fingers. “Well, it’s really hot in here.”

I arched my whiskers at Emma, and she shook her head. I could see goosebumps on her bare legs, despite the denim jacket she’d put on over her sundress. “Really not,” she said.

“Oh, good. Fever?”

“Infection,” she guessed, and leaned forward, talking brightly. “Callum? Let’s go grab a seat, okay? There’s a little bench in the corner there. Will you come sit down with us?”

“Sure,” he said, and followed her to the bench, his attention still on his bone.

“Can I look at your bite?” she asked, once he was sitting down, and I jumped up next to him on the seat.

“I don’t mind.” He kept gnawing the bone as she lifted his shirt. “Ugh. Why are these so hard to get into?”

"Well, I don't like the look of that," Emma said, her voice low. I'm not sure why she bothered – Callum wasn't listening. He was knocking the bone on the back of the seat experimentally, as if he might be able to snap it if he got the angle right. I leaned forward to inspect the bite.

The skin of his belly had taken on a stodgy grey tone, as if he were slowly turning into a bowl of porridge, and when Emma peeled the dressing away some of the skin came with it.

"How're we looking?" Gertrude asked, making both of us jump.

"It's worse again," I said.

"And he's all cold and clammy," Emma said, placing a hand hesitantly on Callum's pale skin.

I looked up at the reaper. "Can you see? His soul, I mean. Is it okay?"

She looked at me, her face shadowed in the hood of her robe, and her voice was gentle. "Can't you smell it?"

I opened my mouth to say that there were too many people, that the old deep reek of dead things was too strong, that I wasn't a damn *bloodhound*, and shut it again. I just breathed Callum's scent, which wasn't his anymore. Cigarettes and old books and silence and magic, that should have been him. But it was all lost under a sneaking rot, like roast chicken on the turn.

"Are there bones in that bag?" Callum asked, looking at Gertrude with wide eyes. "Could I have one?"

We left Callum on the bench, his old bone discarded at his feet and a shoulder of pork in his hands.

"Is that safe?" Emma asked. "What if he gets sick?"

Gertrude looked at her. "More than zombie-sick, you mean?"

"I'm just saying, raw pork—"

I'd jumped onto a pile of packing boxes that still smelled faintly of fish, and now I said, "Raw pork still seems better than human brains."

Emma frowned at me, but nodded. "That's a fair point."

"We need that antidote," I said. "There's more out there. We have to *stop* this."

"But how are we going to find them all?" Emma asked. "I mean, other than the bone fetish, Callum looks pretty good."

"*Excuse* me," Gertrude said, but her tone was light.

Emma stuck her tongue out. "Not like that."

I ignored them, staring down the long, bright-lit yet weirdly shadowed alley of the meat market, fish stalls on one side and butchers on the other. Half-seen shapes walked on the very edge of my vision, old memories and lost things that didn't even qualify as Folk anymore, and the concrete floor couldn't keep in the rich old scent of long years of bloody trade. The market was older and more savage than parsley bundles and organic cotton shopping bags.

A little deeper into the maze of old shops was a zombie, hopefully still shut up in the stall with the twitching remains of another undead creature. Big Ted had been bitten here, his friend killed. Pru's human had been bitten right on this row. Callum had insisted he needed to come back here, and I didn't think it was just for meat. I thought it was for more than the old, deep earth smell of dead things, too. Or maybe that was all it took. I do not claim to be a zombie specialist.

"Gertrude," I said, "How do you see souls? I mean, can you tell from a distance if they're … not well?"

She turned to follow my gaze, the scythe leaning against her shoulder. "You said it yourself," she said. "All souls are damaged. It's the condition of all life." She considered it. "Except dogs."

"Dogs?" I asked.

"Yes, they have lovely snuggly souls," the reaper said.

I managed not to point out that only having half a brain did kind of rule you out of most activities that would damage your soul and just said, "Okay, but you said zombie souls were squidgy. Can you see any out there heading that way?"

There was a moment's silence as we all examined the Friday afternoon shoppers, then Emma said, "Can neither of you actually *see?*"

"Hey, I have *great* vision," I snapped. "Distance isn't so good, admittedly, but low light—"

"What are you talking about, Ems?" Gertrude said over me. "What're we missing?"

She waved a hand at the crowded market. "How many of them are acting normally?"

"That's a big statement for humans," I said, and Gertrude made an agreeing noise. "I mean, is there a normal? Really?"

Emma looked as if she wanted to swat one of us on the

nose, but didn't. "How many are actually shopping? How many are just standing there, staring at the meat, looking confused? And look – there's a woman over there eating chicken hearts out of a bag."

"Ugh," Gertrude said.

"Ooh, chicken hearts," I said.

This time Emma actually did swat me, tapping me lightly on the head. "Pay attention, you muppet."

"Hey! That was a really small bowl of tuna—"

"Look," she said, and picked me up.

Usually I object strongly to being picked up without warning. Think about it. Is there any way clearer way to take away someone's autonomy than by scooping them up and squishing them against you like a stuffed toy? Ask permission, people. No one should be touched against their will.

But, all that said, Emma smelled even better close up than she had when she'd scritched my head, and she was a lot less bony than Callum, so I didn't bite her. Plus, she wasn't fussing. I can't stand fussing.

"Look properly," she said again. "You too, Gertrude."

She strolled along the line of fishmongers, and as much as the scent of the distant sea made my whiskers twitch, I kept my eyes on the shoppers instead. They were mostly turned the other way, toward the meat counters across the aisle, other than a woman in chef's whites pointing at scallops and a bearded man with fleshy tentacles fringing his neck who was buying seaweed. It was crowded down here, but no one was actually moving. Or not moving much. The odd person pushed through the crowd, muttering, but the majority of them seemed to just be *waiting,* like concertgoers before the doors open. I spotted the woman with her chicken hearts, and caught a whiff of spoilt meat as Emma carried me past. The woman's eyes were half shut, a trickle of bloody drool dribbling down her chin.

"Ew," I said quietly, even given the fact that chicken hearts are delectable.

"Her soul is sticky," Gertrude said, lingering near the woman. "Not squidgy yet, but sticky."

I shivered, thinking of Callum gnawing his bones on the bench, and Emma rubbed the back of my head absently.

"Look," she said. "There's another one."

This was a teenage boy, a raw hamburger patty in each hand and headphones dangling around his neck. He alternated bites from each patty, humming to himself quietly while he chewed. I half-recognised the tune.

Emma reached the end of the row and started back along the butcher's side. Not all the stalls were meat stalls, of course. There were places selling spices, a cafe-type place with hand-written menus and tables made out of pallets, and a phone shop, because there's always a phone shop. And from my new perspective, less worried about being stood on, I could see the crowd was gathering in clumps around the display cabinets of meat.

A small girl had her face pushed against the front of one, licking the glass. I could see a dressing on her arm, taped down with dinosaur plasters. Her mum stood behind her, eating a marinated chicken wing. Not a cooked one. Judging by the muck on the girl's face, she'd already eaten all hers. The rotund man behind the counter stared at both of them with a kind of restrained horror, as if he couldn't believe what he was seeing but wasn't about to turn away sales.

"Would you like to try the sweet chili?" he said as we went past. "It's very popular, and not too spicy. Good for the littlies."

The little girl growled and stretched her hands toward him, and he took a step back from the counter.

Further on, an old man sat on the seat of his walker, his dentures on the ground beside him. He was sucking enthusiastically on a lamb chop, blood decorating his immaculate pullover. An equally old lady sat on the ground next to him, and when he reached out to take a bone from her lap she smacked his hand away with a hiss.

All of which was weird enough, but all around them people were just *standing,* staring at the meat counters and the people already eating with an uncomfortable mix of horror and hunger. No one said anything to the eaters. No one laughed or pointed, not even the people behind the counters, who just kept serving and trying not to make eye contact. Some of the waiting crowd shuffled around as if they were trying to leave but couldn't quite manage it. One woman was hugging herself, shaking her head hard enough that her hair flew.

"Vegan," she said as we walked past. "Vegan!"

"Yeah, good luck with that," I muttered, and Emma gave me a rather less friendly pat.

More were arriving, too. Not pouring in, but as we walked back toward Callum a skinny man with a bushy beard hurried through the market doors, his eyes wide. He came to a stumbling halt in front of the meat counters, closing his eyes and breathing deeply, a smile tipping up the corners of his lips, as if arriving home to the smell of baking bread. Behind him, a woman rushed through the door and straight to the nearest butcher, pointing at the lambs' kidneys desperately.

"Those," she said. "Hurry!"

"Would you like 100 grams, or—"

"All of them!"

The young woman behind the counter gave her a started look, but just dished up the kidneys. It was going to be a good day for the butchers.

Emma stepped around a man in paint-splattered work trousers sitting with his back against the wall, three barbecue packs set on the floor in front of him. He was eating his way methodically though a raw kebab, sausages and chicken legs still piled in front of him, and when Gertrude stopped to examine him he growled at her, pulling the meat protectively closer.

"Awesome," I said. "This is just so, so awesome."

19

WE DEAL WITH THESE THINGS IN-HOUSE

WE MADE OUR WAY BACK TO THE BENCH WHERE WE'D LEFT Callum. He was still there, the pork shoulder almost stripped to the bone already. He nodded at us as we sat down, his attention on the meat.

"Well," Gertrude said, rocking on her heels thoughtfully. "At least we know where to find them."

"Some of them," I said. "I mean, we've got *a* zombie in the stall up there, but he can't have bitten all these people. There must be other full zombies, and how do we find them?"

"They all seem to be coming here," Gertrude said. "They must smell it. It draws them."

"We don't know that it's the market in particular," I said. "There might be half a dozen helping themselves to the Marks and Spencer deli display as we speak."

"There might," the reaper agreed. "There also might be four more corpses rising right now with no one there to stop them. There's plenty we don't know. All we can do is deal with what we *do* know."

I stared at the massed almost-zombies, swaying and muttering and scoffing raw meat like doughnuts. "How do we do that, then? And how many *are* there?"

"Forty-three," Gertrude said, then added, "Oh, forty-four," as a man staggered through the doors and headed for the butchers.

"Are we sure they're all infected?" Emma asked.

"Oh, yes. Now I know what to look for, you can see it very clearly. It's like a little sign above their heads," the reaper said.

"Awesome," I said again. "Awesome, *awesome.* Forty-four almost-zombies out here. One real zombie locked up in there. Who knows how many of both still running around. And my partner's a meat addict."

We turned to look at him, and he smiled back at us, displaying pink-stained teeth. "Forty-five," Gertrude said. "I forgot about Callum."

"Forty-five. Perfect," I said, and looked at Callum. "Give me your phone, dude."

"Sure," he said cheerfully, and fished it out of his pocket, holding it out to me.

"Put it down on the seat," I said, as patiently as I could. Which wasn't very, but he didn't seem to mind. He just set the phone next to him and went back to his bone. Well, he was more agreeable as an almost-zombie. I had to give him that.

"I'm calling Ms Jones," I said to Emma and the reaper. "We need that antidote."

"That seems like a good idea," Emma said. "And no one's leaving, so I think if we're careful we can contain things in here."

"That's good," I said. "Yeah, I like that."

"We can tell the other stall holders to leave," Gertrude said. "Clear the area."

"The Folk'll probably go," I said, "But the humans might be more difficult."

"Oh, Gertrude can be very persuasive," Emma said, squeezing the reaper's arm.

"I imagine she can, at that," I said, patting the phone with my paw. I really wanted one with a touchscreen, but Callum said he didn't want to make things too easy for me. He already shut the laptop when he wasn't in the room so I couldn't get online. I mean, it was *one* bad email. Maybe two. "Ugh, can someone help me?"

As Emma picked up the phone there was an explosion of screaming from deeper in the market. The crowd of almost-zombies didn't even look up, but there were some gasps from the stallholders, and one of the butchers pushed out from behind the counter with a cleaver, staring anxiously down the alley.

"What's going on?" he yelled. "It's the bloody greengrocers again, isn't it? They're always at it! Where's security?"

Something smashed, and more shouting broke out.

"Hairballs," I said, and leaped off the bench, racing after Gertrude as the reaper sprinted toward the commotion, scythe in one hand and her robes bundled up in the other. "Call Ms Jones!" I yelled at Emma. "Hurry!"

And if they didn't have an antidote, I didn't know what came next. The end of custard, most likely.

Reapers are *fast*. I guess lost souls require quick action.

Gertrude raced through the maze of alleys and pathways that made up the market, dodging fleeing shoppers and alarmed stallholders with easy, thoughtless grace (although her scythe did catch on an overhead banner at one point, shredding it straight down the middle. It took some fancy paw-work to dodge that one). I was running flat out to keep up with her, my ears back and my tail streaming behind me like a rather more elegant banner than the one she'd just destroyed.

In the muddle of stalls and shops and lingering, confused-looking shoppers, we almost ran straight past the scene of the commotion. Well, *a* scene of commotion. My flicking ears caught shouts from elsewhere, too, but the scream that pulled us on was urgent and visceral, coming from the area of quieter stalls crowded on the edge of the market, near where we'd trapped our zombie. Gertrude changed direction as smoothly and instantly as if she'd been planning it. I overshot the corner, stopped so hard I almost fell on my nose, and took off again, now trailing the reaper by a good stall's length.

We charged down a narrow lane between a pet supply store and a shop selling used CDs and DVDs, dodging a woman with a decrepit, yapping poodle in a pink baby stroller, rounded the corner of the music shop, and came to a stumbling halt on the edge of a multi-hued scene of destruction.

"Oh dear," Gertrude said.

I sneezed.

Wherever the fight had started, it had rolled its way through a greengrocer's, into a spice and international food shop, and back out again. Great drifts of turmeric and paprika and cinnamon swept across the ground, studded with papayas and yams and weird spiky fruit that didn't look particularly edible. Well, fruit is pretty inedible generally, so who knows.

Fragrant clouds of dust spun into the air as cans of coconut milk and jackfruit and lychees tumbled about the place, and the dwarf in a nearby stall was trying to get his shutter down, yelling that his stock was going to be *ruined.* He had a point – he seemed to specialise in cream-coloured embroidered pillowcases and duvet covers. A woman in a spice-smeared apron was hitting a large man about the head with a broom while he protested that he was just trying to help, and a faery in a black apron with hair clips stuck to the straps was waving a pair of scissors and threatening to chop someone's ears off if everyone didn't calm down.

And in the middle of it all, raising plumes of spices and knocking cans from displays and squashing mandarins and strawberries, Big Ted, a woman with no teeth, and a teenager with pink hair were wrestling a small but very irate zombie. A proper one, all groans and grave dirt and snapping teeth.

I opened my mouth to tell them to let go, and sneezed again. Then again. Apparently paprika doesn't agree with me.

Gertrude stepped in. "Stop this right now," she scolded them. "This is not the way to handle things!"

"What do you suggest, then?" the man fending off the shopkeeper shouted. "She just tried to bite me!"

"We're on it," Big Ted bellowed. "We've got this under control!"

"It bit me!" the teenager shrieked. "I'm going to go all night of the living dead!"

"Oh dear," Gertrude said, and I sneezed again.

"Security are coming!" the shopkeeper shouted, hitting the man with her broom again. He grabbed an empty spice tub to fend her off. "This is public disorder, and destruction of property, and—"

"Everyone calm down," Gertrude said. "I'm sure we can handle this civilly—" she broke off as the dwarf ducked out from under his stall shutter with a cricket bat.

"I'm going to brain you *all* unless you stop!" he yelled. "We're just trying to run our businesses—"

"Yeah!" the greengrocer shouted, and started pelting the fighters with potatoes. She looked fairly human, although there was a distinctly green tinge to her hair. That might have been dye, though. "Get out of my veggies!"

"You're destroying our stock! Stop it!" The dwarf shook his bat warningly at the tussling group.

"You don't understand," Big Ted started, and I opened my mouth to tell him to shut up before we had a complete panic on our paws. All that came out was a wheeze, and I clawed Gertrude's robes.

She gave me a disapproving look. "What?"

"Big Ted," I managed, then started sneezing again before I could add, *is meant to be watching the stall.*

Gertrude straightened up. "Who's Big Ted?"

"He is," the stallholders and the man with the spice tub chorused, like some cut-rate pantomime audience. Big

Ted glared at us as he tried to wrestle the moaning zombie into a headlock.

"What? I don't see any of *you* doing anything helpful," he half-shouted at us. "This is the *zombie apocalypse*, you bananas!"

"Yeah!" the teenager with the pink hair yelled, and in the distraction the zombie bit the toothless woman, threw its head back and smacked Big Ted in the mouth, kicked Pink Hair, and scrambled out from under all three of them. Big Ted grabbed a handful of its dirt-caked burial cardigan, but the zombie surged forward with the sound of popping buttons and tearing stitching, ripped itself loose and bolted off between the stalls.

"After it!" Big Ted shouted.

"Everyone *stop!*" Gertrude shouted over the top of him, but no one was listening. The three fighters, the man with the spice tub, the dwarf with the cricket bat, the greengrocer (clutching a bag of potatoes), the stallholder with her broom and the faery with his scissors all legged it after the zombie. Or Big Ted and his team were after the zombie. I think everyone else was more worried about damages for the stalls.

"Hairballs," I wheezed, and sneezed so hard I sat down. By the time I got up and started jogging after them, Gertrude was gone too.

"Hairballs with cucumber pickles on," I mumbled, and pushed faster, still sneezing paprika.

By the time I caught up to them they were clustered in a nervous group around Gertrude, watching the zombie snuffling its way along the front of our undead prison. Or living dead, or whatever. It pressed its hands against the shutter and moaned, and an answering moan came from inside. There was a pause which felt uncomfortably like the two corpses were silently communicating (or worse, *thinking about stuff*), then they both started attacking the shutter. That seemed bad. It had been strong enough to hold against one of them, but two I wasn't sure about.

"What's wrong with him?" the spice stallholder asked, jabbing her broom at the zombie. She was quite a striking shade of yellow from all the turmeric.

"It's a virus," Gertrude said, before Big Ted could say anything. "It activates the aggression nodes in the, um, left lesser cortico gland."

There was silence for a moment, then the teenager said, "Well, that's not even a thing. And aggression's controlled between the amygdala and the prefrontal cortex, anyway. Are you from the government or something?"

Gertrude glared at her. "Do I *look* like I'm from the government?"

"You look like you're from a fancy-dress shop," the woman with no teeth said, and Gertrude drew herself up indignantly.

"These robes are handmade. *Handmade!*"

The dwarf waved his cricket bat. He was wearing white silk trousers and a matching tunic, embroidered with cream thread and decorated with large paprika handprints. "I don't *care* what's causing it. I just want to know who's going to compensate me for loss of stock!" He looked down at himself. "And for my dry-cleaning bill."

"Yeah," the greengrocer said. "And loss of business!"

"And the clean-up," the faery added. "There's cumin all over my dye table. I'm probably going to have to replace all my brushes, too."

I glared at them all, my tail whipping, and wondered how many of them would be shocked if I started shouting. I *wanted* to start shouting. Here they were, squabbling about lost carrots or whatever, and there was a *zombie* trying to set another zombie free right in front of them, and gods knew how many more almost zombies just waiting to get bitey on us. And it wasn't just the humans, either. The dwarf and the faery were being just as useless. What is it with people never wanting to see what's right in front of them?

"Hey," someone said, and Big Ted crouched down next to me, the vast drifts of his beard decorated with dried bay leaves and some snow pea shoots.

"Dude," I said. "Are they all *blind?*"

"Most people are," he said.

"Yeah, well. This the only other zombie so far?"

"Only one we've found. Melody and Terror found it hanging out in the loos." He waved at the teenager and the toothless woman.

"Terror?"

"Tera. With an A. She's the younger one."

"Oh." I looked at his bandaged hand. "How's that bite doing?"

"Seems alright. Kind of fancy something meaty, but no brains yet."

"That's good," I said. The guy really was huge. Maybe it spread at different rates depending on body mass.

He nodded, and looked around. "Where's Callum?"

The paprika or cumin or what-have-you clogged up my throat, and I had to cough before I answered. "Hungry."

"Aw, bollocks. I'm sorry."

"We've got someone working on a cure," I said. "We're going to fix this."

He examined me with red-rimmed eyes, his eyelashes still clogged with dried spices. "So what do we do next?"

I started to say, *no, you've done enough,* then stopped. He'd seen his friend killed, and he'd come back and taken on a zombie. *Two* zombies. People who live on the edges of things don't just see more. Sometimes they're capable of more, too. It's just that no one ever gives them a chance. Not that I'm saying zombie hunting is a good place to start, but it did occur to me that if anyone could handle zombies, this Sasquatch of a man might just be able to. So I said, "Get this one locked up, for starters."

"Good," he said. "Let's do it."

GERTRUDE WAS STILL TRYING to explain that she was a small business owner herself, and so understood the difficulties they were all facing, but they weren't getting anywhere by arguing, so would everyone please just calm down, and maybe if they could all have a nice cup of tea and talk about it in a civilised manner they might make some progress? I decided there was no point distracting her, and that I preferred handling zombies to civilians, so I left her to it and followed Big Ted as he shambled over to Terror and Melody. Or Tera, whatever.

We huddled together while the reaper and the others argued behind us, and the zombies shook the shutter angrily ahead of us.

"Can you all hear me?" I asked them.

"Of courth, no one'th deaf," Melody said. She'd found some novelty vampire teeth somewhere and popped them in her mouth, but they didn't fit very well and made her lisp.

"Don't mind her," Terror said, giving the older woman a one-armed hug. "Dental care's expensive."

"Try being a cat," I told her. "We don't get fillings. We get a general anaesthetic and our teeth pulled out. But anyway, I actually meant most people can't hear cats."

"We're not most people," Big Ted said, which was about as true as you could get.

"Fair enough," I said. "Best option I see right now is we trap the zombie in the stall. We just have to make sure the other one doesn't get out while we're at it."

"Thouldn't we jutht, you know," Melody asked, running a finger across her throat.

"We could," I agreed, "but someone's working on a cure. Three test subjects seem better than two."

"You actually need a bigger sample size than that to really test a treatment," Terror said. "You can't get reliable results with just three subjects."

I breathed out slowly, then said, "It's better than two, right?"

"Sure. Just, you know."

I looked at Big Ted. "We also need to calm the stall-holders down and make sure no one's actually called the police."

"They haven't even called security," he said. "Stuff like this we tend to deal with in-house."

"Stuff like this? Like zombies?"

"Well, no. Not usually them," he admitted. "Just the odd disagreement."

That seemed a weird way to describe a fight with a zombie that destroyed an entire spice stall and half a greengrocer's, but I wasn't about to argue. I glanced at Gertrude, but she was in the middle of explaining the best way to file insurance claims for damaged stock. No one looked in danger of being prematurely reaped, at least.

"I'll distract the zombies," Terror said, pushing her hands back through her hair. "I can get them to chase me into the stall if you make sure they don't follow me out."

"Don't let them bite you," Melody said, taking her teeth out and putting them back in her pocket. "Maybe I should do it."

"No. I'm faster." Terror shrugged, and pushed her sleeves up. "Besides, what's one more bite?"

I looked at the ring of tooth marks on her forearm, still oozing blood. "There'll be a cure," I promised her, hoping I meant it. "There will."

"Good," she said. "Let's do it, then." And she bounced up and ran straight at the shutters, light-footed in trainers, yelling, "Come get your munchies here!"

She hit the shutters hard, pounded her fists on them, then bounced off and danced away as the free zombie spun around and snarled at her. Inside the shutter, I could hear the other one moaning.

Big Ted and Melody raced forward, Melody grabbing the bottom of the shutter and hauling up as Big Ted dropped to his knees beside the latch.

"It's *locked*," he yelled. Terror dodged the zombie and ran back a few paces, then rushed forward again to kick the shutter. Inside, the first undead roared and pounded on the metal. "Callum locked it!"

"Then *unlock* it," I yelled at him, and flung myself at the zombie as it grabbed for Terror. I raked my claws across its face and jumped clear again. It followed me with a strangled moan that was trying to climb into a roar.

"I don't have a key," he shouted back.

I shot between the zombie's legs, its fingers sliding off my fur unpleasantly. It almost overbalanced on its face, but recovered and turned its attention back to Terror. "What? Why not?"

"We're squatters. Why the hell would we have a key?"

"Just get it open!" Melody leaped onto the back of the zombie as it lunged at Terror, wrapping her legs around its torso and grabbing handfuls of its hair. "Hurry!"

"Mel!" Terror ran forward to trap the zombie's hands before it could batter the older woman. "Don't let it bite you!"

"I am trying!"

The creature inside the stall kept up its assault on the shutter, pounding so violently it sounded like the metal was going to tear apart any moment, and Big Ted grabbed the door to either side of the latch, pulling so hard I could see the veins bulging in his neck and forehead.

"It won't give," he yelled at me, as if I could do anything about it.

"Bolt cutters?" I suggested, and even Terror stopped tussling with the zombie to give me an insulted look.

Then Gertrude swept past me, her scythe poised over her shoulder. Big Ted gave a yelp and rolled away, and she brought the blade down in one smooth motion. There was a clink as the padlock split cleanly in two and fell to the ground, and she said, "Quickly!"

Big Ted grabbed the bottom of the shutter and hauled up. Terror ran in before it was more than halfway up, plunging into the dark and straight into the belly of the waiting zombie, carrying it backward like a rugby player charging into a tackle.

"Terror!" Melody shouted, and dropped to the ground, although she kept her grip on the zombie's hair and hauled the moaning corpse into the stall with her.

"Get out!" Big Ted shouted at both of them. "Hurry, hurry, come *on!*"

I shot into the dim confines of the stall, eyes wide. Melody seemed to have decided her technique was working well, and had a handful of each zombie's hair, shouting at both of them. The older corpse had grabbed Terror as she tackled it, and was trying to wrestle her close enough to bite while she braced herself against its chest with one arm. She'd clamped the other hand to the second zombie's jaw, stopping it from biting Melody, and the two zombies and two humans staggered back and forth among the scattered blankets and unidentifiable body parts like some weird deep-sea organism.

"Hairballs," I muttered, while behind me Big Ted lunged under the shutter. "Hang on!"

"What the hell d'you think we're doing?" Terror bellowed, and I gathered myself to leap into the middle of a whole lot of zombie teeth.

I launched myself off the ground, aiming for Zombie Two's face and trying not to think too much about what would happen when I had its full attention, and as I flared my claws and let loose my most threatening screech a hand snatched me out of the air. My yowl went from defiant to alarmed as I wondered if we'd missed a third corpse, then I was deposited in a pocket that smelled of fabric softener and cake and stardust splintering in the infinite, lost reaches of the universe.

20

NO ONE BITES EMMA

I CLAWED MY WAY TO THE TOP, SPLUTTERING, JUST IN TIME to see Gertrude crack Zombie One between the eyes with the stock of the scythe. It collapsed to the ground, releasing Terror, and the reaper dealt the same hard blow to Zombie Two.

"They're not dead, are they?" I asked, my paws hooked over the top of her pocket. "We need them alive for testing."

"I know perfectly well how hard to hit someone," Gertrude said, watching the smaller zombie crumple to the ground. "Well, mostly. There may be some mild concussion. Well, possibly severe. But they're not *dead.*"

Terror wiped her hands on her trousers. "Awesome. Can I have a go with that?"

"No, you may not," Gertrude said, tucking the scythe a little closer to her. "Everyone out."

She herded the humans out of the stall, and gave Big Ted some money to go and buy a new padlock. The stall-holders were comparing notes on their smartphones as they wrote up insurance claims, just as if there hadn't been a battle to the death going on next to them. Well, battle to the unconsciousness.

"Hey," one of them called. "Will you be a witness?"

"Of course," Gertrude said. "Just print out your statement and I'll sign it."

I looked up at her and said, "Can I get out now? I can't help feeling I might fall through a black hole in the bottom of your pocket." I peered down. "Unless there's some cat biscuits in here."

"No eating in my pockets," she said, lifting me out. "One shouldn't feed the black holes."

The faery trotted up to Gertrude and offered her a mug with Tinker Bell printed on it. *Sprinkle a little fairy dust!* it said.

"Tea?" he said. His beard was immaculately coiffed, and had little silver bumblebees dangling in it like misplaced earrings.

The reaper stared at the mug. "Really? Tinker Bell? I thought faeries hated her."

He shrugged. "It's ironic, isn't it?"

"Is it?" But she took the mug and stood there looking awkward while the faery went to ask the dwarf how he'd described the damage to his stock.

"Devastating," the dwarf said firmly, and the faery nodded.

"Seems reasonable."

I sat down to clean zombie from under my claws, and after a few more murmured comments, there was one of those strange pauses that humans seem to suffer from – and reapers, too, apparently. Well, they're former humans,

I suppose, so it just goes to show how long they cling to these things. Gertrude was still examining her mug, looking dubious, and the man with the spice tub rocked back on his heels and looked at the ceiling, and the woman from the spice stall examined her stained nails. The greengrocer was holding her bag of potatoes against her chest like a lumpy child, and even the faery and the dwarf, definitions of damage resolved, looked a little uncomfortable.

"So," Spice Tub said. "Nice weather we're having."

"I heard it's meant to hail by tonight," Greengrocer said.

"Never lasts, does it?" Spice Woman said, taking a sip of her tea, and everyone seemed to relax a bit.

I looked up at Gertrude, who was still staring at her tea. "Are you going to drink that or what?"

"I can't drink it."

"Oh." I thought about it. "Oh, because you're dead?"

"Technically dead," she corrected me.

"That's cool," a voice said next to her. "Explains the scythe. I *love* the scythe. Are you sure I can't try it?"

"You may not," Gertrude said, adjusting her hood a little.

"Fair enough," Terror said. "Can we have your tea, then?"

"Oh, yes." The reaper handed the mug over, and Terror passed it to Melody, who took a loud slurp.

"Take your teeth out," Terror told the older woman, and she did, tucking them into her pocket.

"Are you dealing with this, then?" the dwarf asked Gertrude. "Only we have some stalls to clean up."

The faery glanced at his watch and yelped. "Godsdammit! I'm late for a client!" He turned and sprinted back toward his tiny salon, his carefully styled hair bouncing elegantly.

Gertrude looked at me. "I do suppose we are dealing with it. What about them, though?" She nodded at the humans, who had moved on from today's weather to what the weather used to be like when they were children.

"Now *those* were winters," Greengrocer said, and sighed.

"And proper summers," Spice Woman agreed. "Oh, do you remember the ladybirds?"

"Nineteen seventy-six," Spice Tub said. "My mum still talks about it."

"They'll be fine," the dwarf said. "A cup of tea and some talk about the weather is like a human reset button. There was a goblin brawl in here a few months back. They completely smashed three stalls and started a fire in the kebab shop, and all the humans had forgotten an hour later. It's like it all sort of falls out of their minds after a cup of tea."

It made sense. I'm ninety-nine percent convinced that tea has magical properties. A good thing it doesn't make Callum forget things, though, because the amount he drinks he wouldn't even know who *he* was, let alone me.

"Shall we get back?" I asked Gertrude.

"Hey, you're not just leaving those things in there?" the dwarf said. "I mean, the humans might not remember, but I don't fancy having a … whatever those were hanging over my shoulder when I'm locking up tonight."

"They shall be dealt with," the reaper said.

"Personally, I'd close early, though," I added. "There might be some disruption to regular services, so to speak." The dwarf gave me an alarmed look.

Big Ted jogged up, waving a padlock. "Will this do?"

"I'm sure it'll be fine," Gertrude said, barely glancing at it. "Just get it locked." She turned her attention back to the dwarf. "Gobbelino's right. Can you tell all the stallholders to close early? Try and clear the market?"

The dwarf snorted. "I can try. Don't see it happening, though. Have you seen Butcher's Row? They're having an awesome day— Oh. *Oh.* Oh, hairy elf bollocks."

"There it is," I said and Gertrude gave me a disapproving look.

"The market's going to close in like, half an hour," Terror said. "Why don't we just wait it out?"

"That seems better," the dwarf said. "I, personally, might shut early though." And he hurried off before anyone could suggest he do anything helpful.

"Well, that's very uncooperative," Gertrude observed.

"We can help," Terror said, taking a swig of tea.

"Definitely," Big Ted agreed, showing Gertrude her change. "Did you want this back?"

"No," she said wearily, as the human stallholders turned toward us.

"There should be compensation of some sort," Spice Tub said.

"Or at least reparations," the greengrocer agreed. "You know, they should come and clean up for us." She waved at Big Ted and the two women vaguely.

"We're a bit busy," Terror said.

"Zombie-hunting," Melody added, baring her gums in a grin.

"Well, that's hardly an excuse," Spice Woman said.

Gertrude rubbed her face with one pale hand. "I didn't know I could still feel tired."

"It's amazing the things you learn when hanging around with humans," I told her.

"Evidently," she said.

THE STALLHOLDERS (and Spice Tub Man, who didn't seem to belong to a stall but had made himself at home in the middle of it all, apparently for his own amusement) were still arguing with the other humans when Emma marched out of the maze of stalls, guiding Callum with one hand hooked though his elbow. He was still chewing on a bone, and another couple were sticking out of his coat pockets. Jan hurried along behind them, clutching a blue, hard plastic cooler to his chest and looking vaguely queasy.

"*There* you are," Emma said. "Honestly, I was wondering what had happened to you. Everything's getting a bit weird. Some people started climbing into the butchers' stalls, and a fishmonger bit a policeman, and a florist hit someone over the head with a potted palm. I figured we should leave." She looked at the arguing humans. "What happened here?"

"Humans," Gertrude said, waving at the squabbling group. "Humans happened."

"Also zombies," I said. "But the humans were the main issue."

"Hmm," Emma said, and wandered over to listen to them.

I looked up at Callum. "Hey."

"Hey," he said, still gnawing on the gristle, and he sounded so much like himself that I half-expected him to drop the bone and shove his hands in his pockets, and give me the half-smile that showed his crooked tooth on the left side. But he didn't. He just kept chewing. I could hear his teeth scraping on the bone.

"Well, he's not a zombie yet," Gertrude said. "That's something."

"It's not much, though, is it?" I said, then added to Jan, "Where's the sorcerer?"

He blinked at me. "Who?"

I took a deep breath. "Ms Jones. Who was helping you make the antidote."

"Oh. Um. She left."

"She *left?*" I demanded. "What d'you mean, *she left?*"

"That seems very casual," Gertrude said. "How odd."

Jan clutched the cooler a little more tightly. "She said she had to check something. We came up with a new formula, though."

"You did? Is that it?" I asked.

He didn't quite look at me. "Well, I've got *something.* But I don't know the long-term effects. Or how it'll work on someone who's not actually a zombie. Or—"

"How did it work on your zombie?" Gertrude asked.

"Well. Yes. It … it killed it—"

"It *killed* it?" I said. "That is not the result we're going for."

"I know, I know." I could smell Jan's sweat even over

the lingering dust of spices. "But, you know, it was a corpse. It *should* have been dead."

I looked up at Gertrude. She just returned my gaze, not saying anything. Not that I supposed there was much to say. After all, it had either killed the zombie, or returned it to its pre-zombie state, which was also dead. The only way to tell which was to test it on someone else.

Emma clapped her hands, drawing our attention, and we watched her shoo the humans away. They trouped off in the direction of the ruined stalls and she turned to us, smiling.

"What did you do?" I asked her.

"Just told them to stop arguing and sort themselves out," she said. "Life's too short for squabbling over spilt spices."

"Spilt milk," I said.

"That's crying," Jan said, and we all looked at him. "Sorry." He lifted the lid of the cooler and peered inside, as if making sure nothing had escaped.

"Well done, dear," Gertrude said. "They were giving me quite the headache."

"You can't get headaches, G," Emma said, patting the reaper's arm affectionately. "But that's quite alright."

"What do we do?" I asked them. "This antidote might just kill him." The damn spices were still making my throat feel claggy.

"If I just had more time," Jan started, and I bared my teeth at him.

"I wasn't asking you. And what time? We've got a whole market full of almost-zombies already!"

"Gobbelino's right," Emma said. "How many doses do you have?"

"Well. It's only experimental, you understand, so I still don't know the exact dose, and then there are variables such as body weight and comp—"

"How many?" I yowled at him.

He flinched. "Fifteen. Maybe twenty if we took it right down to the smallest dose that I could imagine would be effective."

"Fifteen. Fifteen and there's ... how many? Forty-five?"

"More now," Emma said. "They keep coming in."

"You ... you parsnip," I said to the mortician. "You mouldy potato. What did you think fifteen doses was going to do?"

"Maybe twenty," he said, his voice small. "But it was all I had the components for. And Ms Jones just *left,* so what could I do?"

I looked at Emma. "You were meant to call Ms Jones."

"I did," she said. "She told me she'd send the antidote."

"Great. That's just *great,*" I said, and when Emma crouched down next to me I pulled away from her. *"Don't touch me."*

"Sorry." She stood up again, tucking her hands into the pockets of her denim jacket. "So, what do we do?"

I watched Callum turning the bone in his hands, looking for a way into the marrow. "I don't know," I said.

I'M NOT sure how long we might have stood there, mired in a swamp of indecision, with two zombies moaning behind the shutters to remind us of where Callum was headed, and Callum happily oblivious to it all while the rest of us tried to decide whether it was better to risk killing him now or take that risk on someone else. I mean, left to myself I wouldn't have minded finding someone else, but I suppose it was a bit of a grey area ethically. I was pretty certain Gertrude wouldn't agree, and I didn't fancy arguing with her, no matter how comfy her pockets were.

But, as it happened, I didn't even have the chance to consider sneaking Jan off and getting him to jab someone down the meat hall while the reaper was looking the other way.

Well.

Okay, yes, I *considered* it. But I didn't have a chance to *act* on it, because just then Callum dropped his bone. It almost landed on me, and I scooted a couple of steps away. He gave an uncomfortable groan.

"Oh dear," Emma said. "I thought the pork might be a bad idea."

"I don't think that's it," Gertrude said, and Jan backed away so rapidly he almost tripped over his own feet.

Callum swayed, his gaze fixed on the ground, and opened his mouth wide, like he was stretching the muscles after all the chewing.

Emma grabbed his waist as he wobbled again. "There we go," she said. "Let's get you sat down."

He moaned.

"Emma, let him go," Gertrude said. "Quickly!"

"He's not—" she started, then gave a yelp as he snapped at her, lips drawn away from his teeth and his eyes rolling.

"Callum!" I yelled, but he didn't even flinch. Emma tried to pull away from him, but he had hold of her jacket with both hands, clawing her closer as she fought to wriggle out of it. He was growling in a way that raised the fur on my spine, and I shouted his name again.

"Emma, *duck*," Gertrude said, and as Emma dropped to her knees, arms pulled up over her head by the sleeves of her jacket, the reaper smacked Callum squarely between the eyes with the butt of her scythe. He crumpled to the ground without even a whimper, taking Emma with him.

"*Hey!*" I yelled, "That's still Callum! We're trying to save him, remember?"

"Sorry," Gertrude said. "No one bites Emma."

"Thank you," Emma said, and leaned over Callum's chest. "He's still breathing."

"He's still breathing?" I said. "So that means he's not a zombie yet, right?"

"I would think not." She looked at Jan. "Let's see your antidote."

He reached into the cooler and produced a syringe, pale liquid half-filling it, and took the little plastic cap off the needle before he handed it to her. She looked at it, then at him, and said, "So, what? I just jab him?"

"Um. Yes."

"Where? At the bite?"

"I … I'm not sure. I've only tried it on a corpse. That wasn't bitten. It was an original."

"I don't even know what that means." She stared at him. "Did it work?"

"It died."

"Your only test subject has been a corpse that died."

"Yes?"

She looked at me. "Gobbelino, your call. I don't know if this is going to work or not."

My chest felt as though the first damn zombie, the one from the cemetery that had started this whole ridiculous thing in motion, was sitting on top of me again, and for the first time in four lives I wanted to chuck up some excellent top-shelf tuna. The spices had really done a number on me.

I looked at the mortician. "Where's Ms Jones? We could really use her right now."

"I don't know," he said. "I'm sorry."

I walked over to Callum and stood staring down at him. I didn't know either, about anything. I didn't trust Jan's antidote, and I didn't know if I was killing Callum, and I didn't know what I'd do if it did kill him, and I wished humans had more than one life, but then it wouldn't help because he'd be a baby, and humans take *so long* to become useful, and—

I closed my eyes and forced my claws down against the hard concrete, listening to the confused noises of the market as stalls pulled shutters down and shoppers filed out into the spring dusk, and someone – or more than one someone – shouted something that I couldn't quite catch. The whiff of old cigarettes and damp drifted from Callum's hideous coat, and under it I could smell rot and poison and a slow, creeping hunger that made my chest hurt.

It was the sort of old hunger that swallowed all else, and for a moment I thought that was all there was, all that was left of him, and my stomach tightened painfully. I leaned a little closer, snuffling at his neck where his hair curled over his ears, desperate for something more familiar. And finally, there. Faint but sure. Dust and magic and a longing for silence.

"Do it," I said, and Emma slipped the syringe into his neck without hesitating, depressing the plunger, flooding his system with something that was kill or cure. Or both, as I guess if he did die, he wouldn't be a zombie anymore. Silver linings and all that.

Gertrude and Jan leaned over us, staring down at Callum's still form. Emma capped the syringe and handed it back to the mortician, then rested her ear on Callum's chest.

"He's still there," she said.

"His soul's still a bit muddled," Gertrude said, peering at him. "Not squidgy, though."

We waited.

I SQUINTED AT CALLUM, trying to decide if he looked slightly less pallid than he had a moment ago, but it was hard to say. He wasn't exactly the healthy glow type at the best of times. Emma was still kneeling next to him, and now she looked around.

"What's that?" she asked.

"What?" Jan asked, wiping sweat off his top lip with a shaky hand.

There was a moan from behind the shutters, then a louder one.

Gertrude frowned. "They shouldn't be up yet. I hit

them *very* hard."

"Yeah, how hard did you hit Callum?" I asked her.

"Not *as* hard," she said, after a moment's consideration.

Someone shouted deeper in the market, a quick short sound that could have been laughter or could have been a scream cut short.

Emma checked her watch. "Um ... are zombies nocturnal?"

We looked at each other, while the zombies in the stall banged against the shutter and moaned again.

"You made them," I said to Jan. "Ideas?"

"I don't really know," he admitted. "They did seem to only come out of the graves at night. But that last one just woke up in the middle of my lab."

"Your *mortuary,*" I said, raising my voice to be heard over the trapped zombies, who had apparently decided to hold an impromptu percussion concert. "Just so we're clear here. Those two in there have been active all along, though. Even when we were here earlier."

"No natural light in here," Gertrude said, her voice thoughtful. "Or in the mortuary. Maybe they feel the difference, even if they can still be active during daylight hours. That's how it is for me. I'm not nocturnal as such, but I don't do well in daylight. Plus I'm stronger at night. Faster."

"You're no zombie, though," Emma said, smiling at the reaper.

"No," Gertrude agreed. "But I am technically dead."

There was another shout from the direction of Butcher's Row, and this one was laced with alarm.

"Why d'you want to know?" I asked Emma.

She raised her wrist. "I've got sunset and sunrise times on my watch. The sun just went down."

There was another shout, this one from closer by, and the crash of something large falling. The zombies behind us started throwing themselves at the shutters.

"Shouldn't the market be closed by now?" Jan asked. "Doesn't it close at five-thirty?"

"I think so," Emma said. "But has anyone actually seen any security? Or anyone management-y?"

We looked at each other over Callum's still form, and a familiar voice said, "I think we could say that normal operations have been suspended."

I spun around to see two cats advancing across the floor, unhurried despite the man in a flour-dusted apron who ran past just behind them, clutching a baking tray and screaming something incomprehensible. One of them was Pru, her naked skin rendered pale and sickly in the fluorescent lighting. She watched the man pass with a distracted sort of interest.

The other was Claudia, a new scar on her nose and a notch in her left ear since I'd last seen her, but her pale, mismatched eyes just as clear and unsettling as before.

I drew myself up to my full height and put my best scars forward. "I was starting to think you weren't coming."

"Officially, I haven't," Claudia said. "But I could hardly pass up seeing what sort of mess you'd made this time, could I?"

And she winked, which could have meant anything, but was the best thing that had happened in at least two days.

21

ZOMBIE POTATOES

"Pru said the Watch weren't interested," I said, nodding at the Sphynx cat. She nodded back.

"They're not," Claudia said. "As far as they're concerned, this is human business."

"Seems a bit harsh."

Claudia gave an amused huff. "You of all cats should expect that."

"Eh." I looked at Callum, but nothing had changed. He still looked mostly dead. "I guess I thought the end of humanity might spark some interest."

Jan gave a wordless squawk, although whether that was due to more talking cats or the end of humanity, I wasn't sure. Emma patted him on the shoulder.

"Humanity's self-inflicted extinction is neither against the Watch's ethos nor entirely against their interests," Claudia said, ears flicking as a fresh wave of shouts broke out in the direction of the gates.

"But their souls are going squidgy," Gertrude said, frowning at the calico cat.

Claudia wrinkled her nose. "I'm not sure we have a lot of regard for souls."

The reaper sniffed, and shifted her grip on the scythe. "I'm definitely rethinking my stance on cats."

Claudia arched her whiskers in amusement. "You obviously haven't known us well enough previously."

"What's happening?" I asked, before the situation could deteriorate any further. "Is it really just us?"

"Just us," Claudia said. "We've sealed the gates. No one's getting in or out. Plus we threw a few hiding runes about, so no one's going to hear anything from outside."

Jan clutched Emma's arm, and Gertrude scowled at him.

"Can you help him?" Emma asked, looking down at Callum.

Claudia glanced at her. "You overestimate the healing powers of cats. Besides, a human made this. We don't have anything that can combat that, even if the Watch wanted to."

I narrowed my eyes at the mortician. "This better work."

He twisted his hands together. "Even if it does," he said, and flinched when I growled, "there isn't enough."

"There are other ways to deal with them," Claudia said. "Reaper? Are you willing to help?"

Gertrude frowned. "I don't reap living souls."

"They're undead," Pru said.

"That's vampires," Emma said, and Pru gave her a disapproving look. "What? It is. These are living dead."

"Oh, I'm so pleased to know the distinction," Pru said, examining a front paw, and Emma stuck her tongue out.

"Whatever sort of dead they are," Claudia said, "They're not exactly alive, either. I understand your reservations, Reaper, but the circumstances are ... exceptional."

Gertrude shook her head. "Actual zombies, yes. Like those two in there." She nodded at the stall, where the shutter was taking on dents and bulges from the assault of the creatures behind it. "Not if I can see the living soul still, like Callum."

Claudia narrowed her eyes. "And I suppose no one else wants to deal with them?"

"Dude," I started, as two women sprinted past in grim silence, both of them gripping shiny new saucepans. Well, fairly shiny. One had a smear of blood on it.

Claudia shook her head. "Not a dude, Gobbelino."

"Sorry. But look, these are *living people.* It's just like ... a really bad flu or something."

"That makes them want to eat each other's brains?"

"Sure. The point is, they're still *them* under it all. They can get better. He gave it to them." I nodded at Jan, who looked as if he were about to faint. "He can fix it." I hoped.

There was silence for a moment, Claudia's tail ticking restlessly. Something smashed in the nearby stalls.

"No one's braining my human," Pru announced, as if coming to a decision. "It took me ages to find a decent one, and I'll scratch the eyes out of anyone who even *looks* like braining her."

Claudia shook her head. "So, what? We just trap them here until we can find a cure?"

"We should *have* a cure," I said, glaring at Jan, who gave a funny little smile and waved his hands about vaguely.

Claudia blinked at him. "Reassuring," she said, and as

she spoke the shutters of the zombie stall exploded open, tearing off the tracks on one side with a scream of metal that made my ears flatten.

WE SPUN around to face them, my tail bushing out wildly. Someone screamed (I was pretty certain it was Jan), and Gertrude said, "Oh dear," like her Victoria sponge hadn't risen.

The zombies tumbled out of the stall, forcing their way through the torn shutter with their moans rising into an excited crescendo, and Gertrude stepped toward them, raising her scythe. The zombies paused, eyeing her. Then they dropped to all fours and charged, one heading to the left of us and the other to the right, their movements fast and sure and horrifying, so far from human or animal that the mind turned from it.

Gertrude stepped into the path of the shorter creature, and it slowed, feinting to one side then the other. She met it each time with her scythe raised, and it drew back before she could strike.

"Gertrude, be *careful!*" Emma shouted, and the zombie switched direction once more, plunging toward us where we still clustered around Callum.

Gertrude lunged after the zombie, scythe flashing as it swept under the thing, lopping its legs neatly off at the knees. They flopped to the floor, bloodless, and the creature raced on without even a pause, using its arms and shortened legs and chattering its teeth hungrily.

"Emma, *run!*" Gertrude shouted, sprinting after the zombie.

Emma grabbed Jan as he tried to flee and screamed, *"Antidote!"* at him.

I flung myself into the face of the second zombie as it charged, its breath foul on my fur, twisting my body away from its mouth as I tore at its face, aiming for the eyes. I didn't know if blinding it would make any difference at all, but I was willing to try. It grabbed me and ripped me away, and I heard Claudia snarl as she joined the attack. The zombie moaned and dropped me as it reached for her, then she was gone, shifting away, and Pru was there in her place. The zombie's moan raised up in pitch, and it staggered in a circle, pawing at her as Claudia reappeared and attacked its back. I ran up its legs, clawing and biting wherever I could reach, and the thing wailed.

"Down!" Emma shouted. She was running toward us, brandishing a metal pole she'd ripped from the construction wall. Claudia and Pru dropped to the ground as I jumped clear, and Emma swung the pole like one of those hammer-throwers you see on TV. It caught the zombie in the throat, spilling it to the ground, and her momentum sent her stumbling over it. The zombie grabbed her, jerking her to the floor as she screamed, and hauled her hungrily toward it.

"Emma!" Gertrude shouted, racing back with her robes swirling in shades of night. I threw myself into the brawl, only to have Jan trip over me as he rushed to the rescue, waving another a pole. He crashed to the ground, losing his grip on the pole, and Gertrude leaped over him as she brought her scythe down in a singing arc.

Emma screamed again, but the scythe whispered past her ear and plunged into the zombie's skull. Its hands fell away from her, and she stared at the reaper, her eyes wide. "That was almost me!"

"Of course it wasn't," Gertrude said, and helped her up. "It was nowhere near."

"I *felt* it!"

"Humans," Gertrude said with a sigh.

Jan sat up and glared at me. "Why'd you have to get in the way?"

"Why'd you have to *kick* me?" I snapped back.

"Ah," Pru said. "I think we have a problem."

"Another one?" Emma said, and we turned to follow Pru's gaze.

The walls of the construction site were collapsing, the metal sheeting sagging outward without the support of the poles. Half a dozen walking corpses in high viz jackets stared out at us over the collapsing wall, looking confused.

"Oops," Emma said.

"Hairballs," I said.

"You sure about the no braining?" Claudia asked, and Pru hissed at her, then scooted over to me.

"I thought you said she'd *help,*" she complained. "Gods-damned chocolate teapot!"

"I can *hear* you," Claudia snapped.

The six new zombies pushed at the wall, which flopped noisily to the floor, and they gave voice to excited moans as they started clambering over the metal, waving at us as eagerly as a pack of long-lost relatives. Deeper in the market, the screams were going from scattered to a chorus.

"We can't just kill them," I said. "They're still people."

"What do you want to do, then?" Claudia asked. "*Talk* to them?"

"We've got an antidote."

"Which may or may not work."

"Time," Jan panted. He'd picked up his metal bar again, and looked like he couldn't decide whether to just run or not. "Takes time."

"*If* it works," Claudia said. "I still think—"

Gertrude cut her off. "We're not killing them. I've reaped these two, even if their souls are ruined and they can't ... well, do whatever souls do after they're done here. The rest we need to save before their souls go squidgy."

"Squidgy?" Claudia asked.

"Like bread dough, apparently," I told her.

"I see," she said, and took a deep breath. "Fine. This antidote better bloody work."

Jan squeaked, which hardly inspired confidence.

The zombies had congregated in a shuffling, moaning group outside the construction site, reminding me of the way a pack of dogs will communicate with sniffs and whimpers, regrouping after you've met them with teeth and claws. The problem is that they then tend to come back with a plan. Not complicated plans, admittedly, and it seems zombie packs have certain things in common with dog packs. Collective intelligence, for a start.

Emma set her feet firmly, brandishing her pole. "Let's do it," she said.

"Do be careful," Gertrude told her, and Emma grinned.

Jan looked at Emma, then tried to twirl his pole in an

impressive manner and managed to knock himself in the head with it.

"Dude," I said, and he scowled at me.

"I'm a scientist, not a fighter."

"You're a mortician," Emma said, bouncing the pole in her hands and looking like she wanted to hit him with it.

I took a last look at Callum, still motionless on the ground with a bruise starting to bloom on his forehead where Gertrude had hit him, then turned my attention back to the zombie pack (or maybe it was a horde, although six zombies seemed a little on the low side to constitute a horde). I stepped up between Emma and Gertrude, feeling Pru and Claudia flanking me as the moaning of the undead faded, and they turned to face us. The noise of fighting, the screams and shouts and the crash of stalls being destroyed was swelling all across the market as the night rose and the almost-zombies rose with it. I could smell rot and un-death and fear and sweat and the sleek furious musk of cats, feel grit and dirt beneath my paws and the throb of my own injured ribs. I took a deep breath.

"Bring it, zombies!" I roared.

THEY SURGED FORWARD, splitting into three groups, two of them charging straight at us and two running to each side, moving with deceptive, shambling speed. Gertrude stepped to the left to intercept the attackers on that side, and Emma stepped right, shouting to Jan to help her. I charged straight for the oncoming zombies, my ears back and teeth bared, hearing the whispered scuff of cat feet following me.

My own footfalls sounded thunderous, and the world narrowed to the corpse in front of me as I leaped at it, front paws hooking its high-vis jacket as I vaulted to its shoulder. It had been – or still sort of was – a woman, shorter than Callum, and I almost overshot and went straight over its shoulder. It gave that awful moan-roar, like it couldn't find its vocal cords anymore, or had forgotten how to work them, and tottered in a circle, grabbing for me. I scrabbled around its shoulders for a moment, clawing for the face, then flung myself to the floor before the creature could catch hold of me, gathering myself for another leap with my heart pounding wildly.

The zombie forgot about me as soon as I jumped clear, and charged for Emma and Jan. The second zombie followed with Claudia and Pru hanging off its shoulders, and I pelted past them, heading for my lady corpse. I scratched my way up its back again and clawed desperately at its neck, trying anything to slow it, but apparently cats aren't much of a distraction when there's a couple of juicy-looking humans to think about.

"Emma!" I shouted, and she spun to meet us.

"Watch out!" she yelled, and I threw myself to the ground as she swung the bar in a short, sharp arc, connecting with the zombie's head with a crack that made me wince. Jan was trying to fend off the other two zombies, flailing around with his pole so wildly that I was sure he was more likely to hit himself than either of them. But the technique worked – he gave a shriek of triumph as he actually managed to knock one over, but his shriek turned into terror as the other leaped on him, carrying him to the ground.

"Gertrude!" Emma shouted, and dropped her bar, grabbing hold of Jan's zombie and trying to wrestle it off the mortician while he held it away with the pole, screaming so loudly that my ears hurt.

I pelted into the fray, attacking the zombie's face and trying not to feel guilty about the fact that, if the antidote worked, someone was going to wake up with a tic-tac-toe board on their cheeks. Claudia and Pru were still harrying their creature, trying to keep its attention as it moaned and wandered in anxious circles. One of Gertrude's zombies was unconscious on the ground and she had been chasing the other toward the marketplace, but now she turned and started sprinting back to us, her hood dropping away to reveal her pale, worried face.

Jan gave a sudden, panicked shove, one of those adrenalin-fuelled, going-to-feel-it-in-the-morning shows of strength that only come at the extremes of things, and Emma, the zombie and myself all went tumbling onto the floor, sending the cooler of syringes clattering across the concrete. Emma sprawled over Callum with a yelp, and the zombie lunged after her, grabbing her arm and dragging her toward it, its teeth chattering eagerly. Gertrude was still too far away. Jan had tried to make a run for it, but the zombie he'd knocked over had seized his foot and was trying to shove it into its mouth. Which kind of served him right.

"*Hey!*" I bellowed, with no real hope that the creature was going to listen to me. I leaped onto Callum's belly, ready to get between the thing's teeth and Emma. "Zombie potatoes! Over here!"

And Callum's eyes snapped open.

CALLUM SURGED UP WITH A YELP, sending me flying (again) and slammed into the zombie so hard that the impact knocked him flat on his back again. The corpse tumbled sideways, letting go of Emma and crashing into the cooler, sending syringes flying everywhere. Emma grabbed one and ripped the cap off with her teeth as she flung herself over Callum. She stabbed it into the zombie, which gave a startled moan then tried to catch hold of her again.

"For God's *sake,*" she complained, and Callum snatched the cooler up. He swung it at the zombie like he might swing our trusty cricket bat, smacking the thing in the forehead and sending it backward to the ground. It hit hard as it landed, and lay still. Callum barely glanced at it, just rolled to his feet with the cooler still in his hands and hit the zombie that was currently trying to eat Jan. Emma followed him, dosing the creature with the antidote before it could recover, then we all stared at it as it struggled back to its feet and lunged for Jan again.

"Bollocks," Callum said, and hit it with the cooler again, which promptly split straight down one side. The zombie forgot Jan and snarled at Callum instead, and he said "*Bollocks,*" again, this time with a little more feeling.

Then Emma cracked it neatly over the head with one of the metal poles just as Gertrude stumbled to a stop next to us. She glanced at the two unconscious zombies, nodded at Callum, then rushed off after Pru and Claudia.

"Clear!" the reaper shouted, and the cats vanished. She swung her scythe with that easy, precise movement, using the blunt back edge, and the corpse crumpled to the ground. She waited to see if it'd get up again, then wandered over to check the one Emma had knocked out earlier. She nudged it with the handle of the scythe, then said, "Well done, dear."

I stared from her back to Callum, who sat down with a groan. "Oh, Jesus, my head hurts. Did someone hit me?"

"I did," Gertrude said. "You deserved it, though."

"Oh, good," he said, and looked at me. "Hey."

"Hey," I said, and when he rested his hand on my back I could smell dust and books and yearning silence, and the world righted itself in small and half-known ways around us.

Right until the rest of the zombies started coming out of the construction site, eight, ten, *eleven* of them, some of them doing the moan-y shuffle and some of them moving with the alarming, spider-like grace of the true walking dead.

"Oh, *hairballs*," I said, and Callum said something distinctly stronger.

Callum rolled to his feet, looking around for a weapon, and finally just grabbed the cooler again. Emma had her pole poised over her shoulder, and Gertrude took a step forward as Jan dithered, looking like he'd much rather leg it.

"Everyone go," the reaper said, her voice calm. "There's too many. I'll hold them off and give you time to get away."

"*No,*" Emma said, in the sort of tone even reapers shouldn't argue with.

"Well, I might," Jan said, and Pru hissed at him.

"I don't know that anywhere else will be any safer," Callum said. "Can't you hear it?"

Jan looked around, apparently just becoming aware of the shouts and screams and crashes echoing under the low roof. He mumbled something and gripped his pole a bit tighter.

"At least you can get to somewhere defensible," Gertrude said. "Hurry *up.*"

"I'm not leaving," Emma said.

"Gertrude, you can't beat this many," Callum said. "Let's *all* try and get somewhere we can defend."

"No time," Claudia said, and as she spoke the zombies surged toward us, splitting to circle around our little group, moving with hungry, grumbling speed.

They were more organised than the others had been, feinting toward us, trying to tease Gertrude out, swatting at me as I dashed forward and back again, grabbing Emma's pole and jerking it away from her as they pressed closer. I could smell rot and rage and my own raw fear, hear the panting breaths of the humans amid the moans of the living dead.

Gertrude stepped forward, scythe swinging at the

head of a zombie, and one grabbed her from behind, lifting her off the ground.

"Gertrude!" Emma shouted, lunging forward, and Callum hauled her back before another zombie could attack her from the side. Pru and Claudia were tearing at the face of a third as it grappled with Jan, and the others were circling in fast. Gertrude tore herself free, moving with eerie, silent grace, and Callum yelped as a zombie pounced on him, pulling him away from Emma and slamming him to the ground.

All was teeth and moans and reeking hunger, and I threw myself at the nearest undead, claws bared. Never mind if they might be human again at some point. There was no time to care about it. Now there was only Claudia yowling and Jan screaming, Emma calling for Gertrude and the high thin cry of the reaper's scythe. Now was Pru spitting and Callum swearing, and dead flesh tearing beneath my claws, and the sour taste of fury and fear at the back of my throat, and there was no way we were getting out of this.

No way at all.

But that didn't meant we weren't going to try.

22

WE'RE ALL GOING ON A ZOMBIE HUNT

I WAS WRITHING IN THE GRIP OF A ZOMBIE, AWARE OF Callum shouting that we needed to run, dammit, *run*, and knowing that we couldn't, when a voice cut across the babble of the zombies and the distant roar of the market.

"*Down!*" it roared, and even Gertrude obeyed (although I had some difficulty owing to the fact that a corpse was still trying to chow down on my legs). Something rolled across us, a flood of wind and power, sweeping the corpses ahead of it and driving them back. My zombie dropped me as it was caught in the torrent, and I skidded across the floor with my claws flexed and aching against the concrete. The undead were flung back into the construction site, slamming into walls and each other, groaning and struggling, but it was like trying to fight against a tidal wave. They were washed helpless ahead of it. I flattened myself to the floor as I let the power roll over me, and looked up to see who our saviour was.

Ms Jones walked past me, one hand still out to hold the zombies in place, the other flicking busily as she piled the walls back, driving the metal sheets into the concrete and growing the edges together. She was frowning, a small twitch showing at the corner of her mouth, and when she dropped her hands she rested them on her hips, blowing air over her face. She looked at the wall for a moment, then turned to face us.

"I leave you alone for what, an hour?" she said. "Was it even an hour?"

"It was a rather critical hour," Gertrude said, getting up.

Ms Jones waved her hand dismissively. "An *hour*," she repeated, and wiped her forehead, then looked at Callum. "You better?"

Callum squinted at her. He kept rubbing his bruised forehead and seemed to be having some trouble focusing. "I think so?"

"Good thing we decided not to kill you," Claudia said.

He gave her a slightly alarmed look.

"Pru and I were very against it," I said.

"Well, I'm mostly against anyone killing *my* human," Pru said. "But, you know. What's gravy for the pudding is goose for the gander, or something."

Callum blinked at her. "Yeah. That."

"What now?" Emma asked, fending Gertrude off as the reaper tried to examine the large graze on her knee. "G, leave it. I'm fine."

Gertrude frowned at her. "You should get out of the market and wait somewhere safe."

"Yes," Emma said. "Because I'm perfectly comfortable leaving you to face the zombie hordes alone."

"They're not interested in eating me," Gertrude said. "You, however, are very tasty."

"Thank you," Emma said, flicking some loose hair over her shoulder, and Ms Jones snorted. She was collecting syringes and piling them into the broken cooler. Somehow, every time she picked up one, she ended up with three in her hand, and they were all full of the same faintly cloudy liquid. She looked pale, though, and there was a slick of sweat on her cheeks.

"At least we know these work," she said. "All we have to do is not get eaten while we use them."

Callum looked at the remaining zombies still sprawled around us. The ones in high-viz jackets were twitching and moaning, but more the way dogs do when they're chasing rabbits in their dreams than in a *wait-till-I-wake-up-so-I-can-eat-you* way. The third one, in tattered funeral clothes, wasn't chasing anything ever again. "We have an antidote?"

"I made it," the mortician said, as proudly as if he hadn't made the *need* for the antidote too.

"Sure you did," the sorcerer said, handing Callum two fistfuls of syringes. "Now I'm multiplying it."

"So what now?" Callum asked, trying to shove the antidote into his pockets and discovering two lamb leg bones and some uneaten pork chops. "And why do I have dead things in my pockets?"

"That one we'll talk about later," I said. "For now, we've got a whole marketplace full of the undead to deal with."

"Living dead," Emma pointed out.

Callum made a face, but managed to fit the syringes in around the bones. He didn't seem to want to let them go, which was slightly worrying. Ms Jones doled out more antidote to Emma and Jan, Emma ignoring the reaper's disapproving look.

"What about the trapped zombies?" she asked. "Do we start with them?"

"They should be alright in there for now," Ms Jones said. "Just the other fifty or so to deal to."

Callum ambled over to the construction site wall, picking up a pole Ms Jones hadn't used to fix the metal sheeting back in place again. Behind it, the zombies moaned and bashed the makeshift wall, but it barely shook. Apparently sorcerer building techniques are better than council ones.

"Alright," he said. "Let's go vaccinate some zombies."

We ventured out of our little corner, heading back toward Butcher's Row. The worst of the screaming still seemed to be coming from that direction, although shouts and shrieks rang out everywhere. Claudia, Pru and I fanned out, checking stores and looking for ambush as we went. Some of the stalls were closed and locked, the owners gone before the zombies went all nocturnal break-out on everyone, but others looked like … well, like zombies had been running through them. Oranges were rolling gently downhill through one alley, and I jumped back with a hiss as a coconut bounced past – it was a little too close to head-size for comfort. We found a zombie in the bag shop, all trussed up with leather belts and canvas bag straps, and it moaned as we went past, snapping at us hopefully. Callum glanced at Gertrude, and she nodded.

"It's a fresh one. An almost zombie. I mean … it's not dead."

"Got it," Callum said, and he stabbed the creature with a syringe while it rolled its eyes and tried to bite him. See, even almost-corpses can roll their eyes, but not cats. It's so unfair.

We kept going. One of the phone shops looked like it had been picked up and shaken out, phone cases scattered all across the floor and the paths between the stalls, and daubs of blood and gunk were splattered about liberally.

"*Ew,*" Emma said.

Claudia sniffed something pinky-white and a bit brainy looking that was stuck to the corner of the counter, then had a nibble.

"*Gross,*" I said, and Pru made a gagging noise.

"Sausages," Claudia said. "The posh ones. Some tarragon in there, I think. Have a taste."

"Pass," I said, and ran on ahead to a clothing stall. All the racks had been piled into the centre, coat hangers sticking out at wild angles and the wheeled bases of the stands waving at the sky. As I jumped across them, intent on checking out the curtained alcove that served as a changing room, the whole lot exploded up around me. I was flung across the stall with an undignified squawk, and a woman surfaced with a metal pole in her hands, the sort the stallholders use to hook clothes up to the top of displays. Her sari was slipping off her shoulder, and it swirled like a luminous wing as she swung the pole wildly.

"I will bash your head in!" she screamed. *"No one bites me!"*

I pawed my way out of a box of cheap white sport socks, glaring at Claudia and Pru, who were watching me with their whiskers twitching in amusement.

"Hi," Emma said brightly. "Has anyone actually bitten you yet? Because if so, we can help." She waved a syringe in a manner that was probably supposed to be reassuring, but given the fact that she had bleeding knees and a couple of sweet wrappers in her hair, and was keeping company with a hooded reaper, a man with bones sticking out of his pockets, a panicked-looking mortician, and a sorcerer who was muttering to herself and looking at her watch, it probably didn't come across as well as she'd have liked.

"No, thanks," the woman said, not lowering the pole. "I don't make it a habit to take syringes from strangers."

"Have you been bitten?" Ms Jones asked. She'd liberated some large satchels from the bag shop and handed them out, and she had one slung across her body. Syringes peeked out from under the top flap.

"No," the woman said.

"Is she lying?" the sorcerer asked the reaper.

"I'm not a lie-detector," Gertrude said. "Can't you tell?"

"How could I tell? You're the one that looks into their souls."

Gertrude frowned. "If she's only just been bitten I can't tell from her soul. These things take time."

"Well, excuse me," Ms Jones said. "I'm not the expert on souls."

The woman sank a little deeper among the clothes,

regarding the little group with wide eyes. "I don't want your needles," she insisted.

Claudia gave a huff of impatience and ran into the stall, leaping onto the mound of clothes and sniffing the bewildered woman, who flinched away.

"I can't tell," Claudia said, and the woman gave a little scream. "Just jab her anyway."

"We can't just *jab her anyway,*" Emma said. "I mean, never mind that we don't know what'll happen if someone who isn't infected has a shot. There's just so much wrong with *just jabbing* someone."

"That cat sounded like it was talking," the woman said. "It wasn't, right? Was it?"

"We can't let her go if she's infected," Ms Jones said.

Claudia leaped off the clothes mountain and glared at us all. "This *cannot* take this long. There's a whole market full of zombies trying to eat all the non-zombies out there, in case you haven't noticed. We can't have an ethical discussion over every single one."

"Well, it's easy to tell when they're trying to eat people," Gertrude pointed out.

Callum had been silent through the whole discussion, his fingers tapping the strap of his satchel absently. Now he reached into his pocket, took out a pork chop, and held it up to the woman. "Hungry?" he asked her.

"I don't eat meat," she said, but she sounded unsure. Her gaze was fixed on the chop.

He stepped forward. "Sure?" he said. "I've got plenty."

"No. I mean …" she let go of her pole with one hand and reached out, her eyes bright, and I was pretty certain she was drooling. Then she drew back. "No. I mean, it's *raw.*"

Callum waved the pork chop a little closer to her, and she dropped the pole entirely and grabbed the meat instead, taking an enormous bite and muttering with pleasure. She didn't even protest when Callum jabbed a needle into her arm.

He stepped back and dropped the used syringe in the outside pocket of his bag. "I'm just going to say that's why I have a pocketful of dead things."

Emma patted his arm, and we headed deeper into the market.

WE BARELY MADE it to the next corner before a man in a greasy apron ran screeching past the intersection ahead of us, pursued by two loping zombies using their hands to help them along. A scrawny teenager ran after them, a bag of sausages clutched in one hand. He was throwing them at the zombies' heads and yelling at them to get their bangers here, but the zombies were more interested in the man in the apron.

"Hey!" Callum yelled. "Kid, *stop!*" He sprinted after them, and I followed. I'd had enough of solo work.

Behind us there was a crash of something big falling, and Gertrude shouted, "*Emma!*" but I didn't look back. They had a sorcerer *and* a reaper. If they couldn't manage with that, there was no helping them.

Callum's deceptively fast when he wants to be. He caught up to the kid easily, snapped "*Wait,*" then gave me a nod that I guessed meant *keep an eye on him,* and kept running. I peered after Callum as the kid slowed, panting, a sausage still clutched in one hand. I didn't really want to stay with him, and was considering pretending I hadn't understood Callum at all when a new zombie came charging out of a food stall, wearing a catering pot on its head. Noodles snaked out from under it like particularly greasy hair, and its eyes were bloodshot from the broth. It lunged at us with a hungry moan.

The kid gave a breathy little scream and turned to run after Callum, but slipped on a sausage and slammed to the ground with a *whuff* as the air was knocked out of him. The zombie reached for him with a satisfied gurgle, and I swore and leaped, hitting its shoulder hard and sending it far enough off balance that its hands closed on nothing. The kid scooted backward across the floor, chest hitching, fetching up against a stall as the zombie recovered itself, turning back. I jumped at it again, scoring its cheeks with my claws, and it slapped me away with one heavy hand, slamming me into the nearest wall with my poor abused ribs screaming. The kid struggled to his feet, still trying to breathe.

"Run!" I yowled at him, and he gave a yelp of fright and fled. The zombie moaned and swung into pursuit, and as I flung myself at its legs, trying to trip it up, Pru came off the top of the stall. She leaped with all four paws down and her legs straight, the way I jump on Callum's belly when he won't get up and let me out. She hit the pot hard, her claws screeching as she slid off and plunged to the floor. She landed lightly, and we both stared at the zombie. Its moans had taken on a questioning upturn, and

as we watched it walked into a curtain display, the pot wedged firmly down almost to the bottom of its chin. It tried to pull it up, but its hands got caught in some gauzy net curtains, and it couldn't seem to get a grip on anything except more curtains. It tugged, and the display collapsed around it. It gave an upset sort of moan.

"Nice," I said.

"I thought so," she agreed, and fell into step with me as we pelted after Callum.

We caught up to him just a few steps behind the kid. Callum was wrestling a zombie to the ground, a needle sticking out of its neck, and when he saw us he shouted, "Get me something to tie it up with! Quick!"

The kid reacted faster than we did, snatching a bunch of scarves from a display and dropping to his knees next to Callum. They trussed the zombie's arms behind its back, avoiding its snapping teeth, and Callum looked at me.

"How long does the antidote take to work?"

"A bit," I said, and the kid stared at me, his eyes wide. He was almost as tall as Callum, but if Callum was skinny, this kid was a waif.

"What does a bit mean?" Callum asked, adding an extra scarf while the corpse moaned with frustration.

"Come on, time's a human construct," I said. "How do I know?"

"More than ten minutes," Pru said, and we all stared at her. "What? I looked at Emma's watch."

"Right," Callum said, and the kid made an uncertain, spluttery noise.

"You alright?" Callum asked him.

"Um. Yes. I think so. Talking cats, though."

"Zombies," I pointed out, and the kid gave me an uncertain look.

"Don't mind him," Callum said, ignoring my snort of disapproval. "You bitten?"

"No."

"Sure?" He got up and fished a syringe out of his bag, uncapping it. "This is an antidote."

The kid shook his head. "I'm not bitten."

"Good," Callum said. "What's your name?"

"Max."

"Okay, Max, so—"

"*Callum!*" I bellowed, launching myself forward as another of the running dead thundered out of a side alley and grabbed him by the front of his coat, bearing him to the ground with its teeth snapping at his neck.

TURNS OUT, it was a short zombie. Its teeth *would* have been snapping at Callum's neck if it had been about a foot taller. As it was, it got a good mouthful of his jacket sleeve as they crashed to the floor, landing on the satchel with the sound of lots of little plastic thingies splitting.

Callum howled and stabbed the zombie in the back with the syringe he'd offered Max, and Pru and I threw ourselves at the creature, tearing at its head and ears while it snapped and squirmed and tried to get its teeth into Callum's throat. He fought to hold it off, trying to find room to push it away, but it kept attacking with a raging, desperate hunger, clawing and biting again and again at anywhere it could reach. Pru bit its ear and it hit her so hard she flew the length of two stalls, and I gave up on thinking about the fact that there was still a human in here somewhere and set to gouging its cheeks as hard as I could.

Then Max yelled, *"Clear!"* and for one moment I thought he'd found a defibrillator somewhere, although how that was going to help I wasn't sure. Then Callum shoved me away with one hand and bucked hard under the zombie, hefting it up and slightly away from him even though it kept its grip on his coat. Max slammed a bottle of flavoured coffee syrup into the side of the creature's head, and it gave an enraged moan as the bottle shattered, scattering glass and the scent of almonds everywhere. Max hit it with a second bottle, sending it sprawling sideways, its grip on Callum finally broken, and they both tackled it. Pru limped up, trailing two more scarves and tripping herself up on every second step, looking slightly dazed, and the two humans trussed the zombie up next to the first one.

Callum rocked back on his heels, wiping syrup and scraps of glass off his cheek. "Nice," he said to Max.

"Thanks," Max said, and watched Callum sifting through his satchel, antidote dripping off his fingers and shards of broken syringe sticking to his hands.

"How many've you got left?" I asked him.

"I'd go with not enough," he said, finding a couple of still intact ones and setting them next to him.

"Hairballs," I said, and he nodded, then looked at Max.

"You should find somewhere safe to hole up," he said.

"Okay," the kid said, but didn't move. Callum found two more syringes, popped them in his pockets, then discarded the bag.

"Well?" he said to Max, who still hadn't moved.

"Yeah, I'm going to stay with you," Max said. "I'll be backup."

Callum looked at me, and I shrugged. It didn't seem like the worst idea.

"Alright," Callum said, and got up. "You alright?" he asked Pru.

She blinked at him. "Should there be two of you?"

"Oh, good," he said. "Can I pick you up?"

"No," she said, and I nudged her with one shoulder.

"Stick with me, zombie-cat," I told her. "You'll be right."

"I'm filled with confidence," she said, but when Callum started jogging down the alley she stayed with us, breaking into an uneven lope and only bumping into me every few steps or so.

Which, you know, could've been worse. Her skin was smooth and didn't feel half as weird as I'd expected.

"Callum," I called, as we ran down the narrow, twisting lanes of the market, avoiding tumbled food displays and broken jars and a small flood that was emerging from one of the loos. There's always a flood. It's like disasters never take into account the unpleasantness of wet paws.

"What?" he asked, stopping to peer around a corner.

"Aren't we going in the wrong direction? I mean, the

reaper and the sorcerer – and more antidote – are all back that way."

"I know, Gobs, but can't you hear that?"

I cocked my head and said, "You mean what sounds like a load of people fighting with the undead?"

"Living dead," Pru mumbled, tripping over a cheap pink alarm clock and bumping her nose on a potato. "Ow."

"That's the one," Callum said. "We can't just leave them."

"And what're we going to do with four doses of antidote?" I demanded, but he was already running again, his ridiculous, stained jacket flaring around him and the kid legging it after him, all knees and elbows. I wondered if you could catch zombie-ism *after* having the antidote, or if we'd all just straight-up get eaten. Either option didn't sound amazing, but I nudged Pru. "Want to wait here?"

She squinted at me. "*No.* I need to find my human. You might brain her."

"Fair enough," I said, and tried to keep her in a straight line as we ran after Callum. It wasn't as easy as it sounds.

THE SOUND of fighting swelled as we ran toward the top gates of the market, the shouts and screams and crashes all underscored by an unsettling chorus of moans that rose and fell like a particularly nasty siren song, setting the hair on my tail bushing out uncomfortably. The overhead lights were unlit, and the glass roof let in only the persistent glow of a city at night, rendering the shadows deep where the stalls lights didn't reach. We'd left the loo flood behind, but now we splashed into the faintly musty water of the trashed flower stands as we emerged into the crowd of stalls under the mezzanine floor, the gates ahead of us.

The floor was strewn with crushed flowers and overturned buckets, all giving off a heavy botanical scent like a rainforest gone to rot, and Callum slowed, boots slipping on the damp leaves. The fighting was just ahead of us, and I looked at Pru, who had stood on a lily and was shaking her paw out distastefully.

"Don't lick that," I warned her.

"I'm con— conk— slightly dizzy, not clueless," she said, and lost her balance, splashing onto her side on the sodden floor with a distressed mewl.

"Right, Callum's picking you up," I told her as she got up. She was dripping, and a small fern was stuck to her ear.

"I'm *fine,*" she protested.

"You're going to be a zombie snack," I said.

"He's got a point," Callum said. "Either wait somewhere safe or I can put you in a pocket."

She narrowed her eyes at him. "I'm not sharing with those bones. That's gross."

Callum shifted a couple of pork chops into a different pocket and said, "All clear."

Pru grumbled, but let herself be picked up and deposited in the pocket. It was too small and she hung half out of it, her four knobbly paws hooked over the top. She looked at me with one eye shut. "This is most undignified."

"But you're marginally less likely to be eaten," I said.

"Quiet," Callum said, and waved Max to stay behind him as he crept to the edge of the nearest flower stall, walking half-doubled over. I padded next to him, my ears flicking at the zombie moans and human screams, and we peered carefully around the corner into the battlefield.

23

WELCOME TO THE HORDE

HUMANS AND FOLK WERE CROWDED ON THE BALCONY OF the mezzanine floor, armed with printers and coffee mugs and bottles of water, brooms and mops and desk chairs. A nymph was clutching a bright pink stapler and a pair of scissors, waving them both about wildly and probably with a lot more danger to the two women next to her than to the living dead below. Zombies were pushing up the stairs near the gates, piling over each other, slipping and moaning with terrible single-mindedness while a faun and a couple of humans forced them back over and over, using a large table as a shield. More of the hungry corpses were crowding down the mezzanine from the other side, being held at bay with a hasty barricade of desks and filing cabinets, and I could see anxious faces peering out of the office caught between the twin tides of the almost dead.

We watched silently for a moment, then I said, "Well. Those four doses of antidote should just do the trick."

"We can't leave them," Callum said again, settling into

a crouch as we watched. "They can't hold out for long like that."

Even as he spoke, the barricade on the mezzanine was breeched. A zombie in skinny leather trousers and one high heel scrambled over the top of one of the chairs, and an enormous bearded man seized her with a roar. She hissed at him, clawing his arms and straining toward his face, and he threw her back among her buddies, sending half a dozen zombies into a tangled pile-up. The bearded man snatched up a desk and shoved into the gap effortlessly, then grabbed what looked like a whole sheep's leg from a bag on the floor, took an enormous bite and roared again, his whole body shaking with the effort.

"Jesus," Max said.

"Big Ted," I corrected. "He hasn't turned yet, then."

"Aw," Callum said. "That's good. I thought maybe we lost him when he wasn't at the stall."

"Looks pretty un-undead. He's good at zombie catching, too."

Callum didn't answer, just went back to scanning the scene in front of us. "We need to get up there."

"We need to get more antidote," I said. "Or, you know, a sorcerer and a reaper. They'd be handy, too."

"I can get them," Pru said.

"You can't even stand up," I said.

She wrinkled her already wrinkly nose at me. "I'll *shift*, you garden planter."

"I don't think we should stay here," Max said. "They're going to notice us."

Pru blinked at him. "Why're you still here?"

"I'm sorry? I'm really well prepared for this, you know. I've read *all* the zombie survival guides."

"Yes, well, that may not be that helpful," Callum said. "Most of these zombies can be changed back if we can get the antidote in them, so we don't want to brain any of them."

"Especially not my human," Pru said, then added, "But I meant, I shifted. Did you all come with me? That's cool. I've never done that before."

"That was a really good bump on the head, wasn't it?" I asked her.

She gave me a confused look and started to say something, then Max yelled, "*Watch out!*"

The zombie threw itself off the top of the stall above us with a triumphant moan, all teeth and grabbing hands. Callum dropped his pole and lunged forward, catching himself on his hands and doing a weird frog-like spring away. He slipped on the mulch of wet leaves and crushed flowers and belly-flopped to the floor with a yelp, Pru squawking and trying to fight her way out of his pocket. Max swung the bag of sausages straight into the face of the zombie, shrieking something that probably sounded a lot more coherent in his head. The creature fell back, crashing into the side of the stall, and Callum scrambled to his feet, snatching a metal bucket up and hitting the zombie hard enough that the bucket folded in on itself. The creature tried to push itself off the stall and he hit it again, sending it to the ground. It gave an anxious little moan then lay still, and we all stared at it.

"I hope I didn't hurt it," Callum said.

"It was going to eat you," I pointed out.

"Eep," Max said, and we both stared at him. Pru was still trying to get out of Callum's pocket, and was cursing zombies, humans, and cats with great enthusiasm and accuracy. *"Urk,"* Max added, and waved past us.

Callum and I spun around.

It seems that zombies have good hearing, even when they're occupied with trying to conquer stairs, and beating a corpse into unconsciousness with a metal bucket is apparently quite loud. A dozen or so of the creatures that had been trying to fight their way up to the humans trapped on the mezzanine were on the hunt for easier prey, charging toward us with snapping teeth and hungry moans, some of them springing forward on all fours with rather more grace than Callum, others running with their bellies out and their heads back, slipping and sliding on the treacherous floor.

"Up!" Callum yelled, and grabbed me. He threw me to the top of the nearest stall while I yowled in outrage, then caught the edge of the roof and hauled himself up, catching me just as I slid past him with my claws screeching on the tin. It was one of those pointless rounded roofs in seamless corrugated iron, designed to make the stall look like it was some sort of country wagon, and with absolutely no grip for a sliding cat.

He deposited me on the top and I flattened my belly to the metal, ears back as I tried to turn myself into a limpet of some sort. He grabbed Max's wrist and helped him up, the whole stall wobbling violently and an alarming creaking and cracking rising from underneath us. There was a breath of stillness, then the first of the zombies hit the stall and it lurched violently to the left, almost sending me slipping off the side again.

"I don't like this!" I shouted, and the stall groaned, leaning still further under the assault of the creatures below us. Pale fingers appeared on the edge of the roof, and I slid down to them, biting the first one I reached. It vanished, but another hand appeared, snatching at me, and Callum grabbed me around the belly and dragged me out of reach.

"We have to get off here," he said.

"No—" I started, and he pointed at me.

"If you say baby goats I'll throw you to the zombies."

"It's no weirder than any human expression," I grumbled.

Max was straddling the curve of the roof as well as he could, methodically throwing sausages at the zombies. They seemed distinctly less interested in them than they were in the two tasty humans, but every now and then he caught one in the eye and they lost their grip. Another one took their place immediately, of course, but we weren't about to quibble about small mercies at this point. The stall was leaning more and more severely, and the only reason it hadn't fallen over completely was that the living dead were apparently not the thinking dead, and were still trying to climb up rather than push us over.

"We're going to have to run for it," Callum said. "Straight off the other side and back down into the market. Hopefully some of them will follow us and we can draw them away from the others."

"Yeah, that's exactly what I'm hoping for," I said, and he gave me a disapproving look.

"There's a snake in here," Pru said, sounding more worried than she had been by the zombies. "Why's there a snake in here?"

"Long story," I said.

"I'm out of sausages," Max announced, and the stall gave another warning creak as heads joined hands on the edge of the roof. A zombie with thick glasses hanging off one ear hauled itself up until it could rest its potbelly on the edge of the roof, and Callum threw a pork chop at it, hitting it on the nose and sending it tumbling back off the roof.

"Let's go," he said, and slid down the opposite side of the little roof, dropping to the floor with a squawk of complaint from Pru. I shot after him, jumping to his shoulder just as half a dozen more zombies emerged from around the corner of a Mexican food stall about ten metres away. They spotted us and broke into a proper zombie charge. Max gave a yelp of alarm, but he was already sliding off the roof. He wriggled wildly, trying to stop himself, but there was nothing to catch hold of and he landed hard, hissing in pain as he stumbled to his knees.

Callum hauled him up, slinging the kid's arm over his shoulders and half-carrying him, breaking into a shambling run as we headed for the nearest stall. The zombies at the flower stand were already racing around and through it, flinging broken flowers about the place like a sodden and slightly warped wedding party, and the newly arrived zombies were thundering after us, their symphony of moans somehow worse than any shouting or screaming could ever have been.

"Gobs! Where can we go?" Callum managed, trying to push himself faster.

"Up," I shouted. "We have to go up!" All of the stalls were open, and they were big ones, with huge open fronts and double sides. None of them had one nice handy shutter that could be pulled down to shut out the zombies. There wasn't even a back room in sight that I could see, just open counters and display tables and nothing we could defend.

Callum gave a yelp and stumbled, and I spun back to him. One of the zombies, smaller and faster than the others, had thrown itself at Max, tearing him away from Callum. The kid shrieked and grabbed the living corpse, holding it off as they tumbled to the floor. Callum dived after them, seizing the zombie around the waist and pulling it off Max, but the thing just wriggled around and attached itself to Callum instead, wrapping its legs around him and snapping wildly at his face. He fended it off with both hands, and Max grabbed a half-price diary with a unicorn on the cover and started belting the creature over the head with it. They staggered back and forth, bouncing off tables and sending multi-coloured stationery scattering to the floor while the pack of zombies flooded up the market toward us, eager and delighted and smelling of butcher shops.

"Incoming!" I yowled, and pelted forward to meet them. I threw myself at the nearest corpse and it slapped me away effortlessly, sending me crashing into a second one. I managed to get a couple of good bites in there before that one threw me off too, and I hit the floor hard, coughing air and struggling back to my feet as the horde

rushed past me. I'm not big on numbers and counting, but, yeah. I was pretty certain this counted as a horde, and it was between me and the two humans. I couldn't see them, but I could still hear Callum shouting, and the crack of the diary on undead flesh, so they hadn't been torn limb from limb just yet. All about me were eager feet and pushing arms and starving, longing faces, desperate to taste the life that was being denied them, and I was having trouble getting my breath back.

"Callum!"

"Gobs! Run!"

Yeah, like that was going to happen. Ms Jones might be our best hope to survive this, but there was no time. I couldn't find her and get back before Callum was zombie-chum. I gathered my feet under me and launched myself at the shoulder of the nearest zombie, screaming, *"Come and get me, you brain-munching penguins!"*

Which was probably insulting to penguins, but hey. I didn't have much time to think about it. I hit the creature's shoulder, laid into its face, and jumped to the next. Maybe I could be a distraction. Maybe that would be enough. And if it wasn't, at least I'd be here. And that seemed better than being alone. For both of us.

I SLIPPED and skittered and half-fell across the heads and shoulders of the horde, scratching necks and getting my claws caught in woolly jumpers and sliding on leather jackets and once landing in something that I sincerely hope was mince. I wasn't about to ask.

The living dead moan-roared their protests and tried to catch me, but cats are fast and slippery, and cats worried about getting eaten are even more so. I plunged out of the crowd and landed in front of Callum just as he whacked a zombie on the head with a pink-framed blackboard. The board popped out, and he wedged the frame firmly around the zombie, trapping its arms to its sides and shoving it back into its fellows.

"Gobs, what're you *doing?*" he demanded. "We need antidote, or backup, or *something*."

"Well, that's just rude," I said. "I fought my way through a horde to get here. A *horde*."

Callum muttered something under his breath and started throwing small tins of paint at the zombies. Max was using an umbrella to fend off a mostly dead man in a tweed suit, and they'd backed into the stall until they hit the wall. There was no way out, the zombies pushing to get closer and closer, the strange undead stench of premature rot following them like a fog of the nastier variety.

"Fireworks," Max managed.

"What?" Callum asked, running out of paint tins and picking up the little wooden display they'd been on. He hit a zombie with it and it shattered.

"There's a box over there. We could use them."

"We don't want to kill them," Callum said, grabbing a table and up-ending it, using it to force the creatures back.

"They're going to kill *you*," I pointed out.

"They wouldn't if they weren't infected," he said, and slapped the arms of the nearest corpse away as it reached around the table for Max. Another caught the back of

Callum's jacket from the other side, hauling him toward it, and I scrambled to his shoulder, striking out at the creature's face.

"We don't have time for *ethics,*" I snapped as he tore free (the jacket unfortunately still intact). "Get the fireworks!"

Max lunged for the box, ducking a zombie and head-butting another in the belly. It grunted and fell back, but the sheer press of the horde kept it upright and it came back again.

"Lighter," I said to Callum, and he scowled at me, bracing his shoulder against the table, his boots wedged against the back wall. He was being forced back further and further, and more arms appeared around the edges of the table, reaching for him with a blind hunger that was beyond nature, beyond even magic. It was the eternal hunger of things that have never known what it is to be full, or safe, or warm, or loved, and it made my heart hurt.

But that was no reason to be soft about it.

"*Lighter,*" I said again, and before Callum could reply Max screamed. Callum gave a convulsive shove with the table, driving back the horde just enough that we could see the kid trapped to the floor under a press of half a dozen of the living dead, all of them clawing and clutching him as if they'd tear him to pieces. Which was probably just what was going to happen.

"Max!" Callum yelled, and I sprinted out from the cover of the table, dodging boots and heels and a surprising amount of bare feet. I leaped onto the back of the nearest zombie and bit its ear as hard as I could. It stood straight up with an outraged moan, and I fell back into the fray. Max was kicking and thrashing like a pilly-wiggin in a spiderweb, and the creatures snapped and pawed at him wildly, trying to get a decent bite in somewhere. Callum made it halfway to us, still carrying the table like a shield, before the zombies piled on top of him. The table slammed against the wall at an angle, and he fell to his knees in the gap beneath it.

"Stay there!" I shouted at him, but he crawled out, kicking zombies away, the lighter clutched in one hand and the other holding a can of air freshener. I thought for a moment he was going to do that homemade flamethrower thing you see in movies, but all he did was spray the air freshener in the undead's faces, which helped the smell marginally but barely slowed them. I started to struggle toward him, and the zombies washed in and around us, and one of them scooped me up and tried to put my head its mouth.

"*Old ones take you!*" I braced my forepaws to either side of the creature's gaping maw, kicking wildly with my back legs, dimly aware of a thud from nearby but more worried about the teeth straining toward my nose. The zombie lifted me away, trying for a different angle, then there was a rather closer *thud,* and it let me go with a grunt. I hissed, but even as I started to fall a hand caught me and deposited me on a large, unfamiliar shoulder.

"Hang on, cat," a deep voice instructed me, and my saviour waded on into the zombies, dealing out blows with a desk leg wrapped in what appeared to be a sequined scarf.

"Callum," I said. "He's under there! Get him, quick!"

"On it." We charged forward, and I caught sight of

Terror and Melody hauling hungry corpses off Max, sending them tumbling back with blows of desk legs that matched Big Ted's. Or I assumed it was Big Ted. I couldn't see his face for the beard, but the very size of the beard itself (and how far away the floor was – seriously, I was getting acrophobia up here) seemed like a giveaway.

He grabbed a zombie by the back of its checked trousers and the collar of its chef's jacket and threw it into two oncoming creatures, then pulled Callum to his feet.

"Alright?" Big Ted asked.

"Sure," Callum said. He had a split lip and fresh bite marks on his hands, but he didn't seem to have lost anything vital.

"Good," Big Ted said, then looked away and bellowed, "You got him?"

I squawked and almost fell off his shoulder. Dude was *loud.* I jumped to Callum instead, and he scratched my chin absently. He had bloodstains on his fingers that made me wrinkle my nose.

"Got him," Terror called, waving her desk leg triumphantly. Next to her, Melody swung at the nearest zombie, chattering her teeth and moaning a little.

"Mel, have some meat," Big Ted said, and the older woman blinked, then dug a large handful of raw mince out of her pocket and gummed it eagerly.

Max stared at her, then at us.

"Hope you've got that antidote you were talking about, cat," Big Ted said. "We need it pretty bad."

I could smell the whiff of rot drifting from him.

We fought our way through the horde, heading for the stairs to the mezzanine. The living dead might not have been some of the great thinkers of their time, but they were wary enough of Big Ted and his desk leg. He charged forward with it in one hand and the other hand grasping one end of Callum's display table, using it as a battering ram. Callum and Terror held the other end, wielding a broom and a desk leg respectively, and Melody and Max brought up the rear, fending off our pursuers. I stayed on Callum's shoulder, shouting warnings and instructions until he told me to shut up before he fed me to a zombie himself, which I thought was a bit unfair.

We left behind half a dozen unconscious living dead, and Big Ted knocked out another four before we made it to the stairs. The horde had mostly abandoned them when they'd caught a whiff of us, so once we were out of the crush in the stall our way was fairly clear. Other than having to bop the odd almost-corpse on the head with a scarf-wrapped piece of furniture, of course, but that was starting to feel like pretty easy going after the rest of the afternoon.

We abandoned the table and sprinted up the stairs, the humans' feet clanging on the metal treads and the whole structure shaking with Big Ted's enormous strides as he took the steps three at a time.

"Open up!" he roared as we got to the top, and a faun glared at us around a barricade formed of a large table and what looked to be half a dozen people sitting behind it. The gate was pushed to, but even from here I could see it was twisted off one hinge.

"Have you got the antidote?" the faun asked.

Big Ted waved impatiently. "Just hurry up, will you?" The stairs were still shaking, but now it was with zombies trying to follow us. Terror and Max were holding them off as well as they could.

"But have you *got* it?" the faun repeated.

"Let us in, you pillock!" Terror shouted. "You'd still be hiding in your back room counting your piercings if it wasn't for us!"

"I might've been *safer* in there," the faun shot back. He did have an impressive array of piercings, although it looked like a few had been torn out.

"We've had to lock two more in quarantine," a rounded woman in a unicorn print T-shirt that read *I will shank you* said. "They're on the turn. We *need* that antidote."

"Yeah," the faun said. "No antidote, no entry."

We glared at each other while the stairs shook and swayed, and the horde moaned below us.

"Let us in!" Big Ted roared, but no one moved.

"Hairballs," I said.

24

IT ONLY FEELS LIKE THE APOCALYPSE

THE HORDE ROARED BELOW US, THEIR UPTURNED FACES naked with hunger, and above us the non-infected glared at us suspiciously, stinking of fear and adrenaline.

"We've got the antidote," Callum said, kicking a tall zombie with a shaved head back down the stairs. "Just let us in!"

"Show us it first, then," the faun said, and Big Ted gave a wordless bellow and charged. "*Hold!*" the faun shrieked, and everyone who'd been peering over the top of the table braced themselves against it. Big Ted slammed into the gate with an awful, fleshy sound, jolting it open and forcing the table back far enough that he got his foot into the gap.

"Push him back!" the faun yelled. "He's infected!"

"I was infected before, you pikelet," Big Ted said, rubbing his shoulder. I could hear everyone puffing and straining behind the table, but he didn't move his foot. "Let us in. None of you would've made it this far if not for us."

"We have to protect ourselves," Unicorn Woman said.

"Ted!" Terror shouted. The shaking on the stairs had intensified. The horde was trying to pull the whole thing down.

"Gobs, you've got to go," Callum said, his voice low. "You have to find Ms Jones. We need more antidote."

"I can't go," I said. "It'll take me too long to find her."

"Okay, so d'you want to tell Big Ted we've only got four doses left?"

"You've only got what?" Melody demanded.

"Ah," Callum said, which was unhelpful.

"Pru!" I shouted. "Pru can go! She must be able to shift by now."

"How many doses did you say?" Melody demanded. She was gripping her desk leg rather threateningly, and ignoring Terror and Max flailing about with their makeshift weapons, desperately trying to stop the zombies ripping the stairs from their moorings.

"Pru?" I said again, and Callum patted his pockets like a magician who'd misplaced his rabbit. "Pru!"

"She's gone," he said, a little uncertainly, and I slid off his shoulder to the step just below Big Ted. I stared at the horde below.

"She *can't* be! We can't have lost her! I told her she'd be safe with me!"

"Maybe she ran off at some point," Callum said. "I mean, I was getting a bit crushed, so maybe she sneaked out."

"Give the antidote to us," Melody said, and suddenly she had a handful of Callum's T-shirt, her ragged fingernails snagging the fabric. "Give it to us *now*." She was spitting over her bare gums and her eyes kept straying to Callum's neck.

Big Ted was still trying to force his way through the gate, and more humans and Folk joined the barricade, bracing themselves against the table, demanding the antidote before they let us through. I recognised Spice Woman and the dwarf salesman among them, but there were no cats, naked or otherwise.

"Pru!" I yelled, perching on the edge of the creaking stairs and peering into the shadows of the stalls. "Pru! *Pru!*"

"Help us!" Terror shouted, and Max added something that wasn't particularly coherent and was mostly unrepeatable anyway. The stairs creaked and shuddered, and with an agonised screech something tore loose on the mezzanine. The stairs lurched, and I almost pitched off them into the grasping hands of the living dead. Callum slipped and fell backward, crashing onto the stairs, and Melody landed on top of him, drool spilling from her open mouth. She lunged at his neck, and Callum yelped.

"*Mel, no!*" Terror abandoned her post and grabbed the older woman around the waist, lifting her off Callum as if she were a child. Melody wriggled and squalled, the sound too close to a moan.

"God*damn* you," Big Ted shouted at the group behind the gate. "You don't *deserve* the antidote."

Callum looked at me. "*Go.*" He was already pulling the syringes from his pocket, a little suction mark on his neck where Melody had tried to gum him to death. Big Ted leaped over him, the stairs shaking violently as he landed, and grabbed Terror and Melody, pulling them apart. Max was being forced back up the stairs as more and more zombies piled toward him.

"Callum—" I was going to protest, to tell him I couldn't leave him to be eaten, to tell him I'd been meant to look after Pru and I'd lost her, and that I'd already lost him once and that was *more* than enough losing people for one day, that it was starting to look careless, but he scooped me up and hurled me straight over the heads of the zombies, which kind of took the words off my tongue.

I tumbled twice as I flew, my legs splaying and tail counterbalancing of its own accord, and by the time I came out of the second roll I already had eyes on my landing. Which wasn't *entirely* reassuring, as although it looked soft, it also looked distinctly wet. But that was better than toothed.

I landed hard, claws shredding through leaves and splashing musty water onto my nose, making me snort. My feet shot out from under me, slipping on torn petals and slick stems, and I scrabbled wildly for balance, almost had it, then the terrible sound of tearing metal jerked my head around and I lost concentration. I snarled as I slammed down in the muck, sliding sideways until I fetched up in a drift of daffodils. I lay there for a moment, panting, then metal screeched again, and I scrambled to my feet.

The stairs were still standing, but it was an only-just thing. I couldn't tell at this distance what was keeping them up, but it didn't look like a lot. They were hanging at a strange, twisted angle, and Big Ted had one arm hooked through the banisters on the mezzanine, as if he could hold them all up by sheer will. Callum and Terror had joined Max, trying to push back the zombies, and Melody appeared to be gumming Big Ted's boot. Which was safe enough, as far as such things went.

I closed my eyes against a sudden, freezing tightness in my chest, then turned and plunged into the marketplace, running as hard and fast as I had ever run in any of my four sorry lives, while behind me the horde moaned, and metal tore, and someone screamed, high and tight and awful.

I WAS RUNNING HARD, my ribs aching and my breath harsh, wondering if I dared try the Inbetween or if that was just a good way to get myself eaten by beasts before Callum got eaten by zombies. I hurtled over the water-slick floor, dodging dropped cans and lost phones and crushed take-away cups, aware of the emptiness of the market like the promise of a world to come. But I hadn't even made it as far as where we'd left the two trussed undead before I become aware of a growl, the threatening sound of a cornered cat or an unseen dog, but something *more*, too. It was the sort of sound you'd expect a tiger to make as it breathes on the back of your neck.

I skidded to a stop, one paw raised, poised to dive into the nearest stall or race off down one of the alleyways, half-wondering if this was going to be some sort of mega-zombie, grown from the ancient, bloody remains of the butcher stalls. Some giant conglomerate of hunger and rage and mindless destruction, which would serve that bloody faun right, but didn't exactly bode well for the rest of us.

Movement in the shadows, and I hunched into a crouch, my heart a staccato in my ears. Cats, by nature, are not superstitious. That's for humans. They get all freaky about throwing salt over their shoulders to spite the devil, and not stepping on cracks, and never walking widdershins around a faery circle, but all that gets you is a salty floor, problems on old pavements, and … actually, the faery circle one's good advice, but the rest are rubbish. As for black cats being bad luck, well, I didn't feel hugely lucky right at that moment, but that was more to do with mortician-created zombies than anything else.

Which is all a long way around to saying that I don't hold with ghostly apparitions any more than I hold with coincidences, but what I saw coming out of the depths of the market to meet me was enough to make every hair on my body stand to attention. I think even my paws pouffed up, and that had *never* happened before.

A cat came first, moving in strong, long lopes, the faint light sliding off her pale, hairless sides, her ears back and her teeth bared, tail whipping behind her and her muscles moving under her shoulders like a threat. Behind her, robes flaring into the shadows and drinking the light like the void itself, ran the reaper, her scythe glimmering in the dark and shattering it to pieces that fell in a fractured trail behind her.

But more frightening still was the motorbike purring up the aisles, sending its growl out to shake my bones. It was like no bike I'd ever seen, and there were no decals or stickers to fasten it to the familiar. I couldn't even tell what colour it was, but I think that was more because it was waiting for me to decide what colour I *perceived* it as than because it was undecided about the question. It was low slung and feral and strangely alive, and I was utterly unsurprised to see Ms Jones didn't even have her hands on the grips. She was flexing her fingers together, her face pale and smudged with blood. I could smell both power and exhaustion rolling off her, and I didn't know which unsettled me more. Emma clung to the pillion, an enormous grin painted across her face and her denim jacket missing a sleeve, and Jan clutched her waist desperately, looking like he was about to throw up.

Behind me, there was a final scream of tearing metal, and a whole lot of shouting. The bike leaped forward like a beast on the hunt, thundering past me up the aisles with Emma's delighted laughter following on behind.

"Hey," Pru said, stopping next to me as Gertrude ran on, calling to Emma to *please* hang on tight.

"Hey," I said. "Thought we lost you."

"I thought we needed some help."

"Us? Nah. We've totally got this."

She cocked her head at the screaming. "Obviously," she said, and nudged me with one bare shoulder.

We broke into a sprint, racing across the debris-strewn floor, chasing the bike and the reaper into the heart of the zombie horde.

We pelted into the flower-choked market entrance hall to a cacophony of screaming people and moaning zombies. Ms Jones was still astride her unsettling bike, her Doc-clad toes resting on the ground and one hand held palm-up to the ceiling as if she were carrying an invisible tray. There was sweat slicking her forehead, and her blue eyes were fixed on the stairs.

The undead were mostly trying to pull the whole structure down, although quite a few were turning toward the newcomers with questioning moans. Callum, Terror, and Max were fending off the creatures trying to drag them from their precarious safety, and the top of the stairs was no longer attached to anything. The frame was frozen in mid-fall, and above it Big Ted dangled from the mezzanine, Melody still gnawing at his ankles.

Gertrude stood next to the bike with her arms crossed. "You should have a helmet," she said to Emma. "It's not safe. Do you know how many souls I've reaped after motorbike crashes? It happens so fast they don't even realise they're dead."

"I hope that's not a comment on my driving," Ms Jones said, not looking away from the stairs.

"I think I'm currently more likely to have my brains eaten by a zombie than to bash them in falling off a magic bike," Emma said, shaking Jan off and climbing to the floor.

"It's not *magic,*" Ms Jones said. "Well, I mean, it is, but that sounds like it flies or something. It doesn't. Well, not exactly, anyway."

"I suppose Jan would have to fall off first, so you could

just land on him," the reaper muttered, and the mortician ducked behind Emma.

I looked at Pru. She shrugged. "I don't know. I'm still mildly concussed, I think. I'm sure they'll get to the zombies at some stage."

As if hearing her, a few of the hungry dead left the stairs, snuffling toward the two humans by the bike.

"Here we go," Emma said, with rather more delight than seemed reasonable. She dug in her satchel and grabbed a syringe in each hand.

"Ready?" Gertrude asked.

"Bring them on." Emma positioned herself next to the entrance of the stall we'd been trapped in earlier, and Gertrude started herding the first of the zombies, pushing them about carefully with the blunt edge of the scythe and keeping all except one back from Emma. That one charged toward her, and Emma side-stepped it neatly, jabbing it in the neck with a syringe. Gertrude caught it with her scythe before it could grab for Emma again, and shoved it into the stall.

"Jan, go and close the other doors," she instructed him.

He'd been hiding behind the bike, still looking like he might throw up, but now he got up and ran to the shutters, closing them quickly to leave just the one Emma stood in front of. Gertrude sent another zombie toward her, and shoved the one that had already been dosed further back into the stall, handling them like some sort of professional zombie herder.

"Try and block off part of that entrance so we've got a smaller gap," she said to Jan. "Hurry, now." He rushed off to find something to barricade it with, and Emma dosed the second zombie. Gertrude sent it into the stall and let another go for Emma. It was all terribly orderly and methodical, and I stared at them for a moment longer, then turned my attention back to the stairs, half-expecting the zombies to be queueing politely at their base.

They weren't. Even with the ones coming to investigate us, there was still a mass of zombies both piling onto the stairs and trying to pull them down, and Callum and the others were still fighting desperately to keep them back. I glanced at Ms Jones. Her hand was shaking just slightly, but the metal frame didn't waver. She raised her hand a little, her face twisting with the effort, and the frame groaned as it lifted itself toward the mezzanine.

"Can you climb up?" she called, her voice hoarse. "I can't just hold you there forever, you know."

"They won't let us up," Terror shouted, and Ms Jones glared at the people on the mezzanine. They all took a perfectly choreographed step back.

"*What?*"

"They're infected," Unicorn Woman said, although with rather less conviction than before.

"So are half of you!" Big Ted bellowed, trying to pull himself up. The faun kept hitting his fingers with a keyboard, but the big man seemed more annoyed than pained.

"You've got a *zombie* on your *leg,*" a faery shouted.

"She doesn't have any teeth! She's not exactly going to lick you to death!"

"But she's *infected!*"

"They've got antidote," Callum shouted.

"So you *say,*" a broad man with green hair said. "I think it's a trap!"

"Yeah!" a couple of others shouted.

"You're going to use us as bait!" the nymph with the scissors screamed. "Like … like chumming for sharks!"

"*What?*" Callum yelled. "Why would we even *do* that?"

"I don't know! But you're going to! I can tell!"

"And she's *psychic!*" an elderly woman in a mint-green twinset shouted. "She knows these things!"

Max screamed something at all of them that was anatomically impossible and quite troubling, genetically speaking. He had a truly excellent grasp of profanity for someone so young.

"Are you War?" a man in a woolly hat asked Ms Jones, leaning over the balcony and aiming a phone at her. "I mean, that one's Death, right?"

"*Oh my God,*" Green Hair Man said, clutching his chest rather dramatically. "*It's the Apocalypse!*"

"Ugh," Ms Jones said. "*Humans.*"

"*Excuse* me," Emma said, shoving a zombie away.

"Present company excepted," the sorcerer said, then glanced at Jan. "Well, mostly."

"Hey, *I* made the antidote," he said.

"I'm sorry? Do you have short term memory loss?"

The mortician subsided, and went back to keeping Emma between him and the zombies.

Ms Jones slammed her hand upward, and the stairs screamed up to the mezzanine, hitting the balcony just beyond the barricaded gate. Callum, Max and Terror let loose with matching screams as they were almost tipped off by both the violent motion and what looked like a particularly steep angle.

"Ooh," Pru said, like an appreciative tennis spectator.

"Get off!" Ms Jones shouted, but the humans were already scrambling up the steps. There was a brief, enthusiastic struggle at the top, where Unicorn Woman and Green Hair tried to push them back down, but Terror leaped over the railing and shook her desk leg in both of their faces.

"I have been bitten *so* many times," she hissed at them, her words carrying over the disappointed moans of the zombies below. "I fought a zombie horde. I saw my friend turned. I survived. I had the antidote. I am not a zombie. But Morrigan help me, I will *bite your faces off* if you so much as *look* in my direction!"

Unicorn Woman and Green Hair exchanged glances then stepped back, both of them being very careful not to meet Terror's eyes.

"*Thank* you," she said, and ran to push the faun away from Big Ted and help him over the railing. Melody was still attached to his leg, but she'd stopped gumming his boot and just looked mostly confused.

Callum and Max scrambled onto the mezzanine, and Ms Jones lowered her hand with a sigh, letting the stairs settle to the ground slowly and taking care not to crush any zombies beneath it. A few of them snuffled around the frame, but mostly they turned their attention to Emma and Jan, advancing with a weird sort of hesitance, as if realising that it might be a trap. Above us, Big Ted was berating humanity in general and the stallholders in particular, and someone was shouting that the quarantined zombies in the office were about to break the door down, and that the barricade on the far end of the mezzanine was about to be breeched, so could they all just *focus?* Callum tried to run toward the barricade as a chair toppled off the top and a zombie in jogging bottoms and no shirt pushed its way through the gap, but a dwarf grabbed his jacket and yelled, "Where's the antidote? *Where?*"

Max shoved his way past Callum, waving his broom wildly, and the nymph screamed, "They're attacking us!"

Even the woman in the mint-green twinset looked a little dubious about that, but other than two women with saucepans who were already attacking the zombie, no one did anything to help.

"Gods," Ms Jones said. "What is *wrong* with people?"

"Lots," I said. "But sometimes it's a good sort of wrong."

As I watched, a dryad shoved her arm in front of the zombie's mouth and yelled, "Chew on *this,* deadhead!" Another zombie flung itself off the barricade and tried to bite the dryad's hard bark leg. "*Yeeesss,* break your *teeth!*" she screamed, which was actually quite a few varieties of wrong.

"Oh dear," Gertrude said, watching the commotion and holding a few corpses off Emma almost absentmindedly. "We better hurry up and get finished down here."

A mobile dinged out some woo-woo tone, all tinkling chimes and bells, and the sorcerer sighed, pulling a mobile from the pocket of her khaki jacket.

"Yes?" she said, rubbing her face. "Yes, I'm late. I *told* you I'd be late." She listened, then snapped, "Well, I'm sorry the fish is ruined, but *zombie apocalypse,* Malcolm," and jabbed the screen so hard I'm surprised she didn't break her finger.

"Alright?" I asked her cautiously, and she ran both hands back over the thick mess of her hair, which somehow seemed to droop a lot more than usual. I could feel her exhaustion, rolling off her shoulders and spilling across the floor like oil.

"Fantastic," she said. "Just fantastic." She raised a hand, and half the advancing zombies stopped as if they'd hit a wall. The rest kept coming, edging around the invisible barrier and heading for Emma and Jan. "Can you handle the rest, Gertrude?"

"Oh, yes," the reaper said, shoving another into the stall and corralling three more. "I'll let you know when to release the rest."

"Good." Ms Jones lifted her satchel from where it lay across her lap and looked up at the chaos on the mezzanine. "Callum!" she shouted, and he stopped arguing with a dwarf to look down at her.

"Hey," he called. "Thanks. Great timing."

"I always have great timing," she said, and hefted the satchel up to him. It was a half-hearted throw and hesitated part way up, but she flicked her hand and it kept going. Callum snatched it out of the air. "Dose them up, will you?"

"With pleasure," he said, and paused for a moment, examining the diminishing mass of zombies. He spotted me sitting next to Pru and raised one hand. I nodded back.

"Aw," Pru said.

"Shut up," I said, and we went back to watching Emma dosing the remaining zombies.

25

IT WAS TOTALLY ALIENS

DOWNSTAIRS, THE LAST ZOMBIE WAS JABBED AND TUCKED away in the stall, where the first were already starting to sit down on the floor, looking around in confusion and wondering where their shopping bags had gone and why they only had one shoe on. Gertrude pulled the shutter down and patted it.

"You just wait a little longer," she said. "Then you can all pop home for a nice cup of tea."

"That'll fix everything," Ms Jones muttered.

I'd been watching the mezzanine, where it seemed everyone had finally ended up having the antidote, although with rather less style and control than down here. I'd watched a woman chase a small boy up and down the balcony about four times, him screaming like she was about to cut his heart out, until a faery lifted the kid off his feet as he ran past and held him there, kicking and shrieking, while the woman jabbed him. Not that I blamed him. Needles hurt.

Now I looked around, and said, "Where's Claudia?"

"She's—" Ms Jones started, and Pru talked over her.

"She probably just left. Watch cats. *Huh.*"

"She *was* with us," the sorcerer said, eyeing Pru. "We left quite a lot of confused humans down in Butcher's Row. They needed tidying up."

"Huh," Pru said again, in a tone that suggested she doubted either Claudia's ability or her commitment to tidying up. Which was a euphemism, although not as bad as the way humans tend to use it. She wasn't about to feed everyone to the fishes. There weren't many of them left in the canals, anyway.

No, *tidying up* meant she'd be suggesting to the bemused humans that there had been a gas leak, or a chemical spill, and everyone had just passed out and had some very weird dreams, but *of course* there hadn't been any zombies, and, what, a talking cat? Ha, sure. Go tell *that* one to your GP. And, humans being as they are, which is to say prone to conspiracy theories and resistant to reality, it always took. It wasn't even hypnosis. It was just realigning their experiences with their belief of the world. Tidying up.

"Huh yourself," a familiar voice said, and we turned to see the cat in question cleaning a paw behind us.

"How long've you been there?" Pru demanded. *"Sneaking?"*

"Dude," I said to her. "I mean, I don't love the Watch either, but Claudia's okay."

"She wanted to reap my human. And I'm not a dude, you leftover pastry."

I decided I didn't want to argue with a naked cat, so just looked at Claudia. "We good?"

"Sure," she said. "Got a couple of police at the gate, too, so they're spreading the gas leak thing themselves."

Jan frowned. "But people will know what happened."

We looked at him, and huffed a selection of feline, reaper and sorcerer laughter, topped with Emma's softer chuckle. "Sure," I said. "Because you lot are so good at believing what you see, and not telling yourself pretty stories."

"Well, *I* know what happened," he snapped, hugging his satchel to him.

Emma patted him on the shoulder. "Yes, but you *know* rather than just seeing it. Trust me, seeing is not believing."

"Whatever," he said, and someone knocked on the shutter behind us. We turned to look at it.

"Excuse me," an elderly man in what had once been a very natty suit said, peering through the slats. "Sorry to disturb you, but we seem to have been locked in?"

"Oh dear," Emma said, and smiled at him. "Not to worry. We'll have you out in a jiff."

"Thanks awfully," the man said, and plucked a squashed sausage off his jacket, eyeing it dubiously.

AND THAT WAS PRETTY MUCH how it went. Everyone got very English and awkward and apologised a lot, except for one man who declared they'd *obviously* all been abducted by aliens, and another, rather larger man, who kept trying to shut him up, preferably by punching him.

Eventually Big Ted resorted to sitting on punchy man until he calmed down, which worked pretty well.

Otherwise, most people were fine. Claudia asked Pru and I if we were any good at suggestion, and I had to admit that my skills extended as far as convincing people they hadn't just seen me open their fridge, and that anyone I tried it on tended to end up with the urge to chase their non-existent tails. Pru sniffed and said she supposed she'd help, but her main concern was finding her human. Claudia just nodded and they ambled off through the crowd that was coming down from the mezzanine and out of the stall.

Pretty soon the story was everywhere, humans repeating it to each other and Folk repeating it back to the humans, everyone adding their own breathless twist – there had been a gas leak, it was a really bad kind of gas, it induced meat cravings, it made you violent, they should write to their local MP, it wasn't the market's fault, they should do *all* their shopping in the market from now on in order to show their support for the trauma everyone had been through … that one was totally from the Folk stallholders, but we weren't about to quibble.

We sat on the edge of the overturned flower stall and watched the market empty, uniformed police guiding everyone out into the night and ambulances pulling up to the kerb outside, handing out foil blankets and shining lights in people's eyes. Everyone looked a little confused, but only the Folk looked really worried, and Claudia was moving among them, assuring them everything was taken care of. I'm sure it helped that Ms Jones was leaning on her big bike watching them go, and Gertrude was sitting next to Emma, still cradling her scythe.

As the last few humans trailed out into the night Big Ted got up and stretched. "We all done, then?"

"There may be more out there," Gertrude said, handing him a satchel. "And they do seem to be attracted to the market. We'll pop by, but …"

"We'll keep an eye on things," Big Ted said, shouldering the bag.

"Can I grab some antidote?" Max asked. "Just in case?" Big Ted shrugged and handed a handful of syringes over. "Thanks," the kid said, and looked at me and Callum. "See you around?"

"Sure," Callum said, and Max gave a weird sort of salute. I hoped he wasn't going to start wearing long tatty coats and forgetting to brush his hair. Then he glanced at his watch, swore, and sprinted for the doors, shouting something about how his mum was going to kill him for not calling, and that was *way* worse than zombies.

We watched him go, then I glared at Jan. "We *are* done, aren't we?" My ribs still hurt, and at some point someone had stood on my toes. They were throbbing.

Jan nodded. Scraps of dust and, for some reason, lettuce, festooned his hair. "I'm done."

"Why did you start all this, anyway?" Emma asked. "It seems strange, for a mortician."

Jan looked at his hands. "My mum. She's got Alzheimer's. It's early still, but … well, sometimes she goes out and gets confused about where she is, or leaves the stove on, or … you know. And no one's *doing* anything."

"So *you* thought," Ms Jones started, and Emma spoke over her.

"I understand," she said, and patted his arm. "But people *are* trying. These things are complex."

"I suppose," he said, and got up. "It just seems like there's never going to be a cure." He thought about it. "I might go back to school. Study neuroscience properly."

"That sounds like a wonderful idea," Emma said. "You'll be brilliant at it." She smiled at him brightly until he turned and wandered off, looking so nervous that if the police *had* been looking for a culprit they'd have spotted him immediately. Then she looked at us and said, "Please make sure he never touches my brain."

Gertrude smiled at her. "I promise he will never get near your brain."

"Thank you," Emma said.

Terror shoved herself off the truck. "Well, we're out of here. Nice hunting zombies with you all."

"You're not staying in the market?" Callum asked.

"There's bits of dead zombie in our stall," Big Ted said. "Besides, the police'll be poking around the place looking for other survivors."

"Are you sure?" Emma asked. "Will you be okay?"

"We're always okay," Terror said. "Come on, Mel."

Melody nodded and got up, linking her arm through the younger woman's as they headed for the gates. A paramedic ran up to offer them some blankets, but they waved them off and slipped into the night, heading for their own quiet, hidden places.

Pru had already left, carried out into the night by her human, who I'd expected to be all tweed and hankies and boiled sweets in her purse. Instead, she'd been the zombie in leather trousers who'd jumped the barricade on the mezzanine. She walked out of the market barefoot, her back straight and her long blonde hair sweeping to her waist, and at least three male emergency workers and one female one rushed to "help" her. She waved them off, imperious as a northern god, and bore Pru away. I could hear her fussing about Pru being out of the apartment, and getting her feet dirty, and that she'd just catch her *death* of cold without a jumper on.

Pru looked over her human's shoulder as they left and narrowed her eyes at me, daring me to say anything. I didn't. Humans are weird, but some of them are good weird. Or compatible weird, however you want to look at it. You can put up with a lot for that. I just lifted my chin a little, and she lifted hers back, and then she was gone.

Now Callum put a hand on my back. "We should probably get going too."

"Are you hungry?" Gertrude asked. "We can pop back to ours before I drop you home."

Callum made a face. "I'm not. I don't want to think about why I'm not, but I'm not."

"You didn't eat any brains," I said. "So it could be worse."

"My jaw hurts, and there's *bits* in my teeth. It's bad enough."

"I could go for some brownie," Emma said.

"You could always go for some brownie," Gertrude said. "You're practically *made* of brownie."

"But you make such nice ones!"

The reaper smiled, her hood pooling around her

shoulders. It should have been at least a little frightening, that smile, with the bones of her jaw so tight against her bleached skin and the shadows etched under her eyes, but there was something sweet about it. “I do, don’t I?” she said.

“I like brownies,” Ms Jones observed, tucking her hands into the pockets of her jacket. “One of humanity’s better inventions, brownies.”

Callum ran his tongue over his teeth. “Maybe brownies would get the taste of … *stuff* out of my mouth.”

“They’re practically medicinal,” Emma said, getting up and holding a hand out to Gertrude. “Come on.”

We slipped back through the empty, devastated market and out the bottom doors. Emma and Callum squeezed into the front seat of the little white van, and I clambered onto Callum’s knee. He barely managed to get the door closed before Gertrude gunned the engine and swung us out of the market square and through the locked gate, missing the nose of a police car by a rabbit.

“A hair,” Callum said, when I pointed that out.

“Which is bigger than a rabbit, and so proves my point.”

He gave me a pained look, but that might have been due to the fact that he was clinging to the door trying not to squash Emma as Gertrude flung us around corners and swiped lamp posts and almost hit a variety of pedestrians, all looking much as you expect people to do at this hour on a Friday night.

It was all refreshingly *normal.*

Ms Jones pulled her bike into the alley right behind us, which made me happy I hadn't been her passenger. Being in a van going at that pace was bad enough. Claudia jumped from the pillion, looking sleek and unruffled, and Emma ushered us through the cafe and up some stairs hidden behind the first of the *Private* doors. We emerged into a tidy, warm flat, filled with the scents of baked goods and coffee and something indefinable that made me want to curl up in the nearest chair and start purring. The floors were polished wood scattered with cheerful rugs, and the little living room housed two small sofas that practically begged to be cuddled into. There were fluffy throws and bright cushions, and an awful lot of doilies.

"I'm trying to break her of the habit," Emma said, as Ms Jones picked up a cushion printed with a ginger kitten tangled in a ball of pink yarn and waved it questioningly. "But she has *so many!*"

"So many what?" Gertrude asked, climbing the stairs behind us with a stack of Tupperware.

"Cakes," Emma said. "So many cakes."

Gertrude gave her a look that suggested she thought Emma might be being a bit economical with the truth, then nodded at the sofas. "Sit down. We'll get some coffee."

Ms Jones sat down in one of the sofas, stretching her legs out in front of her with her booted feet crossed at the ankles. Callum looked from one sofa to the other, then sat down on the floor next to the coffee table, which honestly seemed like a good option. The sofas were pretty cosy.

Claudia sat next to the sorcerer, tail tucked around her toes, and I jumped onto the table.

"*Off,*" Gertrude said, coming back in with a stack of small plates and a larger one piled with brownies and cake and biscuits.

"Aw," I said, but jumped to the arm of the empty sofa while Claudia arched her whiskers at me.

There was some muddling around with mugs and coffee and tea and sugar and milk and napkins and so on, but eventually everyone was settled, Gertrude and Emma in one sofa and Ms Jones and Claudia in the other. Callum looked pretty happy on the floor, a mug of tea in one hand and brownie in the other, and Emma offered me and Claudia cream. Everyone was complimenting the brownies, and Gertrude was explaining it was to do with the quality of chocolate one used, and it was all quite lovely and un-life-threatening, then Claudia had to go and ruin it.

"Zombies," she said, licking cream off her chops. "Pretty amazing some mortician came up with that."

"You saw the formula," Callum said to Ms Jones around a second helping of brownie. "Did it seem … I don't know, *possible?*"

Ms Jones chewed a piece of shortbread thoughtfully, then said. "I'm not a scientist. But it must've been possible. It happened."

"What about the antidote?" Gertrude asked. "If you're not a scientist, how did you make it?"

"Ah," she said. "Yes. That was magic. I had to turn the formula inside out. I created a concentrated form, then left Jan to distil it. It took a bit out of me, though, which is why I had to leave you to it for a while. I wouldn't have been able to replicate it without some recharging. Even then I wasn't sure it'd work, mind, but it did."

I wondered what recharging constituted for sorcerers, and decided I didn't want to know.

"So how come you couldn't just cure everyone?" Emma asked. "Like wave your hand, and *poof.*"

"Firstly, very little magic involves *and poof.* It takes a huge amount of power and effort. And I couldn't even force the cure in Callum, let alone a whole mob. I needed a medium to do it with, and it had to interact properly. Essentially I just re-jigged the arrangement of a couple of molecules, which is a lot easier than trying to create something out of nothing."

She said *easier,* but there were shadows under her eyes to rival the reaper's, and lines on her forehead I hadn't seen before. I looked at Claudia. "You think someone gave him the formula."

"It's more likely than him coming up with it on his own, isn't it?"

"So who gave it to him?" Emma asked.

"Ah, well. That's the question, isn't it?" Claudia said.

"Was it the Watch?" Ms Jones asked.

Claudia tipped her head. "I can't say it wasn't."

"*What?*" I demanded. "That could've wiped *everyone* out. Like, *everyone.*"

"You express it so well," she said, arching her whiskers at me. "Look, I trust the Watch leader, but there's more to the Watch than her and my … division. There are factions. There's unrest. Resentment. Anger at what humans are doing to the world. And it's not just Watch. There are those who'd be happy to see humanity wiped out, even if some Folk were lost along the way."

"It's been rising, hasn't it?" Ms Jones asked. She had her mug cradled in her hands. It had – surprise – a kitten on it. "I keep hearing whispers. There's movement."

"That's why you wanted me to—" I started, then realised that mentioning I was meant to spy on Claudia *in front* of Claudia was probably a Spying 101 fail.

"Yes," Ms Jones said, the corners of her mouth twitching. "Although I can now see that was perhaps not one of my better judgement calls."

Claudia looked from one of us to the other. "Ah. Well, he was either very subtle or didn't do it."

"The second one," Callum said. "*Subtle* is not a word I've used much about Gobs."

"*Hey,*" I said, but really had no follow-through after that.

"I never felt magic in any of the zombies," Gertrude said. "I'd have known."

"Not all magic is magic," Ms Jones said. "Sometimes it's just science no one knows yet. Like tweaking antidotes. You could do that in a lab, once you figured it out."

Callum rubbed his chin, stubble scraping under his fingers. The nails were filthy, and he wrinkled his nose at them. "So what we're saying here is that some Folk – or maybe Watch – came up with the living dead infection."

"I'm saying it's possible," Claudia said. "These resentments run deep and old. And I may be wrong."

"I don't think you are," Ms Jones said.

There was a pause, then Emma said, "Well, we should do something about it, then." We all looked at her, and she shrugged. She'd taken her ripped jacket off, and her dress was splattered with what smelled like sweet chili sauce. "I don't fancy being wiped out."

"Well, no," Callum agreed. "That would suck."

"I would really rather you didn't get wiped out either," Gertrude said, and Emma leaned her head on the reaper's shoulder.

"Yeah, I vote against it," I said.

Ms Jones nodded. "But the question is, what can we do about it?"

"For now, not much," Claudia said. "But maybe the thing is to be ready."

THERE WASN'T a lot to say after that. Claudia left, and Ms Jones followed her down the stairs and out the door, and Emma volunteered to drive us home, which was kind of a relief. I'd had about enough of reaper car trips for the day. Probably for life, to be honest. Gertrude waved us off, an apron already on over her robes.

Emma's driving was a lot slower than Gertrude's, but as it crept on for midnight the streets were empty of cars, if not people, and she dropped us off in front of our tattered apartment building in good time. She leaned over the seat to look at us as we got out.

"I suppose I'll see you soon," she said.

"Seems like it," I said.

"Well, don't wait for the next threat to human existence," she said. "Gertrude's going to make zombie cupcakes, so come by and try them out next week."

"Alright," Callum said. "Thanks."

We watched her leave, then pushed through the juddery door into the damp hall. My ribs hurt and my legs ached, and I looked at the stairs with a sort of despair, wishing I could just shift straight to my bed.

"Lift?" Callum asked me.

I looked up at him. "Please."

He gathered me up more gently than usual, cradling me against him with both hands and not putting me down until we were inside. He deposited me on the desk and picked my microwaveable bed up, wandering into the kitchenette with it. I heard the kettle go on and the microwave start, and smelled his cigarettes as he pulled the packet from his coat.

I sat down and considered my mucky fur, and gave my side a couple of half-hearted licks. Then I said, "Hey, did you find Ifan?"

Callum came back with an unlit cigarette dangling from his lips, and looked at me thoughtfully before he lit it. "No," he said. "Lucky, really. I mean, he was dead. I don't think I could've brained him."

I considered it. "But he was one, right?"

"As far as we know." He cocked his head as he lit the cigarette, inhaling deeply. "Maybe one of the others got him. Maybe he's still out there. I just … I couldn't have."

I watched him for a moment. "Who was he? How do you know someone like that? An old-school magician?"

Callum shook his head, and went to collect his tea and my bed, setting them both on the desk. "Does it matter?"

I examined him, then climbed stiffly onto the heated cushion. "I suppose not," I said, and watched him crack the window before he sat down, taking the snake from his coat. The snake coiled himself around a paperback and looked from one of us to the other, tongue flicking questioningly.

Callum flicked the ash off his cigarette, picked up his tea, and put his feet up on the desk with a sigh I could almost feel myself. The snake investigated his boots, then snuggled up to the edge of my bed. I couldn't even be bothered pushing him away. I just breathed the musty scents of our battered apartment, clinging to reality in its stubborn, tenuous way. Just like the rest of us.

"Alright?" Callum said eventually, watching the smoke drifting toward the ceiling and ignoring the window entirely. For once I didn't mind it.

"Alright," I said, and that was all that needed to be said. Sometimes the whole world turns on what is unsaid, in both good and bad ways, and we both knew what was underneath it, as surely as if we'd said it aloud.

Right now, we are alright.

We'll worry about tomorrow – and all the rest – when it comes.

But, right now, we're together. And we're alright.

I lowered my nose to my paws and let him rest his hand on my back, and breathed in smoke and books and the warm, deep magic that ran between us, and knew that neither of us was lying.

Then I sat up and batted the snake, who'd been trying to crawl *into* my bed, and the snake tried to bite me, and Callum tried to push us apart and got hissed at by both of us.

Which made things exactly as they should be.

FREE STORIES!

Cats always have that air, don't they?

The one that suggests they know something we don't. Possibly a lot of somethings we don't.

And maybe . . . just maybe they do.

Discover eight tales of cats with good intentions but bad execution, cats that may or may not be cats, and cats that could really be a lot more helpful than they actually are (but you try telling them that).

They inhabit some worlds that may seem familiar, or near enough to be only a step away. Others not so much. Or hopefully not, anyway.

But they all share one key characteristic.

They've all got issues with cats.

Disclaimer: your cat may or may not be living a secret second life. But don't say I didn't warn you. And if they wink, *always* wink back.

Download your free book now!

www.subscribepage.com/catstories

AUTHOR'S NOTES

Lovely people, thank you so much for picking up this book. I know there are huge demands on all of our time these days, and I appreciate it hugely that you've chosen to spend some of yours reading about mercenary feline PIs and their human sidekicks.

I have one request, and one gift for you (because that seems fair).

Reviews are a bit like magic to authors, but magic of the good kind. Less raise-the-dead, more get-more-readers-and-so-write-more-books variety. More reviews mean more people see our books in online stores, meaning more people buy them, so giving us the means to write more stories and send them back out to you, lovely people.

So it would mean the world to me if you left a review at your favourite retailer, on Goodreads, or at any other website of your choice. It doesn't have to be long – "liked it" or "would rather watch paint dry" will do just fine. Of course, if you'd like to leave a longer review, that would also be wonderful!

And finally, if you jump to the link below, you'll be able to grab yourself some free stories! You'll need to sign up to the newsletter, but that'll get you first dibs on advance reader copies of new books as well as being able to enter giveaways and receive unsolicited cat photos. Ahem.

The Cat Did It: 8 Tales of Troublesome Felines
(www.subscribepage.com/catstories)

And if you'd rather just jump into more novels, head to my website (www.kmwatt.com) for details on *all* the books, plus to read blogs and short stories, and view potentially incoherent book review videos, because the talking is harder than the writing.

Thank you once again for being so entirely wonderful.

Read on, lovely people!

Kim

ACKNOWLEDGMENTS

Always the first thanks are to you, lovely reader. Thank you for continuing the adventure with me, for taking a chance on yet another zombie story in a world flooded with them, and never questioning the wisdom of reapers running city centre cafes. You are entirely wonderful.

Thank you to my wonderful editor and friend Lynda Dietz, of Easy Reader Editing, who teaches me something new on every single book, and never fails to make me laugh about it. All good grammar praise goes to her. All mistakes are mine. Find her at www.easyreaderediting.com for fantastic blogs on editing, grammar, and other writer-y stuff.

Thank you so many times over to my fantastic beta readers, who never do anything but make my stories better. You know who you are, and I also hope you know how amazing you are. Which is very.

Thank you to Monika from Ampersand Cover Design, who not only makes awesome covers, but is exceptionally patient when I get colors wrong because of certain user errors on my laptop … Find her at www.ampersandbookcovers.com

And, every single time, thank you to my small but perfectly formed family, providers of love, support, inspiration, and laughter. And, in the case of the Little Furry Muse, bites. But I think they're loving ones. Sometimes, anyway.

ABOUT THE AUTHOR

Apparently this bit should be done in third person, but the Little Furry Muse refused to do it for me. She says lending her muse-ship to my writing is more than enough.

So hi, I'm Kim. I write funny fantasy set in a world not so dissimilar to ours (and in fact sharing many locations). I write about mystery-solving dragons with a strong affection for barbecues and scones, and reapers running petting cafes featuring baby ghouls. I write about myth and reality clashing in small and spectacular ways, and about the healing magic of tea and a really good lemon drizzle cake.

I write about snarky feline PIs and the Horsemen of the Apocalypse upgrading to Vespas, and the very real force that are women of a certain age.

Most of all, I write about friendship, and loyalty, and the importance of looking out for one another. Because these, above all things, are magic.

And you can find me rambling on about all this (and more) over on my website (www.kmwatt.com), or join me on Facebook, Instagram and Twitter for bad puns and many, many cat memes. Many.

Come join me!

facebook.com/KimMWatt
twitter.com/kimmwatt
instagram.com/kimmwatt

ALSO BY KIM M. WATT

The Gobbelino London, PI series:

A Scourge of Pleasantries (Book 1)

A Contagion of Zombies (Book 2)

A Complication of Unicorns (Book 3)

A Melee of Mages (Book 4)

Book 5 coming soon!

The Beaufort Scales Series (cozy mysteries with dragons):

Baking Bad (Book 1)

Yule Be Sorry (Book 2)

A Manor of Life & Death (Book 3)

Game of Scones (Book 4)

The Beaufort Scales Collection (Books 1–4, e-book only)

A Toot Hansell Christmas Cracker – a festive short story & recipe collection (Book 5)

Coming Up Roses (Book 6)

Short Story Collections:

Oddly Enough (Tales of the Unordinary, volume one)

The Cat Did It (a free e-book)

The Tales of Beaufort Scales (a free e-book)

Head to kmwatt.com/my-books for details!

Printed in Great Britain
by Amazon

75396636R00232